Dear Peggy!
Be the blessing!
"a be blessed!
Happy Reading
Eileen Petro
10/5/19

THE MYSTICAL ARK

A VESSEL OF BLESSINGS

Praise for The Mystical Ark

A magical journey awaits! You'll be enthralled by the adventure of The Mystical Ark from the start. It's one of those novels that you want to keep reading as it's filled with intrigue, romance, imagination, wonder and spirituality.

The people, the places, and the visions are so vivid that you will feel one with the journey. Readers will have questions and 'aha' moments within the story and then it goes deeper and even more fascinating.

This breakout novel is a tour de force. Your only question at the end will be...where to next?

- Donna Adinolfi, Mindful Adventures

This exciting, inspiring novel swings right into action. Readers will not need to wait to get into the exploits with this story ... a wonderful mixture of mystery, suspense, action adventure, humor, and a sprinkling of fantasy ... highly recommended for adults and teenagers who enjoy a thought-provoking adventure.

~ Janice L. Smith, Book Reviewer

So compelling and so well-written ... I got caught up in the story. Ms. Patra has created an important spiritual message; I hope that message becomes widespread through publication of *The Mystical Ark: A Vessel of Blessings.*

~ Bill Worth, Minister and Retired Newspaper Editor

THE MYSTICAL ARK

A VESSEL OF BLESSINGS

Eileen Patra

SEVENTH
LIGHT, LLC
Royal Oak, Michigan

Seventh Light, LLC
Royal Oak, Michigan

Bible verses, quoted or referenced, are from the New Revised Standard Version unless otherwise indicated.

Cover Design: Eileen Patra

Stock Photography used for cover:
© iStock.com | gremlin, © Aleksey Telnov | Dreamstime.com,
© wacomka | Dreamstime.com,

ISBN: 978-1-54397-611-3

First Edition: June 2019

With great love and appreciation, I dedicate this book to Steve, my husband, partner, earth angel, and best friend who often took our dog up north so I could have the house to myself to work on this book, and who diligently read and proofread numerous drafts.

And, to my children, Stephen and Julie, who have taught and inspired me and who, along with their families, are the greatest treasures of my life.

Acknowledgments

I would like to acknowledge the many kindred souls I have encountered along my path who helped inspire this book, especially:

Joe B., whose prose-like letters I typed as his secretary a couple of lifetimes ago inspired my passion for the creative use of words.

Don Herrin, who asked, "Does Unity believe in the Ten Commandments?"

Ramona Underwood, who asked, "When will you speak about the other commandments? People really need to hear this."

Sharon Connors, whose coaching skills helped bring this book to fruition.

Maureen Dunphy and the members of her class, *Finding Your Way to Writing*, whose feedback on the early chapters was invaluable.

Special thanks to my beta readers whose insights and attention to detail made The Mystical Ark a better book; Donna Adinolfi, Patricia Lawson, Julie Miller, Steve Patra, and Jan Smith.

My heartfelt gratitude goes to my copy-editor, Bill Worth, a retired newspaper editor and Unity minister, whose guidance on the first pages of an early draft of this book encouraged me to expand beyond my perceived boundaries, and whose expertise and attention to detail on the final draft honed this work into a polished piece.

And finally, to God, the Essence of Life, who has placed this story and its ideas in my heart, I give thanks.

CHAPTER ONE

The Discovery

There it was. The prize now sat before them in a hidden chamber of the dimly-illumined, desert cave to which they had escaped. They were hot, dirty, exhausted, and frightened. Most of their research team had perished the night before. Now, they encircled the thing in silent wonder. A box really, made of some unearthly gold-like material, covered with ancient dust, held their undivided attention. Metal loops, nearly worn away by time and use, hung from its sides. The remains of angelic figures that had long since lost their wings and their brilliant, shiny surface, still clung to its top.

Visibly weary, Paul staggered toward the ancient treasure. He stretched his hand toward it, then drew it back. He tried again, but it seemed to be emanating a powerful energy that could not be penetrated. He stared at it, mouth agape, creating a deep crevice in his smooth, oval face. A short crop of hair circled the dome-shaped crown of his head in a way that created the appearance that he wore a permanent skull cap. Now it was dusty and disheveled, but the illusion of a cap remained. His near-black eyes, partially obscured by dark-rimmed glasses, were surprisingly gentle and exceedingly deep. A published journalist of archaeological papers and articles, Paul had joined the field study as the Archives Supervisor, hoping to gain insight and complete research for his first book. He backed away now and leaned against the cave wall, still staring at the box.

Josh reluctantly left his post at the chamber entrance. Apprehension and his vow to protect the team had kept him glued to the chamber opening; curiosity pulled him toward the box. He knew the ancient stories. His father, a minister, had drilled the scriptures into his head, chapter, and verse. If the stories were true, touching this thing might be fatal. Yet Paul had not been harmed, just repelled from it. Josh pushed dusty dreads away from his brown face, then timidly reached toward the golden receptacle. He, too, jerked his hand away, dark eyes widening as he stared from his hand to the box and back again in disbelief. He hastily backed away and returned to his position by the entrance.

Zak adjusted the portable lights to get a better look. A small fragment of an engraved tablet discovered at the original dig site in southern Egypt had led them here, to this unparalleled discovery. His thick brown hair fell unkempt over his eyes, and his usually crisp clothing was rumpled and spattered with blood. As the lead archeologist, Zak was about to achieve the crowning glory of a lifetime devoted to the exploration of ancient civilizations. The exhaustion and trauma from the night before slipped away as he extended his hand confidently toward the box, but then quickly snapped it back again. A strange, invisible energy field surrounded the artifact, repelling any attempt to touch it.

Only Elena was able to pass through the invisible force that radiated from every inch of the container. Shirt torn, chestnut hair in hopeless, dampened tangles, Elena pulled herself to her feet and reached out to run her fingers across the strange substance. She should have been snapping photos to record and log the find, but her camera had been irreparably damaged the night before. Instead, she captured the unfolding scene in the photographs of her mind, storing them for the paintings she would most certainly produce.

The others had pulled their hands away as if the box had emitted some kind of electrical shock. Elena felt only a tingling sensation and then a smooth, surprisingly warm veneer. Her fingers searched the top for an opening. There were no hinges, no seams, no space that divided top from bottom. Her hand moved slowly around until she felt a spark, a surge, like a phantom cell-phone buzz. She tried to pull her hand away, but to no avail. An electric wave of energy flooded her entire body, knocking her off her feet. Then suddenly, but delicately, like a flower blooming in time-lapse photography, the top of the box began to move. It rippled and undulated. The once-solid substance appeared like molten metal; it began to wrinkle and spread apart, reminding Elena of the parting of the Red Sea in the Charlton Heston version of *The Ten Commandments*.

It was open. And from it sprang forth bursts of light in radiating swirls that spiraled toward the top of the cave and gently fell like long-awaited rain upon their weary, sunburned shoulders. As particles of light fell upon them, they felt an energy vibrating through them as if the very cells of their bodies were coming apart and joining in the spiraling dance of light. Then they felt the particles condensing, creating a forceful, pulling sensation. They watched in utter amazement. They had found it. The Ark of the Covenant. The most sought-after artifact of all time. It was open, and it was pulling them inexplicably through its now transparent sides.

Inside this sacred, ancient tabernacle, there were no stone tablets, no walls, no curtains. Just a soft, irresistible glow and bursts of light that danced through it. It was an opening, a portal to the heart and mind of the Divine. It was incomprehensible. It was abundantly clear. God, the Essence of Life itself, had hidden this gateway to all the blessings bestowed upon humankind. The artifact sought for eons engulfed them, and in it were not the commands of a demanding, judgmental god. Instead, there was indescribable, unfathomable, immeasurable peace and wholeness. There was no god demanding homage, but rather an all-permeating Presence that promised infinite blessings and security. They felt rather than heard answers to their unspoken questions. They were aware of one another's presence yet they were somehow intertwined as one. They knew each other's thoughts. They felt one another's feelings. There seemed to be almost no place where one of them left off and another began, yet they were still recognizable as the unique individuals they had always been.

Never had anyone experienced such a feeling. They met each other's eyes and knew they were inseparably one, yet they could see one another as if they were separate. They saw the planets in their rotations, the Earth in its orbit, and they sensed rather than saw the outworking of the evolution of humankind: stumbling, falling, then rising again. So sad, so bleak, yet so perfect in potential. Beautiful.

As they watched, immersed in the unfathomable energy, they began to notice that the activity of their thoughts seemed to take shape around them. They thought of flowers, and flowers appeared. They imagined weightlessness, and it was so. They imagined gravity, and they became stuck to an invisible ground. They imagined flying, and they rose high above what they had been viewing. They thought about planets, and there they were. They thought of stars, and stars appeared. They floated among planets and stars and far beyond. Everything was changing, continually moving, continuously evolving. Yet everything moved in perfect harmony.

Questions arose and were answered as quickly as they could be asked. *Where is this place?* And the answer was ***Here***. *What time is it? **Now***. No words were spoken, but the answers appeared amidst their minds. They looked at one another and saw radiant beings of Light

3

floating like angels in the sky. *Why are we here?* And the knowing emerged. ***Because you chose to be.*** *Can we go back?* ***You never left. There is only one place, one moment, one activity appearing as many, expanding and growing beyond limits and breathing itself back again.***

As they grappled with these answers, they found themselves outside the box again. Its molten lid closed as its images disappeared before their eyes, but the essence of the vision remained in their minds and hearts. They each suspected it would always be carried, carefully, gently, in the temple of their hearts, and they wondered how they would explain the inexplicable. How could one begin to express the ultimate, perfect Truth that lay invisible, hidden beneath the activities of the world?

Hours. Days. No one knew the time, or how long they had been immersed in the energy of the Ark. The box had sealed itself again, but it didn't matter. They knew what was inside. They had understood every word, every thought, every whisper of the Divine. Every question ever uttered by humankind had been answered, and they each now understood. Everything in them had changed. Forever.

Elena brushed the dust from her torn clothing, her tie-dyed field shirt unsalvageable, and wiped tears from her mud-streaked face. The experience had been overwhelming, yet there was nothing more beautiful, more perfect. It was a miracle. Or, was it the stuff that miracles were made of? In either case, it was glorious and real. Even now she could see a faint glitter of light still emanating from the other members of the team. Each looked different somehow. More glorious. More brilliant. More serene. There was no fear, no worry, no judgment, no competition. Only a peaceful glow that seemed to radiate and blend like the colors on her palette when she painted in her studio.

No one spoke. Words were not necessary. They could read one another's thoughts now, as if they were one being. They gathered their gear and began covering any traces of the excavation. This vessel was much too important to be confined to a museum or placed in storage, as antiquities offices and different governments argued over its ownership. It was far too valuable to be the stuff of pirates and scoundrels. It belonged right where they found it, deep within a hidden alcove of a desert cave in a place time had forgotten.

Elena watched Zak as he carefully began placing the last pieces of rock and shale around the sacred object. She didn't have to wonder what he was feeling. She could feel it with him. Even the dedicated archeologist in him, even with the promise of professional acclaim, he could not bear to place this sacred object where it could be mishandled or misused.

Her best friend since that first anthropology class together at the community college, Zak was an archeologist not just by trade but also by his innate nature. As a child, he had loved to play in the dirt and had managed to make that activity his career. Elena often accompanied him on expeditions. She loved the feeling of softly brushing away the years from ancient artifacts. It was like painting in reverse; every stroke of the brush revealing more of the object's hidden form.

Zak had an equal love for art. He attended most of her openings and sometimes came by just to watch her paint. They had been through much together. Now they had been through something indescribable, life-altering.

Zak had grown up in a home much like Elena's, though perhaps more affluent and a bit less dysfunctional. As a child he had played for hours in the mud, building structures, then smashing them down again. He collected stones and dirt-encrusted toys buried in the yard by the former occupants of his centennial childhood home. Zak had an artistic flair, too. Enthralled by the artifacts he recovered, and the lives they represented, he occasionally took to sculpting shapes that emulated their unique beauty but with a sleek, modern interpretation. He loved the feel of the clay. It reminded him of being on a dig, sifting through sand, squishing through mud, discovering what was already there, just waiting to be found. It was a great form of release.

Zak found no greater joy than discovering some relic that told the story of an individual now gone, but because of his work, not forgotten. To Zak, the earth was a treasure chest filled with history, meaning, and messages from ancient civilizations.

Zak touched his hand to the smooth surface of the box one last time before replacing the last of the rocks that lay scattered about its intended asylum. It was still now, seemingly solid; no longer repelling their touch nor drawing them in. No evidence remained of its having opened and pulled them inside. The experience through the portal had been indescribable. He knew he would never be the same. He suspected none of them would. He glanced at the remaining members of the team. Each carried a soft, almost translucent glow about them. The space between them was different, too. He could faintly see the energy that connected them. They moved in quiet unison, each knowing one another's intentions. *How,* Zak wondered, *will we ever be able to explain this mystical experience? How will we go about our lives?*

Zak turned his gaze toward Elena. She was stowing the last of the gear into their packs. The two of them were like magnets, pulled by some invisible force toward one another, yet at times pushed apart by the circumstances of life. After that first anthropology class at the community college where they had met, Elena had gone on to pursue her love for painting. He had continued with archeological studies. Their pursuits seemed like polar opposites, yet remarkably, they found themselves on the same campus for both their undergrad and postgrad studies. Zak was often in the field sifting through dirt and sand, hoping to gain insights into civilizations long gone. Elena lived in the Village now, immersed in the world of art. Somehow though, they had always found time to be together and to support each other.

Zak was immensely grateful that Elena had agreed to come on this particular dig. She had joined him many times before as their lead photographer, but this one he had sensed would be significant even before they found themselves pursuing one of the most sought-after relics of all time. Elena was immeasurably valuable on an excavation team. Her soft touch with a brush insured the integrity of the relics they unearthed, and her talent as a photographer provided them with unparalleled photographs of their work.

Elena, he thought, *she paints the sky while I play in the dirt. How is it that we have found someplace in the middle to be such incredible friends?* They had supported each other through numerous horrid relationships. They had seen each other through the neurotic throes of final projects and Master's theses. Now, they had been together for the most transformative experience anyone could ever imagine.

Satisfied that the Ark was flawlessly concealed, Zak joined the rest of the group. They stepped outside into the light of a gently rising sun casting its warm, yellow rays upon the otherwise bleak and hostile terrain of this remote area of the Sahara Desert, one-hundred-some miles from the Qasr Ibrim dig where their journey had begun.

The trek down the mountainside was quiet. Each team member was absorbed in silent reflection. The peaceful glow from the Ark remained with them as they descended the rocky terrain. They had left what they would call *The Mystical Ark* or *The Container of All Blessings* in the place where they had found it. But the message that had seeped from it into their hearts would never leave them. They had been blessed. They had seen what every earthly being longs to see. It had unfolded delicately from within. To them, it was no longer hidden in a cave but indelibly imprinted on their hearts. The knowledge fortified them as they moved their weary bodies down the path toward the camp.

What had seemed a treacherous and exhausting ascent last night was almost effortless as they descended. The harmonic sounds that had filled their minds in the Ark continued to play in their heads. The sun rising higher by the minute began beating on their backs, but they didn't feel it. The dust that coated the desert landscape and whirled about them with every step was invisible to their eyes. Lack of sleep had no effect. In fact, they felt more energized than any of them remembered ever having felt. Until they reached the camp. There, the carnage they had escaped the night before awaited them.

Wounded team members were being lifted into a helicopter, while the bodies of those who had not survived were being loaded into a larger aircraft. Law-enforcement officials were examining the area and taking a statement from Lucas, their medic who had volunteered to stay the night with the wounded while they had escaped up the mountainside. Exhaustion, trauma, and a full gamut of human emotions crashed down upon their weary shoulders like an avalanche. They braced themselves for the barrage of questions most certainly awaiting them and the grief that could no longer be held at bay. They had seen the Light and were now enveloped in a scene shrouded in darkness and despair. It seemed as though the spell was broken, the blissful energy of the Ark shattered by the scene before them. In the Ark, all was beauty and harmony. In the world, well, there was this.

CHAPTER TWO

No Place Like Home

Elena opened her apartment door. A quiet sigh escaped her as she felt the tension releasing its grasp on her shoulders and chest. Everything was just as she had left it, except for the neatly piled stacks of mail her neighbor, Margot, had placed on the table. Nothing else had changed. Carefully placed shoji screens gave the feel of separate rooms to the open space. In the studio, the easels, piles of paint tubes, half-finished paintings, cluttered counters, and table were still there. The smell of linseed oil permeated the air even after weeks of not painting. She took a deep breath, filling her nostrils with the scent. *There's no place like home*, she thought.

Elena offered a silent prayer of thanksgiving for her Aunt Vicki who had bequeathed her the lease to this apartment in the highly-desirable Greenwich Village artists' community known as Westbeth. Aunt Victoria, the one her father called *Crazy Vicki*, had been one of the original tenants, and like most of the residents, never moved. Inheritance was the only way in. Aunt Vicki had no children of her own and had learned that her niece was a budding artist. *Thank you, Aunt Vicki!*

A flash of black fur descended the steps from the loft above followed by an undulated chirping sound. Moses appeared, tail straight up in the air, meowing, purring, and incessantly rubbing his jaw against her legs as she unloaded her gear. "I missed you too, Moses," Elena whispered. She reached down to pet him and gently rubbed his ears as he wound himself in figure eights around her legs.

Moses was the most affectionate cat Elena had ever known. Well, he was the only one she had ever owned, but that was beside the point. Moses was loveable and hated being left behind when she traveled. Maybe he had abandonment issues. It wouldn't be surprising, because Elena had found him when he was just a few weeks old floating down the river on a discarded piece of wood. He was so small and frightened. He let out tiny, terrified screeches that would have been meows from an older cat. Elena somehow managed to snag the floating debris with a nearby branch, pulling the frightened feline to safety. "I guess I'll call you Moses, drawn from the water," she laughed as the tiny kitten dug his needle-like claws into her sweater. Moses was going nowhere but home with her where she would feed him with an eye dropper and keep him warm. The irony of her cat's name was not lost on Elena, given her recent adventure. She chuckled to herself and thought *if you only knew, Moses.*

Yes, Moses was still there, waiting for her return. The studio looked the same. But something in her was different. She remembered and missed the deep feeling of peace she had experienced in the presence of the Ark. Their return to the camp and then the primary site had been emotional and overwhelming. There were interviews with local authorities, antiquities officers, and university representatives. There had been little time to debrief with the other team members before they had left for home. The memory of Zak's face as they parted ways at the airport haunted her. He looked tormented, divided. Elena sensed he was struggling with having left behind such a significant artifact. She knew him too well not to recognize the thoughts swimming behind those gentle brown eyes. He was already regretting having abandoned the Ark in that obscure, desert cave.

Elena's heart ached as she thought about Zak. He would crave examining it, carbon dating it, and requesting a myriad of tests to prove its authenticity. He was in his element when he was logging and documenting every detail of a newly discovered artifact. But how could he document a mystical experience? There was nothing to measure, nothing to photograph, no data that could be recorded. He would want to share the discovery and what it represented about a lost civilization, but there would be no proof, no object, and no words for what they had experienced.

Elena had no words either, but she definitely had images; her mind overflowed with them. She glanced at the stack of blank canvases leaning against the off-white wall. They called to her, as they often did. She could almost see images taking shape on them. She scanned the tubes of paint, checking for pigments that matched the pictures in her mind. Chromas, cadmiums, bright colors. Most of what she needed was here ….

Her thoughts were interrupted by a subtle, persistent vibration on her right leg. It was Moses, purring and rubbing against her. His yellow-green eyes implored her. "Okay, buddy. I get it. The painting will have to wait. Right now, there are more important things to do, like feeding you, right?"

With Moses fed, and a list of supplies and groceries compiled, Elena climbed the steps to her loft where exhaustion was luring her to bed. She smiled as she remembered having changed the bedding right before leaving for the trip. There was something luxurious and sumptuous about sliding between fresh sheets after a long journey, especially this one.

***

After a day of shopping and catching up with emails and phone calls, Elena spent the next several weeks painting the visions that were deeply planted in her mind. She worked with urgency and a passion unparalleled with her previous approach to painting, ignited by the burning desire to convey all that had been revealed to her in the Ark. It burned until she felt almost consumed by it, but not. No. It wasn't consuming, it was exhilarating.

Elena rapidly drew her brush across the canvas, laying down the most vibrant colors she had ever used. In some places, the paint was thin and virtually translucent, with areas of the canvas bleeding through. In others, the paint was thick, creating its own swirling, glittering textures. There were faint hints here and there of familiar images; people, places, and objects, but all appeared to take shape from swirling streams of light above and around them. The effect was immensely ethereal and intensely enticing.

Elena took a step back to view the current canvas. She tilted her head, squinted her eyes, and took another step back. *Almost*, she thought. *It does draw you in, but it's not quite the same. If I could only reproduce the beauty and multiple dimensions. If people could just see what I've seen, they would be changed. Beautiful beings of light, all of them, yet they are asleep to their grandeur, unaware of their power, oblivious to their connection with one another. Maybe even this small glimpse, these imperfect replicas could make a difference. No doubt the world needs something.*

Elena set her brush in the open jar of odorless turpenoid and plopped herself into her papasan chair. The swivel-chair was purposely placed in the center of the apartment, where Elena could view her work, or turn it to face whichever space a guest might occupy. She turned it now toward the painting and the emerging series it represented. It stood in stark contrast to her earlier pieces that sat off to the side, prepped for her upcoming show. They were a series of abstract, multi-media bridges, spanning vast and seemingly endless oceans, embedded strings stretching across the canvas in an optical illusion of movement. Others, torn apart or crumbling, cast their embedded string-like cables into soft, three-dimensional puddles.

The new painting was incredibly beautiful. It resembled the visions Elena had in mind, but it still seemed a little flat, a poor replica of what she had experienced in that desert cave. However imperfect though, it promised to give birth to the others in an attempt to bring her experience and inner knowing more fully alive on the canvas.

Moses appeared as if on cue. He meowed loudly, then pawed at her leg insistently. The light was fading, and he was hungry again. Moses wasn't like other cats. You couldn't just put down a pile of food for him to last the day. He would gobble it all at once and then meow in pain from his overfull tummy. She gave him a little in the morning and then a more substantial portion in the evening. His anticipation of mealtime was like clockwork, and she swore he could tell time.

"Okay, okay. I know. It's way past dinner time, isn't it?" Elena said as she picked him up. "What do you think? Is it done?" She asked as she pointed him toward the canvas. Moses replied with an irritable meow that said "Feed me. Now!" Elena set him down and headed toward the kitchen to fill his bowl.

Moses chomped ravenously at the tiny pieces of cat kibble, letting out an occasional purr between bites. Elena wrapped herself in a prayer shawl and adjusted her chair for a better view of the most recent painting. Vague images of people, going about their business but surrounded by brilliant streaks of paint that zigged and zagged in colorful, gentle patterns around them, then streamed upward from the tops of their heads into a single stream of light connecting all of them. Around the perimeter, vibrant dots and streaks of light enveloped the entire scene. There was something familiar about those zigzag patterns, something beyond the visions from the Ark. What was it?

Chills ran up and down Elena's arms, and fluttering sensations filled her chest. She had seen these before. She sat up straight. She'd seen them before the Ark! In fact, she had always been aware of this brilliant pattern of light that surrounded people. The goosebumps now reached every part of her body as the recollection unfolded itself.

As a child, drawing had been her refuge. She drew cats and dogs, and flowers, all the things that brought her joy. When things got frightening at home, she comforted herself with paper and crayons. The feeling of the crayon rubbing across the paper, creating something beautiful in the midst of what scared her, was soothing. She ignored what was going on around her and created another world altogether.

In third grade, she had drawn pictures of people with zig-zagged patterns around them. Art period, which only came once a week on Friday afternoons, was her favorite. She longed for it all week as she suffered through math, handwriting, spelling, geography, and religion classes. One week, the assignment was to draw something that looked like a photograph, as realistically as possible.

Filled with joy at the opportunity to record the beauty of the world around her, she fervently filled the page with children playing in the park. Elena's heart was full as she filled the large piece of drawing paper with every color available in her jumbo-size box of Crayolas. She felt, rather than saw Sister Catherine standing behind her, watching. "What on earth are you drawing, Elena?" she asked. "What are all those patterns surrounding the children? The assignment is to draw something that looks like a photograph. It's supposed to look real."

Elena could not mistake the look of concern on Sr. Catherine's face as she explained that this *was* real. She was drawing the children the way they looked to her. "See. This one is excited, and most of her colors are red and yellow. This one is sad because he's all alone and his colors have a lot of brown and gray mixed in with blues and greens," she explained.

Elena had been amazed to learn that other people did not see these patterns of light around each other. Didn't everyone see them? After several trips to an eye specialist, followed by several visits to a community counseling service, the visions began to fade. Elena trained her eyes to ignore them until she completely forgot their presence.

Until the Ark.

Moisture welled up in Elena's eyes as she realized she had always known that people were really made of light and that it emanated visibly from the earthly bodies they inhabited. Tears spilled over her lower lids and ran down her cheeks. She had always known but had forgotten. She had buried this ability to conform to the world around her. Until now.

**

Days later, Moses sat purring in her lap. Tummy full, he appeared content to view the new series of paintings with her. She stroked his head and rubbed his ears absently as she scanned the various works leaning against the wall. Each of the six new paintings had the same ethereal particles and swirls of light as the first. The first two were just color and light. The others were nebulous scenes or objects enveloped in and permeated by the colorful light, images of life itself taking shape and form. Except the most recent one.

Elena's eyes fell upon the unfinished painting of the series, a fountain that took shape amid flowing, swirling patterns of light. Explorers of old had searched for a fountain of youth, deemed to be a priceless treasure to humankind. This was not a fountain of youth. It was far more valuable than that. It was the fountainhead of life itself. A multitude of spouts adorned the fount, spilling light rather than water into an ever-expanding array of basins. The spouts resembled flowers, yet there was something eerily human about them. Tiny lotus blossoms floated about the bowls, each emitting a luminous, peaceful glow.

We are one in an infinite Fountain of Life, Elena thought. *We are its cascading spouts, and It flows through us. Our thoughts, our feelings, and our expressions of love float like lotus flowers into its overflowing basins and then scatter like droplets of water bouncing from its surface.*

Elena reached for the small purple journal on the side table to record her thoughts. She would use them later for a commentary on the series.

> *The ultimate mission of each droplet is to flow back again into the one infinite stream of life that is whole and complete. The bowls of water, floating flowers, and graceful spouts are all connected by the endless flow of this mystical fountain, yet somehow, each*

drop, each spray of water, each delicate flower float-
ing in its bowl believes itself to be somehow separate,
alone, and powerless.

The painting, Elena hoped, would rouse a feeling, perhaps a long-ing, and ultimately a question. Still, something was missing. There was something more she wanted it to express, but there was nothing left to paint. It was done; overworking it would only muddy the scene.

Elena grabbed her cell phone and sent a text to her agent, Renee. "New series emerging. Come by so we can talk about putting in the show." All the marketing for the upcoming show had been printed be-fore the dig, and there weren't enough new paintings for an exhibit of their own. But maybe she could include some of them as a preview for another show. Renee would like that idea. Elena was sure of it.

She tapped her phone a few times to bring up her most recent stream of text messages to Zak. She hadn't seen him since their return. He was busy with paperwork and prepping for the fall semester. His texts had been brief and seemed a bit distant. "Lunch?" she typed.

CHAPTER THREE

Math or Aftermath

Zak Erdmann stared at the spreadsheet on his computer screen. Half-finished cups of cold coffee stood sentinel around the toppling stacks of papers that littered his desk. He absently rubbed his temples and shook his head. There was no data to enter. No measurements. No tests. No proof. Nothing to verify. The decision to return the artifact to its hiding place had been unanimous. There had been no discussion. Even he had agreed at the time, but without it, there was nothing to report, just mishaps, tragedies, and seemingly fruitless labor.

The summer Egyptian Field Study at Qasr Ibrim had unearthed a plethora of worthy pieces to log and research, but he couldn't get the Ark, and the potential for further study it represented, out of his mind. They hadn't even measured the thing before hiding it away again. The box itself was no larger than an oversized picnic cooler, but it was heavy enough to have been made of solid gold. They had tried to shift it farther into the hidden chamber before concealing it, but all their strength and knowledge of physics had not been enough to move it from its initial place. Unable to reposition it, they had carefully concealed it by replacing every rock and stone they had painstakingly removed in discovering it. In the end, they had left the most significant discovery of all time right where they had found it without so much as a word, and no reportable data. There weren't even photographs to review. Elena's camera had been destroyed the night before, and they had left their cell phones at the primary site. There was no use carrying them; the lack of signal made them useless in the open desert. The satellite phones worked, but they had no cameras.

Zak picked up one of the stacks of reports and began rifling through it. What difference did these trivial pieces of parchment and cracked pottery make when he could be logging information about the Ark? Artifacts that usually excited him held no fascination now. He rubbed his bloodshot eyes, weary from lack of sleep, and tossed the pile back on the desk. It was no use. He would not be able to rest until he brought the Ark back. *It's not the glory,* he thought. *It's the science. I need to know. Is it real? Is it the real Ark of the Covenant? Can it be proven? How can I just leave that piece behind with all that it represents, all that could be learned from it, and not verify anything about it? Verify. Humph. If it could be verified. And what the hell happened in that cave, anyway?*

Zak was beginning to wonder if the strange experience had happened at all. *Maybe it was all a delusion, a mass hallucination brought on by the trauma of the night before the discovery.* He picked up the stack of papers again and began entering numbers into a database.

A subtle vibration at his hip caused him to drop the reports. He froze and watched as the papers scattered about. Another vibration! Memories of the sensations they felt near the Ark flooded his mind. His chest tightened, and his breathing grew shallow. Another twinge! He looked down then and saw it was just his cell phone. He unclipped it from his belt. A text message from Elena. "Lunch?" it read. He set the phone down on the desk and started gathering the scattered papers. *Later,* he thought. *I don't even know what the hell to say to her. I've got to go back there, and there's no way she's going to agree to it.*

Lost in his internal battle, Zak was startled by a knock on his office door. "Come in," he said, closing the lid of his laptop. The door swung inward revealing its bronze door plaque, "Dr. Zachary T. Erdmann, Professor of Archaeology and Director of Graduate Studies." Strutting past the sign, Gina, the Research Assistant assigned to him for the upcoming semester, breezed in, pausing at his desk. "Is there anything I can do for you, Dr. Erdmann?" she asked. "More coffee, maybe?" Her tone seemed to be a subtle mix of concern and sarcasm as she viewed the growing population of coffee cups on his desk. "Or maybe I can just help you get a little more organized?" she said as she began collecting the cups. Gina was a very attentive assistant, almost too attentive at times. She'd been with him for a few weeks now, and she was so fast at accomplishing the tasks he gave her that he had trouble keeping her busy. She was continually looking for more work and interrupting his thoughts.

Zak looked at the piles of paperwork surrounding him. Maybe he could hand off some of these reports. That should take her a while, and it would get them off his plate. It wouldn't help him sleep, but at least he could find his coffee.

"Leave the cups, Gina. I'll get them. Have a seat," he said. "I need to get the fall syllabus ready, and I could use your help with logging some of these research reports."

Gina sat. She glanced around the room taking in the rumpled jackets strewn haphazardly about and the stacks of books with sticky notes protruding from their pages covering nearly every horizontal surface. She eyed the professor as he attempted to organize the mass of papers on his desk. A handsome man, he was tall, slender, and had this sandy brown hair that swept back in soft, enticing waves, even when it was disheveled as it was now. She wasn't sure whether he was more attractive clean-shaven or with the beard that had accompanied him home from the last dig. She had been so excited to be assigned to Dr. Erdmann. He was highly respected; his published works were renowned, and his field work nearly legendary. But lately, that was not the case. The news reports of the tragic loss of life during the summer field work clouded his otherwise pristine image.

His most recent adventure had engaged more legal experts at the college than archeologists. So many mishaps, tragedies, and inquiries about the uncharted portion of the expedition. And, it appeared there was nothing to show for it. They had found nothing. The excavation reports were seriously overdue, and Dr. Erdmann looked like hell. He was distant, lost in a dream most of the time, his usually boyish smile buried by the beard and tired eyes. He looked like he hadn't slept in weeks. Gina wondered if there was another professor she could be assigned to, someone whose name might ultimately look better on her resume. Now he was pulling three bulging folders from the chaos that was his desk.

"Here," Zak said, handing her the overflowing folders. "These are artifact reference logs from the Qasr Ibrim field study. Each sheet correlates with one of the pieces stored in the lab. The reference numbers match the drawer numbers. Every item needs to be measured, weighed, and examined. This stack," he said, pointing to the one on top, "refers to items that could be carbon-dated and should be checked for any remaining particulates. It's not likely we'll find any; not much survives the desert sand, but being thorough sometimes reveals the unexpected. The items in the other two folders need more log details and may need additional test requests."

Gina looked a bit overwhelmed as she flipped through the files. Her eyes widened with every page. It was an enormous task, not intended for one person. But the loss of life during the field study had left the job in the hands of just a few survivors.

"Don't worry," said Zak. "Once the semester starts next week, there will be students to help. Here, let me show you where the right drawers are." He stood and slid open the glass door behind his desk that led to the lab beyond.

The condition of the lab was in stark contrast to Zak's office. Everything was immaculate and in its place. Gina followed him to one of the large stainless-steel worktables, gleaming under the sophisticated equipment placed carefully on its top. Hundreds of meticulously labeled drawers and cabinets lined the walls. This was the clean room, where newly acquired specimens were stored in airtight, locked containers awaiting scientific scrutiny. Everything was in perfect order, and Zak's coffee cups and general dishevelment had not breached its walls.

Zak removed a numbered drawer from behind the table and set it down in front of Gina. "This sample corresponds to the numbered sheet in the first set of files. Everything was sorted and labeled at the field lab. You just need to go through the checklist for each item. If a piece calls for more research than we can do here, there are forms and procedures for sending them to the appropriate facility. Everything here is on loan through the American Research Center in Egypt and there is a deadline for their return," Zak said.

Gina nodded, looking at the checklist. "Simple enough," she said as she began flipping through the next several sheets, glancing periodically at the matching drawers.

Zak felt his muscles relax and a wave of relief flowing through him as he watched her reviewing the files. It felt good to get these details off his plate. He had more important things to research. He glanced at the vault behind the table and then back at Gina. She was still rifling through the files, with the folders now spread out on the table. *Should I show it to her? She's bound to see it at some point.* Zak nodded to himself as if he had come to some conclusion. Pulling a key from his pants pocket, Zak unlocked a vault and removed a small, covered, stainless steel tray. Gina looked up at the whooshing sound of the vacuum seal being released and the clink of a metal tray on the table and looked up inquisitively.

"This is a separate project, Gina. It's highly confidential. Those reports have to be finished first, but working on this piece will be the reward."

Gina watched as Zak removed the cover and, with gloved hands, withdrew a beige-colored stone tablet from the tray. Lines and symbols were carved into its chipped and worn surface.

"What do you make of this, Gina?" Zak asked, sliding the tray toward her.

Gina's eyes widened as she examined the piece. "It's a map!" she said. "Glyphs and ... something else." Gina's eyes seemed to focus on something in the distance, perhaps the eidetic memory she tended to boast about. With a background in ancient languages and a keen interest in ancient cartography, some of the symbols on the tablet were no doubt immediately recognizable.

"Yes, a map," Zak agreed. "It's not cataloged yet, and the field lab tests were incomplete, but the little we were able to translate in the field was very interesting." Zak lied. It was true, they hadn't done extensive testing at the field lab, but they had indeed translated the map. That was what led them to the desert cave. But the only survivors of that knowledge were those who had been in the presence of the Ark. The others on the expedition had either been unaware of the full translation, or were no longer among the living.

"Can you contact Dr. Mason and see if he is available this afternoon? I'd like him to take a look." Zak retrieved the tray from her and returned it to the cabinet, turning just in time to see a look of longing in Gina's gray-blue eyes. She wanted to see more of that tablet. It had piqued her interest. *Good*, he thought. *I need someone to get excited about this. I've got to inspire a team to go back. It's just too important to leave there.*

Gina gathered the file folders in one arm and pushed a loose strand of her carrot-red hair behind her ear. "I'm on it, Dr. Erdmann. Let me take these files back to my desk so I can get myself organized before jumping in." She spoke carefully as if trying not to imply that the files were a disheveled mess and would need to be sorted out before anyone could make heads or tails of them. "And I'll let you know about Dr. Mason's schedule."

Zak was pleased with the enthusiasm he heard in Gina's voice. Even through his emotional fog, he had noticed that her interest in working with him had been waning. He couldn't blame her. Who would want to work with someone who had nearly destroyed his own reputation and was so preoccupied that he couldn't complete the simplest research notes? Now she was sparkling and smiling at him in an almost coquettish fashion.

Zak watched through the lab's windowed walls as she walked away, the sound of her high-heels fading with every step. Her red hair gently bobbing about as she walked reminded him of the color of autumn leaves. She was an attractive woman, and her passion for the field was just as alluring as the view of her tall, slender body walking away. For a moment he felt an intense attraction to her, but pushed it away quickly. She was a student. A Research Assistant. He had enough trouble with the school over the uncharted expedition. He didn't need a sexual-harassment case on top of it.

Returning to his office, Zak closed the sliding-glass door and picked up his cell phone to respond to Elena. Two more texts had come in from her. "Helllooo?" and "Stop working so hard, let's get lunch."

Zak began typing a response. "Can't make it. Too far behind. Sorry." He added a sad face and clicked send. He felt his own mouth twisting into a sad face then. He felt bad. He missed his best friend, and they hadn't seen each other since they had returned from the dig.

Crap. I should go. But I can't. I just can't face her right now. I can't let her talk me out of going back. I need to sort out what happened there, and I know where she stands on this.

He flipped through the contacts on his phone, found Josh Pearson, and placed a call. Maybe Josh would understand. Maybe he would be willing to go back. Maybe he was thinking along the same lines: Was it real? Did it really happen? And if it did, doesn't the world deserve to know? And who the hell had tried to kill them? The American papers had theorized it was an ISIS attack, but ISIS had not claimed the shootings. The U.S. investigation had failed to discover anything helpful, and it was unlikely that the Egyptian or Sudanese governments would bother to investigate further. Bir Tawil was of no interest to either country, and neither had jurisdiction. Basically, no one there seemed to care that a bunch of Americans venturing into a no-man's-land had run into trouble.

Zak heard Josh's voice and took a breath before speaking. "Josh? Hey, I might have some work for you ... Yeah, another dig, but it's more than that. We need some investigation first and a very detailed security plan ... Well, yeah. I do want to go back ... I know, but I think we have to go back. I think there's more going on than we realized. I really need your help ... Great. Thanks ... How about Monday? Eleven? ... Yep. That will work. My first class isn't until 1:00 on Monday. Okay, thanks, man. See you then."

Zak breathed a sigh of relief as he fingered a small, sealed package in his pocket. It was the missing piece, the broken corner of the ancient stone map. They had found it almost immediately after the larger specimen, and it described the exact location of the Ark. It had been logged and checked out as a separate piece. Only those who had been in the cave knew what it was and what it contained.

Zak opened his bottom desk drawer, entered the combination to the small desk safe bolted to the drawer and placed the object in it. It felt good to know that he had started the ball rolling and would soon be able to reveal the truth about this small piece of stone and hopefully, the greatest of all discoveries that it pointed to.

A knock at the door interrupted Zak's musings. "Come in," he said, thinking Gina must have heard back from Dr. Mason. The door swung open revealing an unexpected figure. Clad in white leggings and a sheer, green flowered top that flowed into a hemline of random angles and lengths, stood Elena. She wore flat but attractive shoes. Elena had never gone for high-heels. At 5'6" she didn't need them. Besides, she was much too practical to gain a few inches of power at the expense of comfortable, healthy feet. Elena provided the only color in what had been a dull and bland environment for the past few weeks. Even in the field, Elena wore colorful, tie-dyed shirts created to intentionally add flair to the drab brown setting of the desert.

"I'm not taking no for an answer, Zak. We are going to lunch now." As she glanced around the room, her eyes widened. When her gaze settled on him, he stroked his unshaven face as if he could magically clean away the scruffy beard.

"What the hell, Zak? What's going on? You look like you haven't slept in weeks." She began picking up cups and empty food wrappers, tossing them in the trash.

Zak watched as she moved gracefully through the room picking up after him. It was unlike her. She didn't usually notice such things as clutter. In fact, her apartment was an eclectic hodgepodge of art, possible art, and general disarray. Visitors never ate at her kitchen table, as the other chair was always piled high with unopened junk mail.

"You look ravishing," Zak said with a smile, "although you do look like you haven't eaten in a while." She looked thinner than he had ever seen her, and he was sure it wasn't just the illusion created by the billowing green fabric over the tight slacks.

"Well," Elena said. "I have been a bit preoccupied – forgetting to eat. I've been painting scenes from … I've been painting a lot, getting ready for the show and all. I've finished five new paintings and started a sixth since we got home. I've actually considered switching to acrylics because they dry so much faster, but I'm such a purist I can't bear to put away my linseed oil.

"Anyway, I haven't had much time for food, and I'm starving – and we are getting you out of here. Let's go someplace where we can both have a good meal."

Zak stood, brushing off his pants and choosing one of the rumpled jackets from the top of the credenza. He shook it out in a futile attempt to rid it of wrinkles. Things were moving now, and the research files were off his desk. He could use a good lunch and some sunlight. "You're right. I do need to get out of here for a while. Let's …." He paused at the sound of high-heeled footsteps in the hallway. As the echo reached the door, a pair of high black pumps topped with long slender legs were followed by a crop of silky red hair.

Elena could feel rather than see Gina's energy as she poked her head around the door, her hair falling across one visible shoulder as she leaned around the door. She looked piercingly at Elena, scanning her from head to toe as if determining in a single swipe who she was, why she was there, and if she were a threat to any of her plans. It gave Elena a cold, rippling feeling in the pit of her stomach. She suddenly felt chilled all over.

"Dr. Mason will be by at 2:00. I hope that's okay. You haven't made other plans I hope?" Gina said, looking at Elena and stepping fully into the doorway.

"No, 2:00 will be fine Gina, Ele… my friend and I are just stepping out for a quick bite. I'll be back. Thank you. That's all, Gina," he said.

Gina gave another chilling glance at Elena and turned to leave, the sound of her high heels against the hard, institutional tiles drumming a bellicose beat as they faded away.

Elena turned to Zak. Even beneath his ample growth of facial hair, she could see his face turning red. "Woah! Who was that? I think she kind of likes you," Elena said, raising an eyebrow. "Watch out for her. I think she wants a bit more than a date with you."

"Yeah ... Gina. She's my Research Assistant for the year. Don't worry. She's actually lost a little interest since I've been so, umm ... preoccupied. Besides, I'm really not that naïve. It is rather flattering, though. Anyway, she's really quite helpful…."

"I bet she is," Elena said with a grin.

"No. Uh, I mean she's highly capable in her field. She graduated summa cum laude from the University of Chicago where she studied Near Eastern Languages with a focus on Egyptian hieroglyphics. She's doing her grad work here with a concentration on ancient cartography."

Elena stiffened a little. "Cartography? Map reading? Did you show it to her?" Elena sounded incredulous.

"No. Not the broken sherd, anyway. She's seen the main piece, it was inevitable. But no one here has seen the fragment. I have that secured," he said moving toward the door. "Let's go."

"How about the Parthenon?" Zak asked as they walked out into the bright blue light of day. The Parthenon was just down the street from the school. The café on campus was good as far as college food went, but they needed a bit more privacy and definitely better food.

"Great. I love Greek food. Actually, I'm so hungry, I don't really care what we eat, but a gyro with fries sounds amazing right now."

They walked the two short blocks to the Parthenon, chit-chatting and maneuvering through the crowded sidewalks. It seemed everyone on the street was going the other way. In the cool respite of the restaurant, they slid into the green vinyl seats of a small booth. The atmosphere was quiet and homey, except for occasional shouts from the kitchen. The decor was a bit cheesy; greenery hung from the walls, some real, some fake. You could recognize the silk ones by the dust accumulating on their leaves. Poorly rendered abstract paintings adorned the walls. Elena thought they must have been done by a family member. They weren't museum-ready, but they had an aura of love about them, and they added to the charm and coziness of the place.

"So, tell me, Zak. What's keeping you up at night? Why haven't you been sleeping? You look like hell." She knew the answer, but had to ask.

Zak looked pensive. He pulled his lips into a tight line as if he wanted to hold his words inside behind them. Then he let out a long sigh and said, "It's the Ark, Elena. I can't get it out of my head. I feel … I don't know what to do with my thoughts, my questions, the very idea that I had this thing in my hands and let it slip away is driving me crazy." He let more air out of his pursed lips as if he had released some pressurized gas through them.

Elena looked at him, her green eyes softening "I know. It's okay. I knew this would be toughest on you. I have my paintings. Paul has his writing. Josh, well I don't know what Josh has, but you need something we couldn't bring back. But you have your memories, Zak. You know from what we experienced that the value of the Ark is not in finding it, or displaying it, or measuring it, or any of that. It's in the message that it holds."

"But that's just it, Elena. If this message is … well, if it's ... re, um true." He was stumbling with his words a bit. Elena wasn't sure if it was lack of sleep or that he just didn't know how to say what was on his mind.

"If that was the true message of the Ark, doesn't the world need to know it? he asked. Not just in images or books but the actual experience? And if it isn't true, then why the hell did we leave something so important in the middle of the desert where it will either be lost forever or stolen by whoever was following us."

"What do you mean by *if* it's true?" she asked. "You were there. You saw it. You felt it. I know you did because I could read your thoughts."

Zak took a sip of the water their waitress had just set before him. "We were distraught, Elena. We'd just witnessed a mass murder. We escaped from what we expected to be certain death when we headed up that mountain. Has it occurred to you that we may have been in shock, experiencing some kind of PTSD ... an illusion?"

"You mean *delusion*, don't you?" said Elena, the furrow of her brow deepening and the glint in her green eyes sharpening. "How can you think that? Have you closed yourself off that quickly to what we saw and felt? Are you so wrapped up in the glory of the artifact that you can't recall the beauty of the experience? That was no delusion, Zak. That was real. I can still see the energy we saw there. I see it swirling around people everywhere I go.

"In fact, I realized as I got home and started painting that I have always been able to see people's energy. I had just hidden it from myself. I guess because it made me different or something. Anyway, it was real. It *IS* real."

Zak gave a slight nod and took a long, slow sip of water. "What about your show?" he asked. "How's that coming along?"

"Nice segue, Zak. But yeah, let's talk about something else. The show is pretty much set to go. I have several new paintings inspired by our experience in the desert – with the Ark I mean – not the shootings. I'm including them as a teaser for my next showing. Renee is excited about the new pieces. She says they are '... Fantastic, wholly unique, and very marketable,'" Elena said in an impersonation of Renee's voice. "Marketable is, of course, her first concern, but that is why I pay her." Elena pulled her cell phone out to show him the recent paintings.

"Wow. They're great, Elena. They do have some elements of ... They look great," he said, handing the phone back to her.

"The opening is Friday. You do plan on coming, don't you?"

"Of course. I wouldn't miss it."

Their waitress took their order then, and they continued lunch with light conversations about Elena's show and the fall classes Zak would be teaching. Elena was relieved they were able to avoid talking more about the Ark; she hated when they disagreed. Yet, beneath the relief, she had a subtle inkling that he was already planning his return to the cave.

They parted ways as they reached the campus, Zak heading toward the school and Elena toward the train back to the Village. She looked over her shoulder and called to him, "By the way, Zak, I wasn't kidding about being able to see people's energy. And that assistant of yours … hers is really dark and extremely cold. Watch out for her."

CHAPTER FOUR

The Queen of Bir Tawil

Josh pushed the "End Call" button on his cell phone, wondering what he had just signed up for. His slender brown fingers pushed open a slit in the vertical blinds, revealing treetops outside his home office window, their leaves gently fluttering in a welcome breeze. It was still summer, but one lone leaf at the very top of a broadleaf maple was turning a brilliant shade of orange, an indication of what was to come. Change was inevitable, whether it was the seasons, relationships, or just life in general. Josh was pretty sure life in general was about to change – radically.

Releasing the blinds and plopping the phone onto his desk, Josh noticed the folders arranged there. Working as a licensed private investigator for the Braxton & Highwater law firm while finishing his Master's in international law had proven profitable, if a little boring. High-profile international cases didn't fall on his desk often, but working at the firm did afford him access to an almost unlimited investigation network. Most of the cases assigned to Josh involved ill-fated relationships or potentially fraudulent disability claims. What Zak was suggesting was infinitely more interesting and likely more lucrative.

A successful excursion in Egypt would do much to further his experience working with international law enforcement and help erase the stain of the previous expedition. They'd done nothing wrong other than being a bit naïve in their pursuit of an un-researched dig site and lack of proper security. But the cloud that surrounded the shootings in Bir Tawil was no way to start a career in international law.

Josh had joined the recent field study as a member of the security team for credit toward his Masters. It was a pretty sweet deal. He paid tuition, room, and board, and gained experience working with international law enforcement that could augment his thesis. Security was a pretty broad word for what his assignment actually had been. Josh had spent most of his time checking credentials for entry into the site and checking the backpacks and cases of those exiting the site. Local authorities handled anything beyond the day-to-day clearance checks. Until Zak had led them into the no-man's-land of Bir Tawil.

The field team hadn't even issued him a sidearm, which had made Josh intensely nervous. He had seen a lot of action in Iraq and Afghanistan. Combat changed a person, and he had been uncomfortable without a weapon on his side.

Change. Josh hadn't really known what the word meant until now. Every aspect of his life had changed, and it promised to change even more. He no longer slept with a gun by his side. Life no longer seemed black and white. If war had changed him for the worse, the Ark had changed him for the better. He no longer saw enemies everywhere. Instead, he recognized that all people yearned for the same things: peace, harmony, happiness. They just somehow managed to get it all mucked up in the process. It was that mucking up that was driving him now. How could he use his newfound peace and understanding to help others, possibly even the world?

Maybe Zak was right. Maybe bringing the Ark back would make some kind of difference. Their absolute certainty that it was to remain hidden when they left the site was waning now – for him and Zak anyway. Back in the real world, there was still a lot of mucking-up going on. Something had to change, and maybe the Ark could help with that.

Josh flipped open the lid to his laptop, and it slowly began coming to life. Delving into the shootings in Bir Tawil would be an excellent place to start. He'd managed to make some contacts with the Egyptian authorities during the field study, and they might be able to help. There was no way he was going back without making sure they would be safe. And, even though he didn't see enemies everywhere anymore, he glanced at the gun safe on his bookshelf. He wouldn't be going alone this time.

The computer screen was up now, and Josh clicked the web browser icon. In the search box, he entered "Bir Tawil." Pictures of sand and rock and a small collection of links to written articles came up on his screen. The Wikipedia article was at the top:

> *Bir Tawil or Bi'r Tawīl is a 2,060 km (800 sq mi) area*
> *along the border between Egypt and Sudan, which is*
> *uninhabited and claimed by neither country.*

Claimed by neither country. There was the problem. No one was responsible for this area, and almost no one traveled there. It was desolate, dry, and nearly uninhabitable, which made the shooting scene that much more of a mystery. Who had shot at them? Why? And why did they stop? What caused them to leave before finishing the job? He was thankful they hadn't finished the job, but none of it made sense.

Visions of the victims and the handful of survivors began to surface in Josh's mind, but he pushed them back down. He'd had enough nightmares after his military tours and was determined not to experience them again.

Josh began clicking on links, reading whatever he could find. There was nothing of value in this desolate area, which was why no one wanted it. Sudan refused to claim it and kept only a few small military units nearby to maintain peace among the gold miners and armed gangs sparsely populating the outskirts and to prevent entry into their own country. Egypt didn't want it, either. It was just a wasteland, not worth their time or resources to govern, other than guarding their own border and intervening as necessary with Bedouin disputes. Any attempt at jurisdiction by either country would exclude them from what each believed to be rightful ownership of the Hala'ib Triangle, a much more desirable piece of land. Egypt wanted to honor the earlier boundaries drawn in 1899 granting Bir Tawil to Sudan, which would give them legal possession of the Hala'ib triangle. Sudan, also intent on rights to the more valuable triangle of land, wanted to honor the later treaties of 1902 bequeathing Bir Tawil to Egypt.

If these two countries only knew what lay hidden in an obscure mountain cave in that dusty wasteland; an artifact more valuable than anyone in either country could imagine. They'd change their minds quickly if they got wind of this. Josh hoped Zak would be pretty creative with his grant proposals and research designs to gain permission and funding without over-tipping his hand.

***

Hours later, Josh was still flipping through pages on the internet, but now he was researching the Ark itself, its history, and what people believed had happened to it. He was not an archaeologist, so the legends of its whereabouts were a bit obtuse. As a kid, Josh had attended the AME (African Methodist Episcopal) Zion Church whose motto claimed it to be an Ark of Safety, but Josh was pretty sure that reference was to Noah's Ark, not the Ark of Moses. Either way, he didn't recall anyone mentioning where the Ark had ended up. There was the Moses story in the Bible and the movie *The Ten Commandments*, but what happened after that? He didn't even recall his dad talking about it much, and he was a minister. Maybe he needed more books. Jewish books.

Flipping through his browser history, Josh began bookmarking pages for further review before heading off to the library, and then the firm. He would need a lot more to go on than what his personal internet access could provide. As he was closing down the pages though, something caught his eye. It was an image of a makeshift flag stuck in the rocks of a Bir Tawil landscape. It was purple and black with a gold, two-headed eagle in the middle of it. There was a symbol on the eagle's breast he couldn't quite make out.

Opening the article, Josh read about a Kansas City man who had traveled to Bir Tawil, planted the flag in the ground, and claimed it as his kingdom. It had been an outlandish anniversary present for his wife, making her the Queen of Bir Tawil. There were a few similar stories of people staking claims to the area, but no government took any of them seriously. To actually claim the land as an independent country would require resources that were just not available. It would require an army too, one that could hold its own against Sudan and Egypt, an unlikely scenario.

Still, there was something about the picture in this article that captured Josh's attention. What was it? He clicked on the photograph and zoomed in. Oliver Quinn, the King of Bir Tawil, was an average-looking white man, average height, brown hair, square face with rounded cheeks, and an ordinary nose. He couldn't distinguish the eye color. There was nothing extraordinary about the man, other than this outlandish adventure in Bir Tawil.

Josh shifted the photo to the left to get another look at the flag. The symbol on the eagle's chest was still too small to make out. He clicked the zoom button again, 150%. 200%. 440%. It was a little blurry, but he could see it better now. It was a capital *P* with a small *x* crossing the vertical stem. He'd seen that emblem somewhere before, but where? He tapped his finger lightly on the keyboard, not pressing any keys, just keeping time with the sifting of memories. *P and X ... P and X....*

He *had* seen it before! It was the prominent image of the stained-glass window framing the sanctuary of his childhood church. It was the *Chi* something. They had called it the Pax symbol when they were kids. He thought it had something to do with peace. *Chi... Chi...*

Josh closed his eyes and imagined that stained-glass window. He could see the colorful light pouring in through its leaded panes; blues, greens, reds, and golds. In the center, stood a capital P with an x crossing its stem. A vague memory of letters on either side of the P began taking shape on the mental screen inside his head. *Chi ... Rho.* Josh typed the letters, into the browser bar. Wikipedia's definition was again the first to appear:

> *The Chi Rho ... christogram, formed by superimposing the first two letters, chi, and rho, of the Greek word ΧΡΙΣΤΟΣ (Christos) ...*

Josh continued his search. It was an early Christian symbol, still a familiar emblem in churches today, most notably Catholic churches. That made sense. The AME church had purchased their building from the Catholic diocese. Josh jotted some notes on a small pad of paper and slipped it into his shirt pocket. He closed the lid on the computer and grabbed his phone. He planned to visit the library first, then head to the firm. The library would provide more information about the Ark itself. The internet was overflowing with repetitive details of popular theories, but finding the more obscure information from archaeology reports and newspaper stories would require a library collection.

And then the firm. There he could learn more about this Oliver Quinn. It was probably nothing, but he had this feeling deep in his stomach that told him there was something more to this man and his flag. Josh had no idea what Oliver Quinn, the Church, and a purple flag had to do with the incident in Bir Tawil, but he intended to find out.

CHAPTER FIVE

Shattered Images

The gallery was full of people chatting, laughing, sipping wine, and eating dollops of brie on thin, gourmet crackers. Elena's work peppered the stark white walls with one section devoted to the new paintings. The gallery owner, Sheila, was in her glory, going on and on about Elena's latest style and the way she blended the colors to create such depth, such an exciting play of objects, shadows, and light. Red dots began to appear on the paintings. Sold. Sold. Sold. It was a good night for art.

Elena's chest grew tight, her breath shallow as she sipped her wine and listened to the conversations around her. "I love this one, don't you George? It goes perfectly with our new sofa, don't you think?" Over the shoulder of the guest who was currently garnering her attention, she caught a glimpse of a couple holding up paint chips to see if they matched any of the colors in her work. A gallery patron was describing another piece and what the artist meant to say. And it was not at all what she had intended. She couldn't breathe. Her head was spinning. The electric vibrations running through her body that had haunted her since her return became overwhelming. She turned abruptly away from Mrs. Randolph, one of her most devout patrons, and walked away.

***

Renee Cunningham, Elena's agent, stood several feet away, wearing a short pink jacket over a pair of white crop pants with lace edging just above the ankle. Her face, framed by short, black hair that swooped dramatically over one side, looked tense. She had watched Elena's face grow pale, then suddenly red. Then she had walked away in the middle of a conversation with Mrs. Randolph.

Elena seemed off balance, not herself. She hadn't been the same since that dig with Zak. There had been terrible accidents and then the mass shooting. Renee had expected these traumatic experiences to show up in Elena's work, but instead, she painted these incredibly beautiful and ethereal works that exuded peace and harmony. The work was fabulous. The evening was going quite well, but Elena was distant, disengaged from it. She had been unusually agreeable negotiating the prices of her work. She hadn't said a word about how and where they were hung. Typically, she would have been there rearranging and rehanging things until the doors opened. There had been disappointment flickering behind her green eyes over that one painting though, the one that was still slightly wet that Renee had suggested did not belong in this show, but Elena had agreed with no argument.

There was something dark about that painting, almost repelling. Maybe it was the start of a new series, one that would express the horrors Elena had experienced in the desert. *It would be therapeutic for her,* Renee thought, *but hardly saleable.* Renee sighed as she caught a glimpse of Elena walking away from the couple with the paint chips.

The look in Elena's eyes now was something different. Anger? Desperation? Disgust? This wasn't Elena's first show. Surely, she had grown impervious to inexpert art commentaries by now. But she looked almost enraged, then suddenly disconnected, no longer interacting with anyone. All evening she had been walking away in the middle of conversations. And now she was leaving the gallery! *Where on Earth is she going? And what is she thinking? This is no way to sell paintings.*

Renee knew how to sell paintings, and she knew how to engage patrons. She thrived on it. She had found her perfect niche representing artists, combining her immense love for the arts with her keen business sense. Elena was her easiest client, or at least she had been. She was generally amiable, prolific, always producing work that appealed to collectors and high-end galleries. They had become good friends over the years, and Renee had never seen Elena like this.

Elena had tough skin. Anyone who had received an MFA from NYU'S Steinhardt School had learned to endure discouraging commentaries of their work. You couldn't survive the departmental critiques otherwise. And she had paid her dues in the art world, living off the proceeds of crazy schemes and menial jobs to support her work. She'd even done art fairs at one point. If there was any place an artist was likely to hear unqualified comments about her work, that was it. This was totally out of character for Elena, and Renee was genuinely concerned. Maybe the trauma was finally catching up with her. She couldn't follow her. Someone had to attend to the guests. Renee reached into her bag and grabbed her cell phone.

"RU ok?" She texted Elena, but there was no response.

"Have you lost ur mind?" Renee felt her temperature rising and her muscles stiffening when little dots appeared on her screen.

"Not feeling well. Sorry," came the reply.

"Should I send Zak to check on you when he gets here?" Renee texted back.

"Yes."

Renee dropped the phone back in her bag and moved toward a group of stunned guests, picking up the conversation. "You'll have to forgive Elena. She hasn't been well lately. I'm sure she just needed a little air. Aren't you just in love with this piece? It feels like you are standing in the midst of some unworldly realm, don't you think? I mean I've seen some intense Northern Lights, but they pale in comparison to this. I just want to linger here in front of it forever."

Mrs. Randolph agreed. "I can't take my eyes off it," she said. "I was just asking Elena if she could paint a larger one just like it. It would be a lovely addition to my Great Room. Can you imagine the effect on guests as they enter? It would be stupendous!"

"I'm sure Elena would be happy to work with you on a commission, Mrs. Randolph. But this? This is a one-of-a-kind, unlikely to be repeated. Another one could never have the exact same feel and essence that this one does. Are you sure this won't fill the space? Or, maybe another space, something more intimate? I know you will be so disappointed if you don't own this one."

"That's what Elena was saying too, just before she ran off," said Mrs. Randolph.

"Temperamental artists!" Renee said, dramatically rolling her eyes. "But the more unpredictable they are, the greater their work, don't you think?"

Renee continued to work the crowd, feeling both perturbed and worried by Elena's absence. She wanted to run after her, but it was important to console the guests who were clearly disappointed by Elena's sudden departure.

***

The electric, pulsing sensation that had haunted her often since her return from the desert increased as Elena walked the five blocks to her apartment. Tears flowed down her cheeks now. No one. Not one person had even glimpsed the powerful experience of the Ark. They looked only at the surface of the paintings, the colors, the size. But the message? It was lost on them. They could not see what she had seen. They could not feel the sense of wholeness and harmony she had so passionately attempted to convey.

Rows of grated windows softly lit from within lined the darkened street. The soft light seeping through the curtained openings cast an intriguing image that seemed to promise something peaceful and beautiful on the other side. Gazing at them, Elena wondered at these rectangular portholes into the lives of strangers. They always seemed inviting, a refuge from the outer world. She often pondered what was occurring behind the curtains of the houses she passed. Was there a family inside playing board games or watching TV together? Was there a couple lost in conversation about their future? Were there lovers gently caressing one another? Or were there arguments occurring behind those backlit shrouds? Was some distraught mother threatening suicide in front of her adolescent child, like Elena's mother had done, more than once?

A few people stood on narrow porches smoking cigarettes or taking in the night air. Neon signs blinked nervously: "liquor," "cigarettes," "checks cashed." The newsstands still held today's headlines; *MASS SHOOTING IN WESTERVILLE, GLOBAL WARMING DISRUPTS WEATHER, POLICE SHOOT UNARMED BLACK MAN.*

It was a never-ending series of disasters, acts of hatred, and violence. *DOW JONES CONTINUES TO PLUMMET, CEO JAILED FOR EMBEZZLEMENT, NUCLEAR ARMS TALKS STALLED – AGAIN.* Fear and despair seemed to envelop the planet. How foolish she had been to think that a few paintings of blissful light and energy would make a difference. Her peaceful, ethereal images fell on blind eyes and the music they played in her mind landed on ears that could not hear.

Inside Westbeth, as the elevator slowly ascended the multiple floors to her apartment, Elena's sense of hopelessness and defeat turned to anger. *What is wrong with people?* Second Floor. *Why can't they see the beauty of life, the wholeness that holds them all as one?* Third Floor. *No. Instead, they fight with one another, judge one another, kill one another, steal from each other, cheat, lie and fence themselves off into tight little circles of fear and separation. And then they wonder where God is.*

Finally, the Eleventh Floor. Elena flung her apartment door open and slunk down into her papasan chair and swung it away from the studio toward the television. She reached for the remote as Moses jumped up, circled about and positioned himself in her lap.

More crap! Elena thought as the TV came to life. Whatever had possessed her to turn on that blasted device. The news was airing, and it was one horrible story after another. *Whatever happened to human-interest stories?* she wondered. Scrolling through the online guide, looking for something brain-numbing she felt those electronic vibrations again. They were getting stronger now, running up and down both arms. She dropped the remote and swung her chair around toward the studio. Her whole body was vibrating now, and it felt as if the cells of her body were coming apart, doing some insane dance to an ever-increasing beat.

She eyed the blank canvases, the unfinished paintings against the wall, and the finished one that hadn't been hung for the show. What had looked so promising to her just a few hours ago looked flat and meaningless. There was the fountain, overflowing with life, droplets of water sprinkling through the sunlit scene and flowing together again as one. *An excellent metaphor for the human experience,* she had thought. Lotus blossoms filled the bowls, reflecting the innate connectedness of life. But the flowers looked only like tormented faces to her now – floating aimlessly and disconnected from each other. Were they floating in a sea of oneness? Or in a sea of turmoil? No wonder Renee thought this one was too gloomy for the show.

Standing abruptly, Moses falling from her lap with a startled meow, Elena grabbed the utility knife from the table. She felt blood rising, hot in her arms and face. She slashed through the paintings with the knife. She ripped them from their stretchers, shredding the paint-laden fabric into small pieces. She broke the wooden stretcher frames with her foot and tossed them aside. Shaking, she looked around at the destruction and began to sob. She fell to the floor in a heap and cried, "Why? Why would I experience something so beautiful, so perfect, and be so unable to share it? Why can't they see what I see? Why can't they see that they are all one? Why do they continue to hurt one another over and over again? All the work. All the labor. All the yearning to share, to make a difference was all in vain! Why God? Why?"

Amid the ruined paintings and tears, Elena felt the vibrations again. They shook her body until she couldn't distinguish the shake of her sobs from the shaking of the vibrations. They ran through her body, her legs, her arms, and hands. The cells and atoms of her body were throbbing, and the sensation moved down and out through her fingertips. She saw the palette, the brush, and the array of paints on the table nearby. They were glowing, pulsing, calling to her.

She picked up the brush and opened a tube of cerulean blue, squirting a dab onto a pigment-stained palette. She dipped her brush in the paint, added a bit of white, a drop of thinning glaze, swirling them together until the perfect, nearly translucent blue emerged.

No. not blue. Red. She dropped the brush and grabbed another, filling it with crimson pigment and touched it almost involuntarily to the only remaining blank canvas. The brush seemed to lift itself as it reached toward the stark white pebbly surface. The electric energy of the Ark was racing up the brush, and through her arm. The vibrations completely enveloped her. She felt like she was being pulled by a great magnet, every cell of her body expanding, then contracting and finally being torn from her studio, into and through the canvas.

CHAPTER SIX

Nothing in Vain

Suddenly Elena was back in the cave with the mysterious box, transported through time and space. Without moving or touching the Ark, she was somehow inside its mystical realm once again. She thought a question and the reply filled her mind. She thought another and words began to form. Another query and images took shape in her mind with absolute clarity.

Nothing is in vain; she felt the voice inside her say. It was a voice without words, a vibration that answered her questions from somewhere deep within her. *Nothing is in vain. All things have purpose. You are never alone. I am always with you. You cannot take my name in vain, for I am always listening, always giving, always blessing. Nothing is ever in vain.*

Elena felt an overwhelming sense of peace and calm. The words "I am" seemed to emanate from deep within her and simultaneously all around her. She was immersed in a presence that eliminated any sense of separation. She was one with the Essence of Life, one with everything and everyone. *How interesting* she thought, *the words 'I Am' refer to me, yet they also refer to this greater presence. I am that I am.* It was God. It was her. It was the All-ness.

I am that I am, the voice said. *There is nothing else. I am all that is.*

The brush was still in Elena's hand. A translucent canvas floated before her. Elena lifted the brush again, and it began painting the lotus flower that had taken shape in her mind. As the brush moved effortlessly in her hand, the flower came to life as if it were painting itself; delicate petals gently opening, fading and withering, then bursting forth in vibrant color once again. Then the brush became still. It transformed into a chisel and began chipping away at the canvas, now made of stone. A graven image; a flower chiseled in rock that lasts forever and ever, never unfolding, never fading, never withering.

Elena peered beyond the stone and saw herself lifting a bronze artifact from the earth, sifting and brushing the sand gently from its elegant form. There it was! The image of the flower was but a shadow, a replica, formed and fashioned after a living flower, but lifeless, hard, only a facsimile of fragrant petals sprinkled with delicate pollens. No bees or butterflies could be nourished by this. No sweetheart could be moved to tears by its subtle fragrance. No. The true flower is both impermanent and infinite and can never be engraved. *Nothing can be engraved* Elena thought. *It's not a rule, it's a fact, a wonder-filled fact. If nothing can be engraved, then nothing is set in stone.* The words, *this too shall pass,* echoed in her mind.

Of course! Elena thought. *The messages of the Ark can never be fully expressed on canvas.* It wasn't a commandment. It was a statement of truth. Nothing *real* could be engraved. Nothing of the realm of pure being can ever be wholly captured in an earthly image.

Elena smiled as she thought of what a blessing this was. If the essence of something could never be fully captured in the physical realm, it also meant that nothing in life was ever really written in stone. Nothing was permanent. Nothing you did or didn't do was ever engraved. You could ultimately change your circumstance by merely changing the thought behind it.

***

Painting in this realm was a timeless experience. Elena did not feel hunger. She did not feel tired. She merely thought, asked, received images, and allowed the brush to paint. From this place of knowing she could see beyond space and time. The flowers that had first emerged faded into the off-white ground of a blank canvas. She held the brush a mere inch before the canvas and watched as the paint flowed, not like paint at all but like particles of light. They danced down the brush to the tip and then stopped as if waiting for one another. Then, like an explosion, they simultaneously adhered themselves to every square inch of the canvas, forming the image of a door.

Elena had seen this door before. She once sat before it nervously waiting for an appointment with the financial-aid officer at the community college. It was the day when what she had thought was carved in stone had opened to a new chapter in her life. She was working by day as a clerk at a brokerage firm and attending school at night. She wasn't sure yet what she wanted to do, but she knew it was not a lifetime of working at the brokerage firm.

Elena appreciated the income from her steady job, if not the work itself. Her family thought her quite fortunate to land such a well-paying job with only a high-school education. But the work bored her. The night classes helped, but they did not offer an ultimate escape from the monotony that had become her life. She felt as though some vital aspect of her was wasting away. Her anthropology class promised the possibility of an archeological field study, and she loved the idea of studying objects of art from lost civilizations. It was a welcome escape from the rigid world of finance, but still, she wanted something more.

Depressed, desperate to find more fulfillment, she had explored following her greatest passion, painting. She wanted to pursue a degree in art, and she wanted to do it full time. Her parents were appalled. Why would she give up such a great job to become a painter and live like a pauper? Elena's friends in her anthropology class were supportive, but could not relate to her burning desire to paint.

Since childhood, Elena had felt an affinity for painting and drawing. As a small child, it soothed her when chaos ensued at home. In grade school, drawing had been a healing balm against the demanding and sometimes denigrating nuns who taught at her parochial school. In high school, her brush had been her voice, speaking out about the injustice and hypocrisy her maturing eyes beheld in the world around her. Art. Painting. Photography. These were what called to her in the night. But how would she fund this venture? She had no desire to be a pauper. The Bohemian lifestyle had its romantic allure, but she liked being warm when it was cold. She liked having food when she was hungry, and she appreciated having train fare when she needed to get across town. Elena loved her apartment, and she could not possibly move back into her parents' home. That was a nightmare she did not care to revisit.

The brush moved swiftly across the virtual canvas now, painting the scene of the miraculous answer to her prayers and the steps she had taken to manifest it. She hadn't just prayed for change. She had meditated and visualized the life she wanted to experience. She had affirmed it with her thoughts and words. She had set up a small studio in her tiny apartment and stocked it with canvas, paint, and brushes. But just painting the image in her mind and stocking the studio was not enough. She had to do something actively to pursue her dream.

40

She made an appointment with the financial-aid office at the community college.

Elena watched now as the door reappeared on the mystical canvas, and opened to the greenish glow of fluorescent lighting of a small windowless, basement office. "Elena Rowan?" A stern-looking woman was calling her name. She entered the room, taking a seat in the hard-wooden chair as the woman took her own seat on the other side of the desk. "What can I do to help you, Elena?" she asked.

Elena explained that she wanted to leave her job, attend school full time, and change her focus to visual arts. She didn't have the funds for a full schedule of classes, let alone the ability to keep her apartment without a steady paycheck. She would need financial aid.

Elena could glimpse just a small portion of the computer screen as the woman began reviewing her files. She saw her flip through the folder of drawings she had submitted with her request for transfer. "I am sorry, Elena, but you won't receive much in financial aid here. Community colleges don't offer the kind of aid you're looking for."

Elena's heart had skipped a beat, but she had taken a breath and held tight to her vision. She asked what was possible because this is what she had to do. The financial-aid officer closed the folder of drawings and said, "You are very talented, Elena. If you want to pursue the arts, you should consider applying to the Steinhardt School at NYU. They offer a variety of financial-aid possibilities that you may qualify for. From what I can see, you should have no problem gaining acceptance into their program."

The Steinhardt School had been beyond Elena's wildest dreams. She could not have imagined a better result. She had not been college-bound in high school, and her parents had neither the means nor the desire to send her. She knew little about scholarships and application processes. But she had prayed for a miracle. She had envisioned it in her mind. She had released any beliefs in impossibilities. She had lived as though it were already done. She had purchased the supplies, set up the studio, and truly believed it would occur.

Elena applied to NYU and was accepted. She applied for grants and scholarships. When a financial-aid rejection letter arrived, she refused to give up and reapplied, again, and again. She finally received the grants, scholarships, and low-interest loans that opened the door to her dream school and her life took off in a direction she had once only hoped for. It was done. It was good! She had walked through the door and painted away a mask that had been hiding a part of who she really was. She had not accepted that her life script was written in stone. She had not bought into the limited visions of her parents. She had believed that her life could be transformed. And it was. The monotonous life that had felt written in stone had been transformed by her commitment to a greater vision. And NYU? That had been just the beginning.

***

Elena continued to draw her brush across the translucent and ever-changing canvas. The paint seemed to know her thoughts and respond with an intelligence all its own. Elena pondered the questions so prevalent in every human heart: *Why is there evil and what can we do about it? There is so much fear and despair. If there is only God, where does evil come from?*

Even in the afterglow of the Ark experience, Elena had been disturbed to return to her everyday life, engulfed by newspapers, internet, and television as constant reminders of the violence, hatred, and selfishness of the human race. The world seemed to be spinning out of control. She could feel her own fear emerging over global warming and irritation with those who chose to deny its existence. She lamented the prevalence of hunger, violence and emotional pain. Hatred, bigotry, people fighting, stealing, and harming one another contributed to an endless stream of negative, divisive energy clogging the beautiful swirls of Light she had so recently experienced. Religion had failed humanity and ironically appeared to fuel the very hatred it was intended to vanquish. Compassion eluded the world. Peace and harmony seemed an impossible dream. Yet, here she was, once again in this unearthly realm of pure wholeness and bliss. *I am that I am.* As the words echoed in her mind, she relaxed into them once more.

Elena felt a warm sense of peace and calm surrounding her. She knew the answers to her questions now. She felt them quivering down her arm, guiding the brush. All the answers to all her questions revealed themselves, painting a picture of the essence of what she had seen and grasped with each cell of her being.

"What is the purpose of evil and how can the world eliminate it?" she asked aloud, and the knowing flooded her mind and oozed through the brush, forming images of people seemingly gripped by fear. Their eyes formed windows to hearts seized by some shadowy, serpentine shape. Walls of dense energy accumulated between each being, encasing each in its own isolated cell. They were not separate, but they believed they were.

Evil, the voice within her said, *is the outworking of fear that has taken hold and become real in the hearts and minds of humankind. It is the fear of aloneness. It is the fear of being separate from or less than, of knowing the self as outside of the very Essence of Life itself. Fear is a false god held in the mind of humankind, looming over them and threatening to harm what cannot be harmed. It is the shadow carried by those who believe themselves separate from the Whole.*

She considered this and wondered how the brush would paint the idea of the oneness of life that believed itself separate. As the brush moved about, a fresh picture emerged as if by another hand. Two people, filled with dazzling, brilliant light that radiated through them and swirled above them, peered at one another through the eyeholes of elaborate masks. The masks obscured their brilliance and the expansive sphere of greater Light in which they stood. Shadows cast in various directions grew until they hid the brilliance almost entirely and the beings seemed to shrink in size and vibrancy.

How can the masks be removed? Elena smiled at the answer so clear in her mind: *Paint them away.* But had the masks not appeared, she would not have thought to remove them. There would have been no contrast to see how brilliant the Light really was. She might have missed the larger sphere of light in which the beings stood.

Evil, she thought, *the violence, the storms, the hatred, anger, and fear are like elaborate masks. They are painted layer upon layer on an unfolding soul and held before it as a shield from some perceived threat. Without the masks they feel vulnerable, exposed, yet because of them, some small part of them cries out, "Who am I?"*

Elena heard the reply in her mind, *I am that I am.* It sent a chill through her being. Each vulnerable, lonely soul was actually one with the voice that uttered these words, "I am that I am." Each was an expression, an extension of the whole. The masks and separation gave contrast, but looking beyond them was a return to wholeness.

Elena's brush continued to move, painting away the masks and revealing the greater Light and the merging of the two into one. As the images of masks began to fade, streaks of blue and green started to take shape. As Elena's brush moved about upon the mystical canvas, petals emerged once again, forming the delicate shape of a lotus flower. They twisted and unfolded from within themselves. Without changing the brush or the paint, the colors adjusted and the petals transformed into streaming rivulets swimming through a vast and turbulent river that had painted itself into the scene. Crescent shapes of green-blue flowed from the center of the flower and submerged themselves into the flowing river. Then, two of the crescents surfaced and gave way to circular shapes. They shifted from brown to green, flecked with an eerie yellow glow. They were eyes. They were keen and penetrating. They floated nearer. They rose to reveal the glimmers of sharp yellowish protrusions. They were teeth! It was a crocodile, jaws open ready to strike. Elena shivered with fear. It was so real!

A woman appeared from nowhere. She walked fearlessly toward the crocodile. Elena instinctively reached out to stop her, the brush falling from her hand. But the woman grabbed hold of reins that had not been there before. She stepped closer. *Good God,* thought Elena. *She will be devoured.* But she wasn't. She climbed onto the beastly reptile and began steering with harness and bit. The crocodile bucked and twisted then swam, pulling the woman and her billowing clothing with him. He dove and spun into the depths of the turbulent waters, but the woman held tight. Elena was with her now in a horrifying downward spiral, a sea of terror spinning around them. Elena was disoriented, dizzy. She felt herself being pulled into the spiral unable to locate the surface let alone swim toward it. But the woman held on. *How can she keep her balance? How is this even possible?* Elena wondered.

At long last, the crocodile surfaced, water dripping from its sides and jaws, its rider steadfast, fearlessly holding the reins. It swam more gently now, carrying his unlikely traveler as would a gentle steed put out to pasture.

The voice inside her head whispered. *She maintains her balance by keeping her eye on what never changes even as she is spun into the depths. What she teaches you is to feel the spin of fear and ride into the murky waters of life with balance and courage, keeping your inner eye upon that which does not change, that which is whole, and eternal, the Essence of Life.*

44

Elena noticed then that the woman riding the crocodile looked a lot like her. Curiosity drew her closer to the painted image, but the memory of the powerful jaws still lingered in her mind, pulling her back again.

I am here, said the voice that spoke to the deepest part of her. *Nothing is in vain. Nothing is engraved, and nothing outside of you is more powerful than what is already within you.*

Elena felt perfect peace and calm settling over her but found herself still gladly painting away the terrifying crocodile and his powerful jaws. For a brief moment, he appeared much like the golden calf fashioned by the Israelites when they thought Moses had deserted them. But the painted calf began to unravel. Strands of gold spiraled out from the calf as if they were a never-ending skein of golden yarn. Then the strands started to shudder and ripple. A quiet rustling sound emerged from the wavering threads that matched the mounting vibration pulling at the strands of Elena's being.

The mystical canvas before her shuddered. The colors on it undulated and separated into tiny particles dancing about in a great flurry of color and then settled back again. Still. A brief pause and the vibration of color began again. There was a sound accompanying the explosions of color. It stopped, then resumed, disturbing the particles of paint. *It's knocking!* Elena realized, and the thought drew her attention through the dancing colors. Her whole body seemed to be shuddering with the same vibration as the paint. At each pause, she felt herself being pulled further into the vast array of twirling pigments, entangled in the strands of golden yarn, until suddenly she felt as though her entire essence was being funneled through a tunnel of light, through the canvas, through space and time.

As the sound and motion stilled, Elena found herself on the floor of her studio surrounded by the wreckage of her tantrum. Shredded canvas lay in colorful strands surrounding her. Shattered stretchers, brushes and paint tubes were strewn all about her.

CHAPTER SEVEN

A Return to Matter

The sound again. More knocking. And a voice. "Elena! Elena! Are you in there? Are you okay? Open the door!" More knocking.

Elena surveyed the room as she tried to regain her balance. The pull through the tunnel of color had left her dizzy and disoriented. *What the hell just happened? How ...?*

Moses was pawing at her arm. Trails of kitty kibble littered the room leading to a torn cat-food bag. His water dish was dry. Light poured in through the open window, and the TV continued to blast some indistinguishable monologue.

"Elena! Open the door!" It was Renee. The opening must be over. Wait. It was light out. How long had it been? Moses pawed her arm again and rubbed his jaw against her knee. He had helped himself to food. It must have been a while. A night? A day? Two days? She didn't know. More knocking.

"I'm coming," she croaked, her voice soft and cracking. Her throat was dry, and Renee hadn't heard her. The knocking was getting more and more insistent. Elena pulled herself from the floor, then unlocked and opened the door.

Renee's eyes widened as she took in the scene. "Oh my God, Elena! Have you been robbed? Are you hurt? Who did this to you?" Renee put her arms around her and held her tight. It felt good to have some physical contact. She tried to speak, but Renee was talking non-stop. Elena had never known Renee to be quiet or calm, even in the most peaceful times. She continued to fire questions at her so rapidly Elena didn't know which one to answer first. Her head was still spinning from the strange tunnel experience, and Renee's questions were swirling around with the remnants of color in her mind.

Renee had her cell phone in hand now, and her finger was moving toward the number nine. She was going to call 911. Elena grabbed her hand and shook her head. "No," she whispered. "I haven't been robbed. I could use a cup of tea." Maybe fixing her a cup of tea would keep Renee busy long enough that she could think. How would she explain all this? Did she dare tell Renee what really happened here?

She wasn't even sure herself. Maybe Zak was right. Maybe she *was* delusional.

Elena gripped the edge of the shoji screen that separated the living area from the entryway. She needed to feel something solid, to reassure herself she was really here. Convinced, she sank into the futon. Renee set a cup of tea on the table in front of Elena, grabbed a shawl from a hook by the door, and wrapped it around Elena's shoulders. *Am I cold?* Elena wondered. *Am I shaking? I hadn't noticed.*

"Thank you," Elena whispered, sipping on her tea. "Can you please put some water in Moses' bowl?"

Renee replenished the water bowl, then poured a cup of tea for herself and sat across from Elena. "Okay, so what happened here? Tell me why I shouldn't call 911. And where the hell is Zak? I thought he was coming over last night to check on you. He showed up at the gallery right after you left."

"I don't know. I haven't heard from him. If he came by, I didn't hear him." Elena said. She looked at Renee who was still waiting for some sort of explanation. She surveyed the room and had to admit it did look like a home invasion had occurred.

"It's my fault, Renee," she said. "I had a ... well ... a bit of a tantrum I guess you might say. I just lost it at the gallery. So much has happened since I returned from the dig. It was … I can't explain what happened there. I know it all seems so horrible and traumatic, but something else happened there too. Something … beautiful."

Renee looked dubious. "Beautiful? What, did you fall in love or something? Sure doesn't seem like it. What's beautiful about witnessing mass murders?"

"No. No. Not that. That was horrible and I know I haven't really dealt with it yet, but there was this time during the night, before the sun came up, several of us had an experience that was just otherworldly. A mystical experience, I guess. I came home, sickened by the deaths but inspired by this amazing experience. We saw things I can't explain, but I thought I could somehow paint; that behind the turmoil and fear and challenges of human life there is something greater, more powerful, and immensely more beautiful. There is this connection between every living being that transcends even death. I thought if I could paint some of that, I might be able to stir something in people so they could see it, too. Maybe it would make a difference in some way."

Renee nodded. It was "wholeness talk." Not unusual for an artist to see something beyond the ordinary. Not unusual for them to want to portray it. What was unusual was Elena's fixation on it in the of wake a traumatic experience. "Go on," she said.

"When I was at the gallery it was beyond disappointing to hear people going on and on about color and size and depth but totally missing the point of the paintings. Not the earlier works but the new ones. It just hit me really hard. Everything seemed so futile. Then, walking home, all I could see was all the hatred, and fear and evil in the world, highlighted in newspapers, social media posts, and television news … it was just too much. Trying to show wholeness and light and oneness to a world engulfed in fear and hatred seemed such an impossible task. I felt hopeless, insignificant. I came home and destroyed every painting that was left in the apartment. I even destroyed most of the blank canvases, thinking I would never bother to paint again."

Renee stood and put an arm around Elena's shoulders. "You are not insignificant, Elena. *So what* if a few people didn't get the deeper message you were hoping for? Art is subjective. And the message is more subliminal than you realize. Maybe just being in the room with those paintings will have an effect on someone. You may never see it, but it doesn't mean it hasn't happened. The arts have always inspired people and initiated change." Renee paused for a moment, taking in the scene of destruction.

"Elena, why don't you tell me a little bit about what happened in the desert. Do you think there's a possibility that experience is trying to … umm, erupt?"

Elena really wasn't sure. She thought she had things under control. She had believed that her enlightened insights would prevail over the trauma of having watched friends and colleagues and fellow field participants meet violent deaths. It was just the death of their bodies, after all. Elena knew their Spirits lived on. She had seen it while engulfed in the energy of the Ark. But now? She wasn't sure anymore. She'd had another profound experience, heard a voice of great wisdom speaking from within her. She had seen visions much like what had happened in the Ark. But how? How did she get there? "I don't really want to talk about it right now, Renee. I'm totally exhausted, and I guess I need to clean up this mess." She saw the worried look on Renee's face and added, "Don't worry. I'll be okay. I'll paint again. In fact, I have an idea for another painting right now. Something to do with crocodiles and goddesses."

"Let me help you with this," Renee said. She went to the cupboard and grabbed some trash bags. "Are these the heaviest ones you have?" she said, scrunching her nose.

"No. I've got some heavy-duty ones up in the loft. I'll ..." She felt the table vibrating and stopped short. It vibrated again. It was her cell phone on silent. She shook her head. *I really have to think about disabling the vibrate setting on my phone.*

Picking it up, Elena saw it was a text from Zak. There were eighteen of them. *Shit. I missed that many text messages?*

"Where are you? Missed you at the gallery" 10:15 pm

"I'm outside your door. Open up?" 10:40 pm

"Are you okay? Sorry I was late." 10:45 pm

The messages went on and on, with an increasing tone of concern. This one just said "I hope you're feeling better this morning. Call me."

Elena texted back, "Renee's here. I'm okay. Will call later."

Ten contractor bags later, the apartment had returned to normal, although a bit barren, with just one blank canvas left in the studio. Renee slung her bag over her shoulder and gave Elena one last hug. "Really, Elena. You need to talk about this. If not me, someone else. Maybe some grief counseling. You can't pretend nothing happened out there."

"I'm fine," Elena said, but the look on Renee's face made it clear she wasn't accepting that answer. "I'll call someone. I promise. In fact, I need to call Zak back now."

Renee left, closing the door behind her. Elena fastened the locks and breathed a sigh of relief. She was grateful for Renee's help cleaning up. It was pretty horrific cleaning up the remnants of one's own hysteria. A little help and company had been great. But she was still disoriented. Still in a daze over what had happened. She needed some time to herself to think. And to eat! She suddenly felt incredibly hungry. Maybe she could call for pizza. But Zak, first she had to call Zak.

Elena's fingers tapped the cell phone, placing the call. "Hi, Zak. Sorry about last night. I ... umm, went for a long walk and then ... well, I just had a rough night, and then I don't know. I guess I fell asleep and didn't hear you ... I know ... No, I wasn't upset with you. It was the people at the show and their remarks about the paintings ... No. They loved them. They just didn't *get* them."

There was a knock at the door. Elena looked around, wondering if Renee had left something behind. "Just a second, someone's at the door," she said. She unlocked the door leaving the chain on to see who it was. "Well, I guess it's you!" she said.

Zak was standing at the door, cell phone in one hand, a large white bag in the other.

"You brought me Chinese!" Elena exclaimed. "Thank you! Thank you! I am so hungry." She slid the chain off and let him in. She hadn't felt this good in a while. She grabbed some plates and set the coffee table up for them while Zak unloaded the cardboard food boxes. They ate and talked and laughed. It felt good to just hang out, and the food was a delicious elixir for her empty stomach and her tenuous emotions. She told him about the tantrum and the shredded canvases. She shared her extreme feelings of futility over not being able to express their Ark experience the way she had hoped. But she didn't tell him about re-entering the portal, or Ark, or whatever it was. He already thought they had suffered a delusional experience. This might just confirm it. And she wasn't entirely sure he was wrong.

"Enough about me and my hissy fit," Elena said as she began clearing the table. What's happening at school? Are you ready for classes on Monday?"

"Pretty much," Zak said. "It's been tough getting ready. There were so many field-study reports and then there were all the university issues to deal with from the dig. Paperwork like I've never had to do before, insurance reports, incident reports ... and of course the lack of reports on what I really wanted to document." He paused there as if checking for a reaction from Elena. She didn't give him one. She just nodded.

"And everyone was more or less required to go through trauma counseling. Not that it was a bad idea, but it was just one more thing to do. Anyway, the paperwork is finally under control, the classes are all set, and my research assistant will be handling a lot of the minor pieces requiring field follow-up with the students. My office and my apartment are back in order – you know how I like order. I've even had some sleep."

Elena could see that; he looked so much better than he had the other day. "So, this trauma counseling thing. Did that do anything for you?" she asked.

"I guess. I mean just talking about it helps. Those were my friends and students. I know …" He faltered a little. "I know what we presumably saw at the cave, but they're still gone, and I still have to deal with that. I wonder if we'd waited on exploring the site and set up better security …." His face darkened a bit, and his comments trailed off.

Elena flinched a little at the word "presumably," but she let it pass. "Zak, no one could have predicted what happened there. How would you have provided better security? We had the only guides in the region that were willing to go with us. You had permission to survey the area and took reasonable precautions, given the purpose of the expedition. You didn't do anything wrong. It's not your fault."

"I know. So, the insurance company and lawyers say. Anyway, I was surprised at how much it helped to talk about it to someone. Maybe you …."

"Shh." She put a finger to her lips and put her other hand on his. "I might just do that, but I don't want to talk about it anymore right now. Okay?"

Zak nodded in agreement and began picking up the paper food containers and clearing the coffee table. "Stop, Zak. You brought the food. I can clean it up," Elena protested.

"No. You cleaned up after me, now I'm cleaning up after you. Besides, you look like you could use some sleep," Zak said as he placed their dishes in the dishwasher. He wiped the table, hung up the dishrag, and dried his hands. Elena watched as Zak moved efficiently through her small kitchen area with the familiarity of an enduring friend who had spent a great deal of time there. He looked considerably better than he had when she had stopped by his office to drag him to lunch. His eyes looked rested, his clothes were no longer disheveled, and he'd shaved that scraggly facial growth. She wondered what had changed. Had trauma counseling helped that much? Surely it wasn't just her scolding him and taking him to lunch. He looked … *Oh crap! He looks like he does when he's getting ready for a dig! I hope it's just the regular summer field school. He can't be going back to Bir Tawil!*

51

When Zak left for the night, Elena collapsed into her papasan chair and cuddled with Moses, relieved to have time to reflect. "What do *you* think happened Moses? What did you see and hear last night?" she said. He purred and curled into a tighter ball in her lap. She stared at the one remaining blank canvas. "What will I paint?" she asked. "And will it make any difference?"

CHAPTER EIGHT

Impermanence

Morning had arrived, and Elena still felt a little disoriented from the night before. How had she been able to enter the portal from her studio? It seemed impossible. Yet the experience was so vivid, so real. Was it possible to enter that realm from anywhere? Could the others do it? Could anyone do it? Or, was it just her? And if it was just her, was it real? Or was there some truth to Zak's idea about psychotic delusions?

It certainly felt real. While she had been in that realm, everything made so much sense. Even when frightening images like crocodiles had appeared, there had been a deep sense of calm within her as if she were a silent observer. If only she could feel that way all of the time. And if she could somehow share that peaceful knowingness with the world. Back in the world, however, worry, doubt and a sense of disconnect crept in and her peaceful feeling dissipated. From the papasan chair, teacup in hand, Elena stared once again at the blank canvas. *Blank. Just blank. In the Ark, it all made so much sense. But now ... not so much.*

There had to be a way to capture that feeling and integrate into her everyday life. *What if I could enter the portal on purpose?* she wondered. *What if I could choose when to enter it and when to return? How did it start again?* She ruminated about the events of the previous night. She had been feeling the vibrations of the Ark in her body more intensely all night. Then, she had been overwhelmed, distraught, angry, and had totally lost control. She had been destructive, annihilating her own paintings. Anger and destruction couldn't be the key to entering a realm of pure peace. If it were, the world would be at peace now.

Wait! I wasn't enraged when it happened. I was exhausted, empty. Emptiness! Many spiritual traditions taught the importance of emptying the mind. It was the key to mindfulness, enlightenment, and connecting with the Divine. To be empty was to release all thoughts and concerns. She had been taught this practice years ago when she first learned about meditation at a weekend seminar.

Maybe she had never fully emptied herself before. Perhaps last night, at the point where she had felt the most hopeless, was when she had surrendered enough to be totally empty. She mentally retraced the events and emotions of last night, settling on the feeling of emptiness rather than hopelessness. She closed her eyes, began noticing her breath, relaxing her body, and then, with a start, she opened her eyes wide again.

The brush! Elena looked at her brush and palette on the table next to the easel. Picking it up was the last thing she remembered before being pulled into the realm of the Ark.

Gently dumping a startled Moses from her lap, Elena grabbed the dry brush and touched it to the blank canvas. Nothing. It was still. There were no strange vibrations, just a long slender handle with soft sable hairs protruding from its metal collar. She drew the dry brush across the blank canvas as if painting an invisible image. Nothing. No vibrations. No inspiration.

Elena set the brush down. Maybe a walk would help to empty her mind. It might not get her back through the mystical portal, but it might inspire the next painting. As she grabbed her keys from the bowl near the door, Moses leaped to the windowsill. Apparently, he liked to watch a tiny version of Elena walking down the street from his elevated perch. "Be good, buddy. I'll be back soon," Elena said as she closed the door behind her and set out for the park.

***

The park was just a couple of blocks from her Westbeth apartment, and it was always a soothing place for her. She felt her body relax as soon as she turned the corner where the park came into view. Birds were singing their early-morning song, and a small scattering of leaves at the tops of the trees displayed the beginnings of fall colors. The grass felt soft and slightly moist from morning dew beneath her sandaled feet as she left the sidewalk.

The park was generally a lively place, with children playing, artists sketching, and lovers lying side by side on blankets dreaming of their united future. But there were no blankets strewn about yet, no children playing. It was too early. Only a few people were scattered about the park, and food vendors were just beginning to arrive.

In the distance, Elena saw a gathering of monks in their flowing saffron and burgundy robes. Yellow mohawk-like hats bobbed about atop their shaved heads as they gathered under a portable canopy surrounding a slab of concrete intended for games of Four Square. Curious, Elena walked toward them. Stopping a few feet from the gathering, she discovered an intricate design taking shape on one-quarter of the concrete court. There were triangles and circles, boxes and vines, arranged in a myriad of bright colors, all emanating from a center circle. Elena had seen similar designs on posters and in coloring books. It was a mandala, a visual tool for meditation. Focusing on the center of the mandala was a means of centering the mind, *emptying* it of outer distractions. *Hmm,* she thought. *Maybe a mandala will help me to empty my mind. What are the odds of stumbling on this just now?* Visions of the crocodile from her recent unearthly adventure meandered through her mind. The center of the mandala was not vastly different from the focal point of the woman who steered the crocodile by keeping her eye on what never changes.

This mandala was especially lovely, and Elena was becoming mesmerized by the emerging design. *Is it chalk they're using to draw such an intricate design? No. Not chalk. They're pouring something. It's sand!* Using tiny spoons and funnels, sand was being laid in place and then gently blown into precise patterns with straws. She watched with fascination as the design was patiently and deftly completed. It was fortunate that it was such a still day. There was no wind, not even a breeze to disrupt their work.

It was soothing and riveting to watch. No one spoke. The monks seemed to know one another's movements and intentions as if they had joined minds in the process. Finally, the monks stepped back to appreciate their work. They sat down in the traditional lotus pose at the circumference of their grand design, oblivious to Elena and the small gathering of onlookers. Their eyes sought the center of the design, and they seemed to breathe in unison. One by one, they each closed their eyes as if entering an even deeper stillness. Elena sat down on a nearby bench. She didn't want to intrude, but she felt drawn to the peaceful energy emanating from the monks and their handiwork. She too focused on the center of the design, visible above the monks' headpieces, seeking to empty her mind. As her eyes closed, she could still see the outlines of their bodies and the shape of the mandala as if the images had been burned into the inner screen of her mind.

After a time, Elena opened her eyes to see the monks concluding their meditation. They were slowly pulling themselves to their feet. *What are they doing now?* Elena wondered. *Are those brooms? Good grief! They're going to sweep it away.*

"No! Wait!" Elena cried. The sound of her voice startled her as much as it did them. She was moving quickly toward them, her cell phone in hand. "Please! Let me at least get a picture," she pleaded.

The monks stopped obediently and moved away from the mandala, allowing Elena to photograph the design. As she thanked them, the monks resumed whisking away their intricate endeavors.

How long have they been working on this intricate display? They must have started at dawn. Or maybe they've been at it for days? And now, before the afternoon crowds come to appreciate it, they're just going to brush it away as if it had never happened! It baffled the preservationist in her. As an art student, she had been trained to select materials and processes that would hold up over time. Conservators spent countless hours restoring the paintings of early painters who had not been so careful in choosing pigments and materials that would last.

Elena caught a few photos of the whisking away of the mandala, wishing she had a better camera with her. She missed her Leica, destroyed during the dig. She had others but the Leica, lovingly referred to as "Little Leah," was her favorite.

One of the monks turned toward Elena as if he could read the questions floating about her mind. He was not like the other monks. His robe was white, rather than the traditional saffron and maroon. His headdress was a plain white cap. His skin tone was pale beige, and he had the most translucent, penetrating blue eyes she had ever seen. His gaze drew her in, inviting conversation.

"Why would you sweep away all that work before more people had a chance to appreciate it?" Elena inquired. "It was phenomenal!"

"Thou shall not create graven images," the monk replied.

Startled by his response, Elena shook her head as if she'd somehow misheard the answer. "What?" She asked. "What did you say? Did you just quote the Bible? What does a Buddhist monk know about the Ten Commandments? How was that a graven image, anyway? It was just sand."

"I'm not actually a monk. Not yet anyway, and not a Buddhist at that. I'm a visitor at the monastery, and I also know a bit about the

Bible. There are actually more similarities in the different spiritual paths than there are differences." He paused for a moment as Elena stared at him. His blue eyes sparkled as his lips broke into a smile. "Elena?" he asked.

How could he know my name? She squinted, as if to get a better view of him. There was something familiar about those eyes. She had seen eyes like that somewhere. But where?

"Yes?" she answered tentatively. "Do I know you? Have we met before?"

"Yes. It's me, Aidan," he said, and his smile grew wider. "They call me Anurak now, but you knew me as Aidan."

Elena rummaged her brain. Who was Aidan? How did she know this man? As if reading her confusion, Anurak said, "St. Bardo's Elementary School."

Instant recognition! Elena's eyes widened. Memories flooded her mind. Yes, she remembered Aidan Quinn. He was without a doubt the smartest boy in her elementary school. Straight A's every year, every subject. He was an exceptional member of the debate team and the first to raise his hand for every question posed to the class. She had always been attracted to those eyes. They were like lakes that sparkled under the summer sun, daring you to dive into them. But then, the teacher's-pet aspect had been a little off-putting. She remembered being paired against him for a mock election debate and had found him absolutely undefeatable. There seemed to be no end to the depth of his knowledge. And here he was now, a monk? She heard he had gone to seminary after high school, but she had assumed it was a Catholic seminary.

"What are you doing here?" she asked. "I thought you were going to become a priest. A Catholic priest, I mean."

"Oh, I did. But I left the priesthood several years ago. It's a long story. Would you care to join us for tea? The temple is just a few blocks from here. We could catch up a little and talk about the whisking away of graven images," he said, smiling.

Elena smiled back. She had been so isolated since her return from the dig. Other than Renee and a few conversations with Zak, she had spoken to no one. Well, except the patrons at the opening, but that had been a disaster. "I'd love a cup of tea. But, umm … there's a café right around the corner that serves amazing jasmine and lemongrass tea."

Elena was reluctant to get too far away from her apartment and the canvas that awaited her there. "I'd be happy to buy us a pot of tea. That is, if you are allowed to do that?"

"I'm allowed. I'm not a monk yet. Not even a novice, really. I'm not too keen on vows of any kind, other than the private commitments one makes with God. I do enjoy the monastic life, though, and the monks here have been most gracious hosts. I enjoy their classes and ceremonies, and I especially appreciate the quiet solitude of the monastery itself. It gives me a great deal of time for prayer and reflection, and there are no social pressures there."

He paused a moment as if taking in Elena's appearance. She wondered if she looked as tired and bedraggled as she felt. Anurak continued, "So, yes. I'm allowed, and I would love to go out for tea with you."

Elena smiled as she fell in stride with her childhood friend, now known as Anurak. Something about him called out to her, and it was not just those brilliant blue orbs shining from his face. There was a gentle glow about him. It was radiant and inviting. In all the world, for Aidan to show up just then as she struggled with this inner knowing that begged to be shared, yet promised to remain hidden, was some kind of miracle. Out of the mouth of a novice monk had come the words that should have been found on stone tablets in the Ark, but were not. Elena did not believe in coincidences. At least not accidental ones. There was something synchronistic about their crossing paths at precisely that moment. Of that, she was certain.

CHAPTER NINE

Reminiscence

Anurak and Elena lowered themselves onto the plush burgundy floor pillows of the Chenglei Tea Room. Elena ordered a pot of jasmine tea with a touch of lemongrass. With a subtle bow of the head, the waiter left to fill their order.

"So," began Elena. "Tell me more about your becoming a priest and why you left. I mean, if it's not too intrusive of me to ask. Just curious, I guess. I always saw you becoming a politician rather than a priest, anyway. What drew you to the seminary in the first place?"

Anurak laughed. "There's definitely a political streak in me, but there's politics in everything Elena, even the priesthood. And it's not intrusive at all. I'm happy to share my journey. Sometimes sharing one's journey can be especially helpful to others, don't you think?"

Something about that question caused a chill to run up and down Elena's arms. She took a breath to ground herself and held onto the table. It would not be a good time for those vibrations to return and carry her away. She hoped he hadn't noticed, but something in those clear blue eyes sparkled as if they had.

"Absolutely," she replied. "I learn a lot from hearing about what others have experienced. Sometimes as much or more than I do my own experiences. Really, if you think about it, that's what I do as an artist. That's the path I followed, by the way." Anurak nodded in acknowledgment.

"My paintings are my way of sharing my views, my experiences, and what I see around me. Sometimes that's as physical as a landscape and how it looks to me. But more often it is something more than that. It's something I see that is beyond the physical. Maybe it's an emotion I see in someone's eyes or a subtle form of energy I see them carrying."

"Yes. Exactly," Anurak replied. "We all have different ways of sharing our experiences and our perceptions. It is part of our nature to do so. Ultimately, I believe that our shared experiences are what cause us to grow as a people.

"Anyway, back to your question, Elena. I do have a natural talent for politics and debate. It's probably part of what caused my eventual departure from the priesthood. But in spite of my intense interest in politics and world events, it was preordained that I enter the priesthood. My family was old-school in that way. I was the eldest son in a devout Irish-Catholic family. It was assumed that I would take Holy Orders. The expectation is born out of a biblical tradition of giving the first tenth to God, or in this case, giving the first son to God. Just as many kids grow up knowing they will attend college or go into the family business, I knew I would become a priest. There was no other option. I didn't fight it. It was who I believed I was and what I was destined to be."

Sipping on his tea, Anurak continued. "After I was ordained, I spent a short time at a small parish in Wisconsin as an associate pastor. I loved the people there, especially the children. I enjoyed making bible stories come alive not only for the Sunday sermon but for the children as well. I played basketball with the boys, jumped rope with the girls. I could have lived the parish life for a long time to come, but that was not what the Church had in mind for me." He added a little more tea to his cup and offered the pot to Elena.

"My secular studies at the seminary were above average. I excelled in government and legal studies. The priesthood is a little like the military, you see. You don't always get the assignment you want. You are assigned where it is determined you will best serve the whole. So, I was sent to Rome to pursue a juris doctorate and become a member of the Vatican's legal counsel."

"That must have been fascinating! To be a priest and live at the Vatican. I would think that would be a dream come true for a priest," Elena said. "I've never even had a chance to visit there. I imagine just walking through St. Peter's would be an awe-inspiring experience; like you could feel the energy of saintly beings having passed there before you!"

"I guess it was pretty exciting at first. I mean it was quite an honor to be selected to serve in Rome. But I missed the parish life. I missed the connections. But then, I really did enjoy the solitude too, and I relished having access to the Vatican Library. I've always loved books. I can never get enough of them. It doesn't even matter the subject. I just love the connection with another human being's mind and being able to learn what was of importance to them. So the library was a big plus, but it was also the beginning of my fall from grace, so to speak."

Elena listened intently as Anurak spoke of his experiences in Rome. It seemed to her he had a great deal of anguish buried somewhere just below the surface. Yet there was this insistent glow about him, too. As if he had experienced some terrible blow but had risen above it and gained greater clarity. Elena wondered, *Should I tell him about the Ark?* The team had made a vow of silence. The discovery of the Ark was to remain a secret, yet they were to somehow reveal the message hidden within it. *Easier said than done,* Elena mused.

Anurak went on to explain his years in Rome, how he loved the seclusion and the hours it allotted him for devouring the most extensive metaphysical library in the world. It was there that he had discovered conflicting information between doctrine and spiritual teachings. It wasn't surprising in such an expansive collection of religious thought. But the contradictions were unsettling. Some could not be ignored. He began to question the very tenets of the faith to which he had dedicated his life. He had long debates with his superiors and discovered a great deal of disparity between the teachings of the Church and the demonstration of them among his fellow clergy. He hadn't questioned his vocation, but the inability of his superiors to answer his questions about the most fundamental teachings of the Church had troubled him.

"Ultimately, my inner instinct to question and my talent for debate that initiated my being brought to Rome was also what pulled me away," Anurak explained. "I just couldn't defend some of the Church's positions. Especially when the sexual abuse of children was uncovered. I completely lost my ability to defend my client. There was so much fear and such a tendency to hide from the facts that I was in a moral dilemma between my beliefs and the institution I had dedicated myself to serve. There were steps the Church could have taken to protect itself, not from being discovered, but from providing an environment that cloaks aberrant behavior, but the Church refused to take them. I was morally and spiritually devastated and personally shattered." Anurak took a breath and a sip of tea before continuing.

"I say that I entered the priesthood because it was expected of me, but it was more than that. I loved the teachings of Jesus. I still do. Being ordained to further that teaching was a great privilege and to find myself torn between what I believed about those teachings and the way they were being distorted was heartbreaking. I knew the church had a sordid past; the inquisition, the sale of indulgences, and other human failings, but I believed the heart of the Church was in alignment with its role as a leader of the faithful. But this ….” Anurak's eyes became distant as if he was no longer in the room. His face grew somber, and Elena noticed the energy that surrounded him contracted; she could see its movement slowing, with a muting effect on its color.

Anurak blinked, his eyes refocusing on Elena, and continued. “The constant turmoil between my inner guidance and the life I was being compelled to live finally sent me into a deep depression and ultimately to a complete nervous breakdown. To restore my mental health, there seemed to be no other answer than to break my vows and find a different way to serve God. I asked for papal permission to leave the priesthood. My request was denied, but I was granted leave. Eventually, I was laicized; that means I was released from my vows, but that happened much later.”

“I'm so sorry Aid ... Anurak. That sounds like a terrible experience, like having your whole family torn away from you. I can only imagine how you must have felt.”

“Yes. It was. I couldn't sleep. I couldn't function during the day. I had no interest in anything and completely isolated myself. I stopped eating pretty much, too. I was hospitalized and began counseling. That was difficult too, because, of course, my counselor was also a priest. In some ways, he was the perfect person to share with and in others, exactly the wrong person. There were many things I kept to myself. In the end, it seemed the only solution was for me to find new surroundings. I missed parish life terribly, but that was not an option in my current state. It's hard to give and guide when you are feeling lost and broken. With the help of my counselor, we devised a plan in which I could travel and explore other faith communities as an ambassador of sorts from the Church. This idea really appealed to me. I created a proposal that included not only visiting places of worship around the world but writing about their similarities and differences. It took some time and some finessing of the plan but based on my inability to serve in any other capacity and my eagerness to do this work, permission

was granted. I had to make frequent reports and supply supporting letters from the institutions I visited, but I was given the freedom to
follow this passion that was *born out of the ashes,* so to speak."

The energy around Anurak had begun to move and glow at a
higher rate of vibration as he spoke about his passion and his freedom
to explore other faith traditions. Elena could understand how something powerful could be born out of the ashes. She had experienced
what she called the *Phoenix Effect* more than once in her life. Out of
a dysfunctional childhood had grown a passion for artistic expression
that had become her career and her voice. Out of a horrid betrayal in
a relationship, Elena had developed a strong sense of independence
and self-reliance. Ashes from previous challenging experiences did
stick a bit even now, but she knew she was better and stronger because
of them. Self-sufficiency had many advantages, one of which was the
time and space to be creative through painting, photography, and a
variety of other media she experimented with from time to time. Now,
of course, there were the ashes of the nightmare in Bir Tawil. What
would rise out of that was yet to be seen.

"Following your passion seems to agree with you," Elena said. "I
can see your enthusiasm when you talk about it. Surviving an ashes
experience will often do that."

His blue eyes began to brighten, and a smile crossed his face.
"Yes, indeed I am glad in the end that I was able to follow the path
that energizes me. After I left Rome, I continued to read everything I
could about a variety of spiritual paths, and I found myself attracted
first to the simplicity of Buddhism. I stayed for a time in Tibet where
I was encouraged to think, to question, and to continuously grow. The
change I experienced there was so profound I took on a new name –
it's where I changed my name to Anurak. Before Tibet, I had thought
of Buddhism as having no god, but what I found was a deeper understanding of living in harmony with the Essence of Life and not trying
to contain that principle into a super-human personality. This was the
God I had vowed to serve, and Buddhism taught me to do it better."

Elena felt an unexpected thrill at Anurak's words "*Essence of
Life.*" She also used this phrase to define what she had come to under-
stand as God. It seemed a more appropriate name for the Power and
Presence that permeated all of life. She asked more questions about
Anurak's new adventures, traveling around the world to different

places of worship and researching many facets of spiritual beliefs. She found his work fascinating and his insights affirming. She had always thought there was really only one God; one that different cultures and traditions put their own face on.

Anurak clearly enjoyed his new work. He told her about the early part of the journey, how he had continued to have differences with the Church as they tried to dictate his findings rather than just receive his reports. Eventually, he had asked again to be released from his vows. The Church, he thought, had been glad to let him go then, since he could not conform to their letter-of-the-law consciousness.

Without funding from Rome, he relied heavily on the goodwill of the centers he visited and from his own funds, comprised of a small amount of savings and a modest inheritance from his parents. He enjoyed the monastic life, and his needs were simple. Travel was his most significant expense, and that was often defrayed by the ministries interested in his interfaith research. He had traveled nearly everywhere; Europe, Asia, the Middle East, to almost every continent, and many, many islands. Who would have thought the blue-eyed youngster with politics written all over him and preordained to be a priest, would live a life as far-reaching as Anurak's? And how amazingly synchronistic to have stumbled upon him at the park today as she struggled with how to express the profound understanding she had gained in her recent adventure with Zak.

"Tell me more about the Buddhist monks whisking away the mandala, Anurak." Elena hoped to steer him back to his statement about the graven images. Maybe there would be a way to share something with him.

"Well," he began, "impermanence is a central teaching in Buddhism, which claims that everything we experience in this human form is fleeting; bodies, flora and fauna, relationships, careers, and circumstances. Everything is in a constant state of decay and all suffering, according to Buddhism, is a result of our attachment to what cannot last."

"But what does that have to do with graven images in the Bible? Doesn't that refer to the false idols we were warned not to have?" Elena knew better, but she wanted to hear Anurak's view. "Why did you respond to me with the commandment about graven images?"

"Similarities," Anurak responded. "The teachings are more the same than they are different. The truth is, I recognized you the moment I saw you. I could read the question on your face, and I knew the biblical words would be familiar to you and might be a good place to begin a conversation about the concept of impermanence; that nothing can ever be written in stone.

"If you think about it, the biblical quote is more of a blessing than a command. God, or the Essence of Life, is like the stone, the element that never changes. But life as we experience it is continuously evolving, unfolding and expanding. In this way, the law of Moses is not so much a command but a statement of truth. There can be no earthly image that fully captures the Essence of Life and no earthly condition that does not change and unfold over time."

Elena could feel her own eyes widening with every word Anurak spoke. The words he spoke were the same as those flowing through her mind ever since she first encountered the Ark. She, too, believed that the words that had been understood by humankind as commandments were more of a blessing than a list of rules, each one cascading from the other as if they were a never-ending fountain of bliss. But how could you explain this to anyone? Would anyone believe it? And if they did, would chaos ensue? Wasn't this list of rules at the core of social governance? Were they not what kept order in the world? Or were they merely early man's understanding of a Truth too profound for human words?

A barrage of internal questions threatened to explode inside Elena's head. But here was a man who had not been in that desert cave with her, who had not experienced the energy of the Ark, yet he spoke as if he had. *Can I tell him?* Elena wondered. It would feel so good to share this with someone who might really understand. *Maybe ...*

The waiter interrupted Elena's thoughts, asking if they needed more tea. "No thank you, we have to get going," Elena said.

Elena paid for their tea and Anurak graciously accepted the gift. Leaving the tearoom, they walked into the brilliance of a midday sun among throngs of people swarming toward the park or off to handle lunchtime errands. As they prepared to go their separate ways, Anurak invited Elena to visit the monastery the next day for midday tea, and she accepted. She turned the corner toward her apartment with extra buoyancy in her step as she anticipated their next encounter.

CHAPTER TEN

The Karta Project

Gina sat on a high stool, one high heel hooked on the footrest, the other dangling and twitching nervously as she peered through a large-format magnifying glass at the piece of rock that had come to be known as the Karta, a shortened form of *yetekebere karta*, or *treasure map*. A rough translation had been done early in her study, but Gina was now examining the shape and cut of each character. The inscription was a curious blend of hieroglyphs and *Ge'ez*, an ancient Ethiopian script. She suspected that the combination was intended as a code, or a means of confusing the translation. Examining the details of each character, she hoped to determine if the words had been inscribed by one hand or two.

Across the table from Gina sat Dr. Gerhardt Mason. He was taking copious, handwritten notes as he flipped through page after page of data on the computer screen in front of him. They worked in silence not because they didn't want to disturb one another, but because each was so absorbed in their work they had forgotten the other existed. They were in worlds all their own, and their thoughts were wholly focused on the task.

Well, that wasn't entirely true of Dr. Mason. He was absorbed in his work, but he was not unaware of the woman sitting across the table from him. *Mason*, as his colleagues called him, was enthralled with more than the ancient map. He was captivated by Gina. She had awakened parts of him that had fallen asleep many years before. A widower, Dr. Mason had never really recovered from the loss of his beloved wife. He never dated and seldom attended any social events other than those required by the university. He had become a dowdy man, slightly overweight, frumpy and balding. His work wardrobe consisted of ten or twelve identical button-down shirts and five brown jackets, each very much like the other. Although he wore a different shirt and jacket each day, it appeared to those around him as though he never changed his clothes. Except for the bowties. Mason had a rather vast collection of colorful bowties. They were the only hint of color and personality in his otherwise dull attire.

Mason gazed beyond the computer screen, watching Gina work. *God, she's beautiful, even with those glasses she wears in the lab.* She definitely did not fit the stereotype of the female scientist. She had the grace and beauty of a fashion model with a brain nearing genius-level. Her lab coat was unbuttoned and hung loosely at her sides, caressing the soft green curves of the sweater beneath it. The slightest hint of cleavage peeked out from the V-shaped neckline. Her autumn-red hair was tied back in a tidy bun, but errant, wispy strands framed her face. When she was working, she was completely engrossed, but when the work was done, she looked at him in a way that made him feel twenty-something again. There was always a hint or promise of something decidedly not work-related in her words and manner. He was grateful that Zak had insisted that they work together on the Karta project. Mason glanced down at his own clothing and determined it was long past time that he update his apparel.

"It's conclusive," Gina muttered as she entered her findings on the keyboard next to her.

"What's conclusive?" asked Mason.

"Oh," she said, smiling. "Did I say that out loud?" She looked piercingly at Mason as her tongue slipped through her lips, moistening them. She stretched her arms and arched her back. "It's so dry in here. And I get so stiff from sitting in one position for so long." She rotated her neck and shoulders and then pulled both shoulders back which caused the green mounds of her sweater to protrude more fully from beneath the unbuttoned lab coat.

"It's conclusive," she continued "that only one hand carved the writing into the stone. The angle of the cuts, the depth, everything matches from one character to the next. We can be sure it was written by one person, but why he wrote in two different languages, we can only guess. I still contend that it was an attempt to make it more difficult to decipher – which it would for anyone using either language at the time.

"How are things coming on your end?" she asked.

Transfixed by her presence, Mason pried his attention from Gina and forced himself to look at his notes. "The data confirm the rock was indigenous to the area and the remnants of the cloth it was wrapped in suggest it was buried around the tenth century BCE soon after it was written, no doubt purposefully hidden. The copper fragments Zak found embedded in the carving fit the tools available at the time. It appears to be real and what it suggests about a lost civilization is fascinating." *Not nearly as fascinating as the red-haired woman smiling from across the table* Mason thought, *but very exciting.*

"Let's finish up and call it a day, shall we?" Gina asked. "It's been a long day, and I could use a drink." Pulling on the pair of latex gloves next to her, Gina carefully disengaged the stone map from beneath the large-format microscope and placed it in its storage tray. The screen attached to the scope went blank with no object left on its viewing plate. With near worship-like reverence, she prepared the Karta for storage and placed it in the vault, which hissed a little as it engaged the vacuum feature when she turned and removed the small silver key. She walked around the end of the stainless work table and placed the key in Mason's hand, gently squeezing it into his palm. She was standing close enough to him that her lab coat brushed against his knees. "Once you've finished up and returned the key to Zak, meet me down the hall? I hate to drink alone." She squeezed his palm again and turned away walking out of the lab.

Mason was too dumbfounded to remind her that only he was supposed to remove and replace the artifact and lock the vault. He shouldn't have left the key in the lock, but that thought was swiftly drowned by the hot flow of blood that rushed through his veins. Gina had just invited him out for a drink! He slid the key into his lab pocket and glanced through the glass doors to Zak's office. Zak was typing furiously at his computer, oblivious to the scene in the lab. Mason wondered why Gina would prefer him over a man like Zak, a good twenty years his junior and a rather dashing one at that. Sure, there had been some questions about his most recent dig, but he was still the youngest man to ever hold the position of Director of Graduate Studies. His field studies and the ensuing papers had earned him a great deal of respect in his field. Zak was a far greater catch, but the thought was a fleeting one. Mason didn't really care why. He was about to go on a date with the most gorgeous woman he had ever met. He nearly floated through the room as he gathered his notes, saved the files he had been working on, and knocked on the glass doors to Zak's office to return the key. Mason's mind was utterly enveloped in the delight of possibility as he walked by the lab security guard who nonchalantly glanced at him and nodded approval for him to pass.

***

Zak quickly returned his attention to his computer screen following the brief interruption by Dr. Mason. He wished that Mason and Gina would work more swiftly. He already knew what they were taking forever to discover. He knew the Karta would reveal a general area where the long-lost Ark may be hidden. They wouldn't know the details. They would not be able to decipher the exact location – that was only visible on the broken piece of artifact locked away in his desk safe. Zak was anxious for the lab work to be complete and the discovery to be made so they could officially begin plans for a dedicated field study. A partially finished grant proposal sat waiting on the computer screen. He had filled in every blank he could. It was the umpteenth proposal he had prepped in the past week. All awaited the vitally important piece, the rationale behind the proposed survey and excavation.

He clicked the save button and closed the document. All that remained now was waiting. He could jump in with the information but given the circumstances of the previous dig, deciphering by another professional at the university would lend more credence to the proposal. And these two were unlikely to connect the dots and realize what the original team had discovered. Ultimately this would get him back there with a full excavation team, satellite photos, security, everything he needed to *re-discover* the Ark. Yes. He did want to see that discovery next to his own name and picture. But more, he wanted the discovery to be made public. The information this artifact contained – not on the inside – but in its construction, deterioration, and possible particulate data, was almost beyond comprehension. The world deserved to know the Ark existed and they deserved to know whatever it could tell them about the evolution of humankind. The religious aspects of the artifact were not of particular interest to Zak, other than their relationship to ancient history. The Jewish heritage of his family was more cultural than religious, and Zak considered himself an agnostic – having no particular opinion about a supreme being or humankind's relationship to it. The experience in the desert had almost changed his mind but time and reality had set in, convincing him that the entire experience of being pulled inside of the artifact was, in fact, a psychotic episode brought about by the deaths at the campsite the night before.

Visions of Elena wafted into Zak's head. *She believes it with all her heart,* he thought. *But even if it is real, does that mean we should keep it hidden from the world? Either way, this is knowledge the world needs to have. Maybe by the time the grants are approved, and the dig is scheduled she'll come around. I can do this without her, but I don't want to. We're a team – an odd one, but a team nevertheless.*

CHAPTER ELEVEN

The King of Bir Tawil

Josh ran his hand across the top of his buzz-cut. He missed the dreads he'd been forced to cut off after the expedition. They were so caked with dirt there had been no other choice. He felt bald now, but he had to admit his new look was a better fit at the firm. He'd allowed a carefully trimmed beard to grow and stroked it, noting that it was coming in faster than the hair on his head.

The first draft of Josh's thesis lay unattended in a pile to his left. His office at the firm was small, a closet space in comparison to the partners and even the staff attorneys. It did, however, contain a computer with access to a plethora of public and not-so-public information. In front of him, just below the computer screen, was a small notebook already half full of details about the history of the Ark and the man in the Bir Tawil photograph, Oliver Quinn.

Oliver lived in Kansas City, Missouri, with his wife, Barbara. They had no children. He had grown up in New York, attended parochial schools from elementary through high school and then taken computer-science classes at a small community college. He had one brother, Aidan, who had entered the seminary immediately after graduating from high school. His parents were deceased and had left him and his brother a modest inheritance – nothing that would exempt him from the need for employment, but perhaps enough to splurge on a crazy anniversary gift for his wife.

Josh clicked through the link on his browser to review employment records for his subject. A bleak white page with small, unformatted text appeared. Oliver Quinn was currently self-employed – at what, the database did not say. He had worked at a variety of jobs starting with a video-rental store. Oliver had then worked at a car-rental facility for several years. He had one bankruptcy on record. None of this was remarkable – other than the fact that his income did not seem to afford him the luxury of traveling to a foreign land to make his wife the queen of a no-man's-land. The inheritance was likely spent on recovering from the bankruptcy. Maybe his wife had some substantial income. Perhaps his brother had given him his share of the estate. After all, what would a priest do with the additional income?

Josh ran his hand across his scalp again and took a long sip from his now cold coffee. Aidan. The brother. Where was Aidan? What parish? What was his financial status? He entered the details he knew about Aidan and requested a new screening report. It would take a while for the report to process. He glanced at the abandoned thesis paper but chose the Jewish history book on his desk instead. He had made copious notes at the library, since most of the books were "Reference Only," but this one was available for loan. It had an entire chapter on the Ark of the Covenant. He flipped carefully through the pages, speed reading for details.

There were several plausible sites suspected of being home to the Ark. None of them were in Bir Tawil. Hundreds of expeditions had resulted in little or no evidence of the Ark's existence. Solomon's Temple was the last place the Ark had been seen. This particular author assumed that the Ark remained hidden beneath the temple, concealed there during the Babylonian invasion. Beyond that, the book stated there were dozens of baseless rumors about its whereabouts but did not elaborate or list them.

Josh stroked the tidy growth of hair on his chin as his eyes widened and his mouth fell slightly open. It was an unconscious movement. It happened whenever an obvious answer popped into his mind.

Wait. Why am I researching the whereabouts of the Ark? Zak must know the places it's alleged to be. That must be archaeology 101. Josh reached for his cell phone and, pushing the home button said, "Call Zak Thomas."

"Calling Zak Thomas," a female voice replied.

"Hey Zak, I need some details about the Ark from you. I need to compile a list of places the Ark is suspected of being ... Yes, I think it may help ... I'm ready."

Josh wrote in the notebook; Solomon's Temple. He knew that. Mt. Sinai. The Hill of Tara in Ireland, a site near Cairo, Mt. Nebo, Lake Tana, Zimbabwe, Yemen, France, a basilica in Rome, the U.S., and a small church compound in Aksum, Ethiopia.

Josh flipped the page of his notebook and scribbled more notes as Zak explained some theories associated with the sites.

"Which do you think is most likely?" Josh asked. "... Yeah, I know we found it in Bir Tawil – but what if we hadn't? Where would you look first if finding the Ark was your greatest passion?"

Zak had no definitive answer. Some experts believed the Ark was still under the temple in Jerusalem. The church in Ethiopia claimed it was there, hidden away in a private chapel, protected by a guardian who spent his lifetime watching over it – never leaving the sanctuary where it was hidden, until he died. Most archaeologists dismissed Ethiopia's claims because they refused to allow anyone to see it and had no visible means of security for it.

Some of the sites had been excavated, but no valid trace had ever been found. From 1899-1902, a group of British-Israelites desecrated part of the Hill of Tara in Ireland with a poorly planned excavation. They found no remnants of the Ark, only a few Roman coins, the dates of which made them unlikely to have accompanied the Ark.

"Okay, Zak. Thanks. I'll call you when the plans for security are more complete. I found a person of interest related to Bir Tawil. It's probably nothing, but I'm researching him now."

Josh ended the call, musing over the list of the places Zak had mentioned. He circled Ethiopia. It was not far from Bir Tawil. He underscored Sinai. It was not far from the scene, either. What proximity had to do with it he wasn't sure, but a quiet insistence from his gut had him adding a star next to Ethiopia.

The door to the office opened. Jim, one of the attorneys, entered carrying an armload of files. "Hey, Josh. I've got a complicated disability case on my plate, and could use some help. Client says the guy has been working two jobs but claiming he can't work. Guy says he's going to physical therapy and church – nowhere else. Can you do some of your magic and see what the guy is up to?"

"Sure. Of course," Josh said, standing to take the files from him. "I've got a few things on my desk, but should be able to get on this pretty quick."

Jim scanned the office, taking in the stack of file folders, the notepad, and the thick stack of papers that were Josh's thesis. "I hope so. The case is being heard next week."

"Really, Jim. I've got it. It's not a problem."

Jim gave a somewhat dubious nod and closed the door. Josh sighed. Maybe he had taken on a bit too much, but he'd fit it all in somehow. He slipped his notepad in his pocket and began reviewing Jim's notes. Pretty simple surveillance job. He should be able to get started tomorrow. He entered the defendant's address into his phone and began perusing the file for more information.

A chime from his computer interrupted his thoughts. The name Aidan Quinn appeared in blue letters on the otherwise austere background screening page. He clicked the link and downloaded the initial report. It was too soon for in-depth details, but it would be a start.

> *Aidan Quinn. No criminal records found. No bankruptcies. No traffic tickets. Additional names found.*

Josh clicked on "Additional Names Found" revealing a short list.

> *Father Aidan Quinn, Aidan E. Quinn, Aidan Everett Quinn, and Anurak*

Anurak? Just plain Anurak. No last name. No middle name. What kind of name is that? Josh searched the internet for the name. Listings for Anurak Community Lodge in Thailand filled most of the page. Scrolling down, he discovered a few people in Thailand sharing the name; a football coach, a cyclist, even a law firm. He searched *Name Meanings* and scrolled through the A's under boy's names. Not there. He clicked back and chose another name-meaning site. Another. Finally, the name Anurak appeared on the fifth try. He clicked on it and found the name Anurak was associated with Buddhism. Its origin was Asian, and in Thai mythology, it meant *boy angel*.

Josh clicked on the back button, then selected *Known Addresses*, revealing a lengthy list of residences; Brooklyn. Kenosha. Rome. Kansas City. Tibet. *Tibet?* What was a Catholic priest with a name from Thai mythology doing in Tibet? The list went on: Couiza, Tokyo, Bali, Yemen, and Aksum. *Aksum, Ethiopia!* Aidan E. Quinn just became a lot more interesting.

Twisting his mouth into a scrunched up, sideways moue, Josh began tapping his left index finger on the keyboard – not hard enough to type a letter, just a light plunk, plunk. He was lost in thought, coming to a decision. He stroked his chin and widened his eyes. *Tom Majors,* he thought. Tom could access the information he needed. Tom had been his mentor during an internship at the NSA the previous summer. Tom had taken Josh under his wing, encouraging him to seek a career with the NSA after his international law degree was complete. Josh wasn't sure about that, but he was sure Tom could help him now. The question was, would he? It would help that his request involved an international crime scene. There couldn't be any reason not to help. Josh picked up his phone again, scrolled through the contacts and placed the call to his friend and mentor.

The voice on the other end of the call was brief and formal, "Tom Majors."

"Tom. It's Josh. Joshua Pearson. I interned ...."

"Josh! Great to hear from you, son. Have you decided to join us? We could really use a researcher like you. Especially one with a military background." The voice paused in hopeful anticipation.

"Haven't decided yet, Tom. Still working on that law degree and doing P.I. work for the law firm. But Tom, I need your help. I'm engaged in an international investigation – a rather high-profile one actually – and I've dug through all the resources I can access. Some persons of interest just got a little more interesting. Flight records and cell-phone data may help to solve an international terrorist attack investigation."

"The dig for the university? In Bir Tawil? I heard you were there," Tom said. "It's a pretty high-profile case, and I might be able to help, buddy. What've you got so far?"

Josh proceeded to tell Tom about the King and Queen of Bir Tawil, the flag, and a sibling priest who had lived in some rather interesting locations. All just circumstantial but his instincts told him that something didn't add up. Tom took the information Josh had gathered and promised to get back to him with whatever he could lawfully dig up.

Josh reached for the keyboard and switched to his email program. No response from his most recent request for security assistance in Egypt. No one was particularly interested in escorting an expedition into Bir Tawil, and they had no real authority to approve such a dig. Phone calls might be more productive, but also expensive. He didn't have an international plan on his own phone, and he couldn't place international calls from the firm. He'd have to set up shop at the university. Calls to arrange security for a dig would be expected there. He tossed his empty coffee cup and picked up his phone. He'd call Zak on his way.

CHAPTER TWELVE

A Confession

Elena arrived at the temple at precisely 11 a.m., quite a feat, as promptness was not her strong point. She was a night owl and not particularly active before noon, but she had no way of contacting Anurak and did not want to be late for their meeting. The building was an ordinary storefront squeezed between similar buildings, except that it was painted bright red. It looked a little like a Chinese gift shop with its bright exterior and souvenir-like Buddhas in the window displays. Stepping through the door, however, Elena entered an entirely different world.

The interior of the temple was elegant. There were no frills, but the building was impeccably maintained and built with high-quality materials. Mahogany beams and banisters accentuated the ivory-colored walls. Golden statuary rested on ornate pedestals and mahogany shelves. Paintings of Buddhist saints in gilded frames – *were they called saints?* – adorned the walls. A light, fragrant scent filled the air. *Nag Champa, with a hint of something else. Was it vanilla?* The fragrance reminded Elena of a small bookstore she often frequented in her college days, The Lotus Libris. The eclectic name fit the store's contents; stacks and stacks of books from seemingly endless schools of spiritual thought. There was no particular order to the books and shoppers were forced to browse every pile in their search for specific titles – unless of course, the owner was there. He could locate any title in any stack as if he were a human card catalog.

Anurak appeared at the other end of the lobby and walked toward her over the blue, inlaid mosaic design in the center of the floor. It was a lotus flower in full bloom. *Seriously? A lotus flower?* Elena thought. *Lotus flowers seem to be showing up a lot lately.*

"Tashi Delek, Elena," Anurak said with a slight bow.

"Umm... Namaste'?" Elena replied with the traditional bow of the head over hands held in an upright prayer position.

Anurak smiled. "Namaste'," he replied, mimicking the gesture. "Namaste is from the Hindu tradition, not Buddhism. But then, I am not officially a Buddhist, and I appreciate the greeting. I behold the divine in you as well. Come," said Anurak as he turned and gestured for Elena to follow.

They entered a small receiving room with a few low tables surrounded by thick, square saffron pillows. Faux windows were backlit to give the ambiance of outdoor lighting and the spaces between them were filled with various paintings of ornately dressed female figures. "Are they Buddhist saints?" Elena asked.

"They are Bodhisattvas, which are rather like saints but not canonized like a Catholic saint. These paintings all depict different manifestations of Kuan Yin, Bodhisattva of Compassion. Kuan Yin is exalted in Buddhism much like Mary is in Catholicism. She is the embodiment of Compassion, so she shows up in different ways – some say in different people, too.

"But please, Elena. Have a seat. One of the novices is bringing us some tea in a moment. Would you like anything else? Some water, or a biscuit maybe?"

"No. Tea is fine," Elena said as she settled onto one of the golden cushions. They were velvet, and the cording was a gold metallic material. "It's so beautiful here. No wonder you want to stay here. Are you still considering Buddhism as a path?"

Anurak sat across from her, legs tucked neatly beneath his flowing white robes. "No. I'm just visiting. Enough about me. Tell me about you, Elena. Where have you been? What have you been doing? Is church still a part of your life?"

"Whoa. Slow down. One question at a time. I'm still thinking about where I've been. There's a lot of years to cover in that question."

There was a quiet knock on the half-opened door. The head of a novice appeared from behind it, silently seeking admittance.

"Yes. Please come in," Anurak said.

The novice entered and brought a silver tray with a matching teapot and two china cups to their table. He placed them in the center, bowed and left the room. No words were exchanged.

"Pinchau has taken a vow of silence," Anurak said as he poured tea for both of them. "Go on. Lots of years to cover. How about starting with what happened after high school."

Elena blew some breath through her lips. "I got a job working for a broker in Manhattan. It was a pretty sweet job – at least my mother thought so. She always wanted her daughters to have a trade so they wouldn't have to rely on a man to take care of them. Anyway, it was a good job, but I hated it. I was bored out of my mind."

Anurak interrupted, "I can't imagine you in that environment. I always expected you to do something artistic."

"Me, too. I wanted something different and enrolled in some community college classes. It wasn't enough, though. I still hated my day job. So, I took a great leap of faith and quit my job to go to school full time. I got accepted into the Fine Arts program at NYU and never looked back – not even when I was selling street portraits and wait-ressing to pay the bills." Elena chuckled at that, but her memory wasn't quite so amusing. It had been fun in a way, but it had also been challenging.

"My major was painting, but I minored in photography. My mom's insistence on the ability to make a living apparently made an impact on me. My photography skills paid far better than my street art and waitressing. In fact, it was a series of photographs that inspired the paintings that got me my first solo exhibit. Now, I shoot mostly for fun and reference, but I still take some freelance gigs that interest me." She paused to take a sip of tea, then remembered the next question.

"As far as church goes, no. I haven't attended church in years, not a Catholic one, anyway. I've explored a bit, done lots of reading. It's not that I don't believe in God. I think of myself as spiritual, but not religious. Somewhere along the line the Church just seemed to be out of alignment with itself and I couldn't ... it just seemed so ... insin-cere? I don't know. I just got nothing from it, so I found other ways to express my spirituality."

Anurak sat quietly, blue eyes like openings to the universe. He took in every word but gave no indication of judgment, good or bad. He just listened, then without warning asked: "And when did you meet Zak?"

Elena was startled. She almost choked on her tea. Had she said anything to Anurak about Zak? She didn't think so. "How... how do you know about Zak?" she asked.

"Pretty hard not to know Elena. Your names were all over the papers when the story about the shootings in the desert broke. One of the articles mentioned you had accompanied him on many field stud-ies and I was just curious how an artist ended up joining archaeological digs." He stopped, waiting for a reply.

"Oh, of course." Elena blinked to hide the rolling of her eyes. "Zak and I have been friends for years. Best friends." She looked directly into the welcoming blue eyes and added, "Not a romantic relationship.

"We met in an anthropology class my first year at the community college. It was the first class I signed up for when I started thinking about going back to school. It wasn't what I wanted. I was hoping for a painting class, but by the time my registration number came up, it was the only open class left that interested me. Zak and I really hit it off, and when there was an opportunity to earn credits by going on digs together, I couldn't resist. Finding lost artifacts inspires me. It's like having a connection with an artist from another time and place."

"I see," Anurak replied. "So, you are friends. You have some common interests. You are a successful artist – and you still go on these field studies with Zak because you feel a connection to artists from another time. Anything else?"

Elena suddenly felt warm. She wasn't sure she liked where this conversation was going. What was Anurak's interest in Zak? Was he going to hit on her? It seemed unlikely. He was a monk of some kind. She did an internal shake of her head to clear her thoughts and said, "Yes. There is something else, Anurak. It's not about Zak, though. It's about the last dig, not the newspaper story but something else." She paused. Relaxing her focus, Elena saw Anurak's energy. It was peaceful and blue, much like his eyes. *Should I tell him? I think I have to. I'll go crazy if I don't.*

"Anurak. I want to share something with you. It's umm, well, do you still have to keep whatever people tell you in confidence? I mean, you never really stop being a priest, right?"

Anurak smiled. "That's confession Elena. Do you need to confess something?"

"No. Not exactly. But I do need you to keep it to yourself. It's vital that you do."

Elena shared it with him. All of it. The ancient map, the uncharted excursion, the hazards, the deadly encounters, and finally, the Ark, the mystical box formed of mysterious metals that defied the laws of physics. She shared the team's entry into the mystical realm that seemed to exist inside the Ark.

"All the things you said yesterday," Elena began, "about impermanence and graven images, I heard, or felt those things in the Ark. There were no stone tablets in there, just a sense of knowing."

"Knowing what?" Anurak asked. He was listening intently, his face serene and his blue eyes like inviting pools of water on a hot summer day.

"I can't put it in words exactly. It was like knowing everything. No. Not everything, but whatever question came to mind, the answer came with it. Not just any answer, but an unequivocal answer that couldn't be misunderstood. There was a sense of knowing that permeated my entire being. There was no self, yet there was. We were all one; one being, one mind, one thought – yet we were not. The words we had expected to find on stone tablets did not exist. Instead, we encountered a presence that expressed blessings beyond human comprehension and certainly beyond words written in stone."

Anurak had listened silently in the manner of someone who had heard many confessions. Now he spoke. "What do you think it means? That there were no stone tablets? Does it mean that this was not the real Ark, or that the tablets had been removed?"

There was no hesitation in Elena's reply. "Oh, it's real. But I don't think the tablets ever existed. I think they were a metaphor. I've been poring over the words of Exodus for clues ever since we returned. It says that the commandments were written in stone by the 'very finger of God.' What does that mean? God doesn't have fingers or toes. God is so much more than that. So, the finger has to be a metaphor, which means the tablets were also a metaphor.

"When I think of stone, I think of something that is not easily changed, something more or less permanent. A finger is an extension, something we point with, something we touch with. So, I think the finger of God is the point where God meets man and what *is* written is inscribed immutably – not on tablets but maybe in the mind or the heart? Maybe the tablets represent what cannot change and that somewhere deep within us we know these things. I mean God doesn't change, right?"

Anurak nodded in agreement. "God does not change. This is true. What about the commandments themselves? How did they become a part of the story if they didn't exist?"

"Oh, they exist all right. They just don't have to be written in stone. I think the concepts are already written in our DNA. Think about it. Don't most spiritual paths have a similar set of rules? At the very least, a code that prohibits harming one another? The codes written by the finger of God are embedded in our nature. They are irrefutable, but they are not commandments – not in the sense of rules as we understand them."

Closing his eyes for a moment, Anurak seemed to be pondering her last statement, as if trying not to judge what she had said. "Not commandments?" he asked.

"No. They're not." Elena had lots of questions about what she learned, but this was something she was certain of. "They are blessings. They are a list of statements reassuring us that God is with us and nothing can harm us – nothing can harm our spiritual being – or soul, if you prefer. Each one of these blessings is an extension of the first. If we understand that God is all, and we are a part of the All-ness, then nothing can really harm us. I know this. I learned it in the Ark, but I also realize how foreign it sounds when I say it out loud. There are no words to truly describe what I'm trying to say."

Anurak spoke quietly. "You are finding it hard to put into words what you learned? I wonder if you are not alone in this quandary?"

Elena's first thought was of the other members of the team, Zak, Paul, and Josh. But something about the sparkle in Anurak's eyes told her he was thinking of someone else. "Ah. Yes," she said. "I suppose Moses would have had a hard time putting it into words, too. I read that he told God he was 'slow of speech and slow of tongue.' At first, I thought that meant he had a speech impediment, but I think it's more likely he felt inadequate, unable to communicate infinite ideas with the words of a finite language. A set of rules or steps would have been easier to explain, and no doubt imperative to the survival of his people. But in the end, in the realization of what God really is, no human rules are necessary."

"That's very perceptive of you Elena. I've spent years researching the vast metaphysical library at the Vatican exploring exactly what you've just said, that the stories of scripture have more than one meaning. There is much to be learned literally, but even more can be discerned metaphysically. Such clarity is rare among even the most devout pupils."

"It was all obvious to me in the Ark, but I've lost a little of it since we returned. When we found ourselves outside the box again, we continued to move in unison for a while. We didn't speak. We just began concealing the Ark, replacing the rocks that had hidden it. We gathered all our equipment and climbed back down the mountain to the camp where a multitude of questions and turmoil awaited us. We silently agreed never to share the discovery or the whereabouts of the Ark, but felt compelled to share its message. The question is, how? How do you express what is beyond words, even beyond images? I painted what I saw, but people couldn't begin to grasp it. They appreciated the beauty of the colors and shapes, but the message fell on blind eyes."

Anurak smiled. "Perhaps it is only for those who have eyes to see and ears to hear."

Elena looked quizzical. "What?

"It's something Jesus said," Anurak replied. "He said it quite often, actually. He knew that many of his followers were unable to grasp the true meaning of the messages he shared, but it didn't stop him from sharing them. It's like the saying attributed to The Buddha, 'When the student is ready, the teacher appears.' That doesn't mean the teacher suddenly materializes out of the ethers. It means the teacher or the teaching has always been there, but the student is not aware of its presence until he or she is ready. You just need to keep painting and expressing what you've learned. When the student is ready, they will see, they will hear, they will feel. You think you are painting for patrons and those who will purchase your work. But you are working for something much greater than that. The eyes and ears that are open will see and hear. It may be the person who purchases the painting. It may be the person who delivers and hangs it. It may be a visitor who sees it in passing. It may even be you as you paint. If what you share is not understood, that's really not your business."

Elena sighed in relief. These were comforting words. The pressure seemed so much less. It was not hers to explain, it was merely hers to explore and share. Ideas began to form in Elena's mind. Paintings, drawings, installations. What Anurak said made sense. She could feel it inside. It was as if he were confirming what she already knew. She smiled at the man with blue eyes that she had known since childhood, and suddenly she knew what angels were.

But what about the paintings she had destroyed? "I'm afraid I've lost some of the lessons," she said. "I got so frustrated when people were not getting it. I looked around and I ... well, I guess I let it 'be my business,' that people didn't see or hear my message. I shredded them – the paintings. Not the ones in the gallery but everything else in my studio. And now I just feel blocked. I want to paint but what? How do you paint something so perfect? So complete? I think I want to paint God, but there isn't a canvas big enough."

Anurak smiled at this. "Yes, Elena. God is big. Much bigger than the human mind can conceive – at least on a conscious level. But you've seen, you've encountered what few have been able to experience. You've had an experience of enlightenment. Many spend a lifetime trying to reach what you and your friends stumbled upon. Perhaps you need to take it one small step at a time."

Elena shook her head in agreement. "That's for sure. I hadn't thought of it that way, but yes, I imagine people do spend a lifetime trying to achieve something like that. The thing is, I ...." Should she tell him the rest? Why not? She'd told him this much.

"The thing is," she took a deep breath and a long sip of tea before continuing. "I entered the Ark again ... from my studio. It was after I shredded the canvases. I was in a crazy state of mind. I just went out of my mind, I guess. And then suddenly I was back in that heavenly realm again." Elena's heart was pounding now. It was pounding so hard she wondered if Anurak could hear it. If he heard it, he didn't show it. He sat as placidly as ever, just listening.

"And I suppose you want to know how to get back to that place. On purpose. Right?"

This was getting a little weird. How did he know this? It almost seemed as if he already knew everything she had shared, but listened as if hearing it for the first time. "Well, yes," she said. "I would like to go back. Not to the desert, but I'd like to get back into that state of mind again. I can think and see so clearly there. I think it will help me paint whatever it is I'm supposed to paint if I can just get back there again."

Anurak stood and brushed the folds of his robes down, so they draped perfectly to the floor. "You've got the first part of it already, and I might be able to help you with the rest," he said.

"What's the first part?" Elena asked.

"It's easy. You just have to get 'out of your mind.'" He twisted his mouth into an ironic smile and said, "Come on. Let me show you something. There're seven floors to this building, and the seventh is actually on the roof. It's a place I think you'll love. And it's a good place to lose your mind."

CHAPTER THIRTEEN

The Secret Garden

Elena followed Anurak up the six flights of stairs. He gave her a brief tour as they passed each floor. The first floor, where they had begun their visit, housed the temple and several small rooms used for receiving guests and for small, intimate classes. There was also a gift shop, displaying a variety of Buddhist books and statues.

The second floor was used for larger classes and meetings with visiting dignitaries. The rooms were similar to the first floor but with larger windows and more lighting. More golden statuary was displayed throughout, and paintings similar to the Kuan Yin pictures, but with clearly different subjects adorned the walls.

The third floor housed the dining hall where three vegetarian meals per day were served. Breakfast and dinner were for the residents and visiting dignitaries, but lunch was available and free to anyone who chose to attend. The meals were prepared by the residents, primarily the novices under the direction of the head chef, a monk, and resident for many years. Anurak believed the chef's cooking skills exceeded the abilities of any New York chef and was confident he would win if he appeared on the Food Channel competition, *Chopped*. Elena wasn't hungry, but the aromas on the third floor were definitely enticing. She would have to make her next visit at lunchtime.

The fourth through sixth floors were primarily dormitory rooms with a few offices scattered throughout. These floors looked more like a convent than a Buddhist temple, from what Elena knew of convents anyway. She and some friends had snuck into the convent at St. Bardo's one afternoon thinking the nuns were all in a meeting. They peeked in the doors of the austere bedrooms that contained nothing but a small bed, a bible, and a crucifix. They had been skipping joyfully through the dining room, wondering which nun sat at which seat, when through the kitchen door stormed Sister Marie John, wooden spoon in hand. Weeks of extra homework and zillions of written lines, "I will not invade the privacy of others," motivated Elena and her friends to never again enter a restricted area.

On the sixth floor, the stairway ended, and Anurak led her to double doors around the corner. Pushing through the doors, they climbed the final flight of stairs. Elena wondered if there was an elevator but thought better of asking. At the top of these stairs, there was another set of double doors, but these had frosted windows at the top. Light poured through them, and as they swung open, Elena was thoroughly disarmed by the beautiful sight that appeared on the other side. The rooftop was covered with a lawn of soft, lush bluegrass. It was real grass! Planted on the roof! Raised flower beds were everywhere, peppering the meadow-like scene. Beautiful wrought-iron benches were carefully placed – most of them stood alone, inviting a lone monk or seeker to spend quiet, private time on the roof. A few were gathered in clusters, apparently arranged for quiet conversation. Statues of Buddha were carefully placed throughout, most with a sitting area nearby. The perimeter of the roof was lined with potted trees, a visual obstruction to the cityscape beyond them.

"Come." Anurak motioned toward a small area with two opposing seats. They were not wrought-iron benches. They were more like the cushions in the receiving room but slightly raised, probably to avoid early morning dampness. She wondered what happened when it rained but the feel of the pillows assured her; they were waterproof and comfortable but a little crunchy.

"It's beautiful! It's hard to imagine there is something so beautiful in the middle of the city. I mean there's the parks and all, but this is ... It's breathtaking."

Anurak sat across from her, tucking his legs into a lotus position. He gestured for her to do the same. As she did, the sound of sirens below screamed up at them, horns honked, brakes squealed, and metal clanged as delivery trucks below unloaded their contents onto loading docks. "If it weren't for all that noise, I would think I was in Tibet," said Elena.

"The noise is not really a problem, Elena, unless you allow it to be. In fact, in true mindfulness meditation, the noise can be conducive to the goal – total silence. You begin by paying attention to the sounds, listening to them, allowing them to take you wherever they will. And then, you begin to listen for the space between them. The space between outer noises is often easier to find than the space between your own thoughts."

Elena nodded. "Sounds good. Kinda makes sense. I often find my meditation time is so full of thoughts I can't really call it meditation.

It ends up being more like *concentration* on whatever is going on in my life."

"Let's begin then." Anurak sat up even straighter than before. "Begin by sitting straight; your spine is curving forward too much. Straighten yourself as if there is a string above you lifting you just a little off the cushion so that all your vertebrae are perfectly aligned, one on top of the other, as straight as can be."

Elena straightened herself and was surprised at how bent over she had actually been.

"Now, close your eyes and breathe with me. That's it ... take a deep breath in ... and now let it out ... keep letting it out ... more ... until there is nothing left and your abdomen feels like it is touching your spine ... Now do this again – four times."

This Elena had done before. She knew how to push all the breath out of her lungs and abdomen and did so.

"Now listen to all the sounds around you ... let them fill your mind until all you hear is the sounds ..." He waited a bit for her to do this and then continued, "Now pick one, single-out one sound, just one, and follow it. Let it take you wherever it will ... until you find the silence."

The most prominent sound that Elena heard was metal clashing on metal. It sounded like the doors of a large delivery truck slamming shut. *They must be delivering food to the kitchen,* Elena thought. Then she caught herself thinking and listened only to the sounds of the truck, the motor starting, the gears squeaking as they shifted into reverse, the grinding noise as they shifted forward. She could hear the tires scrunching along the pavement, the blinking of the turn signal, the air whooshing out as the hydraulic brakes were engaged. Just the motor running and the blinking of the flashers now. Then the gears engaged again and she followed the sound, down the street, into traffic, and beyond, onto ... the highway? The sounds were smooth now, almost monotonous. They grew fainter and fainter ... until... they transformed into something else ... a quiet chirping sound ... she was in a forest ... far, far away ... she listened to the bird song and felt the vibrations of the tune ... and then she was absorbed into the resonance of the song ... she was the song ... then there was silence....

In the nothingness, there was movement, a quiet pulsation. Elena focused on it. She knew this vibration, it was the energy of the Ark. It was the way in. Her heart leaped within her as the familiar pulses began to shroud her body ... and then she stopped. *Not here. Not now.* She thought. *Later, when I'm at home. Not now.*

A different vibration rang through Elena now. It filled her ears and ran down through her shoulders and spine, then faded. *Was that a gong?* she wondered. Then another sound began to penetrate her eardrums, quiet at first, then louder, more insistent.

"Elena ... Elena! Come back."

It was Anurak. She opened her eyes and felt the smile spread across her face. "Anurak! Thank you! That's exactly what I needed. It's been so long since I was able to let go of everything – on purpose, anyway. Thank you."

"You were able to stop it, weren't you?" he asked.

"Yes! But how did you know?"

"I was with you, Elena. I didn't want to send you on that journey alone. I followed you. So much has happened to you I felt you needed an outer guide. It's possible to do that – to meditate and travel together." Anurak smiled a gentle and serene smile.

"Wow," she said. "I love this place. I'm so glad we found each other at the park and I'm so grateful you brought me to this incredible secret garden."

"You are welcome. And it's not really a secret. You are welcome anytime, Elena. The Garden is open to anyone who knows about it. We can meditate together whenever you wish – and you can come on your own, too."

Elena was anxious to get back to the studio. She wanted to try this method again while she was close to her canvases, but the invitation to return was also irresistible. "I will absolutely come back. I enjoyed the meditation, but I also enjoy our talks. It's been wonderful to be able to share this thing about the Ark with you. I hope you don't mind if I spend a lot of time talking about it. It just helps so much to say these things out loud. I think between talking about it and getting more focused – or unfocused, I guess – with my meditations, I think the paintings will flow much more easily. And I won't forget that it doesn't matter if everyone gets it – but it is nice to know that *you* understand."

"Anytime, Elena. I'm glad we met, too." He paused a moment as if he were trying to decide something or gather his thoughts. Elena waited.

"Elena, may I ask you some more questions about the Ark?"

"Of course." She smiled at her newfound – or was it *re-found* – friend.

"Where exactly did you find this Ark anyway? I'm just curious – there are so many places it is believed to be."

Odd question, given the details she had shared earlier, but someone who had dedicated his life to religious study was bound to have questions. She had already broken the vow of silence – how could this information hurt?

"It was in Egypt. Well, not exactly Egypt. That's where the original dig was. We made a side trip to a place called Bir Tawil. It's a little piece of unclaimed land between Egypt and Sudan that neither country wants. It's pretty barren. Not much good to either country I guess, and both believe claiming it would exclude them from possessing a more valuable piece of land."

"Ahh. Hala'ib Triangle." Anurak shook his head in understanding.

Anurak had excelled in geography just as he had in government, politics, and all of the sciences when they were in school. It should be no surprise that he knew about the standoff between Egypt and Sudan. Elena, on the other hand, did not excel in geography. If she hadn't been to a place, it barely existed in her mind. But Bir Tawil, that existed.

"And you left it. Right there? How did you find it? What drew you to Bir Tawil in the first place?"

Elena hesitated. This was more than she was comfortable sharing. What could she say without betraying Zak and the others? "Uhm ... the team found some evidence that there might be some artifacts in the general area. We went to scout it out. We actually stumbled on the place where the Ark was hidden when we tried to escape the shootings." *That's true. It doesn't give too much away.* She didn't share about the map or the broken piece. Even if someone knew the location of their campsite – and many people knew that – finding the hidden cave would be impossible. Even with the map, they had only discovered it because it had called to them.

"That's quite a coincidence, stumbling upon the greatest archae-ological find of all times by accident, don't you think?" Anurak was smiling now. He seemed to be looking through her and seeking a spe-cific response, like a teacher knowing the student had the answer at the tip of their tongue.

"There are no coincidences. I know. Like you and I finding each other in the park. It's meant to be. Souls calling to each other at the right and perfect time. I believe in the synchronicity of all things. That resonates with me. But the Ark? Us finding it? Me? That I haven't figured out yet."

"Tomorrow then? At lunchtime? You'll love the food. It's delectable."

"I think so. But I might get involved with a painting. Is there any way to contact you here? I mean, is there a phone, an email, some way to reach you?"

Anurak paused a moment as if trying to think of an answer, right hand deep in the hidden pocket of his robe, fingers touching the top of his cell phone. He pulled his hand out, empty. "I'll know," he said. "If you don't come tomorrow, I'll know you are painting – and I'll know when you are ready to visit. We are connected in Spirit, Elena."

Elena wasn't sure if *being connected in Spirit* with Anurak was thrilling or disturbing, but it would make meeting with him easier. "Okay then, hasta la vista, or see you later." She reached out to hug him, but he drew away from her. It was apparently not appropriate to touch, but it wasn't necessary either. She could feel a gentle, energetic embrace.

They left the garden, descended the stairs and Elena said goodbye once again. They bowed slightly toward one another and Elena walked out the temple door into the bustling city street outside. The energetic difference was overwhelming. She took a few breaths to calm herself and headed home.

***

The cell phone in Elena's pocket vibrated and let out a cricket-like chirp. A text message. She pulled the phone out as she walked through the park. It was Zak.

"U okay? Painting yet?"

Elena smiled and felt something in her abdomen relax.

"Yes K," she replied almost running into an elderly lady walking the other way. She saw an empty bench and sat down. The sun reflecting off the concrete surface was so bright it caused Elena to look away as she sat. The seat felt warm from soaking up the sun languidly crossing a cloudless sky. *Thank God for Indian Summer,* Elena thought. She wasn't looking forward to the cold weather.

"Not painting – but ready," she added.

"Lunch tomorrow?" Zak asked.

Elena hesitated, thinking about the possible meeting with Anurak – and painting.

"Dinner ok? Have plans for lunch."

Elena could see Zak was texting something. Little dots were doing their incoming text dance. She waited – and waited.

"Only if you let me bring something. Not in the mood for ramen."

Elena laughed out loud. She didn't stock much food in the apartment. She didn't like to cook, but there were always stacks of ramen in her cupboard.

"Great! Surprise me." Then she added, "but no raw fish."

Zak's reply was a laughing face. They both knew she hated sushi.

CHAPTER FOURTEEN

A Bubble in Time

It felt good to be painting again. Elena's meeting with Anurak had helped to clear her mind and deepen her meditations. This morning she had reached the same still, quiet place she was able to attain at the rooftop garden. She felt the same ripples of energy moving through her, but instead of following them into the portal, she brought them out of the meditation with her. Along with the peaceful sensations, she brought vivid recollections of her last visit to the Ark realm and the images that had appeared on the magical canvas.

Now, with the perfect southern light pouring into her studio, Elena looked deeply into the eyes of the crocodile she had just painted. They were deep and brown and beautiful. They were missing just the slightest bit of golden glint, and so she picked up the brush and dipped its tip into the white paint, mixed it with a bit of yellow and raw sienna, creating a perfect shade of amber.

She lifted the brush and gently touched the pupil of the eye … and then she felt it. Rippling through the brush, into her hand, up her arm, and through her whole body. The irresistible vibrations of the Ark. Should she control it? Stop it? She knew how now. No. She relaxed every muscle in her body and released her thoughts. She let go and allowed the power rushing through her brush to draw her in, through the canvas, to another space and time, the place where the heavens waltzed a dance of love and light, where she could see beyond time and space. She felt as if she was inhaling the breath of the very Essence of Life. It was exhilarating. It was a place that transcended the world of form, a place where things were drawn into form as the thought of them danced through her mind. She thought about the mystical, translucent canvas, and it appeared.

Touching her brush to the magical palette, Elena saw herself appear on the canvas, but in a different time. She did not appear as a static image but as a moving picture. It was the day, long ago, when she had first caught a glimpse of something utterly unworldly; a great white ball in the sky, like a giant bubble floating through the currents of air, resting, bouncing, circling, then hovering right before her.

She must have been five or six years old when she'd first encountered the bubble. She hadn't been afraid, just curious. As the bubble rested in front of her, it seemed to speak, but it did not use words. It became still, then seemed to expand and envelop her. Inside the bubble, she could see the stars, the moons and planets, and far beyond. In fact, she could see forever. She could see the past, the future, and the present all tumbled together in one exquisite, pulsating vision. Then she saw what words could not describe.

It was a feeling more than a vision. It was *a knowing* that surpassed what her human eyes could see. She was whole. She was complete. She was at one, one with all things and magnificently unique. She was filled with a sense of freedom and joy that surpassed anything her childish years had yet experienced. She knew she was one with the stars, one with the world, one with all things, living in a grand symphony of life not contained by bodies or ruled by time and space, but uncontainable, unlimited, unfathomable, more magnificent than anyone might ever have imagined.

And then the bubble was gone. The world stood seemingly motionless though Elena knew it had moved. The trees gently swayed in an invisible breeze and the grass lightly rippled, brighter than it had been just seconds before. The sturdy maple standing next to her seemed the same as it had always been, but somehow it was less solid. When she looked in a certain way, she could see past the dark brown bark to a glittering substance breathing in a harmonious rhythm, not unlike her own.

"It was just a weather balloon," her mother had told her. But in her heart, Elena knew that the bubble was so much more.

***

The magical brush pulsed in Elena's hand now. She held it toward the floating canvas, and it painted a translucent image of the bubble in a vast expanse of sky already visible on the mystical canvas. The bubble called to her. It beckoned her and Elena found herself pulled inside the magical orb that had floated before her as a child. She felt, rather than heard, the voice that had spoken to her there so long ago.

You have a million images at the tip of your brush that all reflect what you know to be true; that there is but one Essence, one thread that lives, and yes, weaves through each of us. It is beautiful, whole, and never separate. I am here. I have never left you. Together, let us paint the story of how beautiful everyone is and help them to see it. If only one person realizes that there is more to life, and that there is nothing to truly fear, what an incredible gift that would be.

The voice became still then, and the bubble began to rise, carrying her through a vast ripple of light. Elena could see all the moments of her own life appearing as little vignettes. One vignette grew larger, and Elena found herself immersed in a scene from her past. Her mother was cooking supper, cleaning the kitchen as she worked. Her mother seemed to be in a world all her own, a world that contained porcelain appliances, aluminum-clad pots, and bowls full of vegetables. It was a world that seemed to begin and end with the faded, papered, walls and miniblinds of Elena's childhood home.

But now, immersed in this memory, Elena could see the brilliant glow of the spiritual being that animated her mother's actions. This spiritual being was alive and active, yet hopelessly entrapped by a swirl of dark and heavy emotional energy. She saw her mother's pain, her mother's passion, her mother's longing, and deep sadness. She also saw her mother's courage, her strength, the incredible sense of love that fueled her actions as she went about the business of caring for her family.

Elena's mother had been abused by her own father and cheated on by her husband. She had, in fact, been disenchanted by life as a whole. Yet her love for her children sustained her and inspired her to action. She saw all three, Elena and her older siblings Rich and Jenny, as perfect and had immensely higher hopes for them than they had for themselves. Unaware of the inner power to change her own life, she selflessly cared for her family as if they were the only thing in the world worth living for. Elena was suddenly overwhelmed with compassion for this woman who worked tirelessly at her role as mother and wife, all the while asleep to her own inner grandeur.

Tears flowed down Elena's face as this memory revealed a woman she had lived with, but had never really known. *Honor thy mother and thy father,* she felt the voice of the bubble exclaim. *Honor all mothers, all fathers, for in their Essence they are the expression of the Mother-Father Essence of the One.*

The bubble moved a short distance, depositing Elena a short time later in the same, gray-tiled kitchen. "Mommy, I'm hungry," young Elena was saying. "When can we eat?" Dinner had been on the stove for a very long time. Elena's mother absently stirred a pot, then returned to her vigil at the window, peering through the slats of the miniblinds. "We'll eat when your father gets home, Elena."

Elena knew this could go on for hours. It would start with a peek or two through the blinds, the sound of irritation growing in her mother's voice with every peek. Dad was late. Again. Supper would be late and cold. Later, hours later, Elena's father was delivered to the front door by his coworkers, flopping around on the front porch like a fish. Momma had forgotten about dinner altogether as she angrily went about putting Daddy to bed. Elena wondered why she was so mad at Daddy for being too sick to walk. It would be many years before she understood the effect of the grown-up drinks Daddy smelled of that night.

As the years went by, the aroma of alcohol radiating from Elena's father became synonymous with his presence. It exuded from him like steam from a clothes iron on a Saturday afternoon several years later when Elena was sewing a dress for a high school dance. In her bedroom, away from her father's ranting on and on about spending all his money on some new rugs her mother had purchased, Elena was running bright blue taffeta through the sewing machine when it jammed – again. It jammed frequently, and Elena's patience had run out. She swore at the machine. She screamed at the fabric. She cried at the knots that had formed along the seam, damaging the fabric. "Fuck! Fuck! Fuck!" She cried. Then she fell silent as the sound of her mother's screaming reached her ears.

"No. Stop. Stop. No!" The screaming was followed by the shuffling of feet and the sound of bodies struggling and bumping against the walls just outside her bedroom door. Then she heard her mother crying "My leg. My leg!" as her father burst through the door, slamming Elena onto the bed. He grabbed the iron from the ironing board and viciously raised the steaming block of steel toward Elena's head. "No! Please! No! I'm sorry. I'm sorry," she sobbed as she covered her face with her arms, inching away as far as she could toward the head-board. *My God!* she thought. *He's going to burn me with that thing!*

Suddenly, Mother's screaming from the hallway seemed to penetrate her father's anger. He lowered the iron and placed it back on the ironing board. A look of remorse crossed his face as he mumbled an apology and walked to the hallway where Elena's mother lay crumpled on the floor. Her leg was broken.

Even in the comfort of the bubble, Elena's heart was pounding. Tears were forming at the rims of her eyes. Elena had forgotten the intense fear and anguish buried with this memory. She could feel a familiar knot forming at the top of her stomach. It had been beyond terrifying at the time, but shock, denial, and time had somehow lessened the horror. Until now. As she ruminated on the scene playing out before her, it was clear just how close she had come to not only being burned by a hot iron but having her life cut short at the hands of her enraged father. For years she had carried a burden of guilt over the event, convinced that her swearing at the sewing machine was the cause of her father's outburst and her mother's injury. She wondered now which was more frightening; that she would think *she* was responsible for such an act of violence, or that her father had nearly killed her because she had cursed at a sewing machine.

How do you honor that? Elena wondered.

Watch again, the voice within her replied.

Elena watched again, but from a higher vantage point, as if she were floating above the scene as it unfolded. From this view, she noticed that the moment her father was about to bring the iron down on her, something bright and luminous surrounded him, and it wasn't just outside of him. As the brilliant glow began to enfold him, light burst through the top of his head. The look of remorse she had seen had been much more than that. In that instant, with a total loss of control, her father's inner light had risen up to stop him. It wasn't her mother's screaming, after all. It was some sleeping part of him that was somehow awakened. This was the father she was being asked to honor, the spiritual being that inhabited her father's body, the Truth of him.

Elena's mind was spinning with an awakened knowing. It wasn't the physical mother and father a person was commanded to honor – though that was important, too. It was their Essence, which in its purest state was both mother and father, an expression of the One.

The brush was now moving madly about in Elena's hand. Colors poured out of its tip, and the bubble gave way to images of people at work, people in stores, people traveling, airplanes taking off and landing, factories pumping out toxic smoke, and houses, empty with no one at home. There was a frenetic energy about it. Everything was moving. Nothing was still. It was not a painting so much as it was a video on infinite repeat. Children came home to the empty houses, turned on TVs and plugged into video games. Alone. The sky grew dark as night revealed itself, but the frenetic activity failed to cease. Workers continued to work. They didn't dare stop. Jobs were scarce. Competition was fierce. There were bills to pay and savings to build.

The stores did not close, their checkout lines did not thin. The children continued to play their games. Alone. Some grew restless. They searched the house for pills or alcohol to fill the persistent void growing inside. As the stars grew brighter and the moon rose higher, exhausted mothers and fathers drove endless hours in serpentine masses of automobiles to bring home fast-food dinners. The stores remained open, and the activity did not cease.

The brush slowed a little. It hardly seemed possible, but everything in the scene grew just a bit gloomier. Elena could see into the darkened bedrooms now. Sleeping pills were swallowed in preparation for another exhausting day. Bottles of scotch were drained to stop the obsessive worries over the next day's work. It was quieter now, but the motion continued as a nightlife awoke to the start of midnight shifts. Addicts emerged from neglected houses, searching unlocked cars for unattended cash and valuables, on the prowl for another fix. There was a deeply disturbing feeling of hopelessness radiating from the endlessly moving scene. It was exhausting. It was depressing just to watch.

The brush remained motionless in Elena's hand, but it had ceased to paint. Instead, she found herself floating again in the bubble, carried back to the soft green grass in front of her childhood home. She could feel the breeze that rippled through the maple trees adorning the lawn. She could smell the scent of the tiny pink flowers on the Spirea bush just behind her. Her mother had called it the "Little Princess" bush. Elena believed it was planted just for her.

As Elena peered through the picture window of the gray, cement-block house, she saw her family dressed in their best clothes. Her mother was checking everyone's attire, handing out white gloves for the girls and straightening her brother's tie. Her father was putting some cash into an envelope and licking it shut. It was Sunday, the Christian Sabbath. They would go to church and then spend the rest of the day at home. Perhaps there would be a little yard work left over from Saturday. There would be some preparation for supper. But most of the day would be a time of rest. Her father might listen to the ballgame as he tended to the weeds in his garden. Later in the day, he would help her learn to ride her new bike. Her mother would have time to sit and read the newspaper. There was no more shopping to do. Most of the stores were closed except for a few at the mall, the pharmacy, and some gas stations. They might even play a family game together at the old kitchen table after supper.

Sundays were like that back then, Elena thought, a day of rest and rejuvenation for the week to come. It was a day of connection and respite. There was no internet, no video games, and no makeup softball games to be played. People 'Remembered the Sabbath.' They understood there was a time to work and a time to play; a time to toil and a time to rest; a time to think and a time to be quiet. It was peaceful. It was balanced. It was heavenly.

Elena was lifted higher, out of the scene. From this vantage point, Elena could see the entire Earth as it floated in its orbit around the sun, creating the illusion of time. She could see the days and nights flashing by so quickly that the difference became imperceptible. The tilting of the Earth created what was experienced as seasons, and this too occurred at a frenetic pace so that the leaves on the trees sprouted almost simultaneously with their changing color and falling to the ground. It was all an illusion, an experience unique to one's position on the Earth. In the realm of the Ark, she felt no time, no frantic pace, no need to slow things down or hurry them along. There was, in fact, no time at all. There was only now.

Time, Elena thought, is an illusion. There is no time except in the mind of the human experience. The Sabbath, a time of rest, is meant to be a respite from the delusion of sequence. As a blessing, it is an awareness of the space before time where the mind was at one with the Essence of Life. This is a rest more revitalizing than any spa, vacation, or retreat could begin to replicate.

She wondered how it would feel to experience life and all of its illusions of time with this knowing – that there was really only one moment. Was it possible to walk through time yet be fully aware of it all being now? She thought about the mindfulness meditation Anurak had taught her. If it was impossible to stop the machinery of life on Earth, to honor an actual day of Sabbath, maybe one could at least take time each day for a Sabbath of the soul – time spent remembering the place without time.

Click ... click ... click ... The mystical canvas had reappeared, and Elena's brush was forming melting clocks in the style of Salvador Dali's *The Persistence of Memory*. To Elena, the painting had always suggested time melting away. *Maybe time melting away is not about hurrying, or even slowing down. Maybe it's about dissolving the illusion and returning to the state of oneness that transcends time.*

Click ... click ... click ... The deformed clocks were ticking. Click ... click ... click ... The particles of paint began to shudder with every click. With each sound, they spread further and further apart, and a vast gap of nothingness appeared between them ... click ... click ... click... Elena's ears were filled with the drum of the clicks. The sounds came closer together, deeper ....

Wait. They're not clicks. They're knocks. Elena's studio became visible in the space between the particles of paint. She felt the whooshing, pulling feeling that had now become familiar to her. It was Zak at the door with dinner.

CHAPTER FIFTEEN

An Invitation

Knock, knock, knock. The clicks were knocks, and Elena was back in her studio standing before her painting of the crocodile, paint drying on the brush. "Shit," she said, as she set the brush in the thinning jar, wiped the paint from her hands, and headed for the door.

"Took you long enough," Zak said entering with bags of food in his hands. "I got Paninis, but they might need warming up by now – between the walk here and waiting at your door."

"Sorry. I was so engrossed in the painting, I didn't hear you right away. I know that sounds crazy but sometimes I get so into it I'm ah ...." Elena hesitated. "It's like I'm in another world." Elena felt an inward smile at the white lie ... *It was another world all right!*

"So I've noticed. Yikes!" he said peering over her shoulder at the crocodile painting. An open throat with dastardly looking yellow teeth filled nearly the entire canvas. The rest of the crocodile was a massive blob of dark green and brown scales, his pudgy feet and sharp claws penetrating the mud and sand at the edge of some murky body of water. Yet, at the very edges, there were traces of the earlier paintings, the ethereal ones from the show. Wispy strands of colorful beams of light gave the only hint of brightness in the otherwise sinister looking painting. "That's about the darkest thing I've ever seen you paint. What's it about?"

Elena took the dinner bags from Zak and headed toward the oven. "Let's get these warmed up. I'll explain over dinner. How's the research going?" Changing the subject would buy her some time. She wasn't sure if she wanted Zak to know about her returning to the realm of the Ark or not. He already thought she might be losing it and she didn't need to encourage that belief. She hoped that what was happening to her would not drive a wedge in their relationship. They'd been friends for far too long to let that happen. *I'm not delusional, just transcending everyday thought a bit.*

Zak hung his jacket on the coat rack by the door and plopped onto the futon. He eyed the chairs by the kitchen table which were, as usual, stacked with unopened mail. "You know, you really ought to open your mail more often, Elena. You could get an eviction notice and not even know it until someone comes and starts piling your stuff at the curb."

Elena laughed. "I open the ones that I know are important, Zak. That's just the pile of junk mail. I get a ton of it, and it just takes me a while to sort it and recycle it. Besides, I like eating in the living room. Sitting alone at the kitchen table is just ... well, pitiful."

"So, what's with the croc?" Zak asked as he kicked off his shoes and loosened his tie.

"He represents fear, the reptilian brain. He's about to swallow you up, kind of like what happens to people when they focus too much on fear."

"He's so real." Zak stood up and moved closer to the canvas. "It really does feel like he's about to swallow me. So, your intention is to scare the fuck out of people?"

Elena laughed. "Well, yes, in a way. He won't be alone, though. There's a second painting – one that brings him under control." She paused for a moment wondering, *How much should I tell him?*

"Elena. I know that look on your face. There's more. What else? This painting is really a huge break from your style. What's up with this?"

"Yes. There's more. I know you're having second thoughts about what happened in the cave, but for me, the memories are really vivid. I know we all saw and felt the same things, but I think we all saw some personal things, too. I don't know what you or the others saw, but I saw a series of paintings." She was lying a little. The images that were coming out now were not from the cave. They were from her more recent travels through the portal, but this was a safer way to explain it. He wouldn't be calling Bellevue.

"And you saw *this*?" Zak exclaimed. "I know I've been questioning what happened but Elena, everything I believed I saw and felt was wonderful, beautiful. Not scary. Are you sure you remember it correctly? This painting is kind of disturbing – maybe the crap from the desert is trying to come out. Have you contacted the trauma counselor I recommended?"

"No. It's not about the shootings. Really," she assured him. What I saw in the Ark was a series of contrasts. This crocodile represents fear, the kind that immobilizes you, swallows you, or threatens to drown you. The *contrast* will illustrate what happens when you connect with the realm we encountered in the Ark. The crocodile is still there, but tamed."

"No one can tame a crocodile Elena," Zak said. "People who think they can are the ones with missing arms and legs – or worse."

"Always the realist, aren't you? Okay, tame is the wrong word. But harnessed maybe, or conditioned. We can create a conditioned response in ourselves that conquers our fears. Right?"

"True. Actually, that's a pretty powerful statement." Zak walked to the kitchen to check the oven. "I think we can eat now," he said. "That is, if it's okay with Mr. Crocodile." He smiled. "Really, Elena. It is a powerful idea. Let me know when the other one is done. I want to see it."

Elena reached into the cupboard for plates while Zak pulled their dinner from the oven. "Absolutely," she said, grateful he hadn't asked any more questions about her inspiration. "But you haven't told me how the research is going? Have you waded through the stacks of reports yet? Is anyone working on the map?"

"Gina took on the pottery and bone artifacts. She assigned groups of them to other grad students, so those are off my plate. Now, I've got her and a visiting professor working on the map. We're calling it the Karta Project. They've confirmed what we already believed, that there was only one author to the map."

Elena cringed at the name Gina. She didn't know why she didn't like this woman. Was it jealousy? She didn't think so. She'd never been jealous of any of Zak's students or assistants before. She'd never been jealous of any of his girlfriends, for that matter. She thought most of them weren't good enough for him, but that was another matter. Just something about that woman bothered her. Maybe it was the way she played up to Zak when Elena had visited him in his office. She just seemed pushy or something. And then there was the dark energy she had seen around her. But maybe she had only imagined that. She dismissed the thought. "Do they know about the broken piece yet?" she asked.

"No. I have that piece secured. There's no reason for them to see it."

"Good. It would only make them want to go there."

"Elena, we are very close to going back even without the fragment. The Karta itself indicates archaeological finds that beg to be discovered. I can't ignore the potential it represents, a lost civilization and a connection between Jerusalem and Ethiopia? And once the rest of the research team recognizes the full message, there won't be any stopping the process. I'm getting ready for what has to happen, another trip to Bir Tawil. But this time we'll have a lot more security."

Elena put down her fork. She was sitting cross-legged on her papasan chair with the plate balanced in her lap. She took a breath and gave him a worried but knowing look. "And how exactly do you propose to keep everyone safe? What kind of security?"

Zak finished chewing, took a swig of the soda Elena had set on the coffee table and answered, "I've got Josh working on a detailed security plan. He's in touch with the Egyptian police and military, and they're helping to arrange a large group of guides with military backgrounds. I'm also coordinating with the American Research Center to vet and employ local archaeologists and workers."

Elena hoped there was time to talk him out of it – but she knew she couldn't. Connecting with ancient civilizations was Zak's life. Stopping him would be like eviscerating a part of him. "And when are you going?"

"I was hoping we could go over winter break, but it's just not feasible. The grant applications alone will take us to almost the end of the term. My guess is we'll have everything for this summer's field study. Probably for many summers to come, actually."

Elena was becoming resigned to Zak's going back. In fact, after several trips through the portal, she was beginning to think he was destined to return. She didn't know what the results would be, but she did know that Zak was the right person to get there first if someone was going to unearth this sacred object from its hiding place. She gave him a tentative smile.

"I know. I know you have to go back. I've known it since we landed at the airport. I could see it on your face then. But please ... be very, very careful. I need you in my life."

Zak's shoulders lowered themselves an inch or so from his earlobes. "You can't imagine how relieved I am to hear you say that. I've been struggling with this since we got back – the need to go and the ... I don't know ... guilt? The feeling of betraying the group for going back. I've searched myself for reasons; am I going back for personal accolades? Or am I going back to satisfy curiosity, to confirm or deny the bizarre experience? I'm still not sure what really happened there. I finally decided the reason I'm going back is because I have to, because the only way I can communicate what we've been ordained to share is to bring it back, to measure it, to examine it, and to make sure it is safely guarded against those who would use it for other purposes."

"I don't like it, but I understand," said Elena.

"I'm glad you understand. I really needed that from you. And there's one more thing I need – or at least I would really like, anyway."

Elena stood up, took Zak's plate from him and headed toward the kitchen. She knew where this was going, and she didn't want to hear it. Over her shoulder, she asked, "What's that?"

"I want you to come with us. We'll need the best photographer we can find, and I think you need to be there, anyway."

"Nope." Elena didn't even have to think about it. There was no way in hell she was going back there. It was one thing to support Zak's desire to return, but she was not going. Didn't need to. Didn't want to.

"That's it. Just nope. You don't even have to think about it?"

"No. I really don't, Zak. I understand you need to go. I really do. But I just can't go. I can't be there in that place again. I'm still trying to get the images, the ones of the victims, out of my head."

"What about Mr. Crocodile and conquering fear?" Zak teased.

Elena glared. "It's not just fear, Zak. No one should be going back. Besides, I've got this series I'm working on and I can't stop right now. I've got Renee working on a new show for them. And ...." *Oh God, should I tell him this?* How could she not tell him? They shared everything. *Here we go...* "I've met this man ...."

Zak's eyebrows arched. "Oh? And who is he?" His eyebrows twitched a little, followed by a friendly smile.

"It's not like that. He's ... actually, I've known him for a long time. I went to grade school and high school with him."

"Ahh, the young lover returns?" He was teasing her now.

"No... no. He became a priest after high school ...."

"So, is he stationed around here? How did you find him? Is he helping you ... sort through things?" Zak sounded hopeful.

Elena shook her head. "No. He's not assigned anywhere. He left the priesthood, studied in Tibet for a while, traveled a lot, and now he's staying at a Buddhist temple near here. We just stumbled on each other at the park. I guess you could say he's helping me sort things out."

"Okay. So, he's not a priest. Does that mean there *is* some romantic interest? I mean, why does having met some guy from high school mean you can't go on the dig?"

"No romance involved. He's not a priest, but he is some sort of monk, not Buddhist, but some other sect. I'm not sure exactly, but it's not a romantic thing at all. I just need to stay here, work through all this and get the paintings out of me. I don't think I'll be able to rest until I do."

"Okay." Zak sounded resigned. "I get it. I know how you are when a series of paintings start coming through – and these must be way more intense than anything you've experienced before. But don't let this guy... what's his name?"

"Anurak."

"Anurak?" Zak made a quizzical face. "Let this Anurak guy know he better not mess with you or your friend Zak will take care of him."

Elena laughed. "I'm sure you will. Want some more soda?"

"Nah, I've gotta get back. Tons of work to do tomorrow." He slipped on his shoes and started to gather his things. "I'm really bummed you can't go with us. But I'm glad you've got someone to talk to about it. And I'm glad the paintings are helping you get it out, too. I think you're on to something – but if you change your mind...." A coy little look formed as he opened the door to leave.

"Not a chance. But if I do, you'll be the first to know."

CHAPTER SIXTEEN

It's in the Stars

Mason unlocked the vault containing the Karta and slipped the key into the pocket of his lab coat. He'd been careful not to leave the key in the vault, since Gina had blatantly broken the rule and removed the key herself. Not that it mattered much. She would just put her hand in his pocket and sensually remove it and give him that look that made his manhood rise. He wasn't sure if he was pocketing the key for security sake or for that moment of fondling that he knew would ensue. In either case, Gina didn't seem interested in actually keeping the key – she just liked playing with him. And he didn't mind at all.

Carefully removing the tablet, Mason carried it around the table to his station. Gina had been deciphering the text, but he had noticed something yesterday that intrigued him. There were markings beneath the glyphs that at first glance looked like scratches in the stone, unintentional. But something about them seemed calculated to him. He was actually kind of surprised that Gina hadn't noticed it, or if she had, why she hadn't mentioned it. With her keen interest in cartography, the hint of constellations scratched into the surface should have caught her eye.

He placed the tablet on the viewing board and adjusted the microscopic camera lens, bringing the scoring into a closeup view. He moved the camera up, then down, left, then right. Yes, these were not scratches, not natural lines in the stone. They were carved, carved with a light hand before the glyphs were added.

Gina was really bright. She had exceptional abilities to recall detailed information about hieroglyphs and multiple ancient written languages, but she was young and inexperienced. That was why she was here. To learn from experts like him. Mason had been studying the use of measurement and navigation in ancient cultures for most of his career. These inscriptions were fascinating. If he was right, they might very well prove the theory that ancient civilizations had devised a way to measure precise degrees and latitudes. This map was not an ordinary treasure map. It appeared to have precise directions to a specific place, maybe even a particular object.

The door to the lab opened, admitting conversations from the hallway. Gina was bringing students to the lab this morning. Mason looked up and met her gaze. She smiled at him, then glanced at the open vault and the tablet on his viewer. Her brows narrowed for a moment. A frown? And then it was gone, and she was pursing her lips in a feigned pout. Mason couldn't blame her. This piece was far more interesting than the bits of clay and bone she would be helping the students study this morning. He smiled at her, then returned his attention to the tablet.

He began taking notes, slowly at first, then furiously. Most archaeologists these days typed their notes into the computer as they went, but Mason still preferred his yellow legal pad. He would have to type them eventually, but there was something he liked about the feel of pencil on paper. It was faster for him. He could get his thoughts down before they passed. If they passed, he might not remember them later.

Hours passed as Gina guided her students and Mason gathered data. His scribblings now filled several pages. There were words, symbols with translation notes, and theories about angles and direction. He'd found glyphs for Orion and Sirius, and what looked like a rough outline of a rock formation against a horizon line. It had long been suspected that the ancient Egyptians somehow used the constellations as a tool for navigation. Mason's notes had circles drawn around some of the symbols and arrows leading from one, to another, then another. It would have looked like a set of modern hieroglyphics to anyone else, but what was taking shape on those pages had Mason's heart beating almost as fast as it did when Gina moved close to him. He drew multiple circles around the last word that he had written on the page, *Menelik.*

Mason stared at the circled word. He glanced back at the viewer, then down at the page. By God, this wasn't just a map. It was a map to the ... It was impossible. No, the findings were irrefutable. He'd checked his work ten times. There was no doubt in his mind. The symbols, the names, they all pointed to the Ark of Moses. But something was missing. Some of the inscriptions that defined the location ran off the edge of the stone. They had thought this was just the shape of the rock, but now it looked glaringly like a broken edge. He couldn't believe they'd missed it before. They'd need to do some studies to see if they could determine the time of the break compared to the age of the piece itself. Mason entered several test requests into the computer in front of him, then began to transcribe his notes. He stopped before he wrote the word, *Ark*. Zak should be the first to know this, if anyone.

Mason saved his work and carefully lifted the tablet from the viewing table. He could feel Gina's eyes on him as he secured it in the vault. Averting her stare, he grabbed his notepad and knocked on the glass doors to Zak's office.

Zak looked up from his computer and motioned Mason to enter. "What's up?" he asked as Mason carefully closed the sliding glass door behind him. He moved slowly, yellow notepad in hand, and sat in the leather chair facing Zak.

Mason peered over his reading glasses at Zak, tapping the yellow pad on his own knee. "What exactly did you know about the inscription on this rock, Zak?"

"What do you mean, Mason? You've seen the notes from the field lab. It's a map, found in Qsar Ibrim, square 113, level 9, that seems to indicate a possible dig site. Have you found something more?"

Mason was skeptical. He knew field labs were limited in their capabilities, but he also knew the skill of some of Zak's team. And he knew Zak. Just a suspicion of a possible site would not have taken them away from their initial assignment. What the hell was going on here? "You knew, didn't you?"

"Knew what?" Zak looked sincere, but a flash of something crossed his eyes. Mason wasn't a new kid on the block. He may be a recluse, but he knew people. Zak knew what the map suggested, Mason was sure of it. He stared at him, tapping the notepad on his knee, waiting. Sometimes silence was the best tool for getting more information.

Zak drew a breath, glanced through the glass door at Gina and the students. They were involved in their work and Gina had her back to them. "Yes. We knew there was ... something more. What did you find?"

"I think you know. What else could have taken you to that God-forsaken ... apparently not God-forsaken, place? Why haven't you told anyone?"

"I'm just not ready to reveal the information, Mason. My reputation is a little shaky right now after all that happened out there, leading the students and volunteers into a dangerous situation and all. I intended to reveal what we were looking for, but not until we got a little closer to the trip. The last thing we need is the Egyptians getting wind of this before we get there. They might just make it impossible for us to enter Bir Tawil. It may be its own country, but there's no other way in. Sudan is too volatile. The airspace is too close to border lines, and even if we could fly in, there's far too much equipment needed to enter by air.

"We need to feed enough information to the regents and enough information in the grant proposals to get approval for a more in-depth expedition, but not share the details until we're ready to go. I needed someone with your expertise onboard and connections in Egypt to lend credibility to the project. I knew you would discover the significance of the map. That's why I called you in. I've just been waiting for you to figure it out."

Mason felt a little used, but his excitement over the ultimate find overshadowed it. "So, what's next then? Where do we go from here?"

"We need satellite shots, LiDAR if possible – but the airspace may be a problem for LiDAR."

"LiDAR?" Mason pursed his lips. "I can probably find some locals to fly over the area, but how will you get the cost approved?"

"Already done. I showed this brochure to a small group of donors," Zak said, handing Mason a copy of *Understanding LiDAR: Light Detection and Ranging for Archaeology. O*nce they saw the detailed landscape photography possible with laser light pulses, they understood it would save money in the long run – less time wasted surveying and sampling nonproductive sites. When I showed them some detailed mounds in the shape of Neolithic hut circles, they were geeked."

Mason nodded as he reviewed the brochure. "The desert is a perfect place for it. No trees to interfere with the light pulses. I'll make some calls and see what we can do about a plane willing to fly over the area."

"It would be great if we could get some drones out there too," said Zak. "But that may have to wait until we arrive. I don't know what you've deciphered in terms of location so far, but what we found

110

at the field lab was pretty sketchy." This was a lie, but Zak had no intention of letting Mason know that he had the broken sherd – not yet anyway. "We discerned the general area but nothing precise enough to home in on. Our intention out there was to do some site surveys, and get some ground penetration data for future digs. We just didn't expect to be ambushed on the way."

"Well, I've just started deciphering the navigational data, but it appears it will get us pretty close. Drones are a great idea. I'm sure I can find some contacts in Egypt willing to get some initial shots for us. Once we cross the border into Bir Tawil, we can fly them without a permit so we'll be able to get really detailed data." Mason tapped his pencil on the yellow pad as if there were more, but didn't mention his suspicion about a broken sherd.

"Mason," Zak said. "I need you to keep this between us for now – until we get closer. That means no one knows besides you and me." He tilted his head toward the lab, indicating Gina. He wasn't blind. He had seen the developing relationship between the two of them. They worked longer hours in the lab than anyone needed to. They were often there at the crack of dawn, sometimes one of them wearing the same clothes as the day before. Although that didn't mean much with Mason.

"Got it," Mason said. "But I do need her help with some more research on the tablet itself. That's okay, right?"

"Sure. Just no mention of the Ark. For now."

"I can't guarantee she won't figure it out, Zak. I'm actually a little surprised she hasn't noticed yet. But I won't let on."

Mason handed Zak the vault key and pocketed the yellow notes in his upper breast pocket beneath his lab coat. His side pockets were much too vulnerable. Gina glanced his way just in time to see his hand depositing something behind his lab coat.

***

Gina lay covered in just a sheet, her red hair spilling over the silky white cloth. "He's using you, you know," she said.

Mason rolled over facing her and caressing her beneath the sheet. "Who is?" he asked.

"Zak. I mean Dr. Erdmann. You're twice the archaeologist he is. He's using you to get his grant money. You're doing all the work, and whose name will be in the journals when the site gets excavated?"

"Hmm. I hadn't thought of it that way. I suppose my work is helping him – especially since the school was not particularly happy with him after last summer's expedition. But it's not about whose name is on the dig. It's about getting there and seeing what we can find."

"Well," Gina said, returning the caresses and swirling a strand of her hair in his ear, "just the same, you should be first on the grant proposals, or at least on the credits for the expedition. Just keep your eyes open, Mason. I want you to get the credit you deserve. You are such an amazing man – at work *and* at home," she said with a sly grin.

With that Mason sought her mouth and gently slid his tongue inside, where her tongue met it in a gentle, wrestling motion. Gina withdrew her tongue and kissed him all over his face and neck, then, without warning smacked his butt cheek and said, "Hey, it's time for work! Don't you think you better get in the shower?"

Grudgingly, Mason peeled himself away from Gina and walked, manhood slightly stiffened, to the bathroom.

When the shower started, Gina tiptoed to the dresser and pulled a folded yellow paper from Mason's pocket. She didn't need to copy it. She would recall the entire series of words, circles, and arrows later. She just looked, folded the paper, and replaced it just in time to wrap herself in the sheet as if waiting for the shower.

Mason came out of the shower whistling a tune Gina had never heard before. *Something before my time,* she thought. She let her lips lightly graze his cheek and neck as she took over the bathroom.

"Now stop that," Mason said. "We've got to get to work."

"Yes. We do," Gina said. "And you remember what I said. You are the genius of this expedition and don't let Zak, I mean Dr. Erdmann, forget it."

Mason's face flushed red. He looked embarrassed by the compliment.

"I mean it. I've never worked with anyone so brilliant. You just blow me away every day. I wish I would have had you for classes at the University of Chicago. I would be much further along in my studies. You really have to start giving yourself more credit, Mason."

112

With that, she gave him a quick kiss, closed the bathroom door and began humming a tune of her own.

CHAPTER SEVENTEEN

The PAXman Connection

A small office had been set up at the university for Josh. It was even smaller than his office at the firm but contained all he needed. A small wooden desk, an older but functioning computer, and a phone. He preferred his own laptop, but the school computer had access to a printer. Plans, maps, and protocols would have to be printed. His phone calls to the Egyptian authorities had finally produced the beginnings of a workable plan. The school would provide security volunteers, but arrangements for several local guides would be essential. Josh was working with the Egyptian military stationed nearby and they had agreed to remain in close contact – though they would not enter Bir Tawil except for evacuation purposes.

Josh looked up from his work, startled by the vibration of his phone. He wondered if he would ever feel a cell phone buzz again without thinking he was about to be sucked into another dimension. It was a text from Tom, his contact at the NSA.

"Encrypted message. Check NSA email – still valid."

"Thx!" Josh replied.

Josh pulled his laptop from his backpack and set it up next to the ancient university computer. He clicked through to general settings on his phone and activated his private hot spot. He had no intention of using the school computer or WiFi network to access NSA email. Even this was a little risky, but he didn't want to wait to get home to see what Tom had sent.

The report started with a long list of airline tickets purchased by Oliver Quinn. Some looked like a partial list of his brother Aidan's residency list; Brooklyn, Kenosha, Rome, Kansas City, Tokyo, Bali, Yemen, and Aksum. That made sense – if you had enough money to visit such places. But there were more. The list looked more like the flight history of a travel writer or an international spy than a self-employed, bankrupt guy from Kansas City: Jerusalem, Cairo, Dublin, London, Thailand, Machu Picchu, Jamaica, Madrid, Dubai, Zimbabwe, Yemen.

Aksum was the last flight purchased, according to the records. It was from two years ago, and there had been no return flight booked. Was Oliver still in Ethiopia? What was he doing there?

A summary from Tom followed.

"Oliver Quinn Work History: Subject has had a series of small business startups, most of which failed, except for his most recent one. Self-employed status turns out to be owner and CEO of PAXman International, a computer technology company. He pays his taxes. No arrests. No name changes."

PAXman. Interesting name. Josh made a note to research more about the company. He didn't know what he might find that Tom hadn't already summarized, but PAXman was jogging something in his mind. He read on.

"Oliver Quinn Travel History: Early indicators showed extensive travel, but Oliver was not the passenger. Nearly all of the destinations listed his brother, Aidan E. Quinn, as the traveler. A few additional, mostly in the states, appear to be work-related conferences."

Josh let out a long breath he hadn't realized he was holding and ran his hand across his growing crop of afro-textured hair. Aidan Quinn was becoming much more interesting than his brother Oliver. Together, his list of known addresses and flight destinations covered nearly every suspected location of the Ark. Josh scrolled down to read the information gathered so far on Oliver's brother.

Aidan Quinn: Ordained by the Roman Catholic Church and assigned to a parish in Kenosha, Wisconsin. After serving a year and a half, reassigned to Rome where he completed a law degree and was assigned to the Vatican's legal counsel. Several years later he took a medical leave. Medical records are protected by the Vatican. Later assigned to study and report on world religions. The Vatican paid for most of his expenses until he wrote a series of papers that grew progressively more contradictory to Church dogma. About four years ago, the Church cut his funding entirely and censored his articles.

Aidan's travel history made a little more sense in context with his work for the Vatican, but something still bothered Josh about it. If they cut his funding, why did the King of Bir Tawil pick it up for him? Josh had a brother, too. He would certainly help him out if he was in need, but fund a travel itinerary like Aidan's? Not likely.

Flipping through the bookmarks on his browser, Josh selected the Bir Tawil story he had found about Oliver. There it was. Oliver Quinn standing on a rocky mound in the middle of nowhere with a purple and black flag, sporting a two-headed eagle with the Chi-Rho symbol, or PAX as it was popularly known. A man whose travel purchases included nearly every alleged location of the Ark of the Covenant was claiming the land where Zak's team had actually encountered it.

PAX. PAXman. PAXman International! thought Josh. *I wonder if there's a connection between Oliver and the Church. Maybe he's just a devout Catholic. Or is it something else? Could there be a reason the Church wouldn't want the Ark to be exposed?*

It didn't make sense. Finding the Ark would confirm the teachings of the Church – the basic history of the Judeo-Christian tradition, for that matter. Or would it? The contents, or lack of them, didn't support the biblical story, but how would the Church know that? Unless they already knew where it was and what it contained. So many questions. Josh's head felt like a spinning top or whirling dervish. Questions, possibilities, more questions, but the biggest question right now concerned the brothers Quinn.

Josh scoured the report on Oliver Quinn. He searched the internet for PAXman International. It was large, a Fortune 500 company. Information on what the company actually produced, however, was a bit vague. They were involved in computer technology, that was clear. According to the report the company had an array of international clients. Business was good – booming in fact. And the company logo was a two-headed eagle with an altered Chi-Rho symbol, an additional horizontal line creating the letter A in the bottom half of the X.

Josh entered "two-headed" eagle into his browser bar and tapped the enter button. A list of links came up, but he didn't click on them. He just viewed the first few lines of each. They all seemed to indicate the symbol meant power. The most-used word was "empire."

He clicked on the "images" link at the top of the screen to view two-headed eagles. Some were ornate flag pole ornaments or sculptures, but most were flags. He scrolled down, looking for one on purple and black but found none. What he did find was an image with a remarkable resemblance to Oliver's flag. It was on a black ground, and it was labeled, "Flag of the Holy Roman Empire."

The owner of PAXman International, whose logo resembled the flag of the Holy Roman Empire, had a vested interest in Bir Tawil. He had a tie with the Vatican through his brother, Aidan. And he had funded extensive travel to locations where the Ark was believed to be hidden. *What,* Josh wondered, *do Rome, an international computer technology company, a censored priest, and a man with an outlandish claim to the no-man's-land where we encountered the Ark all have in common?*

Josh sent a text to Zak. "Need to talk. Got a minute?"

CHAPTER EIGHTEEN

The Missing Sherd

Zak placed his Starbucks, Dark Roast cup on the corner of his desk and hung his jacket on a hanger on the back of the door. His office was almost back to normal; just today's coffee cup and no rumpled jackets lying around. There were a few neat folders in his hot file, and the rest of the desk was clear. It felt good to be back in his own world – everything in order.

Opening the top folder, the one for today's team meeting, Zak took a sip of his coffee. Over the top of the cup, he saw Gina flipping through a large book of log files. Across from her Mason had turned on the computer and hung his jacket over the back of the chair. It was blue! In all the years Zak had known Mason he had never seen him wear anything that wasn't brown. Zak chuckled to himself and went back to the folder in his hands.

A text from Josh interrupted his thoughts.

"security update 4u."

"Great." He texted back. "Join us in lab – meeting in ten minutes." Zak started to set the phone down but then added, "if ur in building."

He clipped the phone to his belt and made a few final notes for the meeting. He swiveled in his chair to see Gina and Mason moving toward the conference table carrying their own notes and file folders. *Time to roll,* he thought as he slid open the door, folder in hand and coffee cup left behind. No food or drink were ever allowed in the lab. Zak joined his team at the conference table, and Josh entered the lab just as Zak took his seat.

"Hey, Josh. Glad you're here. This is Gina Edwards. She is our Research and Teaching Assistant." Turning toward Gina, he said, "Josh is heading up security for the summer field school and coordinating with Egyptian law enforcement and the Ministry of Antiquities."

Gina and Josh acknowledged each other with nods.

"And this is Dr. Gerhardt Mason, Associate Director of Egyptology at Brown University. He's visiting us this term as an adjunct and assisting with grant proposals. Dr. Mason has just agreed to stay on through the winter term and accompany us on the summer expedition. His expertise and long-term relationships with the Ministry of Antiquities will be a tremendous asset to us in this endeavor." Heads all around the table nodded at Dr. Mason.

"Brandon and Jessica are grad students. They've both been to Qasr Ibrim several times and the three of you will be working together on the logistics of the two field sites in Abu Simbel and Bir Tawil."

More acknowledgments were made, and Zak began: "At this point, you are all aware that the Karta Project has revealed evidence of a potential excavation site between the Egyptian and Sudanese borders, in an area called Bir Tawil. Our goal is to begin onsite surveys during this summer's field studies. That being said, we will need to work fast to meet the November deadlines for grants and for permissions from the university, not to mention approval from the appropriate agencies in Egypt. This is a much bigger endeavor than simply joining a preplanned college field study. We will be working from scratch, providing detailed plans and long-term goals. It's a lot of work, but I guarantee it will be rewarding."

There were nods all around the table. "Mason, why don't you start with an update on the satellite images?"

"Well, we've just begun getting satellite images but what we have so far indicates some very interesting variations in the land," Mason began. "Several areas indicate the possibility of underground structures, mostly square – some round, definitely not natural formations." Mason stood and used a remote to pull up an image on the large LCD monitor on the wall. Using the laser pointer, he circled an area in the rock formations.

"Here," he said, "there appears to be some sort of structure built into the side of this mountainous area. It looks like nothing but a blip on the photo, but a detail shot suggests there is something there that is inorganic – perhaps manmade. It's impossible to tell without LiDAR or maybe some drone shots, but I've seen images like this turn out to be a structure built into the side of a mountain cave, maybe a place of worship or a burial chamber. It's difficult to tell, but there is definitely something there."

Zak squinted his eyes a bit to see the area Mason was pointing out. It was indeed interesting and would certainly help with their excavation proposals, but it was not the area where they had found the

Ark. He knew that formation like he knew his own apartment. He saw it in his sleep.

"Does it look like there was some sort of communal living in the area?" Zak asked.

"Yes. It does. The area is arid and barren today, but there is a long winding formation that might well have been a riverbed at one time." Mason clicked through a few slides and pointed to an elongated area on one of the images. "This is the area where there may have been a river, which would make what the Karta indicates possible. The topographical variation is so subtle it's easy to miss so it's not likely a wadi, but more likely a dead river. One of the things we will want to explore is how it dried up. Was the water diverted to another place? Or was there some other change in the terrain that could have caused it. The fact that it's there, though, and of course the inference of the Karta, indicate the possibility that a thriving community may have once occupied the area – and then something happened to diminish their water source."

"Fascinating," Zak said. "This is great work, Mason. Thank you for joining us on this project. I'll need you to create a full report of your findings for the grant proposals, the satellite images, the technical data on the Karta, and the overall history and rationale. Will you need some help with that?" he asked, knowing the answer.

"Yes. Yes. It's a lot to put together, but Gina and I have been working on the project from the beginning. If you can spare her, she would be a great help in getting the technical data ready, and she can include all the details about the translation and the dual languages."

"I do have a few other things for Gina, but I'm sure she can handle both. Right?" he asked, looking at Gina.

"Oh, yes. Of course, Dr. Erdmann. The Karta Project is all I can think about. Whatever I can do to be of help, I'm yours," she said.

"Great. The first task does not involve research. We need to find some photographers for the trip. See what you can come up with among the grad students – photography students, I mean. If you can't find anyone here, try NYU. We'll need at least six of them, and we can probably work out credit for them and possibly some scholarship money, too."

Gina made notes and started to ask about Elena. "But Dr. Erdmann, will your ... friend be attending? Will she be in charge of the photo students?"

"No." The answer was abrupt. Zak did not want to discuss Elena not coming on the dig. Turning to Josh, he said, "Where do we stand on security Josh? What have you got so far?"

"I've been working with Egyptian law-enforcement since our return. They've not been able to discover any helpful information about the shootings. They believe the attack was most likely from a remote Bedouin tribe, protecting their territory. As barren as the land is, some tribes use the area as passage, and they may actually reside there but how they sustain themselves is a mystery. The Egyptians are cooperating with investigations here in the states, and I have more information about that as well."

"So, no trace of who attacked us, then?" Zak asked.

"Not really, but I haven't stopped there. In my digging around, I found an American who has become a person of interest in the investigation. He is the self-proclaimed King of Bir Tawil."

"Seriously?" Zak asked. "How does one get to be king of a no-man's-land in the middle of the Sahara Desert?"

"Well, the area belongs to no one and no one wants it – that's a story in itself and politically driven. Anyway, this guy took the American homesteading idea to Egypt. He plopped a flag in a pile of rocks and named himself king. It was a stunt, really. He says he did it to make his wife a queen for an anniversary present."

"And how is this person a possible threat?" Zak asked. Mason had lost interest in the conversation and was making notes on his printed satellite images. Gina, however, was listening intently.

"It seemed innocuous, but something about the flag itself kept nagging at me. The flag is very similar to the flag of the Holy Roman Empire, and he adopted it as the logo for his company. I also discovered that he has funded a rather extensive travel history for his brother – mostly to destinations where, umm ... that are rather curious. It's probably all coincidence," he said. "But I'm gathering more information on both of them."

Zak knew Josh was exceptionally adept at finding information that routine background checks and internet searches could not uncover. He also knew that the "help" Josh referred to meant his contact at the NSA, but there was no need to spill those beans. That would likely get people upset about privacy.

"Okay, so we'll need some final information on your guys. We'll also need full background details on everyone from the last dig, and everyone, including ourselves, who will be involved in this new excavation. Background checks will be required by the school and by the American Research Center in Egypt if they partner with us on this. Treat this as a high-level security clearance, Josh."

"You've got it, Zak," Josh said, closing his notebook. "If that's all you need from me, I've gotta run. I have to put in some billable hours at the firm this week, too."

"That's all for now Josh. Just keep me posted – especially about this King of Bir Tawil." Zak was beginning to wonder about the guy, too. If he was triggering Josh's radar, there was likely more to the story.

"Gina," he said, turning toward her again. "We are also going to need detailed excavation plans, cost projections, and a conservation plan. I'll need some of our own grad students to work with me on those. I'd like you to find three or four that can handle the extra workload and who won't mind working on mind-numbing plans and numbers. See what you can find for me."

"I'm on it, Dr. Erdmann" Gina said with a flip of her silky red hair. She stretched her back, pushing her chest slightly forward. Zak was sure the gesture was intended for him and not Mason, who was too busy with his satellite images to notice. He thought about telling her she should have that back looked at but thought better of it. He forcibly controlled his eyeballs, not allowing them to roll.

"That's it, team. We have a lot of work to do in a very short timeframe, but the reward will be unrivaled."

***

Gina unlocked the vault with the replica key from her 3D printer. It hadn't been hard to get a wax impression of the key while she was working with Dr. Mason. He was so busy watching her ass; he hadn't noticed her hands slipping into her own pockets with the key. She wasn't planning on doing anything unethical. She just wanted more time with the artifact. Dr. Erdmann was so fricking paranoid about it he would only let them work on it together and only when he was there watching from his office. It was like working in a fishbowl.

Gina slid the precious stone tablet from the vault with gloved hands and carefully carried it to the stainless-steel work table. She ran her gloved finger over its etched surface as she waited for the computer and zoom camera to come to life. Small tingling sensations ran through her body. Her anticipation and growing excitement could hardly be held back now. Mason and Zack knew something about the tablet she had not yet figured out – and she was determined to discover it.

She reviewed the reports one more time and scrolled through her translation notes. There was no doubt that the ancient map led to a valuable treasure, but its identity was still a mystery to her. Had Mason figured this out? Was that why he had that clearly private meeting with Zak? Translating the writing had been easy for her. She had a remarkable ability to recall a vast variety of ancient texts. Her eidetic memory allowed her to retain every textbook and translation code she had ever read. Even the two different languages on the tablet had not thrown her for long. But there had to be something else – something Mason was not sharing with her.

And what the hell was going on at that meeting? Sure, it was fascinating that they had found a brand-new potential dig site, but what was this "treat it as high-level security" thing about? She wondered if she might be able to get something out of this Josh character. Boy, was he ever an enticing piece of eye-candy!

She went back to her translation notes, wondering if she had missed something. It wasn't even that hard to translate. The field lab should have been able to gain the general gist of the map. What had Mason seen?

She let her mind focus on the notes she had spied in Mason's jacket. If she looked at an inner screen in her mind, every detail of a page she had read came back to her like a photograph. The yellow notes came in to focus now.

There were lines and arrows all over his notes. They were like a personal set of hieroglyphs. One word stood out, though. It was circled multiple times. She'd seen that word. It was on the Karta. "Menelik." Whatever or whoever that was. Ancient texts she was an expert on. Ancient history, not so much.

Gina opened a browser on her cell phone. She didn't want the school IT department to know what she was looking up. She typed "Menelik" into the search bar and clicked enter.

As usual, Wikipedia's definition was at the top of the list:

> *Menelik: Illegitimate son of King Solomon and the Queen of Sheba. It is believed that Menelik was either given or stole the Ark of the Covenant and brought the sacred tabernacle home to what today is called Ethiopia.*

Ark of the Covenant! Holy Christ! Gina's eyes grew wide as she backed away from her phone. No wonder there was so much security and secrecy over The Karta Project. But why would the team last summer have gone off into a no-man's-land in search of it without more data – like the satellite images and artifact research they were doing now? It didn't make sense. So many miles of barren land and only a general idea where it might be.

Unless! Gina's eyes moved from the cell phone to the monitor. She zoomed in on the lower right edge of the tablet. They had believed it was just an irregular shaped stone or that a piece had been broken off before the map was inscribed. All of the text was contained in the main section. It didn't appear that anything was missing. But what if there was something else on that missing corner?

Gina zoomed in tighter. The edge showed signs of a break. She increased the magnification, hoping to find some trace of the fabric remnants they'd found on the stone. The presence or absence of fabric particulates on the edge might indicate whether the break occurred before or after the artifact had been buried. There was no apparent difference between the broken side and the other surfaces. She entered a series of commands on the computer and started a more detailed scan. It would take a while, but maybe something would be revealed.

While the program ran, Gina contemplated the secretive nature of the meeting. She recalled Josh's report about the King of Bir Tawil and wondered what it was that had captured Josh's attention. She entered "Bir Tawil" in the search bar of her cell phone browser and waited. She scrolled through a long list of boring articles about the land and the reluctance of Egypt and Sudan to claim it. Then she saw it. "Man claims Bir Tawil as Kingdom. Makes His Wife Queen of Bir Tawil."

Gina clicked through to the article, scanned it, then zoomed in on the picture. Oliver Quinn was an ordinary looking guy, a little short – maybe a little pudgy. It was hard to tell with the baggy desert clothing. He held a purple and black flag with eagles on it. No, not eagles – just one eagle with two heads. She bookmarked the page for further review, then returned her attention to the Karta.

There was a soft clicking sound from the institutional clock above her head, made louder by the silence of the early-morning hours. Gina looked up. It was nearly 7 a.m. Mason and some of the grad students would be arriving soon. She could explain being in the lab, but not having the Karta out of its vault. She gave it one more adoring look as she prepared to return it to its little tomb, then noticed something she hadn't seen before. She couldn't believe she had missed it. She had been so intent on translating the visible characters she hadn't noticed the faint lines that ran off the edge – the broken edge. They looked like an ancient attempt at defining degrees and directions. That was definitely something that would have caught Mason's attention. That must be the information he had taken to Dr. Erdmann.

The test results wouldn't matter much now. It was obvious. There was definitely a piece missing from the map. Without it, the exact location of the Ark would be impossible. It could take years of excavation on the areas they'd discovered in the satellite photos. *Unless*, she thought, and another thrill ran up her spine, *unless someone already had the missing piece.*

Gina flipped through the log pages. There were hundreds of entries. One-by-one, she read the descriptions of objects retrieved from Dr. Erdmann's dig. Nothing. No small piece that matched the size and shape of the missing chunk of stone. Did someone have it? Had someone hidden it? Or stolen it? The fame alone in such a discovery could tempt just about anyone to conceal it. Did Dr. Erdmann have it? Had his team followed this map and discovered its treasure? No. They would have brought it back. They must have been attacked before they found it. But either way, what were they waiting for? Why would Dr. Erdmann have taken so much time to reveal the message of the map? It would have spared him a lot of scrutiny by the university and the archaeology community.

EILEEN PATRA

Maybe he just needed as much detail as possible before requesting the grants and permissions to return. It wasn't surprising that he
would want everything in perfect order, considering what had happened in the field. Or, maybe not. Maybe he was stalling for time to
find the highest bidder.

CHAPTER NINETEEN

The Power of a Comma

It was November, the air was chilly, and snowflakes skittered about in an attempt to find a place to land. Elena wrapped the ties of her coat more tightly around her as the wind threatened to transform its front flaps into reluctant wings, wondering why on earth she was headed to the park on such a blustery day. She still had no way of contacting Anurak other than just showing up at the temple, but he was always there when she arrived. Sometimes he would show up in the park, and they would walk together, or just talk about her paintings and the metaphysical ideas behind them. It was getting too cold for this though, and she considered hailing a taxi when she noticed the crowds. The sidewalk was blocked by a throng of shivering people standing in line. They were clutching their coats and jackets, too. The line snaked around the block and into the door of a bookstore, a brick-and-mortar store, though the front of it was mostly glass.

The walls and windows were plastered with posters. Apparently, it was a book signing of some sort. Curious, Elena peered through the mob trying to read the signs, which were nearly obscured by the crowd. Bright blue background. Yellow Font. *THE TO* ... Elena moved a little to the right ... *MB*. She was trying to make sense of the letters when a man stooped down to tie his shoe revealing a full poster; *THE TOMB* was printed in large red block letters. Beneath it in larger letters spaced out, so they took up the same amount of space, it read *OF GOD.*

A chill ran up and down Elena's arms, but it wasn't from the wind. Vibrations began to rise from somewhere deep within her. Beneath the words was a highly stylized, golden box with winged angels on its top. The last line read ... She missed it. The man stood up, blocking the rest of the poster. There were more posters inside the store on the back walls. She backed up, nearly falling off the curb but finally saw the last line, *by Paul Emerson Silva.*

It was Paul's book! What the hell was he thinking? What did he mean *Tomb of God?* She hoped he wasn't revealing the whole discovery. More, she hoped this book was not another "God is Dead" story. It didn't seem possible that anyone could experience what they had and still believe God to be dead. Quite the opposite, they had to know that God was all there is and everything was connected and rooted in that pure, unlimited, harmonious Light. She had to see this book – and talk to the author!

A glance at the growing line of people told her she wasn't going to get anywhere near Paul today. Those at the end of the line couldn't possibly hope to get inside the tiny bookstore anytime soon. Elena reached for her cell phone, tapped it a few times, found the book online and bought the eBook version on the spot. She would read it when she got home. Satisfied, she slipped the phone back into her pocket and continued toward the park.

"Magnificent day don't you think?" It was Anurak. His white linen pants and robes flapped violently against his body as relentless gusts of wind blew through the park. He looked as though he might be blown away at any moment.

Elena scowled at him. "Seriously?" she replied. "You look as if you're about to take flight! I'm freezing. Let's go somewhere warm."

"How about your studio? I'd love to see what you're painting."

This took Elena by surprise. She was thinking tea or the library or even the temple, but her apartment? Her paintings? She had become quite an introvert over the years. Few people were invited into her sanctuary, especially men. Except Zak, of course, and some of their mutual friends. After years of shallow relationships, Elena was enjoying her single, independent life. She had no room for a romantic relationship. So, what was she worried about? Anurak was a monk – well, as good as a monk. He wasn't interested in a romantic relationship. At least she didn't think so. And she was not interested either – except for those blue eyes. She always felt as if she was falling into them and had to focus on some other part of him when they spoke.

"If you're not comfortable with that it's okay," said Anurak.

"Oh, no. It's fine," she lied. "I was just surprised you would want to see the paintings and I was trying to remember if I'd picked up the clutter enough for company this morning. Come on. We've got to get out of this wind. It's not far."

The walk was cold, but they didn't notice. They were too busy talking about the series Elena was working on and the thoughts that had inspired them. Anurak listened, asked questions, and offered some thought-provoking concepts that reflected similar ideas.

Inside, warm at last, Elena dropped her keys in the clay dish by the door and motioned Anurak toward the small futon that faced the kitchen and overhead loft, as she went to start a pot of tea.

But Anurak did not sit down. He was taking in the whole apartment: the shoji screens defining the different spaces, the south windows, the active studio with easels, stacks of canvases, finished paintings, jars and tubes of paint on every shelf and flat surface nearby. Above, there was the loft, Elena's bedroom. It also had south windows, but they were draped and dark. The kitchen was small but efficient with a small café table and two chairs. Stacks of magazines and unopened mail sat on one of them, leaving only one chair usable.

"Doesn't look like you get much company," Anurak said, gesturing toward the obstructed chair.

"Oh. It's not that. I hardly use the table. When I have company, we usually sit in the living area, not at the table." She caught the penetrating look questioning her words.

"Well okay," she said. "You're right. I don't entertain much. I like my solitude. It allows me to get lost in my paintings." It allowed her to keep from getting hurt too, but she didn't mention that. "I have a few close friends and an agent who visit from time to time. But for the most part, this is my sanctuary."

As she spoke, Anurak carefully observed the paintings lined up against the wall. He stopped in front of one in which the focal point was a large sphere with a rounded streak dangling from its right side and curving to the left. The shape was stippled with multiple colors, giving it both transparency and dimension. Beyond it, there was an inky black background sprinkled with flecks of light. Floating in the space between the shape and the night sky were the slightly transparent shapes of three letters, *I, A*, and *M*. The letters were spaced so they vaguely suggested the words *I AM*.

Anurak lingered at this one, apparently mystified by it. "The sky, if that's what it is, seems to draw me in. I feel as if I could fall into the painting," he said. "But then, I am confronted by the shapes and letters. What is this shape in the foreground? It looks like a tadpole or a seed of some sort."

"Ah, a seed," considered Elena. "I hadn't thought of it that way, but that could work. It's actually a comma."

"A comma? What is so significant about a comma?"

"Well, a comma can make a great deal of difference in written language. Maybe you've seen t-shirts in catalogs with the saying 'Let's eat, Grandma' followed by 'Let's eat Grandma.' The placement of the comma changes the whole meaning of the phrase from something inviting to something terrifying."

"Okay. I get that. But it's just a comma and three letters ... or I suppose two words, I AM. Where does the comma go? Between *I* and *AM*? What difference does that make?" asked Anurak. His brow was scrunched into a series of ripples as he tried to comprehend the difference a comma would make in that phrase. It was a look Elena had never seen on his face. In elementary school, he always knew the answers. During their discussions about the Ark, he seemed to grasp everything she shared and frequently offered his own vast knowledge of sacred texts and teachings. But the "comma painting" seemed to have stumped him. She smiled at the opportunity to share an idea with him that he might not already know.

"No, the comma goes after the whole phrase, 'I AM' ... comma," Elena said.

"But what's the rest? What comes after the comma?"

"Everything."

"Everything?"

"Yes. EVERYTHING else," Elena said. "But, let's just start with the first of the laws one would expect to have found in the Ark. I am the Lord your God. This has been interpreted through the ages as a command from a deity that is a super-human in the sky, one that judges, punishes, demands to be held above all others and worshipped. Placing the comma after the word 'I' or the word 'Lord,' reinforces an external God, separate, Lording over humankind. But, placing a comma after 'I AM' places God within you.

"In Moses' first encounter with God, God says his name is 'I AM that I AM.' What if *I AM,* a name we also use to refer to ourselves, is an indwelling expression of the greater *I AM?* What if each of us is the temple of God and the *I AM* consciousness within us is our direct connection to the higher power and presence of God? Then this statement, with a comma added, says in effect that the *I AM* is the Lord your God. The *I AM,* the still, small voice inside of you, minus the ego consciousness, is the God of your being. The *command* becomes a blessing – a portal to the place within where God dwells. A comma makes all the difference."

The wrinkles in Anurak's forehead relaxed, allowing a smile to form on his face. "That's an incredibly astute observation, Elena. It's a very simple painting, but its message is … beyond limits. I think you're on to something with this. How will you explain all that, though? I mean, the painting says so much more than the viewer can imagine without your explanation."

"It's not mine to explain," said Elena. "It's just mine to paint. I've been thinking a lot about what you told me. I can't control what some-one gets from my paintings, or even who the message affects. People may not capture the meaning on a conscious level, but the image speaks to the *I AM* within them. The *I AM* recognizes the message because it *IS* the message."

"So… It doesn't matter to you if they understand the message consciously, then?" Anurak asked with a knowing smile.

"Sure. I would love it if everyone understood my art, but that's more about ego than it is about what I paint. I paint because I have to; because the message inside me has to come out and be seen. If it doesn't, it screams inside of me until I can't sleep or eat. What happens after it comes out is not really up to me. It's like you told me, 'when the student is ready, the teacher appears.' If the viewer is ready, they will get the message – if not from my painting, from somewhere else."

Anurak nodded as if this made sense to him and moved on to the next painting. He was standing in front of the crocodile painting; large, sharp projectiles of a yellowish hue formed a concave curve at the top and bottom. Between them, an array of dark, murky colors swirled in discomforting patterns toward a blackened space near the center. The previous painting had drawn him in, but this one caused him to back up.

"This one is very different from the comma painting. It's actually a little terrifying. It reminds me of what the inside of the whale must have looked like to Jonah."

The depth of the image seemed infinite, as though the bony tunnel reached into eternity. That was disturbing enough, but around this cav-ernous image were yellow and brown-stained stiletto teeth poised to grab and spear. Above the upper teeth were two small, reptilian eyes, yellow and brown.

Anurak moved to the left, then the right, as if trying to see if the eyes would follow him. Elena knew they did.

She had given the beast life-like scales with a palette knife; thick globs of olive and umber with hints of ochre applied with just the right depth and curve made them appear quite real. The spikes along the crocodile's back stood at attention, giving him a ready-to-strike appearance. The overall effect was that you were standing in front of an enormous crocodile who was about to devour you.

"It's frightening – except for the colorful edging," Anurak said, backing up to get a better view. At the outer perimeter of the painting was a colorful array of rainbow-like rays. "The colors seem to exist in spite of him as if they are endeavoring to penetrate his scales," he paused, then looked at Elena thoughtfully.

"I thought you were in a realm of perfect peace and harmony when you traveled through the realm of the Ark," he said.

"I am," Elena replied. "But I also find at times, because I feel so safe and whole, I am able to face some of my deepest fears and my most troubling thoughts and emotions. They come to me as paintings, and then I see through them to a higher understanding. I find that I am ready at that moment to gain a deeper understanding of things that have happened in my life or things that are occurring in the world. It begins with my tapping into the image or feeling and then recognizing something else that has been there all along, a deeper meaning or a lesson being learned, or some soul growth or expansion occurring. And that inspires the next painting, the one that answers the troubling one."

"What's the answer to this? This looks like a crocodile about to swallow you up. Have you always been afraid of crocodiles? I wouldn't think you would come in contact with many in New York unless those sci-fi movies are true and they're lurking in the sewers somewhere." Anurak chuckled at his own humor.

"No. I don't have more than a healthy fear of crocodiles. They are just a symbol of something fearful, anything that one might believe can swallow them up or drown them. The answer is the painting across the room." She pointed to the painting on the other side of the studio where a goddess stood atop the crocodile, steering it as if it were a tamed horse.

Anurak walked toward the painting, taking it in as he strode. He turned toward Elena, his eyes wide and eyebrows arched. "What do you know of Hindu gods?" he asked.

"Nothing, actually. I mean I know that Brahman is the main deity and the others are the many expressions of him, or at least that's my understanding. I've seen paintings and sculptures but never really studied them. Can't really name a single one."

"This image. I've seen it before. Not the way you've painted it. That's original. But the woman who is riding the crocodile. She is a Hindu goddess. She is often portrayed riding a crocodile."

"I had no idea," Elena replied. "She was part of the experience. When I thought I would be swallowed by the crocodile in the portal, she appeared and drew me in alongside her. We both spiraled to the bottom of the river together on the back of the crocodile and then emerged, triumphantly steering him to land. The message she gave me was to keep my eye on what didn't spin, like what a ballerina does to keep her balance while performing a pirouette. It was a metaphor for keeping your eye on God when things seem to spin out of control. That's what I was painting."

"Her name, the Hindu goddess ..." Anurak went on. "It's Akhilanda. It means *Never Not Broken.*"

"*Never not Broken!* That's exactly what I discovered when I was sprawled out on the floor of my studio surrounded by the wreckage of my canvases. I was just lying there like a broken heap – but I wasn't broken at all. I was just empty – and empty made me open up. It let an incredible light shine in, and I was suddenly able to see things more clearly than I ever had before."

"Will you display the paintings next to each other, then?"

"I don't think so. I keep putting them next to each other but then I get this inner voice, the *I Am,* I suppose, guiding me to put space between them. I think it's because people need time and space between experiences to understanding what they mean. I'm not sure, but I don't think they are meant to hang side by side, at least not yet."

***

It was a delightful afternoon. Elena and Anurak talked at length about each of the paintings in the studio. It was so amazing to have someone to talk to about the Ark and the fantastic revelations she had experienced. She and Zak had always shared their deepest secrets with each other, but this was different. Elena could share the portal experiences with Anurak, and he understood like no one else, not even Zak, could. There was no judgment. There was no hint of thinking she was delusional, which seemed to be Zak's attitude since they'd returned. It was easy with Anurak, comfortable in a way that had previously only been possible with Zak.

Elena looked at Anurak over her cup of tea. Anurak had settled on the futon, and Elena sat cross-legged in her papasan. He was a handsome man. His brilliant blue eyes sparkled as he scanned the photographs on her wall. She wondered if he planned on taking his final vows or not. She mused briefly about what it would be like to have an intimate relationship with him. Was that even a possibility? No. Intimacy was unlikely with Anurak and even if it wasn't, would she want it? Wouldn't that change everything? Intimate relationships were not exactly her strong suit. This was easy. That would be complicated. *Oh, but those eyes.*

Anurak turned toward Elena, eyes probing. Had he heard her thoughts? Elena looked away, unable to meet his gaze.

"It's getting late," Anurak said. I should get back to the temple. It will be time for vespers soon, and I have chores to do before then. He pulled himself to his feet and took a few steps toward the kitchen with his cup.

"Oh, let me get that," Elena said taking the cup from him. She placed both cups in the sink and turned to watch him wrap an extra layer of robe around himself. It was getting quite cold, and even that extra layer didn't seem to be nearly enough to keep him warm.

"I hope you'll be warm enough heading back. The wind is crazy out there today," Elena said as she moved toward the door with him.

"I'll be fine. I have inner warmth," he said with a serene smile.

They stood just a foot from each other now as Elena prepared to bid her guest goodbye. There was something magnetic happening in the space between them. Elena felt an incredible pull toward him. She softened her eyes and could see their energies melding as one. It was beautiful – breathtaking. Neither of them spoke for some time. Anurak's blue eyes met Elena's green ones, and they, too, seemed to meld together until Elena could no longer see any separation between the two of them.

Anurak spoke first, drawing his energy back toward himself. "It's late, Elena. I have to go, but I'll be back. Tomorrow?"

Elena took a breath. The room seemed to whirl around her as she drew her attention back into her own body. The magnetic pull toward Anurak lessened slightly, and she whispered, "Yes. Of course."

CHAPTER TWENTY

The Tomb of God

The locks on Elena's door made a metallic sound as she slid the bar lock in place and fastened the deadbolt. The noise was a stark contrast to the warm and gentle energy she had been immersed in as Anurak had prepared to leave. She reached for the prayer shawl draped over a hook by the door. It felt warm and comforting as Elena wrapped it around her shoulders and fell shakily into her favorite chair.

It had been a long and somewhat confusing day. She still felt a little breathless over the intense energy between her and Anurak. It was all a little bewildering. He'd made it clear on their first meeting that celibacy was an essential choice in his life but what she had just witnessed between them certainly didn't feel platonic. She didn't know if Anurak felt the same way, but she didn't remember when she had felt so intensely attracted to someone. Maybe it was just the closeness they seemed to have formed over their deep, theological discussions. Maybe it was just the profound sense of trust she was developing in him. Did she want it to be more? She didn't think so, but ... No. Relationships were too much trouble. Difficult. Draining.

Desperate for a distraction that would quell her jumbled emotions, Elena opened her eReader. Her thoughts drifted back to the bookstore earlier in the day. Paul's book. *What the hell did he mean, "The Tomb of God?"*

She flipped through the first few pages of front matter and stopped at the Forward.

> *It is human nature to create organizations and concepts that worship a god that doesn't exist. Until this erroneous image of God is laid to rest, the human mind will not grasp the enormity of the God-ness that gives life to all that is. This is a God that cannot die, a God that has no need to judge, no desire to punish, no human frailties to overcome, and which has no opposing force. This is a God that is the very Essence of Life.*

Elena stopped, relieved to find that Paul's book was not another *God is Dead* dissertation. His premise made sense, the old must always give way to the new. God did not change, but human understanding of God must change. It was the principle of evolution, and evolution was continuous, infinite.

Hmm... infinite, like God, she thought. Maybe God is more a principle than an entity. A principle doesn't change, and God doesn't change. It is only our understanding that varies. Maybe there was a purpose to the God is Dead phase of human consciousness. She flipped the page and read on.

> *CHAPTER 1: IN SEARCH OF TOMBS*
> *As an archaeologist, I search for tombs, remnants of expired life, in the hopes of understanding the culture that placed them there. But a crypt holds only remains, not the life that once inhabited those remains. To discover what lived, and ultimately what continues to live, I must reach beyond what has been laid to rest, and grasp what transcends that earthen cask. Perhaps then, a tomb is not a tomb at all, but a place in which everything that is not real is left behind. Maybe a tomb is ultimately a portal to what is real.*

Apparently, Paul had made radical changes to the informational book about ancient Egyptian tombs he had been working on when they discovered the Ark. It wasn't really surprising. How could anyone return to the mundane after experiencing the profound? She wondered how Paul could have written, published, and marketed a book so far from its original intention in such a short period. But then, she had been painting at a fantastic pace herself. In fact, she was getting closer and closer to purchasing acrylic paints. The oils – she loved them – just took too long to dry, and the paintings were flowing far faster than her slow-curing pigments could record them.

Words emanating from the next page suddenly stood out, grabbing Elena's attention. *The Ark of the Covenant.* She tensed a little, wondering what Paul was about to reveal.

If an archaeologist were to discover the Ark of the Covenant, what would they find? Would they find disintegrating tablets outlining an ancient set of laws to please a god made in the image of humankind? Or would they discover it to be a tomb, a place where false images of God are laid to rest, a portal for transcending the limitations of an archaic concept?

Paul wasn't giving away the discovery, only suggesting a possibility, creating a platform for sharing the wisdom he had experienced. Paul was a part of Zak's circle of archaeology friends. Elena knew him only from the few times they had been on digs together, but she suddenly felt very close to him. The connection they had felt when they first left the Ark seemed to open up, and she could feel his feelings, hear his thoughts. She knew they were both trying to share the same wisdom – wisdom that could only be partially delivered through human words or images.

Elena laid the e-reader on the paint-laden table beside her. She closed her eyes and allowed her inner eyes and ears to open. She let the connection with Paul fill her mind.

No. God is not dead. But civilization certainly seems to be living as if it were so. Elena had felt the same when she had walked out of her art opening. Leaving the gallery that night, she'd been confronted with the stark contrast of the world compared to the realm of love and oneness she knew existed. Maybe it was somehow necessary for humanity to hit bottom before rising up into a new understanding. Most people today seemed to have little regard for the rules they believed were set in stone. Maybe it was somehow necessary to thoroughly experience spiritual blindness before a culture with eyes that could see the perfection around them would be born. It was this concept that was giving birth to her series of contrast paintings.

Elena listened for the silent space between thoughts. Moses, as if on cue, jumped into her lap. He seemed drawn to the shift in her energy when she meditated and often sat purring in her lap when she did. His purring now was reminiscent of the vibrations preceding her entry into the portal. She felt them now, mixed with the rattling of Moses' purrs. She didn't resist, allowing them to permeate her whole body. Every cell in her body began to move in unison with the pulsating rhythm.

Suddenly, there was a tremendous pulling sensation and then silence. She was back, standing before the translucent, ever-changing canvas.

Elena marveled at the weave of the canvas standing before her. The threads were woven together, one strand at a time to prepare a ground on which she could paint. *Love is like that,* she thought. *It draws two things together and creates something new, a blank page on which to write a new story or paint a new vision. Love, not romantic love, not even brotherly love, but Divine Love, accessed through the portal of the heart, draws together and creates anew.*

Perhaps a new canvas on which a portrait of humankind, filled with compassion and reverence for one another, could be painted, one in which the subjects were fully aware that there was more than enough of all the things they so desperately believed they needed to possess. The theme of this portrait would be a world in which fear and weapons of mass destruction were obsolete and love prevailed; a world in which all beings were safe, secure, and well. She lifted the brush to paint, and the canvas wove itself, drawing together strands of sparkling jewels, into a fabric of love and exquisite joy.

Elena remembered her mother telling her to never pull on a loose thread because the entire fabric might unravel. She had not listened. She had pulled threads and seen the result; a long thin empty gap had appeared where the broken thread had been. Again, she had ignored her mother's words and pulled on a string that was not yet broken. The surrounding threads had moved with it, creating a puckered mess. *Never pull a loose thread. The results will not match your intention,* Elena mused.

Elena watched the tightly woven canvas as loose threads began to appear and were pulled by some invisible force. They did not, however, create gaps or puckers. As a thread was removed, it was instantly replaced by another. The strings were woven in multiple directions, moving up and down, left and right, forward and back, stretching into a multi-dimensional fabric until there was no space where this seamless, sparkling fabric was not; no place that was not filled with the continuous movement of light-filled strands. The threads were infinite. They could not remain broken. All that appeared frayed mended itself; the fabric stretched beyond the horizon as if it had no end. It was a seamless, eternal, infinite fabric that could not be torn. It was the very fabric of life, and it had no end.

Elena noticed then that the threads were not really threads at all. They were string-like shapes made up of countless specks of light. Each speck of light vibrated and moved in cohesion with those around it. If one moved out of place, the others pulled it back. Elena wondered which was more magical, the canvas or the brush that began pulling her hand toward it.

The scene that flowed onto the blank canvas before her seemed to draw its colors from the undulating threads of light beneath it. The lights took shape at the touch of the brush, as a multitude of human forms appeared, in an endless variety of skin tones and colorful clothing. Each human figure appeared to be taking something from another, but the process was futile. Whatever they took was soon taken by another. It was fascinating to watch. What each one took looked eerily like what was already around them. They clung to these items, which were almost instantly wrenched from their grasp. In their clinging, they missed the sight of identical objects floating right in front of them.

The brush began pulling the multitude of shapes into one form; a child, gaunt and hungry, creeping into the back of a small grocery store. He placed a loaf of bread in his worn, oversized jacket and then ran from the store. The clerk failed to notice, as he was busy pocketing the cash from a sale he had not rung up. Outside there were hundreds of people glued to their cell phones. None of them looked up to see the small child run off with his treasured bounty. Some were chatting with friends. Some were checking their GPS. Some were making stock trades. Others were delving into the world of the dark web, buying and selling identities. In the distance, transparent walls revealed people in houses, stores, and office buildings. Tax evasion, video piracy, shoplifting, embezzlement, fraud, and government corruption were rampant, pulling steadily at the now invisible strings of light. None were aware that what they stole was in turn stolen from them. They couldn't see the futility of their actions. They believed that there was not enough of whatever they sought; to have it, they must take it from someone else.

The images on the canvas shifted like one of those magic pictures behind a piece of rippled plastic. Tilted up it revealed one image, tilted down it displayed another. Like the first painting, this alternate image showed numerous people engrossed in a variety of activities, but this was different. In this image their connection to one another was visible – their separation by human bodies was transparent, revealing a common thread of light woven through each of them. In this image, everyone was giving something to someone else. The shopkeeper was giving bread to the little boy. People on their phones were donating to charities. Many were pocketing their phones to give their attention to one another. Where cash was being given, cash was being received. Where food was given, food was instantly received. Where love was given, a glow of love was received from multiple people along the connecting thread. *"... the measure you give will be the measure you get,"* Elena thought. It wasn't just a pious suggestion; it was a fact.

For the first time, Elena witnessed the mystical brush drawing a set of stone tablets. They were somewhat transparent and floated over the scene. The words that flowed from the brush to the painted tablets were "Thou shall not steal." But, as soon as the words had taken shape, they began to dissolve, and a new phrase took its place.

> *You cannot steal, for all that you seek is already yours. What your neighbor has is what you have, for you are one and the same.*

The words resonated with something deep within Elena's consciousness. In a culture of theft, the commandment to not steal made sense. But in a culture of love and wholeness, it wasn't even necessary. Who would steal anything in such a culture? The desire to give would grow and expand – and wasn't that what humanity was being called to do? *In an I AM consciousness, an awareness of oneness with ALL, you shall not steal for there is no need; nothing is lacking.*

The image on the canvas shivered and twisted, giving way to a swirl of colors; pinks, greens, and golds, whirling in a never-ending spiral of ribbon-like energy. Through the spiral, Elena saw herself standing before two blank canvases. On one she painted *A Culture of Theft*. On the other she rendered an image of infinite giving and receiving; *A Culture of Giving*.

Inspired to begin the next two paintings in her series, Elena began to focus attention on the space between the two canvases. She became completely still and then felt drawn through the colorful spiral of time and space until she was sitting in her papasan chair. Putting pen to journal, she wrote:

> *It is in the space between the polarities of life, that wholeness exists. In the space between, there is neither taking nor giving. There is only being.*

I wonder, Elena thought. *Can the Ark be stolen? Maybe it can only be given.* She wrote a few more notes about the two paintings she would begin tomorrow and then started a shopping list. She would need to buy those acrylic paints. When she felt the stirring of fur in her lap, she added cat food and litter to the list.

CHAPTER TWENTY-ONE

The Melding of Souls

Anurak was at the door. Elena saw his peaceful presence through the peephole and began the process of unlocking the door, slipping the chain, sliding the bar, and turning the deadbolt. A spontaneous smile spread across her face. She was happy to see him.

"Come in. I'm so glad you came," she said.

"I said that I would be back," Anurak replied as if confused by her statement.

"Oh, I know. It's just that ...." She didn't know how to finish the statement. She felt awkward after their intense exchange of energy yesterday. Anurak appeared so calm, almost aloof; she wondered if he had even noticed what had happened yesterday. Maybe it was all her. Maybe it was all in her head. Doubt began to seep into her mind again. Did she imagine it? Was she imagining everything?

Anurak walked toward the two blank canvases and scrutinized them. "You've been pulling at the threads of this one," he said. "There are gaps. Is that intentional?"

Elena filled the kettle with water and set it on the stove. "Yes. I saw ... I was inspired by a thought about pulling threads. You know, how if you pull a thread a gap appears in the fabric?"

Anurak nodded and turned, his hands tucked into the flowing sleeves of his robe and his eyes focused on her.

"If you think about life as a fabric, with everyone and everything as a thread in the fabric," she continued, "then pulling any one person, place or thing out of place would create a gap. The threads around the gap would be less stable, and the whole fabric would be weakened. The canvas with the gaps will illustrate the energy of stealing and taking. The other will be about the energy of giving."

Anurak noticed a skein of yarn on the table next to the canvases. "And this?" he asked, pointing to the yarn.

"I'm going to weave additional threads into the other canvas. When there is an energy of giving, the fabric becomes stronger, more stable."

Thinking about energy, Elena drifted back to yesterday's experience with Anurak and the energy exchange that had passed between them. It had been exhilarating – then a little deflating when it stopped abruptly. She looked at him now as he pondered her blank canvases with a somewhat confused look. His energy was, as usual, peaceful, calm, and vibrant. There was a healthy glow radiating from him in shades of gold, turquoise, and pink. It wasn't just any pink. It was a Gauguin pink, one that sang a sweet, harmonious song. Yes, his energy was beautiful, except for that small gray area that tagged along after him. She wondered if he was aware of it.

He turned then as if he had heard her thoughts, but didn't respond to them. Instead, he asked, "The Ark has shown you this contrast between giving and taking? It's very intriguing that you are preparing the canvases this way before painting them. I like the fabric analogy. It reminds me of a Buddhist teaching, called *Indra's Net*. It is a net made of jewels, and each jewel reflects the others. It is a symbol of interconnectedness. Everything we do has some effect on everything else around us – like what you're saying with the threads. What will the painting on top of the threads look like?"

"I don't know yet," Elena said. "How are you with elephants?"

"Elephants?" He looked genuinely surprised by the question – and there was little that seemed to surprise him.

"Yes. Elephants. Like the one in this room right now." The tea kettle began to whistle, so she missed the way Anurak's eyebrows arched and the slow smile that spread across his face.

"There's an elephant?" Anurak said to Elena's back.

With great difficulty, Elena set the tea kettle down without slamming it onto the stove. She was trying to remain balanced as she broached the subject. She set the two cups of tea at the kitchen table and cleared the junk mail from the extra seat. "Sit," she commanded.

Anurak obliged, sipping his tea and peering over the cup at her. *Damn those blue eyes,* she thought. *It's hard to be assertive when there are two inviting lakes staring back at you.* "What the hell happened here yesterday between you and me? Don't pretend you don't know what I'm talking about. We stood at that door," she pointed at it, "and the energy around us began to meld together. I know you saw it – or felt it. Then you just cut it off or something. It just stopped, and you left. I've never experienced anything like that with anyone. I want to know what that was and why you forced it to stop."

144

Anurak set his teacup down and absently placed his hands inside his sleeves again. It looked like a form of withdrawal as if wished to remain detached.

"Well, it's exactly ... well, not exactly what you think," he said. "We are of the same ... umm, thread, let's say. Our energies are similar in many ways, and so we are attracted to that. We have much in common. We are both interested in spirituality, in energies, in ways to communicate something we know or feel to others. That's an energetic match, and so we are drawn to each other."

"Then why stop it?" Elena asked. She hated how that sounded. She didn't want to sound like a jilted lover, but she knew she did. She looked at Anurak's sleeves, sheltering his hands. She wished they were exposed because she wanted desperately to touch him.

"There are many kinds of attraction, Elena," Anurak said. "There is romantic attraction, sexual attraction, and there is a higher frequency of attraction. Let's just say that my attraction to you is primarily of a higher frequency. I am attracted to your spirit and the activity of it. I enjoy our conversations and our time spent in meditation together. I enjoy being the teacher, and sometimes being the student. But yesterday, a different frequency occurred – for both of us. And for me, that cannot be. My vow was not to the Catholic church. It was a vow between myself and the God of my understanding. I do not choose to break that vow. It was necessary to break the energy or the vow may well have been compromised."

There was a soft thumping noise over their heads. Moses was trotting down from the loft. His tail brushed across the planter by the door and then snaked about in the air as if testing for wind direction. He approached Anurak and sniffed his robes. He sat and lifted a paw, lightly tapping Anurak's leg. It was his way of asking for attention – or food.

"Well, hello there. And who are you?" Anurak asked as he reached down to rub the cat's ears.

Elena was dumbfounded. Moses rarely appeared when there was another human in the apartment, except for Zak and Margot. Zak, because he'd just been around so much that he seemed to belong there, and Margot, because she fed him when Elena was away.

"That's Moses." She was still staring at the cat with a quizzical look.

"Moses? Really? You're kidding, right?" Anurak looked up then and saw the surprised look on Elena's face. "What?"

"No. Not kidding. I found him in the river. I know it's ... ironic. But I've never seen him respond to anyone new like this. He usually hides upstairs until people leave."

At that, Moses jumped uninvited into Anurak's lap and settled in for some serious ear rubbing. "Must be the energy," Anurak said, laughing.

"Right. So, energy...." Elena said. "Are you saying that what I was – or what my energy was doing was some kind of lower vibration, like it was wrong? Like adulterous or something." She was more than a little peeved. Who was this guy, anyway? She had felt something intense coming from him yesterday. Pheromones were jumping all around them. And now, it was her energy that was bad?

"No, no, Elena. That's not what I meant at all. There's nothing wrong with what either of us felt. It was actually a higher part of each of us causing the attraction. It's not unusual for a spiritual attraction to manifest as a physical attraction. That's what the ideal romantic love is all about, two souls with similar paths recognize each other's energy and sometimes reach out physically to one another. But for me, that cannot happen because I have made a specific choice to not give physical expression to that attraction – not like that, anyway. You have a similar kind of attraction with Zak, but for some reason, you both choose not to give it expression. There seems to be something in the way of that, and I don't want to be a part of what gets in the way."

"Zak? We're just friends. How can you know that about him anyway? You haven't even met him. He's ... like a brother." Elena was feeling a little calmer now, but the reference to Zak was confusing – and a little unsettling. She didn't know how Anurak seemed to know so much about Zak, but then he did seem to know her. She had hoped to let him know her a lot better, but that was clearly not going to happen.

"How do you do it?" she asked.

"Do what?" he replied.

"How do you just stop that intense desire to ... meld together. I mean, I've been attracted to people before, but this was irresistible. How do you stop it?"

"I draw my attention inward. I remind myself of my intention to remain celibate and to express only higher realms of love. As I shift my attention, my thoughts change, my feelings change, and my energy changes. I just sort of draw it in. When celibacy is a choice, it's usually quite easy."

Usually. Elena held on to that word. Did that mean it was more difficult with her? She felt her own energy seeking his, flowing across the kitchen table toward him, her eyes searching the depths of those sparkling blue orbs. She felt a stirring in her body, an irresistible urge. And then a wall.

She had seen Anurak's energy begin to respond and flow toward her, but it stopped, abruptly. A filmy sort of wall had appeared as he blocked her energetic advance. Moses hopped out of his lap, sniffed the shadowy energy ball that followed Anurak wherever he went, then climbed into the papasan chair like the little king he thought he was.

"Sorry," she said. "I don't know why I ... it's just that I've only recently remembered that I could see people's energies. And, I've never seen this melding-energy thing. It's like a new toy." It was more than that, but she didn't know how to else to say it.

"It's okay, Elena. I feel a similar attraction to you. But our paths are meant to meet only on a soul level, not the other level you are feeling drawn to. With practice, two people can meld their energy without melding their bodies. It is a very spiritual experience. In a sense, you and your companions merged in the Ark. You thought together, felt together. You were one, but there was something still separate, not out of the need to be different, but out of an awareness of individualized expression.

"Individualized expression," Elena repeated. *"*Those words have been floating around in my head since we returned from the dig. I don't think I had ever heard them before that. What do they mean?"

Anurak's gaze seemed to search for some place beyond the room as he replied, "If you think of God as the All-ness, the source of everything in the manifest world, and humans made in the image of the All-ness, then each must be an individualized expression of the whole. We all think, feel, speak, move, and grow, yet we do not all think, feel, speak, move, and grow alike. The same, yet different. Individualized. So, we are individualized expressions of the whole, or God."

Anurak had put into words what she had learned in the Ark. She had tried to paint it with the Fountain of Life painting. That one was gone now, shredded in her rage after the opening. She had touched on the idea again with *The Power of a Comma*.

"Anurak, the contrast paintings hinge on what you've just said. Each pair illustrates something with and without this understanding. But ... the understanding itself. I don't know yet how to paint that. I don't know what that looks like. Except ... maybe it has something to do with the space between them."

Anurak smiled, a look of satisfaction on his face. "Well done, my student," he said with the air of a master. "The space between, the gap, the invisible essence, is where all answers reside."

"Invisible is great, but my *path,* as you call it, is to make things visible. So how do I paint God? Or this All-ness?

"Making God visible is the true path of all individualized expressions, Elena. But I understand your question. I think you may need to explore what God is. Many people find it helpful to think about what God is not. But I find the best definition of God comes from the Gospel of John ... God is Love. Not romantic love, not physical love, not even parental or brotherly love – though those are all good visible expressions – Love with a capital L, the essence of what love is. Love is wholeness, love is balance, love is the harmonious blending together of what seems to be separate."

A revelation flashed in Elena's mind. She saw in her mind's eye Anurak and his unusually bright and balanced energy. He was an expression of this wholeness in a profound way. She saw him guiding others into this awareness, deflecting anything and anyone who might deter him from this task. It didn't make him more whole or better than anyone else. It just made him more on purpose. Except for that little gray cloud of energy. She wondered if she should ask him about that. Yes, she would ask, but maybe not today.

"More tea?" Elena asked, picking up the pot.

"Always," Anurak replied. Elena filled his cup, added some water to the pot and set it back on the stove to simmer. She walked toward the blank canvases, stroking Moses as she passed him.

"In the space between these, let's call them *The Culture of Theft* and *The Culture of Giving*, what exists?"

"Abundance," Anurak answered. "More than enough of every-thing. The invisible substance that gives shape and form to the visible."

"And this invisible substance, it can never run out? It is infinite?"

"Yes. It is not possible for it to run out. It simply *is*," Anurak answered.

Elena pulled another thread from the canvas on the left. "So, the only place where something can appear missing or stolen is in the visible?"

"Excellent, apprentice," Anurak said with that master-teacher quality to his voice

Elena turned toward Anurak. She scooped Moses from the chair and sat. "Nothing can be stolen, then?"

"No. Nothing can be stolen in Spirit. But of course, that is not the experience of the physical world."

"I'm wondering, Anurak. Zak is determined to go back and re-discover the Ark, to bring it home for research, display, and protection. Does the Ark need protecting? Can it be stolen?"

"There are several answers to those questions, Elena. Which would you like first, the physical, the metaphorical, or the metaphysical?"

Elena threw up her hands as if to say "Your choice," then added, "You tell me. I don't know where to begin when it comes to the Ark. I'm still trying to wrap my head around what happened in the desert and what I'm able to do now – entering and exiting at will when clearly there is no ark here in this room."

"Okay, so let's start with the physical. Legend has it that the Ark is powerful. It was carried by the Israelites through the desert to house God and his commandments. But they also used it to ward off enemies. It was said to have had powers that would kill anyone who attempted to touch it. Only the priestly tribes were allowed to approach or carry it. A man named Uzzah was killed just for touching the Ark in an attempt to keep it from falling. Yet much later, David, the one who killed Goliath, asked the question 'How can the ark come to me?' and he let it sit for three months. Then he danced in front of it and ultimately took it with him to Jerusalem. No harm came to David through his contact with the Ark. What the stories suggest is that it's not the touching of the Ark which causes harm, but the intention behind it."

"Well, what was wrong with Uzzah's intention? It sounds like he just wanted to protect it," Elena said.

"True. But if it is the temple of God, does God need protection? From whom?"

"How were we able to touch it, then? We didn't ask how it could come to us, and we didn't have any intention of returning it to Jerusalem. I'm not sure we had any intentions at all just then, but I'm pretty sure Jerusalem was not on the list. And none of us is a part of the priestly tribe."

"Are you sure?" Anurak asked. "Let's look at the metaphor. Does the priestly tribe refer to specific people from one Tribe of Israel? Or did it signify those with priestly intent or those on the path of guiding others to God? In that case, you and your friends may have been destined to find the ancient relic, destined to enter its powerful energy. Clearly, none of you intended to steal it or harm it. Your curiosity was innocent, unadulterated, a desire of your higher selves to experience and share something that would be given to humankind."

"How can you know that?" Elena asked.

"You didn't die," Anurak replied with a saintly smirk.

"Okay. What about the metaphysical story then? And what's that mean anyway?"

"Metaphysical means beyond the physical, where all things visible are symbolic of something *invisible*. In this interpretation, the Ark exists, but only as a visible symbol of something that cannot be seen. It is a realm of being. Since the Ark is referred to in scripture as the place where God dwells, then it is a realm of being in which God exists – or rather, in which the existence of God is experienced. That is something that cannot be stolen, it can only be ... achieved or experienced."

"So, is this why I can enter and exit at will, right here in my studio? Then ... I could, if I chose to, enter it from anywhere, anytime?"

"Yes. You could do that." Anurak paused as if there was more, but then offered another thought. "Going back to your original question Elena, 'Can the Ark be stolen?' The answer is first, why would someone steal what belongs to everyone yet belongs to no one. Ultimately, the Ark cannot be stolen because it cannot be found, or if found it cannot be touched by anyone who does not understand this. You, Elena, understand this. You may not know yet how to express it the way you want, but you know it. You already knew these things deep within you when you reached the Ark. Entering it just brought what was already in you to the surface. It is still doing that."

"Is it safe for Zak to return to the Ark, then? He wants to bring it back, and I'm not sure he understands any of this. He seems so closed off to it. He doesn't even believe it really happened now. He thinks the whole experience was a delusion and he wants to bring it back for research. He also wants to get to it before anyone else can steal it."

"His intentions are noble, Elena. He wants to protect it. And while that is a little like Uzzah, he also wants to understand its message and make it visible to others. He just has a different way of expressing it. He is like the part of you that questions things. We all have a questioner within us. Zak is just more finely in tune with his questioner."

"What about the people who tried to kill us, Anurak? I'm terrified that Zak will be hurt or killed trying to find it again."

"The Ark will protect him," he answered.

How? Elena wondered. *It certainly didn't protect the people who lost their lives on the first expedition.* She sensed that at least some of what Anurak said was true, but the questioner in her was balking.

CHAPTER TWENTY-TWO

Real or Unreal?

Renee didn't know what to make of the painting leaning against Elena's wall. It gave her chills, but not the good kind. She felt vulnerable, afraid, as she gazed at the open jaws so life-like they seemed as though they would swallow her whole in the next second. But then, there was the faintest glimpse of something else, some glowing light at the edges of the monstrosity that radiated a different look and feel. Beyond the edges of the crocodile, there were colorful swirls reminiscent of Elena's ethereal paintings. Was the crocodile consuming the peaceful glow? Or was the peaceful glow about to devour the crocodile?

Renee didn't know, but the feeling was unsettling. As she continued to examine the painting, Renee realized she had been holding her breath. Every muscle in her body was tight, and a cold feeling ran through her whole body. But as she began to explore the outer edges of the painting, her breath became more relaxed, as there was something reassuring about that glow. She felt her muscles relax and a warm, fluttery feeling entered her chest. Well, this was a promising direction. A painting that could evoke terror and peace? *There's potential there,* Renee thought. *I can promote it, but can I sell it?*

"Tell me about this piece, Elena," *Renee* said turning away from the frightening painting. Renee knew better than to criticize an artist's work without first hearing their intentions. It didn't make selling it any easier, but it did set the ground for an honest critique.

Elena was sitting quietly in her blue papasan chair, drinking a cup of Jasmine tea. Two new paintings were in progress in front of her, and there were paint smudges on her brow as if she had wiped the sweat from it during a painting frenzy. Her thick chestnut hair, pulled up into a loose bun, left unruly strands trickling down on her shoulders. She took a deep breath and set the cup down on the table beside her.

"Well," Elena said, "there are a lot of monstrous things happening in the world. At times it seems as if all the light and joy are being swallowed up, as if there is little hope. There is hatred and violence, poverty and pain. There are times when it seems these things will swallow us or drown the bits of kindness that still exist. But the painting suggests there is something else; that just beyond what we see as evil and darkness, there is light, shimmering and alive with peace and harmony. The question the painting asks is, 'Which is real? The monster or the light?'

"Most people would say the monster is real since he is big and overwhelming," Elena continued. "He has shape and substance. You feel as if you could touch him if you relished the prospect of losing an arm. But just behind him, there is something that promises peace, security, and harmony. Even though the swirls of light lack what we consider to be substance, they have an effect on the viewer. They change the focus. They pose the questions, 'Which is real? Which is an illusion?'"

Renee eyed her quizzically. She had her own questions firing through her brain. "Are you suggesting that the ethereal lights are real and the monster is not? Do you mean that some unearthly vision is real and the actual evil and horrific stuff happening in the world is not?"

Elena picked up her cup again, taking a sip. "Ultimately, yes," she said. "In reality, everything is made of light. Waves, particles, protons, all come together to form what we see, feel, hear, and touch. So, ultimately, what we experience as solid is actually light moving at an extremely slow rate of vibration. Behind everything we experience is light. So yes, the light is real, and the monster is not."

Renee felt the blood warming in her veins. Confusion suddenly gave way to outrage. "Try telling that to the person whose child has been killed. Or, to the person who has been abused or robbed of their identity. Hell, try telling that to me. Does that mean that asshole that cut my husband off the road because he was busy texting his girlfriend is not real? Does that mean my husband's death was not real? My loss is not real? I still deal with that every day and let me tell you, Elena, it's real!"

Renee's heart was pounding. She wasn't sure she liked this painting at all. "You may want to come up with another explanation for this painting if you want to sell it, Elena. Who is going to buy something that tells them that everything they fear and everything that has caused them pain isn't real?"

"I'm sorry, Renee. That's not what I meant. Of course, what you experienced was and is real. But in the greater scheme of things, beyond our human experience, there is something else, something that transcends the loss. Think about it this way. Tanya Canfree, the talk-show host and philanthropist, experienced great trials in her young life. That's a fact. Everyone knows her story. The experience she had was real. No one can take that away or cause it to be undone. But in a greater reality, what has she become because of what happened to her? How has her experience influenced the exceptionally generous person she is today? It seems to me that she learned what it means to be exploited by someone who has power over you and as a result chooses to use her affluence and power in positive ways. What would she be like without the difficult childhood? Which is more real? The traumatic experiences, or the transformation of the soul known as Tonya Canfree?"

Renee felt her shoulders and face soften a little. She pursed her lips and looked back at the paining. "It's still a tough sell, Elena. Some will get it and some will not. Maybe you just don't explain this one. At least with the real, unreal thing."

Elena stood, setting her cup on the table. "Let me show you what I've painted in contrast to this image. All but the first painting in the series will have a contrasting image." She walked to the other side of the studio and uncovered the goddess riding the crocodile. It was a beautiful painting. The glowing swirls that only framed the outer edges of the first painting gently shrouded the entire canvas. The positive and negative spaces played off each other in a way that created the appearance of continuous movement, the glowing swaths of paint fluttering like the crystalline wings of a hummingbird. Translucent waves of color subdued the beast of the former painting and formed an ethereal female shape with flowing, sparkling garments. She held silvery reins in her hands harnessing the frightening creature as if he were her exhausted steed. The overall effect was tranquil. It was exquisite.

"Oh, Elena. This I can sell. It's beautiful! There's so much power in this second one. Actually, there's tremendous power in both of them, but the strength in the second one is personal and desirable. It's more palatable. You've got something here with the juxtaposition of the two ideas; powerlessness and power. I like it. Will you hang them together? They would make a great diptych." Renee was excited now.

"No. I don't expect to hang them side-by-side. I think they need the space between them. I'm living with them apart for now and letting the empty space speak to me. There's another idea taking shape about how the contrast paintings will be displayed. I'll explain more when I've had a chance to work it out," Elena said as she led Renee to the other side of the studio and unveiled the first of the next pair of paintings. "This one is titled *A Culture of Theft*," she said.

A Culture of Theft had areas of bare canvas, scattered threads removed, and openings that revealed an empty space behind the painting. Renee stepped back to take in the overall effect. Layers of paint depicted various scenes of people stealing something and having something stolen from them. The colors were dark; blacks, muted greens, and muddied blues. The details, the people, and their actions were colored by their clothing, skin tones, and the activity itself – but these also had a darkness to them achieved by an umber-tinted glaze. The only brightness to the image was the colorful wash Elena had applied as a ground, still visible around the edges. The painting evoked a feeling of despair, yet the empty spaces and the colorful border inspired curiosity, and *maybe,* Renee thought, *hope.*

"Powerful," Renee said at last. "Very powerful and a little less frightening. It doesn't make me want to run and hide. I really like this texture you've created by pulling at the threads. There's a statement even in that. I like it. Show me the contrast painting."

Elena led her to the other side of the studio and removed the cover from the painting next to the tamed crocodile. "This one is *A Culture of Giving.*"

Renee felt a dramatic shift in her own energy as she viewed this one. "A Culture of Giving" was a bright and cheerful canvas, the rainbow wash visible throughout. Additional threads woven into the canvas gave it an intriguing texture and added dimension. Here, figures of people were in the process of giving and receiving. Their clothing was brighter, their skin tones glowed, and sparkles of energy surrounded each of them. There was a faint hint of a silvery thread emanating from each of the people in the painting. The painted threads all connected – one to the other. The activity felt seamless and infinite.

The faces of the people emitted unmitigated joy. This was an image that would speak to art connoisseurs – and buyers.

"The series is compelling, Elena. There's no question about that. But I still can't imagine why you're insisting on hanging them separately. They would work so well together in sets."

"Trust me," Elena said. "There is a purpose to the space between them. I'm still working on how to present the concept, but I know you'll love it."

Renee wasn't so sure, but she did know artists. They had to follow their inspiration. Whatever Elena had in mind, Renee hoped it wouldn't be too outlandish, or if it was, that she could talk some sense into her.

CHAPTER TWENTY-THREE

How Do You Paint Love?

With two fresh canvases mounted on opposing easels, Elena lifted a dry brush toward one of them. Sometimes it helped to draw an invisible image first, one that she saw only in her mind. Sometimes it was just an obligatory swirl, like now, when she wasn't sure what she would paint. Still holding the dry brush, she sat in her chair and began focusing on the space between the two canvases. She held the brush in the air and drew an invisible swirl over the empty space.

This set of paintings were to depict love; pure, unadulterated love, in contrast with the love of the senses. Her recent conversation with Anurak about the space between the contrast paintings replayed in her mind. She had mentioned God, and he had defined God as Love. Now she wondered, *how do you paint Love?*

Focusing on the space between the canvases, Elena let her eyes fall out of focus. She began to breathe deeply and allowed the question to become a sort of mantra in her mind, *How do you paint love? What is love? Love. I love. I am love. Love. Love. Love.*

And she felt it, the exquisite vibration of love, similar to the feeling she experienced with Anurak, but even more intense. She could feel this sweet, harmonious vibration throughout her being. A vibrant shade of pink flooded her mind and she followed the color as it led her higher and higher until she was no longer in her body, but floating above it – and then, in one rushing flow of energy, she was back in the Ark again, standing before the mystical canvas holding the enchanted brush.

The love she felt in this place was indescribable. It seemed to not only enfold her, but it moved through her in a way that reminded her of the visceral feeling she experienced looking at the brilliant pinks and greens of a Gauguin painting. Exquisite. Sweet beyond words. So serene you could almost hear the harmony seeping out of them like an angelic voice rippling through your heart.

Elena reached for the palette floating near her. The golds and pinks and lime greens on the board seemed to mix themselves, yearning to be placed upon the canvas. Bursts of golden light danced around her head, lifting her into a vibration of wholeness that transcended space and time. She was in a state of pure knowing, resting in an energy of love so pure, so profound, so powerful she could only relax fully into it and allow it to enfold her.

It was pure, unadulterated, divine Love. Pure, absolute beingness. Pure and simple. Grand and beautiful. How could she paint an image of what was absolutely pure and whole? What pigment could emulate what had nothing out of place, nothing missing?

The brush jerked in her hand and began to paint. Broad strokes, then tiny dots of light. A Paris street emerged into view. She sighed. It was the place she had met Trey, a romantic walkway along the Seine river. That was certainly not the kind of love she was trying to illustrate, though it had seemed so at the time. She had fallen *head over heels* for him, as they say. Handsome, worldly, a fellow artist, he could appreciate her painting. They spent nearly every waking moment together during her semester there, visiting galleries, sipping wine, strolling the streets of Paris amid sweet romantic evenings alone.

When the term ended, Trey visited her in New York. She had taken him to the Statue of Liberty, Coney Island, and on leisurely strolls through the park. Then, one afternoon she had come home early from class to find him wrapped in the arms of her roommate! She was heartbroken. Devastated. Angry. She threw them both out. She hadn't asked where they would stay or how he would get back to Paris. She hadn't cared. She had left both their belongings in the hallway and changed the locks.

The apartment had seemed empty then. Like the apartment, what followed was a series of empty relationships, ones in which Elena invested nothing, expected nothing, and projected her own hurt and anger onto. In fact, she found herself almost deliberately trying to hurt the men that came into her life, drawing them in – then shutting them out. Only Zak was exempt. But then Zak was not a boyfriend. Theirs was not a romantic relationship. Zak was her best friend, intricately bonded to something much deeper within her. He was there when she took ridiculous jobs when her paintings weren't selling; hotdog vendor, kite-flying instructor, even her failed street-artist attempts. He was there for her after the heart-shattering love affair with Trey. Zak grounded her in a way no one else could.

Elena's parents were baby boomers who had come of age in the sixties, the time of *Free Love, and Make Love Not War,* a whole generation that had questioned the validity of religious structures and the nature of monogamy. *Make Love Not War* was an admirable mindset. It was love, after all, that would eventually heal the ravaged, war-torn heart of humanity. *But,* she scoffed, *there's nothing "free" about love, not romantic love, anyway.* Divine Love was free, but its romantic expression came with commitments and a desire to hold one another in high regard, to work together to create something astounding, whether it be children or the coming together of two creative, loving minds to manifest what one could not achieve alone. That required commitment and trust. Elena knew the pain associated with the breaking of that trust.

Elena's trust had been broken long before she had met Trey. Her father had cheated on her mother. Later, Elena discovered that he had fathered a child with another woman while he was still courting her mother. Somewhere in the world, she had a half-brother she never met.

Elena's grandfather had been a despicable man. He drank. He abused his children. He neglected and humiliated Elena's grandmother, staggering into his family home with prostitutes on his arm. Elena thought Trey was different. He made her believe she was the most important person in the world to him. He had mended her mistrust in men and then torn it open again. The pain, the sense of desolation and loneliness, had been devastating.

The love and peace she felt in the energy of the Ark was something much sweeter than any experience of romance. It was unadulterated love, a pure and enduring expression of the essence of love. It could not be altered or changed. It could not be broken. It simply was. She could feel it. She could breathe it and be wholly immersed in it.

Love, Divine Love, she realized, had nothing to do with romance, nothing to do with relationships at all, except perhaps her relationship with herself. Perhaps adultery was as much about cheating on one's self as cheating on another person. In fact, maybe seeing yourself as separate from the unadulterated wholeness of life was the most devastating form of deception.

Paint began to flow from the brush, rendering the shapes and forms of Elena and Trey on that romantic Paris pathway. They held each other, but there was no exchange of light or energy between them. Instead, there seemed to be a draining or siphoning of one another's energies. The more they siphoned, the flatter and grayer their own images became. At Trey's feet, a ball of dark matter like a small cloud clung to him. It too, drew energy from him. The more it took, the more he took from Elena. Elena had seen a gray cloud like this before. It looked like the murky cloud that followed Anurak wherever he went.

The streetlights in the Paris painting began to stretch into shapes that roughly resembled human forms shrouded in swirls of clouded energy. Thin, wispy threads connected them like an endless string of darkened Christmas lights. Most had dark little clouds around their feet that tugged and pulled at them, forcing them to cling tighter to one another to maintain their balance. As they clung to one another, they extracted energy from one another, and then broke away as their shrouds became more cumbersome and more opaque. Some reached out and clung to several others at once. Others jaunted from one to the other, clinging, siphoning, and separating. With every act of siphoning, the shadowy clouds grew larger, and the lights grew dimmer.

The little lights were all separated now and the thin silky threads connecting them faded until they were almost invisible. Elena's heart began to ache for the once brilliant lights that had isolated themselves from one another. They seemed so alone, so desperate.

The lights grew dimmer still, then faded away, yielding to the sandy ochre and sienna tones of a desert landscape. An image of Zak took shape on the canvas, extracting from the dirt the kind of artifacts that made his heart sing, remains of human culture, clues to what had been, and insight into what might be.

What Elena felt for Zak, when she let herself feel it, was almost like the love of the Ark in a way. They were more than friends, yet it had never been romantic. They were *those* friends, the ones who swore they would marry each other if they hadn't found their perfect mate by some distant date in the future. Zak grounded her. She inspired him. They didn't complete one another; they mirrored the completeness *in* one another. What was already whole in each of them was reflected more powerfully when they were together. Yes. The love that enveloped her in the Ark was something like that, yet more. It was the essence of what took form and shape as various types of love, each an imperfect expression of perfect, pure, unadulterated Love.

160

The brush went to work again, drawing brilliant blooms of light from the center of the magical canvas. Golds, yellows and whites bloomed ceaselessly, dissolving the previous image until only a glowing ball of shimmering light appeared. It throbbed and stretched. It grew larger and more intense, then divided in two; two lights throbbed and glowed on the mystical canvas now. The golden orbs took on vaguely human shapes. They showered one another with their golden light, and they grew. And they multiplied.

Millions of lights filled the canvas each showering the others with its rays and each becoming brighter as the light shone on them. Lovers sharing and reflecting one another's light appeared. Mothers caressed their infants. Fathers held the tiny hands of tinier lights. People shared their food and clothing. They sought those whose light seemed faded or alone and shared their brilliance with them. Those who carried little clouds of gray energy were lifted up and freed as the light of others penetrated and dissolved the murky little blobs. This was humankind in love with one another, in love with itself, in love with life. The pair of paintings that had taken shape on the mystical canvas were not unlike the paintings, *A Culture of Theft* and *A Culture of Giving*.

The shimmering beings of light began to grow. They connected and melded together, becoming one vibrant glow of indescribable light. It was gold. It was a rainbow. It was white. Then it was still – or nearly still. Elena was drawn to the subtly undulating light with an irresistible desire to be one with it. She stepped into it and allowed the light to surround her. Particles of light began to separate and shapes appeared in the spaces between them. Elena could see an image of herself in her studio, clothed in a mirror-like substance, standing before two blank canvases. A voice deep within her whispered, *You are Love. What will you reflect?*

The stream of light pressed in on her and she felt the intense vibration of being drawn through the Ark energy. It was familiar now. She didn't fight it. She just rested into it until she found herself in her papasan chair, dry brush still held in her hand. She opened her eyes, stood and began dry painting on the canvases again, but it was not obligatory. She knew that she would paint the contrast between a love that seeks to be filled and a love that seeks to reflect Light.

It is impossible to paint Divine Love, she thought. You can't paint it; you can only experience it and reflect it. Divine Love is what fills the space between – between the duality of love and hate, oneness and separation, harmony and chaos – there is the essence of Love seeking to draw together what seems apart.

CHAPTER TWENTY-FOUR

Winter in the Garden

Elena was surprised when the young monk led her toward the seventh-floor garden of the temple. She hadn't been there for a while and thought the weather was so cold they would have closed the rooftop sanctuary for the winter. She braced herself for the cold wind as the double doors opened to the garden, but there was no variation in the temperature. In fact, it seemed a little warmer on the roof. Looking up, she saw that the monks had erected an inflatable roof, painted to look like the sky. She noticed for the first time the baseboard heating units attached to the short brick wall of the perimeter. It was amazing. She was outdoors, feeling warm, and it was December. In New York!

Anurak was sitting on a golden cushion in front of a golden stupa near the center of the garden. If not for the white robes, he would have looked like the Buddha himself. Mums and other hearty plants continued to bloom around him. His eyes were closed, but she felt him becoming aware of her presence. They had been experimenting with consciously connecting with one another in their meditations together. Whenever they were in close proximity, they became aware of one another's energy. Elena no longer felt an urgent, physical desire for Anurak when their minds and energies met. She just felt peaceful and at home.

"Hello, Elena. I've been expecting you," Anurak said as his eyes fluttered open.

"I anticipated seeing you too, but I didn't think it would be here." Elena gestured to the domed ceiling with a smile. "This is amazing!"

"It may not be real, but the illusion is quite comforting and very conducive to peaceful meditations." Anurak pointed to a pillow adjacent to him and said, "Please, sit. Join me."

Elena sat on the gold cushion and folded her legs and feet into a lotus position. She was facing Anurak and rested her hands, palms up and open, on her knees. She closed her eyes and began breathing in the way Anurak had taught her. She searched for a sound to follow but found none. The effect of the dome muted the outdoor sounds. Instead, she found a soft humming, no doubt related to the air pumps required to keep the roof inflated. This was an easy sound to get lost in. It had a soft, monotonous tone that Elena thought must be like the muted sounds a fetus hears in the womb.

With that thought, Elena's heartbeat and the sound of the pumps became one, and she was soon floating in a formless space of silence. In front of her floated the beautiful, flowing energy of Anurak. His image looked more like a colorful fountain than the form of a physical man. There was a glowing white light that formed a tall column running from the ground to an area above where his physical head would be. The column fanned out into a crest-like shape with streams of light flowing continuously. From this central core, a variety of swirling lights appeared. There were brilliant greens, blues, oranges, yellows, and reds. A subtle violet disc rotated near the place where his forehead would be. The colors flowed gently in an upward stream and then fell softly down around him, then traveled up the column again. Unaware that her own energy looked much the same, Elena reached out to touch the beautiful array and light, the tip of her finger joining the display that was Anurak's. Their energy melded and their thoughts became one.

She could hear him in her mind now. His voice soft and subtle, chanting, *Om vajrapani hum.* It was a chant to encourage enlightenment; a wisdom chant. Elena fell into the rhythm of Anurak's mantra. Eventually, she felt something loosening from her own energy as if something had become lighter and floated away from her like ... *like a pink balloon.*

Later, as Elena's thoughts returned to her, she began sensing her surroundings. She felt the cushion beneath her, the air that surrounded her body, a gentle brush of air as faint currents descended from the domed roof. She wriggled her fingers and toes, assuring herself she was indeed within her body and opened her eyes. Anurak was already back, his eyes smiling as brightly as his lips.

"Welcome back," he said.

"That was so powerful, but so gentle, Anurak. It feels almost like the experiences I have at my studio – like the Ark experiences – but the liftoff and reentry are so much more gentle."

"Unlike a rocket ship, we do not have to break through gravity," he said. "Only through our own thoughts and beliefs. It is said that when two or more pray – or meditate – together, there God is. Together, they form a breach in the illusion of separation, entering the space in which the Essence of Life is felt or known. Nothing is different physically, but much is different spiritually and energetically. It is an awakening to the reality of oneness. The chant is conducive to that awakening."

"I felt something unusual during the meditation. I felt as if something in me floated away – like a balloon or bubble floats away from you. What *was* that? It was so ... *tactile,* I guess is the word. I could feel it leaving me like it was being pulled out of me, like a tooth but without the pain. In fact, it felt...." She searched for the word, "wonderful."

"You were letting go of something. Something you had probably been holding in your consciousness for a long time. It was probably something heavy, someone or something you had been unable to forgive, perhaps. In that moment you were ready and willing to let it go, so the suffering you had been holding onto, left you."

"Suffering," Elena repeated. "If there is any spiritual teaching that is more confusing than suffering, I can't imagine what it is. I was taught I was supposed to suffer and whatever I suffered would somehow give me a better chance of getting to heaven. Yet other traditions teach something else; suffering is part of life, suffering is a choice, suffering is a requirement. It is so difficult to understand."

"In a sense, they all have a point, Elena. Suffering is indeed a part of this life. I suppose it doesn't have to be, but it most often is. But it is in a way, a choice. Suffering most often comes from judging something as either good or bad. Lose the judgment, lose the suffering. I don't see it as a requirement – but learning to release it or the judgment that causes it is most definitely a requirement, not for the sake of entering a place called heaven, but for entering a more enlightened way of being. It makes you lighter – as you just discovered."

Elena thought about it. She did feel lighter. As if something she had carried around in a backpack for a hundred years was no longer with her. She wondered if it was Trey. After her recent excursion into the Ark realm, she had returned feeling less angry with him. The painting that was emerging from the experience gave her a new perspective on Trey. He was no longer mean or evil in her mind. He felt small, insecure, unhappy, isolated, reaching out – albeit in unhealthy ways – but reaching out, just the same. She wasn't angry anymore. She no longer saw their relationship as bad or wrong. She wouldn't repeat it for a million dollars, but it was no longer a source of suffering. It was just an experience that had taught her what she did not want. It had also given her some perspective on the *Love* paintings.

"Anurak," Elena said as she looked past his physical appearance to the energy she could see emanating from him. It was lovely and serene right now, mostly blue with an interesting upward glow of gold about his shoulders that gave a vague impression of ... wings. Near his feet though, a small, cloudy ball of energy held fast to him as if chained to his legs. "May I ask you a question ... a personal one?"

"Of course, Elena. I have no secrets from you."

"You know that I can see energy, right?" she asked

"Yes. I am aware of this gift in you." He replied. His eyes did not blink, nor did they avert her gaze.

"In my recent Ark experience, I saw the contrast between a needy, human kind of love and an expression of ... let's call it *Unadulterated Love,* the kind of love that is a perfect expression of the very idea of love. In the painting of human love, the individuals portrayed had varying amounts of dark, gray, and heavy energy about them. For many, it clung to their feet. For others, it seemed to clog different areas of their energy. The areas you would call chakras were completely enveloped by it in some of them. But mostly, it clung to their feet and the more they tried to draw positive energy from another person, the heavier and larger the shadowy cloud became."

"An interesting illustration of clinging to suffering," Anurak commented.

"Yes. I see that now," Elena said. "But my question is, well ..." She paused, uncertain of how to proceed. "Your energy is bright and beautiful, almost angelic," she said, referring to the wings. "But I see this dark energy around your feet too, Anurak. I've noticed it since we first found each other in the park. It never goes away. It follows you everywhere."

"Is there a question then?" Anurak asked, his eyes smiling just a bit.

"What is it that you are clinging to?"

"Ahh. That is a question. And the answer is long with many questions of its own. How much time do you have?"

Elena needed to know the answer to this. It seemed vitally important that she understand this energy that clung to Anurak. If she was going to authentically paint the energies that clogged the heart and prevented pure expressions of love, she needed Anurak to share his experience with her. How could she paint about perfection without understanding imperfection? "I have all the time in the world," she said.

"Okay then. Let's go inside. We can use one of the receiving rooms downstairs. This is not an energy I wish to explore here." He looked around at the scattering of monks in meditation and those tending to the plant life. "This environment is sacred, and my words do not belong here." He stood and waited for Elena to join him.

They each bowed slightly to the sacred space in acknowledgment of their shared experience and walked toward the double doors. Elena felt a thrill climb up her legs and spine. She wasn't sure if it was excitement or dread, but she walked through the doors intent on discovering Anurak's secret.

***

Inside the private sitting room, Elena settled in on a soft burgundy cushion near the wall, against which she was able to support her back. Anurak sat across from her; apparently his spine never tired of erect posture.

"Elena, when we first spoke here in this room, you asked me if I could treat what you told me as a confession – never divulging what you were about to say."

"I remember.,.." she said.

"I'm asking the same of you. You will be hearing a sort of confession from me. Divulging the information cannot hurt me, but it may harm others or disturb a growth process that I am not destined to disturb – at least I don't believe I am. If I did, I would have made very different choices over that past few years."

Elena wondered what he could possibly be about to share with her, but she forced her eyes to remain softly focused, not allowing the pupils to enlarge. "Go on." Elena thought she sounded a lot like Anurak when he encouraged her to talk.

"I told you about my breakdown in Rome. I was continually in a state of conflict over my growing understanding of God and an environment that would not allow me to express it. That was difficult and emotionally draining to be sure, but there was more."

Elena made no sound but nodded, encouraging Anurak to continue.

"The abuse cases," Anurak said as if the statement itself was all the explanation necessary. He glanced behind him as if checking for eavesdroppers. "The abuse cases took me over the edge. I told you I found it impossible to defend my client, but I didn't tell you about the research."

Elena could feel Anurak's anxiety level rising. Hers was increasing too. She couldn't imagine what delving into the details of child abuse would do to someone, let alone someone like Anurak, who was so sweet and pure. She focused for a moment on a calm, quieting energy within herself and imagined it surrounding Anurak. She brought her attention to her heart where she exhaled peaceful energy into the room and directed it to envelop Anurak. It was something she had learned a long time ago in a workshop called HeartMath. A person's harmonious energy could have the effect of calming another person in close proximity to them. Elena had found that focusing on this energy helped in times of conflict; now it seemed to help Anurak.

Anurak got that far-away look she remembered from their first meeting as if he were time-traveling to a not-so-pleasant place and time. "The claims were horrendous, Elena. It was beyond belief that anyone, let alone priests and bishops, could cause such harm to a child. It was one thing to have your knuckles rapped with the metal edge of a ruler – it was quite another to be sexually abused and threatened as these children had been.

"One of the stories, one of the men who came forward, told of events that had a particularly visceral effect on me," Anurak said. "I could feel this boy's pain, his anguish, his fear. I felt it so intensely I couldn't read any further. I had nightmares. I stopped sleeping. Then, encouraged by my superior, I read some more. He thought it would help me get past the nightmares if I just finished reading the report. He was also concerned about my building a defense which, of course, I couldn't do without continuing the report."

"That must have been very difficult for you Anurak. I'm so sorry," Elena said.

"Yes. Difficult but also in a very sick way, enlightening. The initial reports contained sequestered information. In other words, they did not give the names of the plaintiffs. But the final report, the one I had to read before preparing a defense, shared everything. The church – it was St. Bardo's." He let those words hang in the air and allowed Elena to comprehend what he was saying.

Elena's eyebrows arched uncontrollably. Her eyes widened even though she swore she would not let that happen. She wanted to listen without emotion, to create a safe space for Anurak to share, but she knew what he was waiting for. He was waiting for her to comprehend what he just said.

"Our St. Bardo's?" she asked.

"Yes. Ours. And the boy – it was someone I knew, someone I had served with as an altar boy. Memories flooded into my mind, memories I had vaulted away as if they belonged at Fort Knox. It wasn't just that I didn't want to defend my client – I could no longer do it morally or ethically. I had been abused in much the same way."

Tears formed in Elena's eyes. She breathed some of that heart energy toward herself then and tried to hold them back, but one errant tear rolled down her cheek. "Oh Aidan, I mean Anurak. I am so, so sorry." She didn't know if she felt his pain, but she knew she felt pain, and a tremendous sadness permeating the room.

Simultaneously, Elena and Anurak closed their eyes in an effort to find the silent place from which this energy could be lifted. They remained in a meditative state for a few minutes, then opened their eyes. The energy was lighter, but the gray cloud around Anurak's feet was throbbing and pulling at him. Elena could see the enormous effort Anurak was expending trying to push it back down.

"Stop that," she said. "Stop pushing it back down. You have to let this go ... somehow, you have to let it go."

"Undoubtedly," Anurak replied, "but it is very stubborn energy. There is much pain, and I have held it for a very long time. I have chosen suffering I guess, and I know I must choose otherwise if I am to be free of it. I just ...." He trailed off without finishing the sentence.

"Did you tell anyone? Your superiors? Your counselor?"

"I did. We prayed. I recused myself from the case – actually my superior orchestrated my being recused."

"What about telling your story to someone outside the church? Shouldn't you confront them with this? Shouldn't you join with the others who are revealing what happened to them? You might be able to help those who are having trouble prosecuting their cases."

"No. I will not do that, Elena. Ask me to support those who've been abused, and I will do so, but join with them in prosecuting a case? No. To what end? That will only extend my suffering. No, I must release the pain and find forgiveness, for only forgiveness can unleash me from this energy that I carry with me.

"Ask me to assist with ways of preventing this from ever happening again, and I'm there one hundred percent, but dredging it up to confront someone who is no longer living – I cannot do that."

"Doesn't forgiveness require confrontation? Or bringing things into the open?" Elena asked.

"I've already facilitated that, Elena. I was able to anonymously divulge the information – not to the public – but to the individuals, their families and their attorneys, in a deposition. It is important that they pursue their cases for their own sake as well as the children of future generations. Multiple, high-profile cases will help to move immovable organizations to positive action. But I ...." Anurak hesitated. His eyes grew distant, then returned with a solemn, but peaceful look. "I may not be available when this case goes to trial. I am only here for a little while longer."

Only a little while longer?! Elena was surprised at the feeling of loss that surfaced in her heart. She had grown attached to Anurak. They were meeting two or three times a week, sometimes more, and their time together was so special. It was peaceful and healing. It was profoundly comforting to spend time with him. It had only been a few months, but she couldn't imagine life without him now.

"You're leaving? When?" she asked.

"Not right away. But I cannot stay here forever. I must continue my journey. This is not my path – and," he smiled gently, "it has become far too comfortable."

"You'll let me know, right? I mean, I won't just show up one day and find you gone, will I?" Elena could hear the tension in her own voice. She sounded like a child about to be abandoned by a parent. She took a breath to calm herself.

Anurak's face emitted a soft glow, forming a serene sort of smile that gently traveled from his lips to his eyes. "Yes, Elena. I will let you know. Our time together is not complete. I believe we will both know when it is done. And who knows, maybe the little cloud that follows me will be gone by then."

CHAPTER TWENTY-FIVE

The Dark Closet

The television in Elena's apartment had remained off since her breakdown after the fateful gallery opening. She glanced at it now and wondered if she should just wheel it out of her apartment like the final scene in the movie *Poltergeist*. Returning her attention to the stack of junk mail, the headlines from a weekly news magazine buried in the pile caught her eye. Another prominent member of the government had been charged with lying to Congress. *It seems as though the world itself is caught in a web of lies,* Elena thought as she tossed the magazine into the recycling bin without reading it. It was impossible to tell who was lying and who was telling the truth anymore – even the news media could not be trusted.

Satisfied at the space she had made at the small kitchen table, Elena wrapped her hair into a twisted bun, stuck a hair stick in it, and walked over to her painting area where two new canvases awaited her. She selected a broad, dry brush and began slowly moving it over the first canvas. Anurak had been coaching her on the use of mindfulness beyond meditation; being mindful of every action, even the simplest of tasks. She was applying this practice to her usual dry-brush exercise. Rather than the obligatory swipe when she didn't know what to paint, she mindfully covered every square inch of the canvas, allowing the still unformed images to reveal themselves to her. She watched as the dry bristles flickered against the weave of the canvas. She noticed the muscles in her hand and wrist and how they articulated with the movement of the brush. She noticed every hill and valley of the weave, the texture of the stretched cloth. It was stretched evenly, yet there was an almost imperceptible pucker at the points where the staples fastened it to the wood frame. Elena was an excellent craftsperson when it came to stretching and preparing canvases. No one could have seen these puckers, not even Elena, except during this slow, intentional exercise. The movement was almost hypnotic, and Elena began to feel one with the brush as if she herself were rippling against the canvas in a rhythmic waltz of artist and painting. She felt the soft vibration of inaudible music moving through the brush into her hand and up her arm. It was an exquisite feeling. She craved the vibration, sought to increase it and become one with it. She closed her eyes and allowed the vibrations to wash over her and draw her into the magical realm of the Ark once more.

Before her now was the familiar mystical canvas, awaiting her thoughts and questions – ready to reveal insights and profound wisdom. The brush in Elena's hand moved toward the canvas, drawing her attention to a dark space taking shape there. It was a rectangle and looked like a closet, with three solid sides, with a dark curtain defining the fourth. A tiny glimmer of light emitted from a square shape on one side. Elena recognized the space. It was the confessional, the place where she had revealed the sins of her youth to her parish priest. She saw herself there now; kneeling, trembling, her little list of sins in hand, waiting for the window to slide open revealing a frightening shadow looming on the other side of the frosted, pin-holed window.

Would this list be sufficient? Would the priest believe her? What kind of penance would she receive? She wasn't sure she had sinned at all since her last visit to the box, but a list was expected. She had run through the list of commandments. She didn't really know what a false god was, but she was pretty sure there weren't any in front of her. She kept the Sabbath. Mom and Dad made sure of that. Oh yes, Mom and Dad. She didn't always honor them. They reminded her often that she was sassy and disrespectful. "Don't talk back!" She'd heard that at least five or six times since her last confession.

Don't lie. Well, she knew she had done that. She lied about homework. She lied about brushing her teeth. She lied about cleaning her room, taking a bath, and just about anything she didn't really want to do but could appease her mother by saying it was done. Ten times seemed like a good number for that one.

Adultery. Well, she wasn't sure what that was, but it seemed to be about adults, so she was okay there.

Thou shall not steal. She hadn't stolen anything, except maybe a look or two at Bobby Miller. And covet was a strange word. She must not have committed that since she didn't know what it was. So that was it then. *I lied ten times and dishonored my parents six times* she said to herself as the door to the frosted window opened, casting its terrifying shadow of the man who would dole out her penance and absolve her of her terrible sins.

It was a lie. Elena had no idea how many times she had lied to her parents. Her confession itself was a lie building upon a habit of untruth. It wasn't entirely her fault. It was what she saw all around her. Her parents had lied and called it stretching the truth or, as her mother liked to say, "white lies." Apparently, there were degrees of lies, and some were acceptable depending upon their nature or some perceived greater good.

Streams of white and gray began to flow from the brush in Elena's hand. The brush swirled and raced about the canvas drawing a tangled mess of strings. Behind them an image of the planet emerged, strangled by the web that surrounded it. *Web of lies,* Elena thought. *One leads to another until the web becomes so prominent that its power is nearly inescapable.*

Details began to take shape beneath the web. Elena as a small child, telling a lie that caused a small web to start spinning around her. People, thousands, millions of images of people, all spinning the energy of deceit around themselves, forming webs that joined together as one massive mesh encompassing the globe. The webs thickened and became masks, like the masks Elena had seen in an earlier revelation until no one could see the truth of anyone else.

Thou shall not bear false witness, the inner voice whispered. *False. It means that which is not the Truth,* Elena thought. The highest truth she had learned was that everyone was an individualized expression of God and everyone was connected. If that were true, then the greatest of falsehoods would be *not* witnessing this greater Truth in one another. Witnessing only the mask, the false identity, was a lie that was disguising the entire world.

At that thought, the web on the canvas began to dissolve, as did the individual webs and masks. The millions of beings glowed now, brilliant in their perfection. The only strings that remained were beams of light connecting each of them into a greater, all-encompassing light. The light was so bright that the beings saw each other for the first time and as they did, the light grew brighter still.

Elena began to purposefully draw the mystical brush over the canvas, pulling the images into the brush with every stroke, like a vacuum cleaner sucking something up. As she swiped it to and fro the images disappeared into the brush. She could feel the grain of the bare canvas emerging once again. She could smell the pigments on her nearby palette, and she could hear the gentle purring of Moses, curled up in her papasan chair.

She was back. The blank canvases stood before her, and she knew what these two paintings would be. One would be *Web of Deception*, and the other would be *Emergence of Truth*.

CHAPTER TWENTY-SIX

Holiday Gatherings

Zak stood by the punch bowl dressed in a rented tuxedo. No trace of the scruffy field beard remained and the ponytail that had been threatening to grow had been neatly shaved away from his neck. He filled two cups and handed one to Elena.

"So glad you could be here, Elena. I can't imagine doing these university parties without you," Zak said. "You look amazing, by the way. A breath of fresh air in a stuffy room."

Elena took the cup and pushed back an errant strand of her chestnut hair, trying to reattach it to the bun she had painstakingly wound at the top of her head. Her fingers touched the rhinestone-studded hair sticks she had purchased to match the colorful sequins at the neckline of the silky white dress. She felt festive and just a bit like a goddess.

Elena smiled and took a sip of the punch. "I love a good party," she said. "Especially holiday parties." She gestured at all the holiday decorations, mostly Christmas-related with a few Hanukah items thrown in for political correctness. She was used to attending these events with Zak. They didn't bother her – they weren't much different than art openings. But Zak was much more introverted than she was. He hated these things.

Gina came gliding over to them in a green gown that wrapped snuggly around her voluptuous curves and ended in a dramatic flare at her feet. The neckline dropped well below her cleavage and was flourished with lace holly leaves that formed the single sleeve and flowed around the neckline and waist.

"Oh, Dr. Erdmann. I'm so glad I found you! I wasn't sure if you would be here. I know how much you hate these things. I've got ... Oh, I'm so sorry," she said, glancing at Elena. "I didn't mean to interrupt. I'm sure you don't want to hear details about our project while you are on a date."

Zak stiffened as if controlling an urge to roll his eyes and said, "It's not a date. I've told you before, Elena and I are friends. She comes to these God-awful things with me to keep me from running out the door. What have you got Gina?" His irritation was not even thinly disguised.

"Well, you needed some grad students for photography on the dig, and I've got four of them from the Fine Arts program. I'll need your signature on the forms so they can get credit and apply for grants. I'll have them ready for you on Monday."

"Great, Gina. Is that it? The pressing news?" Zak asked.

"Oh no. It's not just that. I've found someone willing to be the lead photographer, to direct the students and work with you on a strategic photography plan. His name is Allister Barrette." Gina cast a poorly-hidden glance at Elena as she mentioned the photographer's name. "Maybe you've heard of him? He's a top-notch commercial photographer, and he seemed to be excited about joining the team. He said it would be good for his portfolio and he'd like a chance to do something fun for the summer."

Elena held her smile in place. Inside she was wondering what this red-headed woman was trying to do. Did she know that Allister Barrette had been her major competitor when she was relying on photo shoots to pay the bills? Did she know how much they didn't like each other? *I bet Allister was happy to join the team. He would do anything to piss me off. He probably thinks he's beating me out of another shoot – but boy, is he wrong. There's no way I would go on this one.*

Zak caught his breath and shot a quick glance at Elena, then turned back to Gina and said, "That's great, Gina. Thanks for the update. Put his information on my desk on Monday, and I'll review it. Where's Dr. Mason? Did he go back home for the holidays?" Mason lived in Rhode Island but had taken a small apartment nearby for his stay as a visiting professor.

"Oh, no." Gina shook her head, causing her silken hair to fall gently over the bare shoulder on the sleeveless side of her dress. "He's here. Over there talking to some of the donors. We're spending ... umm, he's spending the holidays here. He's just going home for a day or two to check on his house, but then he'll be back. He wants to enjoy the holidays in New York. Can't blame him. It's stupendous, don't you think?" She looked at Elena, as if seeking agreement.

"Yes. Christmas in New York is special, I guess," Elena said. She wanted to say more, but she held her tongue and sent rays of positive energy from her heart toward Gina, but the rays of light seemed to fall downward toward the green folds of fabric concealing Gina's feet.

"Thanks again, Gina," Zak said as he placed a hand on Elena's back, steering them both across the room. "Good God, that woman can be annoying," Zak muttered.

"Do you think she knows about Allister and me?" Elena asked. "I mean, that can't be a coincidence, can it? Who would look for that level of a commercial photographer to go on an excavation? It doesn't even make sense."

"I don't know. Gina is brilliant with translations and ancient languages, but her people skills are a bit off. I think she would flirt with a mannequin if she thought it would get her somewhere. I'll be glad when the year is over, to tell you the truth. And, I'm glad she's taken a liking to Mason – though I can't imagine why. It keeps her away from me, and the attention seems to be doing him a lot of good."

"Mason? You mean Dr. Gerhardt Mason? Wasn't he your professor at NYU for a while?"

"Yes, now he's the Associate Director of Egyptology at Brown. We brought him in as an adjunct for the year, and Brown was willing to give him leave. He's helping with the Qasr Ibrim research, and he's going with us to Bir Tawil."

"I remember him. He was kind of a mousy little guy, right? The one that wore bow ties to school every day? He always looked exactly like I thought an archaeology professor would look – until I met you, that is." Elena laughed out loud.

"Yeah, that's him. But you should see him now. He looks totally different. He's wearing colorful jackets, lost the bow ties, and he even shaved that ancient goatee." Zak ran his fingers over his own recently shaven face.

"Yeah, wouldn't want to let a scruffy field-beard become your signature," Elena chuckled. "I do like you much better with a clean face. Like my mother always said, 'You have such a beautiful face – why hide it?'"

Zak smiled. "Hey, there's Dr. Patterson. Let's go talk to him. I need to do a little schmoozing. Lots of grants and permissions in the works."

"That's why I'm here," Elena said. "Though I don't know why I agreed to this. I don't want you to go back, you know. I get it. I understand why, but I'm so worried about you and the others. I wish you'd just give it up – but I know...."

Zak blew some air through pursed lips. "I know. I know. But I'll never be able to let it rest if I don't go back. You've got your painting to express what happened." His eyes wandered for just a second as that nagging thought that it was all a delusion came back to him. "But I've only got this: science, numbers, measurements, protocols. I ... I can't explain how intense the desire to go back is. It's like, well it's a lot like the feeling we had when we were there, pulled into something we weren't expecting. I'm being pulled by something. I have to go."

Elena nodded. She knew this in her heart. She really didn't want him to go, but she did understand.

"It's actually a pretty done deal now, other than the paperwork and schmoozing. Mason has pulled some amazing satellite images. The area is more than just the burial ground of the Ark. There's evidence that a whole civilization once lived there. We've even found traces of a dried riverbed, which would have made a settlement there plausible. There will be years of research at this site, and the university will get great publicity from it."

Elena felt a sudden twinge in her heart. Bringing another culture to light, connecting with artisans of ancient civilizations, were the reasons she enjoyed the digs. A part of her suddenly wanted to go – certainly, she wanted to be there instead of Allister. But no, she wasn't going. She had no desire to relive the nightmare of the shootings, and she had another task before her. She needed to convince Renee that her next show would be an installation – not something art agents were eager to support.

Zak and Elena joined a group of tuxedoed men. They laughed at their jokes, listened to their stories, and carried on light conversation about previous digs. They even shared a little about Bir Tawil, Zak hinting there was more significant potential there than anyone might imagine.

CHAPTER TWENTY-SEVEN

Installation Proclamation

Elena's musings over a paragraph she had just read in Paul's book were interrupted by a knock at the door. Peering through the peephole, she recognized Renee's back. Renee was chatting with someone on the phone and had turned away from the door. She was wearing a red wool coat, belted at the waist and flaring out over crisply creased, gray slacks. Her short black hair was trimmed perfectly at the nape of her neck, and the open black bag over her shoulder was enormous. Elena wondered what she carried in that thing and how expensive her chiropractor bills must be.

At the sound of the locks sliding open, Renee turned around, ended the call, and opened her arms to Elena, bag sliding to her armpit. "You look enchanting, Elena! No more deep crevices under your eyes. Not skin and bones anymore, either."

She held Elena in a long embrace, then dropped her bag and slipping out of her coat, walked briskly toward the studio. "And you've been painting!" Her brilliant smile grew more luminous as she nodded approval toward Elena and began surveying the paintings arranged purposefully about Elena's studio.

On one side of the room sat seven canvases with dark images, colors unlike Elena's typical style – except for the colorful auras at the edge of each of them. She stopped at the canvas in the center, the one Elena had shown her previously, the jaws of a crocodile ready to swallow the viewer as its powerless prey.

Walking from one to the next, Renee studied the first set of paintings. "Dark. A little unsettling, but the colorful edges are intriguing," she said, her enthusiasm wavering a bit.

Looking away from the dark canvases, Renee moved toward the opposite side of the room, where the contrasting images were displayed. She glanced back and forth, noticing that every dark painting had a matching one filled with colorful light; the same, yet very different. Her step was noticeably lighter, as was her energy. She seemed to pick up the energy of the brighter, more colorful paintings.

"I love this series, Elena," she said. "There's a similar feel to the ethereal teasers we placed in the last show. And those were really well received. But I still don't get why you want to hang them across the room? Wouldn't you want the sets to hang side-by-side so the viewers will see both perspectives? If you hang them this way, people will flock to the beautiful ones and quite honestly, they may be repelled by the others. You will be taking up valuable gallery space with paintings no one will ever want to buy. Who would put these in their homes or offices, or anywhere, for that matter? She paused a moment, and Elena waited silently for her to continue.

"Maybe, if you hung them side-by-side someone might think about hanging them together as a diptych. They'd make great conversation art that way. But even then, these gloomy images are going to be a hard sell."

Elena smiled. She watched Renee's responses as she looked from one side of the room to the other, shaking her head almost imperceptibly. Elena gave her a moment and then started.

"Renee, I need you to set something up for me. The paintings are going to be a part of an installation. All of them. It will have to be a large space, much larger than this room. There will need to be at least two or three hundred feet between the dark set and the light set. And I'll need the better part of a month to install it." She paused. Renee's eyes were darting back and forth as if considering the space. Her brow was crinkling, and her head was moving in a much more obvious "no" than before. Elena could almost see the words, "not possible," taking shape in Renee's mind.

Elena went on, "The paintings will not be for sale until the last day of the show." Renee's brow crinkled more tightly while her eyebrows arched, revealing the next word forming behind them which was probably something like "*incredulous!*"

Before the word could escape Renee's mouth, Elena continued. "And ... umm, I need an advance on the sales."

Renee's mouth fell open at this last part. "Have you lost your mind? How do you expect me to sell this to a gallery? Are they supposed to just give up a month's revenue and hope for the best? And then give you money on a show that might possibly sell only half of its pieces? What gallery is going to host this show, Elena? Installations are for museums. They don't sell. Installations can't be taken home at the end of the show. And even the pieces that can be taken home ... Who is going to come back on the final day to buy the paintings? If they like them, you need to close the deal while they are so enthralled that they don't want to take a chance on someone else buying it. I don't think I'm your girl for this one, Elena."

"Trust me, Renee. People will want to come back. They will mark it on their calendars. There is a place for this show. If not a gallery, a museum. But I still need time and money up front. This is going to happen Renee. You will want to be a part of this."

Elena knew what she was suggesting was unusual, over-the-top even, but she waited for Renee to get past the shock and begin considering the possibilities.

Renee glanced again at the paintings lining the walls of Elena's studio. "Why not here at Westbeth? They've got a large space, and their mission is to support the arts without concerns about profit. Have you checked the schedule?"

"It's not about the schedule Renee. The space downstairs isn't large enough for what I have in mind, and it has too many windows that would have to be blacked out. Besides, Westbeth tends to shy away from highlighting an individual resident – especially for a long run."

Elena began to explain the details of her installation. "The darker paintings will be at the front of the space, the light-filled ones would be hung in matching order at the back. The area between the two sets will be a walk-through experience. The viewer will be enveloped in swirls of light as they pass through carefully placed lasers, holograms, and 3D projection screens. In the final chamber, there will be a promise of something to be revealed on the day of the closing." Elena spread out a series of sketches and explained in detail how the show would be designed.

"I promise you, Renee, the experience will be transformative. People will not leave the gallery without purchasing the limited number of tickets available for the closing day."

Renee watched as Elena explained the experiential artwork. It was as if the lasers she described emanated from her as she spoke. Her entire face changed. Something was glowing that appeared to shine through the cells of her face and arms and legs. Renee opened and closed her eyes. The light was still there. A tingling sensation ran up and down her arms. "How long do you need?" she asked reluctantly. "And how much of an advance?"

Elena smiled and motioned for Renee to sit with her at the table. Renee cast an astonished look at the empty chair – she'd never seen it uncovered before – and took a seat as Elena put the kettle on for tea, then opened her notebook with details about timing, space, and costs for the project. It was an enormous undertaking and a considerable risk. But then, Elena was unique. She was the client art agents longed for. Galleries fought over her. She had a large following of extremely wealthy clients who bought her paintings as if they were red-hot investments. They loved her, and they loved her work. Her paintings fit well in their homes; not just complimenting their décor, but providing unique conversation pieces. The proposal was definitely a risk, but Renee quickly realized it was one worth taking. She would sell the idea to someone. Somehow.

***

Across town, Judith and Blake, owners of the Whitmer Gallery, sipped caramel macchiatos and looked around their expansive space and the exhibit that was about to close. Less than half of the paintings displayed *sold* stickers. Paintings, in general, were not selling very well. Even the most sought-after artists did not bring in enough revenue to support the gallery's considerable expenses. They pored over the spreadsheets in front of them, wondering what they could do because something definitely had to be done if they were going to keep the business open.

Judith stood, leaning her tall, slender body over the work table. She wore skinny black leggings and a burgundy blazer that highlighted her short crop of white hair. Sparkling diamond studs adorned each ear. "Maybe we should consider a pottery exhibit. Utilitarian items tend to sell well," she said.

Blake's head was moving back and forth in a negative response. Blake, Judith's gender-fluid partner, was wearing a short skirt, tights, and a colorful tank, a stark contrast to yesterday's skin-tight black jeans, starched white shirt, and Texas-style belt buckle. Blake's short brown hair worked with whatever the day's desired gender presentation was.

"No," Blake said. "I love creative clay work as much as anyone, but that's not what we started here. Our whole reason for starting the gallery was to support fine art and still make a living doing it. Shifting away from conceptual art might bring in more money, but it's not who we are. We need something new. Something edgy and entirely unique."

Blake pointed to the spreadsheet in front of them. "I think we can afford one more extravagant venture that will either make us or break us. What do you think?"

Judith straightened up, a tenuous smile on her face. "I think it's all or nothing. Let's go for it. Let's look for something out of the ordinary and embrace the next truly brilliant idea that comes through that door," she said, gesturing toward the gallery entrance.

They agreed to remain open-minded to infinite possibilities and even the most outlandish ideas. Little did they know just how outlandish was the idea headed their way.

CHAPTER TWENTY-EIGHT

Bearing Truth

Elena slid the bar lock back, unfastened the chain, and opened the door to Anurak. He wore no jacket but donned heavier robes than usual. It was March, and even though spring was attempting to emerge, it was still quite cold.

"I was just thinking about you," Elena said. "And here you are. It's like magic."

"Not magic at all, Elena. You should know by now that your thoughts anticipate and create the world around you."

"Oh. I do," she replied, "but it is still such a surprise sometimes. Really, I was just finishing up these paintings and wishing you would come by to see them."

"And so here I am," he said, his clear blue eyes sparkling. He took off an outer layer of robes – it was apparently like a coat, and walked toward the canvases in the studio area of Elena's apartment. The sun was pouring in through the windows, casting them into a silhouette from the doorway. He stopped when he got to the point where the light was just right. It was the angle that Elena stood to the windows when she painted.

"Stunning!" Anurak said. "The colors are so vibrant, especially in the second one. It seems as if they cast as much light as your window does today. I love how the streams of light all connect into one brighter stream. It reminds me of a wedding ceremony I watched once. The bride and groom were touching the flames of two candles together to light the unity candle. As the smaller flames touched, they created one bigger flame."

"Exactly!" Elena exclaimed. "That's exactly what it's like when two people see the light in one another. They each become brighter."

"Like you and Zak?" Anurak's tone seemed to be half asking and half mocking. Elena still could not understand how Anurak knew so much about Zak without having ever met him, let alone about who they were together. Yet, as much as he seemed to know, he always seemed to be seeking more information about Zak. It was perplexing, to say the least.

"Yes. I guess so. But that's not what I was getting at. What I meant was that when people fail to see the light in one another, they diminish the effects of light in themselves and in a way, the world. The first one is about deceit, or about seeing only what is false and, I guess, believing what is false. It builds a kind of energetic wall until no one can see anything that is really true."

"Profound thought, very insightful," said Anurak. He was backing up from the paintings now to get a better view. He almost tripped over Moses who was wrapping himself in figure eights around his legs.

"He's hungry," Elena said, heading toward the kitchen to give him his third breakfast of the day. "He thinks anytime there is someone near him stirring in any way it's time to eat again. It's amazing he can still jump to the windowsill, he's getting so fat."

Anurak was still standing by the paintings when Elena leaned down to pour a bit of food in Moses' bowl and noticed that the cloud that usually clung to Anurak's feet was dissipating. It was almost gone. It hadn't occurred to her before, but it was the first time Moses had ever curled around Anurak's legs.

"It's almost gone," she said.

"I know," Anurak answered without turning around. It was uncanny how he knew her thoughts. It was as if he had been in the Ark with her and the team. Sometimes she could hear him too, and at other times it seemed as if there was a soundproof wall between them.

"Good," said Elena. "I'm glad you're working on it. Seems like you're letting go of some of your anger. It's no wonder that you've held on to it for so long, but it is a beautiful thing that you're letting it go. Your energy is so much brighter. In fact, you've inspired some more colorful images that I might just add to the second painting."

Anurak smiled and took a seat on the empty kitchen chair. "How are the excavation plans coming? For Zak and his team, I mean."

There it was again. That never-ending interest in what Zak was doing. It was understandable, she guessed. Anurak knew nearly everything about their discovery. He knew about their commitment to sharing the message but not the Ark itself. And he was an advanced soul, probably interested in helping them keep their promise. It was no wonder he was concerned about what Zak would be doing next.

"Pretty far along now. Several grants have come through, and the university is behind the project one hundred percent. In fact, the regents are in their glory, anticipating the prestige that discovering a new site will bring to the school – and of course, they expect that will bring in more donors."

"And what about their safety? I know you are concerned about that," he asked.

"Josh Pearson is heading up their security team. Josh was one of the members of the team that entered the Ark. He has ongoing communications with Egyptian law enforcement. They've been pretty cooperative, according to Zak, and he expects them to get much more so once he reveals the ultimate subject of the dig." She tensed as she said this, then let out a semi-constrained sigh.

"It's that part that worries me," she said. "It makes the trip more dangerous, and I'm not sure bringing the Ark back is the right thing to do. I feel so conflicted over it. I want to be there with him, but I just can't go. It's as if my feet were planted in cement. Every time I even think about going, a heavy weight seems to gather around my feet, keeping me planted right here. And then, there's the upcoming show. The installation is taking up most of my attention. I couldn't leave now if I wanted to."

"When you close your eyes, Elena, what do you see?" Anurak asked.

Elena plopped into her papasan and swiveled it to face Anurak. She closed her eyes and brought Zak into her mind. She paused there, just reflecting on his energy. Always so bright and blue and peaceful. She loved looking at this view of him. Within the radiating rays of blue and purple light streaming from him, a great white stream of light rose up. It reached into the sky, joining other streams as it rose. It merged with hers, and she could feel the connection. It felt good. It felt right. But then, she noticed other energies around Zak. They were not so bright. They were cloudy, murky even. They were dense, so dense that the light was difficult to perceive within them, even though it was there. This did not feel so good. She opened her eyes.

"I see Zak in all his truth and light," she said. "But I see others around him that are not so bright. They reach for him and try to steal his energy."

"And do they succeed?" Anurak asked.

Elena closed her eyes again, though she really didn't want to. The shadowy energy was painful to watch when she was not inside the realm of the Ark.

"No. They don't," she answered with a partially reassured look on her face. "They don't succeed. In fact, they grow more dense with every attempt."

"And that is the way of it," Anurak said. "Those who steal, lose. Those who give, gain. You've painted this in an earlier painting, yes?"

"Yes, *The Culture of Giving* and *The Culture of Theft*. It seems that everything really comes down to the theme of those two paintings," she said. "In fact, I think that if you give directly to someone who is trying to take something from you, you not only receive more than you gave, you help to dissipate some of the dense energy that binds them." Elena paused as a thought popped into her mind. She was suddenly reminded of the energy exchange that didn't take place between her and Gina at the holiday party. Anurak waited silently as if he knew she had a question.

"Anurak. When I was at the holiday party last December, I ran into Zak's assistant. There's something about her that bothers me. Her energy is so, hmm, not exactly dark, but definitely not vibrant. It seems contained in some way that keeps it dim and cold. She did something that seemed to be an intentional affront to me – even though we don't know each other – and I attempted to send her some peaceful energy. It seemed clear that she wasn't coming from a good place and I thought if I went to my heart and radiated some loving energy, it would make a difference. But I could see the energy that I sent. It fell to her feet and just dissipated. It was the strangest energy exchange – or non-exchange – I had ever seen."

"Is there a question?" Anurak asked.

"Yes. Of course, there is. What was that? Why did the energy just fall to her feet? I've used this flow of heart energy before and had people shift their energy before my eyes. I've had insulting clerks suddenly become helpful. I've seen scary people on the street suddenly look less menacing and lift their heads to smile at me. What happened when I sent this energy to Gina?"

"Gina?" Anurak said as if it was a word he had never heard of before and was trying it out to see how it sounded. Then he went on, "Sometimes, a person becomes so entangled in their false beliefs about themselves and others that they build a sort of energetic wall. It's a wall made of fear, and it can be quite powerful – a false god protecting a false image, you might say. And that false image can make the inner light, that which might receive the energy you were sending, more difficult to reach."

"I wonder," Elena said. "Do you think Zak bringing the Ark back or showing it to the world will help people to see the light in one another? Or will it cause more fear and the kind of walls that fear encourages?"

"That remains to be seen," Anurak answered.

CHAPTER TWENTY-NINE

Traveler of Interest

Josh turned the steering wheel a little to the left and cut the engine, settling in for a long afternoon. Sometimes surveillance assignments required the use of a car and Josh was grateful there was one available from the firm. He didn't own one, and neither did any of his friends.

It was a cushy vehicle; satellite radio, onboard Wi-Fi, and dual climate control – not that anyone was sitting in the passenger seat, but it was a cool feature anyway. He positioned himself so he could watch the revolving-door entrance of the building and still work on his tablet. Double-duty for the firm, and the university had him multitasking like a workaholic.

Editing an Excel file of initial excavation groups and security teams, he noticed the notification icon on his NSA email. *Tom. He must have finished his research on the new team.* Josh opened the email, surprised to find it was additional information on Aidan and Oliver Quinn.

The report began with Tom's informal summary and ended with detailed cell phone activity. *Awesome! He got the cell phone information.* Josh's excitement quickly waned as he realized Tom would not have sent this to him if he didn't think it was significant. He glanced up at the revolving door. There was no activity. Still, he had to keep a line of vision on the door while he read the report.

> *AIDAN QUINN – ADDITIONAL RESEARCH: More information has been uncovered about Quinn's departure from the Church. His writing became increasingly challenging, and the Church didn't just dissolve his vows – they excommunicated him. After that, the subject spent time at a Buddhist monastery in Tibet, where he changed his name to Anurak. He then continued his travels using an inheritance from his parents to fund some of the expenses, but most of it, as we know, was paid for by his brother Oliver.*

Interesting. Excommunication might be a motive to cause trouble, thought Josh. He scrolled further, one eye still on the revolving door.

CELL PHONE RECORD SUMMARY:

OLIVER QUINN - We finally gained access to subject's call records. They indicate many international calls but mostly to a number that has been confirmed as his brother's. Others, primarily to numbers in Egypt may have been to set up his Bir Tawil trip and possibly some business calls for PAXton International.

AIDAN E. QUINN – Subject has had the same cell phone number since his parish assignment in Kenosha. Most of the calls over the past few years are to his brother. GPS information matches travel locations except for the last one which is a bit of a mystery.

A man in jogging shorts and T-shirt exited the revolving door. It was not his subject. Josh scrolled down to the cell-phone records on the next page, confirming that most of Oliver's calls were to his brother. The GPS information for Aidan's cell phone began on the next page.

The list of locations matched the travel history and included all of the alleged Ark locations. He scrolled further through several pages of similar places and then to the last page. There was just one. It was listed as his current location or last known location. Josh's mouth fell open when he saw it. He clicked back to the phone call location. He opened the previous report and reviewed the dates and travel records, then returned to the GPS records. The current location couldn't be right? Could it?

Josh watched as a woman in a very short skirt and stiletto heels exited the revolving door. She wasn't his subject either. He picked up the cell phone and texted Tom.

"WTF?" he clicked send.

The response did not come as a text. Instead, Tom was calling him. "How is that possible? The location, I mean," Josh asked.

"Dunno buddy." Tom's voice was a bit warbled by the car's audio system. "It doesn't make sense. His last record of travel was to Aksum. He made calls from there. He hasn't left Aksum – at least by air or ship. But his phone has. He's definitely an interesting character. Not that any of this makes him a suspect, but the information is interesting."

Josh was running his hand across his scalp. His hair was getting a little longer now, and he liked the spongy feel of it. "Okay. Thanks, Tom. Let me know if you find anything else. And let me know if he moves."

"You bet, Josh. We're watching, but funny thing. The GPS signal cut out completely a couple of months ago like the battery went completely dead – or it was disabled."

"Shit. This is beyond coincidence, Tom."

"Yep, we think so too. Keeping an eye out as best we can. If anything surfaces, we'll let you know."

Josh ended the call and stroked his chin. He was tapping his finger lightly on the tablet. Something definitely did not add up about Aidan Quinn. How the hell did his phone end up in New York while he was still in Aksum? There were no travel records of any kind after he went to Aksum. Yet here he was in New York, and his GPS was disabled.

Grabbing the phone again, Josh sent a text to Zak.

"More information on our traveler of interest. Need to meet. Busy until 4pm."

The reply came a few minutes later. "Here? At 4:30?"

"Yes," Josh typed. "cu then."

***

Zak entered the missing details on the most recent conservation plan submitted by one of the grad students. *Greg will be an asset in the field,* he thought. There was little missing from this plan, and only Zak could have filled in the blanks. The day was getting closer, and Zak's excitement was growing. Finally, he would be able to begin this journey into the unknown civilization referred to on the Karta and maybe, reveal the Ark to the world.

A knock on his office door interrupted Zak's reverie. He jumped at the sound. The school had grown quiet over the last hour. Most of the students were gone, and only Mason, Gina, and a couple of grad students remained in the lab. "Come in," he said minimizing the file on his screen.

It was Josh, a file folder and tablet in his hands. If a black man could look pale, Zak was convinced this was what it looked like. Josh's face was the color of ashes the morning after a campfire.

"What's up, Josh? You look umm, troubled." Terrified was more like it, considering the look on Josh's face, but Zak was minimizing.

"I told you I thought there was something odd about the guy who claimed ownership of Bir Tawil and his brother. I've been following up on that angle, and I just got some very odd and concerning information from ... from my sources." Josh never said NSA aloud, but Zak knew that's who he was talking about.

"Fill me in." Zak hoped the information wouldn't stall their plans, but he was glad that Josh was being so thorough.

"Well, take a look for yourself." Josh opened the latest reports on his tablet and passed it to Zak.

Scrolling with his index finger, Zak began reviewing the reports. Airline travel showed a startling similarity to alleged Ark sites. Cellphone data confirmed one of the brothers was in Kansas City and the other in the locations listed. That was intriguing, but Josh had been hinting at this for a while. It didn't seem entirely new.

"So, this confirms the locations you were concerned about then?" Zak asked.

"Oh, yeah. For sure, but there's more. Take a look at the last page of the cell GPS data."

Zak's eyes narrowed, wondering how Josh was able to get GPS data on a hunch. He swiped the tablet to bring up the last page, his eyes scanning the text. His eyebrows arched slightly as he looked up. "He's here in New York?" Zak asked, his curiosity growing.

"Yes. In New York. But here's the thing. None of the travel information indicates his return to the states – and the search was pretty thorough. He shouldn't be here. He should still be in Ethiopia."

Ethiopia? Zak hadn't really paid much attention to the destination concerns, but Ethiopia was more than just a possible Ark location. It was reasonably close to Bir Tawil and had ties to Lake Tana, another location mentioned on the Karta. He squinted his eyes to get a better view, and then remembered to just swipe his thumb and index finger to make the screen larger.

"I see," he said. "That's odd. Who is this guy again?"

"The King of Bir Tawil is Oliver Quinn. He lives in Kansas City. He owns an international business that has something to do with computers called PAXman International. He placed a flag...." Josh reached for the tablet. "Here, let me show you." He brought up the image of the flag. "He placed a flag in the ground in Bir Tawil that bears an uncanny resemblance to the flag of the Holy Roman Empire."

Zak looked up from the image. "Holy Roman Empire? That's ... I don't know *what* that is. Interesting? Concerning? You think he's here trying to see what we're up to?"

"Not him," Josh replied. "His brother, the ex-priest, Aidan. There're copies of everything for you in the file folder."

Josh took the tablet back as Zak began flipping through the folder. Clicking through to the background information on Aidan, Josh handed the tablet back to Zak. "Aidan is the one who has been doing the traveling under the guise of writing articles about world religions for the Vatican," he said. "But they excommunicated him four years ago and cut off all ties with him. Oliver has been funding all of his travels ever since."

Zak began scrolling through the background information on Aidan E. Quinn. He stopped on the page that showed additional names.

Aidan Quinn. Aidan E. Quinn. Father Aidan Quinn. Anurak. *Anurak! Holy Christ!*

Zak felt the blood in his legs turn to ice and travel up his arms, spine, and neck. He could hear the blood rushing through his ears and feel his eyes bulging in their sockets. He dropped the tablet on the desk and grabbed the file folder as he strode to the door and grabbed his jacket from its hanger.

"What? What did you see?" Josh asked. His voice sounded alarmed by Zak's reaction.

"This guy has been hanging around with Elena. They're together all the time. He's a monk – or posing as one."

194

With that, Zak was gone. He left Josh sitting in the leather chair by his desk, the tablet in one hand and the other hand running itself over his scalp.

CHAPTER THIRTY

The Grass Is Greener

The view outside Elena's studio window was a welcome one. Winter had been harsh, dumping mountains of snow on the city and blowing frigid temperatures through its streets. Finally, spring temperatures were beginning to melt the snow. It was an unusually slow process here by the river where it remained much colder than areas farther away, but Elena wouldn't have traded her apartment or its view for any other place on earth.

Amidst the still melting mounds of snow, verdant blades of grass were beginning to unfold in small patches across the street. Apple trees lining that portion of the road had tiny hints of buds, and the minuscule flecks of purple on the ground beneath them hinted that crocuses were about to burst through the winter mulch. Her own side of the street was obscured by her eleventh-floor view, but the scene on the other side of the street lent certainty to the hope of spring.

Admiring the view and the brilliant blue sky behind it, Elena could hear her mother's voice saying "The grass is always greener on the other side of the street." Elena chuckled as she thought, *No mom. The grass is greener right where I am.*

It was true. She loved her apartment. She loved the studio where a freshly painted series was accumulating against the walls. She had been blessed with a truly amazing friendship with Zak, a terrific agent, galleries that sought her work, and she had this wonderful budding friendship with Anurak. He was her mentor, friend and confidant and she believed the feeling was mutual. Yes, she was abundantly blessed, and there was nothing that anyone else had that she desired.

Two freshly stretched canvases were lying on the ever-present drop cloth that protected the floor of her studio. She placed one on an easel, then looked doubtfully at the other. She wasn't quite sure what the contrast would be for this set. One would be about the deepest needs and desires of a person being met. The other would depict need and unfulfilled desire.

As she had done for several of the other sets, Elena picked up a dry brush and began pulling it across the surface, intentionally left un-treated to allow the washes of bright color to penetrate the outer edges the way she liked. Inspired by the metaphors of greener grass, Elena began making short upward strokes with the dry brush as if she were laying down individual blades of grass. With every stroke, she felt her own energy shift, her heart opening more fully, and her sense of wholeness increasing. Still holding the dry brush, she backed away from the blank canvas and sat mindfully in her papasan chair, closing her eyes. Following the sound of her breath, Elena quickly found the quiet place where images of blades of grass rippled on the inner screen of her mind, gently blowing in an invisible breeze. The undulating blades fell into a peaceful rhythm with her breath, and the subtle vibrations that had become so familiar carried her through the no-longer-strange portal to the realm of the Ark.

Standing before the mystical canvas that had become the backdrop for her Ark revelations, Elena watched a vast expanse of greenery taking shape on the canvas. The vibrant landscape reminded her of the many times she had looked out her mother's kitchen window, wondering what magic their neighbor used to keep his grass so green. Two yards, side by side, separated by a shiny chain-link fence, exhibited varying lengths and shades of green. Yes, Mr. Field's lawn was the most beautiful shade of emerald green she had ever seen. The grass in her own yard was a little bent, the blades often scorched, and shades of ochre and umber blemished their natural green. The lawn needed cutting. Patches here and there required more seed, more shade, or more sun. She laughed gently to herself as she heard her mother's voice again, "The grass is always greener on the other side of the fence, dear."

But there it was. It really did seem greener. But it wasn't. In fact, crossing over the fence had revealed that her own yard was greener from her neighbor's point of view. From his side, he could see the brown patches in his yard and the apparent lush greenery of hers.

"The grass is actually greener right where I am," she reiterated. By grass, she meant more than plant life covering the earth and, by "where I am" she meant more than her childhood home, more than her Westbeth apartment. She meant a place in mind, and that place had been forever changed by the experience of the Ark. Since encountering it, she had discovered a place within her mind where the grass was greener, the sky bluer, and everything was unfathomably more beautiful. It was the place where the perfect idea of color originated.

197

Here, there was the sweet, exquisite idea of green. It was a perfect green, and it was so incredibly vibrant it seemed to almost sing to her. And though the colors of her earthly palette were lovely, the hues of nature stunning, they could never achieve the same brilliance and perfect vibration as the divine idea that manifested them.

The verdant blades of grass on the mystical canvas began to shudder as if a husky wind were blowing their tiny shapes against one another. Elena wondered, *Does a blade of grass ever wish to be the one standing next to it? Does it look at itself and see something inferior. A streak of brown that should have been green? Preposterous. They are all the same. No. Not the same. Each slightly different on the outside, but each the expression of one perfect divine idea of a blade of grass.*

The blades of grass stretched and grew taller. They changed both color and shape. The view telescoped, the blades of grass blending together, forming large areas of land, then masses of land, and finally, a speck of green on a planet that receded even further into an expansive field of stars. From this view, the blade of grass could no longer be seen at all. It was not separate from the other blades of grass, nor was it separate from the planet it grew upon. Neither were the people who populated it separate. Elena wondered from how great a distance could she behold this scene? Was there a space where even the planets and stars would seem to merge together into one mass of light and energy? The desire to be something else, to have something else seemed absurd from this point of view.

Elena recalled times when she had wished to be someone else, something other than herself. Some desires were an inner calling to be more of her true self. Others were a distraction, things that drew her away from who she really was. She remembered wanting desperately to be more like her friend Krystal when they were very young. Krystal was a musician. She played the flute and piano. Krystal had a collection of music that made Elena's head spin, everything from pop to classical. *How could she afford to buy it all? How could she even listen to it all?* Elena wished to be Krystal. But alas, Elena's attempts to play an instrument were disappointing. They sounded like music only to her own ears. No. That was wrong. They didn't even sound like music to Elena's ears. She tried to learn. She took a variety of classes. Guitar.

Voice. Piano. But nothing sang to her like the streams of paint that flowed from her brush when she began to paint.

Frustrated. Sad. Elena had taken to heart the words of her guitar teacher, who said, "There's nothing more I can teach you, Elena. While you are so busy trying to make music where there is none, who will paint the images you have been sent here to render?"

Elena had set aside the guitar that day. *Who was this man?* she had wondered. What had he seen in her that she had missed herself? How could a guitar teacher have had such insight? Had she even told him she loved to paint? She didn't remember having done so.

There is nothing my neighbor has that I do not already have, she thought. If I am one with all that is, what could possibly be missing? And, what can be gained by the practice of jealousy, of wanting what you think you need?

With a sudden whoosh of light, the image on the mystical canvas reversed its motion, zooming into the previous images, the stars, the planets, Earth, masses of land, yards, and blades of grass. The blades were huge, towering over Elena until she felt as though she could walk through them. They quivered and pulsed, and the motion drew her in toward the canvas. She was surrounded by undulating streams of emerald light; subtle, familiar vibrations stirred within her. Through the blades of grass, the tarp on her studio floor came into view. The shuddering colors became still, and Elena could hear the breath moving through her body. She felt the sensation of fingers and toes and a solid brush in her hand. Her eyes fluttered open, confirming her return to the studio. One blank canvas sat before her on an easel, the other lay waiting on the floor next to it.

Wouldn't it be funny, Elena thought, *if these two paintings were identical other than the perspective?*

One painting could be a view over a fence looking toward the setting sun, the other could be the opposite view, from the other side of the fence, the sun reflecting off the trees. Two sides of the same fence, each displaying a perfect, lush lawn and an abundant garden.

That would be a good start, but there would need to be more, much more. For viewers to truly understand the message, they would need to feel empty – and not in a good way. The first painting would have to foster the feelings of lack, despair, desire, jealousy, a burning desire to have what was just out of reach. The other would have to inspire an assurance of abundance.

Unsure how the paintings would take shape, Elena began pouring the colorful wash that would underlie both paintings; one would remain prominent, the other nearly obscured. Maybe they would be titled *The Grass is Greener* and *Right Where I AM.*

Setting the jars of paint aside for a moment, Elena wrote in her journal:

> *When you know you are one with the All-ness, centered in an "I AM" awareness, you will not covet anything, for you shall realize all that you desire is already yours.*

CHAPTER THIRTY-ONE

A Warning

The train to Greenwich was packed. The smell of body odor was stronger than it would have been earlier in the day or later at night. A full day's sweat radiated from bodies dressed in suits with ties, pretty blouses, trim blazers, tattered T-shirts and skin-tight gym gear.

Zak gave his seat to an elderly woman with a cane. It wasn't an inconvenience. He was too nervous to sit anyway. The ride was agonizingly slow. Zak had been calling and texting Elena since he left the school, but she wasn't answering. *Where the hell is she? And what the hell is this Anurak guy doing with her? How many more stops, for Christ's sake?* Zak already knew the answer. There would be at least a dozen more and a significant delay at each one. It was rush hour, never a good time to make the trip, even by train.

Finally, Zak saw his stop coming into view. He glanced at his phone. Still no answer from Elena. The brakes screeched as the train came to a halt, Zak was at the doors like a racehorse hoofing the dirt at a starting gate. The doors opened, and he ran through the station and onto the street. Usually, a short, enjoyable walk, it seemed like a marathon now; *4th St., 8th St., Hudson, Greenwich, Washington ... finally!* The wind coming up off the river was cold, but Zak didn't feel it as he flew through the main doors. *Elevator or stairs? Eleven flights.* He pushed the elevator button, pushed it again then stood back where he could watch its progress. *Come on!*

There was a thump, a ding, and then the sound of the heavy, off-white doors sliding open. Zak rushed inside and hit the "Close Door" button, hoping no one else would enter. His hopes were dashed by a man carrying a grocery bag and a man-purse who grabbed the door and slid in just before the doors were closed. He pressed five. Zak grimaced and sucked in a breath.

The ascent seemed to take forever. He'd never noticed how slow and rickety the elevator was. The stop on five was almost unbearable; finally, the bell rang at eleven. The doors opened so slowly Zak reached for the edge, trying to pull them faster. As Zak stepped off the elevator, he saw a man dressed in white robes walking toward him so slowly, he appeared to be moving in a slow-motion replay.

Zak was not one to see auras or energy. In fact, other than his experience in the Ark, he'd never seen anything remotely like that. But this man seemed to be surrounded by a gentle, blue glow. Zak blinked his eyes, thinking he was witnessing some kind of optical illusion created by the lighting in the hallway.

The monk, if that's what he was, was not exactly smiling, but his lips had a peaceful upward turn to them. His eyes, the color of what? The sea near Hawaii? Lake Placid? They were blue, clear blue. You could almost see through them. Everything about this man's presence conflicted with what Zak had just read and surmised about him – or who he believed the man might be.

As they passed, *like ships in the night,* Zak thought, Anurak nodded and smiled. Zak instantly felt the pressure in his chest lessen and the pulsing of blood rushing past his ears slow down. The thunderous thumping of his heart quieted. He nodded back and continued toward Elena's door as the monk disappeared behind the elevator doors.

She must be home if he's just leaving. Unless he couldn't find her, either. But if she's there, why the hell didn't she answer my calls? His heart sped up a little, and so did his feet. Finally, at Elena's door, Zak began knocking, softly at first, then louder and more rapidly, his heart rate increasing with every unanswered knock. Finally, Zak heard the lock sliding open, the chain being removed.

"Where's the fire?" Elena said with a welcoming smile and a twinkle in her green eyes as she opened the door.

Zak looked positively terror-stricken. He was breathing hard, as if he'd just finished a long session on the treadmill. A file folder was clenched in his right hand. The brightness in Elena's heart quickly diminished as concern washed over her instead. "What's wrong, Zak? Are you okay?" she asked.

"I'm fine. Well no, I'm not fine, but it's not me. Why the hell haven't you answered your phone? I've been calling since I left the school," Zak said as he walked into the apartment.

Elena closed the door, the concern in her eyes becoming more of a question mark. "I'm so sorry," she said. "I put my phone in 'Do Not Disturb' mode and forgot to switch it back. Anurak and I were at the museum, and you know how I hate when cell phones go off there. But why are you so worried?" Zak's demeanor didn't make sense to her.

It certainly wasn't the first time she'd forgotten to reset the ringer on her phone. It wasn't unusual for him, either. "What's so urgent anyway?" she asked.

Zak moved toward the small kitchen table, noticing the other chair no longer held junk-mail but offered an open place to sit. He raised an eyebrow at Elena.

"I don't know." She knew what he was silently asking. The chair had been her junk-mail receptacle for the past few years. Instead of inviting visitors to sit, it shunned them. She felt safe that way. She hated sitting alone at the table facing an empty chair, and somehow the stacks of unopened mail had made it okay.

"It just seemed like it was time to open the space," she said. "It always felt kind of pathetic to sit across from an empty seat. It seems different now, more comfortable. Anurak and I have tea at the table a lot and talk about art and umm ... spiritual ideas."

"Anurak. There's the problem," Zak said, plopping the file folder on the table as he sat in the emptied chair. "He's not supposed to be here, and he's not who he says he is."

Elena scrunched her face and squeezed her eyebrows in a look that matched her words. "What the *hell* are you talking about?" she said. Zak had never been jealous. They'd never had that kind of relationship. He'd sometimes shared his dislike of the men she dated, but that was after he had at least met them. He hadn't even met Anurak, and she hadn't shared much about him with Zak.

"It's a long story, Elena. But I'm worried. I don't think he is who he says he is. Josh discovered something very concerning." He pointed at the file again.

"So now you're investigating my male friends?" she asked. Elena could feel heat surging through her veins, the hairs on her arms and back rising in anger. *Who the hell does he think he is?*

"No. It's not like that at all." Zak shook his head. "Really. His name just randomly appeared in Josh's research about the shootings in Bir Tawil. It all seemed like a coincidence at first, and I didn't even know the person he was investigating was Anurak. Josh just referred to him as Aidan Quinn."

Elena sat down in the other chair. Her temperature was slowly returning to normal, but a light chill began crawling up her spine. "Aidan is his given name," she said. "We knew each other as kids. We went to the same parochial schools. I think I told you that, but how did his name come up in Josh's research?"

Elena was genuinely curious now, but not frightened. It was Anurak after all, and he couldn't hurt a fly – literally. She'd seen him at the temple coaxing insects out of the building, but never squashing or spraying them. It was against his nature to harm anything.

Zak opened the file and turned it toward Elena. He pointed out the highlights, the destinations, the alleged Ark locations, Anurak's excommunication, and the bizarre GPS information. He explained the story of the King and Queen of Bir Tawil and their implied connection to Rome.

"I think Anurak, or Aidan, is here trying to get information out of you about the Ark and our return trip," Zak said when he was finished.

"That's impossible, Zak! Anurak is the most ... honest and spiritual person I've ever met. I can see through him, his energy, his essence. What I see is good, not some dastardly person with a deceptive plan. I think you're just paranoid." Elena's voice was an octave higher than usual. She could hear the stridency in her own voice and feel the rapid fluttering of her heart.

Zak's eyebrows arched at her last statement. "Paranoid? Really? I'm the one ready to go back into the desert again." He paused, and his voice softened a bit. "Look, I know this seems crazy. It may all be a bizarre set of coincidences. I just passed the guy in the hall – at least I'm assuming it was him. You don't see many monks visiting an apartment building. He does give off a peaceful presence, like ... well like what I think the Dalai Lama might exude. But people *have* been known to project an image of themselves that's not quite true. And look at the facts, Elena," he said, pushing the report closer to her. His brow was wrinkled, and his eyes had a worried look that Elena had never seen before. His energy was jagged, with streaks of red and orange spiking out of his ordinarily peaceful aura.

Reluctantly, Elena began scanning the report. She shook her head several times as she read. Her heartbeat had slowed, but a knot of anxiety was forming in the pit of her stomach. "I see what you mean, Zak. I have to admit there are a lot of coincidences here ...."

"Coincidences?" Zak said. "I thought you didn't believe in coincidences."

Elena rolled her eyes. "You know that's not what I mean. When I say that, it's about the synchronicity of things; someone or something showing up at just the right moment."

"Call it what you will. Just because it's synchronistic doesn't mean it's positive or good. Look!" he said pointing a finger at the up-side-down report. "All the places the Ark is alleged to be, also show up in his travel history – ALL of them. His brother plants a flag near the Bir Tawil site, claiming the land is his. And not just any flag!" He flipped the pages until he found the one with the image he wanted. "The flag of the Holy Roman Empire? And now," he said as he flipped to another page, "with no explanation of how he got here, Anurak is back in the states – hanging around with you, a member of the team that found the Ark. The world may not know what we found, but they definitely know where we were and who we are. Our names and faces were all over the news when it happened." He paused for a moment, then added "And now, the GPS signal from his phone has gone dead. Completely. Like it was disabled, according to Josh."

Elena felt a small chill traveling up the side of her head, and then an unpleasant, warm sensation washed over her. It still seemed impossible. She knew Anurak, she knew his intentions were pure, but Zak did have a point.

"It's all so bizarre, Elena," Zak continued. "I mean, think about it. What kind of monk visits a single woman alone in her apartment?" He let out a long, slow breath. "I wish I could convince you to come with us, if only to keep you from being here alone with him."

Elena saw the jagged streaks of orange and red diminishing a little, but they were still there. Zak must be truly afraid for her safety. She drew what peaceful energy she could from her own heart and with a quiet breath, sent the calming energy his way.

"I understand why you're concerned Zak. I can't blame you, and I'm grateful you shared this with me. I will be cautious – but I am not going back to the cave. Besides, if the Ark is what Anurak is after, don't you think he will follow you instead of staying here with me?" As she said it, Elena's mind touched on how many times Anurak had asked about Zak and the plans for the trip. Another chill arose, this time up her arms.

Elena was more concerned for Zak now than she was for herself. She didn't believe that Anurak was planning anything dangerous, but the whole thing was bringing the trauma of the previous trip to the surface. She silently worked at stuffing it back down again.

"I get it," she said in an attempt to quell his concerns. "The whole thing does look strange, but there has to be another explanation. Maybe the flight records are incomplete. He told me the places he visits sometimes fund his travel. If you're only looking at what Oliver purchased, you might overlook something. Anurak is a peaceful, loving person. I'm actually more concerned about you and your teams. If you focus too much on this list of coincidences, you might miss a clue about who was really behind the attack."

Zak sighed with apparent resignation and closed the folder. "Josh is investigating every possibility. We've got much stronger security set up. Collaborating with the American Research Center in Egypt and the Ministries of Antiquities in Egypt and Sudan is providing us with much more cooperation than before. And Josh has made great progress with the Egyptian police – particularly in finding locals for security. But I'm still worried about you. If you ask me – and Josh agrees – this whole thing with Anurak looks very suspicious. I want to trust your feelings – hell, even my own feelings when I passed the guy in the hall – but my gut is saying something else. Can you at least agree to only seeing him at the temple and not here, alone, while we're gone?"

"That I can do." Elena smiled and touched his hand. He turned his hand around and held hers, his eyes meeting hers, searching for something.

Elena could not look away. She had never seen that look in Zak's eyes before. The look was a jumble of emotions, but one sentiment reached out toward her and unleashed a feeling deep within her that she had never felt about Zak before.

As if the dinner bell had rung, Moses came bounding down the stairs from the loft and sat staring at them, meowing for dinner. Zak released her hand and said "I know, Moses. I'm hungry too. It's way past dinner time." Then looking at Elena, he said "Thai?"

CHAPTER THIRTY-TWO

And Then There Was One

Elena tossed her keys into the clay dish by her door and kicked off her shoes. Dinner with Zak had been delightful. They had put both the discussion about Anurak and their worries about the dig behind them for a little while. It had felt like old times; good food, good friend, and great conversation. But now, home alone with her thoughts, everything seemed to be crashing in on her. Her chest felt tight, and a ball of frenetic energy was snowballing in the pit of her stomach. *Anxiety. Oh God, let it pass.* She took some deep breaths and placed her hand on the kitchen table. It was solid. She needed solid. She scanned the room for more things that were solid; the sink, the refrigerator.

Lightly running her hand across the table, then the wall and counter, Elena felt her way to the stove and her canisters of tea. She turned the pot on to boil and rummaged through the teas, selecting one that would calm her nerves. Lavender Chamomile. The lavender added a strange, floral flavor, but it really did help.

With her cup filled she sat at the kitchen table and set the cup aside to steep. The empty chair across from her screamed a silent cry of loneliness. She grabbed some junk mail from the recycling bin and threw it on the chair. "There. Stay that way!" she said aloud.

But the stack of papers and flyers did nothing to quell the ball of anxiety still festering within her. Zak's story was outlandish. It was impossible. But the mere thought of losing Anurak as a friend was heartbreaking, the sound of silence it evoked was deafening.

Sipping the tea, she allowed it to warm her fragile nerves. She followed the warming sensation as it slid down her throat into her stomach, radiating throughout her body. Focusing only on that warming sensation, her anxiety was quelled a bit. But on the next breath, it returned, with thoughts about Zak and Josh. They were headed back to that place, back to where their friends and colleagues had perished, and they still didn't really know what happened or why. It was a foolish venture. What good could it possibly do? And at what cost?

She piled more mail on the chair. The thought of life without Zak was worse than living without Anurak. But the image of life without

Anurak was bleak, as well. Her childhood friend turned monk had become her mentor and confidante. She enjoyed the freedom with which they shared their thoughts and ideas about life, about God, and about the future of humanity. But Zak. Life without Zak was ... she couldn't put it into words even in her own head. It just wasn't possible. It was ... it was empty, but not a good empty – just empty.

She picked up the recycling bin and poured its remaining contents over the chair. It didn't seem like enough. Maybe she would just get rid of the chair altogether.

"Meow?"

"Oh, Moses. Yes, you can fill some of the emptiness, that's for sure. Are you hungry again?" The cat never seemed full. If he wouldn't eat himself into oblivion, Elena would just keep his bowl filled. "I guess we have that in common too, Moses," she said. "I can't seem to feel full either." She poured a bit of food into his bowl, rubbed his head and ears, and walked to her painting area.

For a moment, she flashed on the night she had shredded and destroyed her own work – but the memory receded. She still felt an emptiness inside, but she knew the void was only an illusion. She knew she could not really be alone. She set the unfinished *Grass is Greener* paintings against the wall. She would finish them later. Right now, she was feeling a different image taking shape in her mind. She would need a painting to tie the opposing sets together. Maybe it would be an Ark.

A single, large canvas lay partially hidden behind the finished paintings along the east wall. She pulled it out and laid it down on the paint-spattered tarp. Eyeing it and swiping an invisible brush over its surface, the image in her mind grew more vivid. *Color. Lots of it.*

She selected several jars of thinned pigment and set them around the canvas. Opening the yellow one first, she poured a small puddle of paint near a corner, then lifted the stretcher and tilted it in circular motions, allowing the paint to stain the untreated fabric in a swirling pattern. She repeated the process with red, then blue, then purple, then green, letting the colors run over one another, creating gradations of color in a rainbow effect.

With most of the canvas covered in a thin and colorful wash, Elena stood, backing away. She was satisfied that the ground she had created was exactly what she had seen in her mind. It was light, re-fracting off some invisible prism, creating waves of color that drew you into them. It was a large canvas – eight feet wide and four feet high. Hung at eye level, it would fill a substantial portion of the view-ers' peripheral vision, inviting them into its waves of light. This would be the ground for a semi-transparent image of the Ark.

Elena capped the jars of paint and placed them on the work table. The painting would have to dry for a while before she could begin the foreground. She propped it just enough that she could sit in front of it and get the feeling of being immersed in it without tilting it so much that the wet paint would run. It was a painting. It wasn't real. But it did evoke a feeling of deep peace and harmony. She may feel alone, but she was not. She may feel disconnected and separate, but she was not.

The words *I am never alone. I am that I am* echoed within her. *I am that I am.* She allowed the words to fill her being. She repeated them over and over as a mantra, *I am that I am, I am that I am, I am* ... and the colors began to ripple and expand until they were no longer pigment on canvas, but light surrounding and enfolding her. *I am that I am, I am that I am ...* and she was gently drawn into the rays of light and into the realm of the Ark once more.

In disbelief, Elena stared at the mystical canvas floating before her. In this perfect state of wholeness, aware of the Oneness of All, she was viewing a self-portrait in which she appeared wholly and utterly alone. She saw herself painting her own image with a bleak and empty hole where the heart should be. Tears were running down the face of the Elena in the portrait. The tears ran faster and faster, filling the entire canvas.

Memories. They flooded Elena's mind. Family members, friends and *oh my God,* the victims in the desert – all those whom she had known that had departed the earth. She knew that their leaving was not an end. She could feel it deep inside. She had felt their presence, some-times lingering, sometimes just passing through. Nevertheless, their departures from the physical world had left her feeling sad, immersed in the sense of loss and separation. But she hadn't cried.

Her grandparents had died when she was very young. It hadn't really bothered her, as she hadn't known them well. They were very old, and it seemed somehow okay in light of their age. The only thing that disturbed her was the emotions of the adults around her and their efforts to shelter her from the experience. And then, of course, there were the empty bodies in the funeral homes. That was very odd. She wondered why the adults were so attentive to the empty shells when she could feel her grandparents' energies all around the room.

But then there had been Rose. They had both attended St. Bardo's elementary school. Rose was thirteen, a year older than Elena the day she died, hit by a car on her way home from a shopping spree with friends. Elena's parents had given her bus fare and sent her off alone to the funeral home to "pay her respects."

Entering the building, Elena noticed the scent of flowers. They were sweet – too sweet. A tall man had appeared, dressed in a black suit and somber tie, gesturing toward the room where Rose's body was. Elena had stopped short; then her breath caught in her throat, overcome by the roses and carnations filling the room with their suffocating scent. Elena could feel that stifled breath now as the scene from the past took shape on the canvas before her. As she watched, Elena experienced the scene as if were happening now.

A bronze casket glowed eerily in the overhead spotlights. Candles flickered nearby. Hearts formed of white carnations stood like sentinels on either side of the coffin. And there was Rose. Still. Pale. Dark hair combed perfectly. Lifeless. A girl almost her own age. It was surreal. It was frightening. And yet, there was something deep inside her telling her it wasn't real, that there was nothing to fear. Elena couldn't move. What was that feeling bubbling up inside her? More than one; the emotions seemed to tangle themselves in a writhing mess that threatened to explode from within her. She could not move. Rose's mother came and put an arm around her shoulders. "It's okay," she said. "Rose is with Jesus now. She wouldn't want you to cry."

Cry? A voice had screamed inside of her. No tears were welling up. Amid that tangled web of feelings, there were no tears! *What's wrong with me?* she had thought. No. Tears were not there, at least not at the top of the pile. Sadness maybe. Fear, for sure. Anger? Not yet. But there was this crazy notion that if she didn't bottle everything up and seal the lid tightly, she would start to laugh! Good God, why on earth would she want to laugh? This was a tragedy. It was just so wrong. But the feeling persisted.

210

The sweet scent of the flowers was overpowering now. Elena turned, hoping for a breath of fresh air, but movement in the corner caught her eye. There behind a vase of red roses perched on a tall white pedestal was a faint outline of a pink, glittering bubble. Elena's eyes widened. She knew this shape. It was the bubble that had appeared in her backyard when she was very small. It had returned. Indoors! Didn't anyone else see it? She scanned the room. No. Everyone was talking in low murmurs. Some were crying. Some were hugging. Others touched delicately embroidered hankies to the corners of their eyes. Rose's friends stood around looking frightened. But no one was looking toward this ball of light bobbing about behind the pillar of flowers.

And then the bubble began to shift. It didn't open. It didn't draw her inside as it once had. But it started to writhe and twist. It stretched and pulled, and then gently transformed before her eyes. It was Rose! There she was. Translucent. Pink. Sparkling. Made of the same stuff as the mystical bubble. She was smiling! No. She was laughing! "It's okay," Elena heard her say in her mind. "I'm fine. It was time. I was complete with this one. I've returned to where I came from. I am free! And I am so ecstatically happy! I'm sorry that everyone is so sad. Sorry that the man who hit me will spend a lifetime drowning in guilt no matter how many therapists he sees. But I am fine. You want to laugh because you know. Deep inside you already know where I am and what I'm doing. You know that my time was complete. You know the joy of the other side. You are right, though. No one would understand if you burst out laughing right now. They would be shocked. Offended even. And some people would say you need to see a shrink."

Elena had drawn a long-awaited breath, and the bubble-like Rose had disappeared. *Was that for real? Did I really see and hear that or did I just imagine it?* Did I make it up to explain that insane urge to laugh? Whatever the truth was, Elena determined it was best to put a tight lid on that inappropriate emotion and seal it away. Forever. It would be another six years before the seal would threaten to open, and a good many more before she would understand the relationship between grief, joy, and hysteria.

A single tear began to form at the rim of Elena's eye now, as she recalled the scene that had threatened to open the seal. At eighteen, Elena had moved into her first apartment away from home. In the middle of a dinner party, the phone call had come. It was about her niece, Aria, just nine years old. She was in a coma, not expected to live. The waves of shock had overwhelmed her. The days that followed were like a dream, a frightening one. She watched now as the nightmarish scene unfolded on the mystical canvas and drew her into a replay of the past.

Another funeral home. Inside, men in black suits and ties ushered people toward the viewing room. Walking as slowly as she could, Elena neared the room. Through the archway, she could see the casket. It was white, not bronze. It was filled with poufy white satin and embroidered pink flowers. The scent of funeral flowers permeated the air. There she was. The tiniest little thing. Eyes closed forever. Blonde hair brushed perfectly about her tiny shoulders, white Catholic missal and pearl rosary wrapped in her diminutive hands. Lifeless. Cold. Gone.

It was horrifying. Elena felt terror, anger, confusion. *How could this happen? How could her time possibly be complete? She was only nine! How will her parents go on? How will any of us go on? What kind of God takes a beautiful child from her loving parents and causes such incredible sadness?*

Elena had been angry then. Angry with God. Angry with the doctors who couldn't save her darling niece. Angry that she would never see her grow up, get married or have children. But there again, very deep inside, was this insane urge to laugh. *What the HELL is that?!* Elena had screamed to herself. *What in God's name is wrong with me?*

There was no bubble this time. No sparkling visit from Aria. There was just a ride in a black limousine to an ominous hole in the ground where Elena had been told to drop a flower inside and say goodbye. It was insane. It was just so wrong. There was no way anyone could go on unless they bottled up these horrific feelings and sealed them away. The container of emotions within her trembled. She shut them down, increased the seal, and hid them away. Forever, she had thought.

Weeks later, Elena felt it. She didn't see the bubble again, but she felt Aria's presence. She sensed the touch of a tiny energetic hand to hers. It was a vibration of joy and gladness. The scent of flowers drifted through the air and swirled around her. Though her heart ached for the physical touch of Aria's hand, she knew the little girl she had loved so much was still nearby, brilliant, glowing, radiating love. Her journey had been completed. She had left a story on the hearts of all who knew her. Each of them would carry a piece of Truth with them that had been revealed by Aria's presence in their lives.

More loss would occur over the years. A brother-in-law killed in an accidental shooting. A sister-in-law succumbed to cancer at the age of thirty-six. A nephew hit by a car at sixteen. Just like Rose, gone in an instant. Another nephew, years later, would take his own life. Elena's father had a massive heart attack in the hospital while taking a stress test. Her mother would finally make her transition after years of living in the prison of dementia.

Elena had become somewhat hardened to death. The bottled emotions were so well sealed she barely noticed them. Until that is, Elena's sister Jenny, the rock of her life, had succumbed to breast cancer at the age of fifty-six. Elena had stood at her bedside. She hadn't slept in two days and had left her sister's side only to relieve her own bladder. Each stir from Jenny's body prompted Elena to rub a bit more morphine on her sister's gums and touch the moistened sponge to her parched lips. Elena prayed to a God she hadn't acknowledged in years. She talked to her sister as though she were conscious. *It's okay, Jenny. You can leave. You'll be safe. You'll see the people you've missed for so long. We'll all be okay. We'll miss you, but we know you have to go. Don't be afraid. I love you so much. Thank you for sharing this life with me. Aria is waiting for you. Angels are surrounding you.*

It wasn't a lie. Elena could sense the angels. It had been many years since that first experience with the scent of flowers. It wasn't surprising to smell flowers in a funeral room full of carnations and roses, but when she was nowhere near a flower and caught its scent, Elena knew that angels were surrounding her, either preparing her or comforting. The scent had wafted around her then, though there had been no flowers in the room other than the plastic orchids on the bed-side table, gathering dust among the prescription bottles and hospice notes.

The transition was slow. Jenny had been torn between two worlds, the one she was leaving and the one to which she was return-ing. Her fears of not being complete, of not remaining to help those she left behind, fought with her desire to move on. A list of wrongs she thought she had committed had permeated her muddled thoughts. Fear had enveloped her ravaged body and tired mind. Her belief in a place of torment had battled with the knowledge of a place of peace. At last, the place of peace had won. She had taken a deep and guttural breath, and then she was gone.

Once again Elena wondered where the tears were. They seemed to want to surface but could not. Her heart was aching. The pain was physical. Jenny had been her champion. Her best friend. Her pseudo-mother. She was gone. But again, there were no tears. Thankfully though, there was no urge to laugh. That emotion was well-sealed now. Instead, Elena left the room, allowing others to come in and pay their respects. She went about the planning of the funeral and called the priest.

That evening, when Elena brushed her teeth at the bathroom mirror, she was startled to see her sister's face where her own should be. She felt her sister all around her. But it wasn't a good feeling. It was suffocating. It was frightening. "What the hell?" Elena had said to no one in particular. And then slowly, the image began to recede. Empty now, sadder than before, Elena had stared at the mirror. Yes, she did look a bit like her sister, but not like that image she had just seen. The image in the mirror had been strange, even for Elena, who saw bubble-like images of deceased friends and held flower-scented meetings with angels.

Fear. Her sister was still afraid. She had not yet fully integrated into the ethereal realms. She had tried one last time to hold on by per-meating Elena's energy body. Elena had felt her sister's sorrow. She was sorry to have caused fear in Elena. Jenny was ready now. She would let go and finally release a lifetime that was complete. "Good-bye", Elena had whispered as a lone tear rolled down her cheek.

The most recent hole that seemed impossible to fill was left by Elena's brother Richard, a man who had shouted "No" to death for decades, a man who had lost his wife and two children but kept on going, now dead. He was the last member of her birth family to go. She had felt utterly and completely alone. There were friends and ex-tended family. There were colleagues and fellow artists. There was Zak, but she was somehow, still, very alone. The words ... *and then there was one,* rattled through her mind – over and over. *And then there was one.*

She had known that Richard was ill, but she had thought they would have more time. The moment he had died, Elena knew. Before the text message appeared on her phone, she felt him. It was a bright and sunny morning. Not unusual on a desert dig, but brighter, somehow. No clouds, not even a wisp of one. As she brushed the dust from an ancient relic, the scent of roses permeated the air around her. She stopped. *Roses. Why? Had someone died? Was it Richard? Too soon. Not yet!* And then she had felt him. It was the most joyous feeling! It permeated every cell of her being. It passed through her, then danced about and came back again. The waltz continued for several moments before she heard the vibration. They weren't words. There were no words that could describe this. But she knew their meaning. *I am free! I am free!*

Richard was free! A long and challenging journey had come to a close. He was leaving her with gratitude and gifts. He gave her the gift of strength and courage. He gave her the gift of joy. He gave her the gift of knowing that the physical realm was but a fleeting moment to be cherished and then released. He gave her the gift of remembering that she was whole, that she was on the right path, and that she was loved beyond comprehension. She had laughed out loud, right there in the middle of the desert, holding a piece of human history in her hands, she had laughed. *It was about time that laugh had escaped!* And then she had cried.

Why? The question still lingered in Elena's mind. It was the question everyone asked of untimely and tragic deaths. Even knowing that life continued, this question still arose when she faced or read about someone's untimely death. *Why?*

***

As the mystical portrait before Elena continued to reflect her own image back to her, she realized that the question, "Why" was the packing tape that had sealed her emotions and with them, her understanding of oneness. Its adhesive grip loosened, Elena now pulled the mystical brush over the canvas, and a tall, golden canister appeared, its lid removed and her long-imprisoned feelings escaping their tomb.

She was surprised by the tangle of emotions being released from the painted container. There was sadness. There was fear. She had figured that. But there was something else. As the feelings of grief and anger and fear escaped, the emotions of joy and peace and happiness were also released. Holding the negative emotions captive had also held her more positive feelings hostage. It was very freeing to set them loose, on the canvas and within her own heart.

And then there was one. The thought returned. The feeling of being the only family member left and being alone in the world had returned with it. *And then there was one.* Elena's attention was drawn to the brush in her hand as it danced across the magical surface. The lonely self-portrait reappeared, but it was taking on a deeper dimension. The shapes and forms of the portrait began to blend into streams of Light and sparkling particles, dancing as one ceaseless waltz of harmonious movement. *There was always only One ... one Power, one Presence, and everyone and everything a part of the One, never separate, never alone, always whole and complete – and always present.*

Elena felt them now. Every one of them. Everyone she had ever known and thought she had lost. She could feel their presence, hear their laughter. They were in her mind, and they were all around her. They had never left. Invisible to her human eyes, they lingered, moved on, and then returned. They were eternally one with the invisible realm of Light, taking shape as desired or called upon, and then returning to the dancing stream of Light. There was a sense of joy and peace and harmony surrounding her now as she watched formless energies take shape as streams of Light, ascending and descending into the self-portrait.

CHAPTER THIRTY-THREE

Deadly Encounters

Ochres, umbers, and a variety of earthy colors flowed from the magical bristles, transforming the portrait and streams of light into a vast landscape of desert sand and rock. Crevices appeared in the rocky terrain and then the colors grew darker: burnt umber, raw umber, gray, and black. A cave. The cave. And light, not portable excavation lights – an ethereal glow that radiated from the deepest part of the cave. Yellow ochre, orange, gold, cream, Naples white; all flowed from the brush, forming the shape of a box. The box. The Ark. Right there, just as they had found it. From its closed top, a stream of light and energy arose.

The magical brush continued to paint, drawing the memory from Elena's mind and placing it on the mystical canvas as if it were a social-media live event. The rock and sand beneath the image of the Ark began to vibrate. The motion reminded Elena of a cornstarch and water experiment on top of a stereo speaker. The grains of sand bounced and danced. They moved in undulating waves as if a strong wind were blowing across the desert, creating ripples in its powdery ground. The movement was mesmerizing. The brush in her hand stopped moving. She felt the sands pulling her toward the canvas, into the scene. Then she was there. Back in the desert. Surrounded by the team. It was the night before the discovery, the night of the shootings.

Although Elena was enveloped in the harmonious essence of the portal, her heart began to ache again. Sadness and hopelessness crept into Elena's mind as memories of the desert expedition erupted like hot lava spilling over the sides of an active volcano. Despair engulfed her as the tragedies that had preceded that horrific night came to life again on the canvas before her. No assurance that life continued could relieve the horror she felt as she watched the scenes replaying before her.

The first was Tara. They were just a few days away from reaching their goal when she had awakened in the middle of the night, screaming and holding her head. The look of pain and anguish on her face were terrifying. Then just as suddenly her face went slack, her eyes rolled back, and she fell to the ground. Unconscious. Unresponsive.

Barely breathing. Her long blonde hair lay in tangled strands across her face. Her clothing was soaked with uncharacteristic sweat. Lucas, a medical student who had signed on as their medic, ran to her and began assessing her vitals. It wasn't hopeful. Hours later her lifeless body was air-lifted from the campsite and returned home to her family.

The group was deeply saddened and disturbed. Lucas had told them it appeared to be an aneurysm, a weak blood vessel in the brain that had burst. It was rare, given her age – just twenty-five – and the lack of diagnostic equipment made it impossible to confirm, but the symptoms fit. Later, they would discover it had been a snake bite, the fangs so slender the marks had not been noticeable.

Shock, grief, and fear overwhelmed them and cast a shadow over their expedition. They each wondered if they should go on. But they had made a pact and felt they owed it to Tara to continue.

The next was Trevor, just two days later, one moment standing in front of them explaining the implications of the terrain; then the next moment crushed by a falling rock. He was just standing there talking. And then he wasn't. A day later they had sent what was left of Trevor home.

The shadow of pain and loss grew thicker, and the journey became at once more difficult and more vital. They were driven by the group's pledge to see the quest through whatever obstacles appeared before them. There had been no turning back once they had deciphered the words and shapes scrawled out on the tablet uncovered in Qasr Ibrim. The message seemed to have an energy all its own. It beckoned. It called. It could not be ignored.

The heavy shadow continued to hang over the team as they reached the proximity of their destination. They could see the mountainous rock formations resembling those carved into the tablet. It was just a few hours ahead of them. Exhausted, they set up camp for the night. The final steps of their journey would be best taken in daylight, and the sun was about to sink into the horizon. When it finally fell behind the gentle curve of the sandy horizon, chaos had erupted.

It was dark, except for the campfire and a few strategically placed battery-operated lights. They were sitting around the campfire, sharing the remnants of dinner and late-night conversation when the shots rang out. Lots of them. Screaming. Chaos. Scrambling for shelter ensued, but the cover of tents and Jeeps was not enough. Team members fell to the ground, some only injured, some in a feeble attempt to avoid the terrifying barrage of bullets. Most fell, never to rise again.

Flat against the ground, hidden behind only a flimsy tent, she lay as still as her pounding heart would allow. *Was it a lone gunman? A piece of humanity gone mad? Or multiple gunmen with some hidden agenda?* What could be so important that it justified the ending of another's life? The shots seemed to go on forever, then just before they abruptly stopped, all four of the battery-operated floodlights were shattered. Other than the dim light of the now unattended campfire, they were in total darkness. The silence was filled with the mental echo of gunshots and Elena's fingers moved ever so slowly until they were planted in her ears.

Hours later, there was a quiet rustling audible to Elena's still plugged ears. It was just to her right. Terrified, she listened intently. Was someone else alive? Was it one of the team? Or had the shooters come to look for survivors? She barely took a breath, afraid she would be discovered. A hand gently touched her shoulder. She froze. She held her breath. "Are you okay?" It was Zak.

She took a breath and whispered, "I'm alive." She was far from okay.

Elena and Zak had discovered four other team members alive with minimal injuries. The rest could not be moved or had not survived. The shooters apparently had left, but it was too dangerous to linger there. Lucas urged those who were able to head up the mountainside toward their goal and away from the open area that had served as a shooting gallery; they owed it to those who had lost their lives to complete the journey. He, and his assistant Chris, would stay to care for the wounded and call for help.

Reluctantly, Elena, Zak, Josh, and Paul had gathered minimal supplies and equipment and moved on foot toward the mountain. It was dark, but the clouds that had covered the full moon were dissipating, and they could see without the aid of flashlights, which would have made them moving targets.

If grief had shadowed them before it completely engulfed them during the final few hours of the climb. The violence had made no sense. Were they terrorists? Had they been guarding the Ark? Impossible. No one knew what they were seeking. Even if they had known, wouldn't they have rampaged the camp to find the stone tablet and its broken sherd? So many lives lost. Families would be forever haunted by the deaths of their loved ones. Elena had been haunted by them. The sight of team members falling to the ground had replayed over and over in her head as they had ascended the mountain. Her heart was aching for the lives that had been cut short. Students who would never graduate, marry or raise children. Husbands and wives who would never return home or grow old with their spouses. Survivors who would never erase the sight from their minds. Tears had streamed down her face. Memories of her own losses had flooded her heart and mingled with the ones that had just occurred. She cried until she could cry no more. There were no tears left when they reached the small cave hidden behind tumbled rock and sand.

Emptied of any lingering tears, Elena emerged out of the scene and stood once again before the ever-changing canvas. As she watched, the scene began to recede until she was hovering high above the camp, watching the shooting, but no longer embedded in the scene.

From this vantage point, Elena had a broader scope of the melee. She could see beyond the small area of the camp where devastation had occurred. Here she could see the surrounding area and several piles of rock a short distance from the camp. Behind them were men dressed in white robes made of what looked like a coarse weave of a bleached, natural fiber. Draped around the robes was another cloth of the same color. It fell from the right shoulder around the back, looped over the left hip and then fastened at the right shoulder again. Another piece of the cloth was draped over their heads and wrapped about their shoulders as if to protect them from the scorching sun that was no longer in the sky. If not for the semi-automatic weapons in their hands they would have looked like monks.

Who were they? Why were they shooting at this innocent group of people on a quest to discover a link to humanity's spiritual past? She watched with renewed horror as her friends dropped to the ground. Their bodies lay limp on the desert sand. She could feel the ache in her heart and the rush of adrenalin as if it were actually happening again. But something calm washed over her as the brush in her hand began to draw something else. Their bodies were still, but the light that had once animated them hovered nearby. There were brilliant beams of light exuding from each of the lifeless bodies. The beams joined to-gether just above the violent scene, and the camp appeared to be engulfed in their light.

Where was all that light then? It had been so dark she could barely see her own arms when she and Zak had searched the ground looking for someone, anyone, still alive.

Then something in the scene shifted. Elena's brush began furi-ously painting something emanating from the monk-like characters. At first, it was a series of small masses of dark particles that emerged from them and then hung over them like a lightless cloud. As each plume of darkness slithered out of them, their human shapes became more cloudy. With every shot, another plume flew from the shooter's body, the physical form growing grayer. It was as if tiny parts of their souls fled from their bodies with every pull of the trigger until there was almost nothing left. Faint traces of energetic bodies fell to the ground as if their souls had died, leaving a hollow core dressed in robes. A dark cloud rose above each shooter until it completely en-gulfed them and then began to connect with the clouds of other shooters until there was one massive cloud of darkness hovering over a group of empty husks. It was as if they had succeeded not only in murdering the team members, they had also killed some integral piece of themselves.

Elena's brush drew back and dipped itself into a cup of sparkling white paint. Nearing the canvas, the brush began dotting the inky cloud with bits of glittering pigment. The shining dots grew, opening small cavities in the massive cloud revealing small swirls of light, one hovering above each of the monk-like shapes. The cloud separated into millions of tiny dark particles resembling a dust storm and then vanished. What remained were tiny slivers of light flickering within each of the white-clad men. A greater light engulfed them, kindling the dim lights within them and as it did their arms became limp. Their weapons fell to their sides, and they were still. The light within them had stopped them from shooting, just like it had stopped Elena's father from harming her so many years ago.

The men ambled away, single file, into the dark night. As their dark faces slipped into the night, Elena saw something else – one pair of eyes that stood out. From the front of the group, appearing to lead the others, two crystal blue orbs glinted in the blackened night. They

221

peered in her direction as though they could see her – even now, even here, in the peaceful energy of the Ark. Elena's heart skipped a beat and chills ran up and down her spine. She knew those clear blue eyes.

CHAPTER THIRTY-FOUR

Confrontation

It was morning when she landed on the paint-spattered tarp. Elena hadn't waited for the scene on the mystical canvas to resolve into something more peaceful. The sight of the blue orbs had sent her tumbling through a misty blue tunnel that emptied abruptly onto her studio floor.

She sat there now, shaking, her mind racing. *Why? Why do people harm one another? Why would anyone choose to kill another human being? Isn't that one of God's laws? Thou shall not kill?* She did not recall there being a "but" or a "when" or an "if" to that statement.

She eyed the kitchen chair, overflowing with the junk mail she had dumped onto it. It didn't seem like enough to shelter her from the emptiness it symbolized. She spilled the mail onto the floor and carried the chair to the door. Leaving the door open, she walked to the stairwell, lifted the chair over her head, and thrust her arms forward, intending to pitch it down the stairs. But something stopped her. Destruction was not the answer. She turned and walked back to her door and set the chair down in the hallway. She quickly poured some kibble for Moses, grabbed her keys, locked the door, and headed for the temple. She could hear Moses abandoning his breakfast and pouncing across the room toward the window. *Crazy cat. The only thing he likes more than food is watching me from his eleventh-floor perch.*

***

She found Anurak in the seventh-floor garden. He was wearing white robes and sitting peacefully on a stone bench surrounded by a well-tended flower garden. Elena charged up to him. She didn't care if he was meditating or not. This was no monk. This was a murderer. Before she reached him, Anurak opened his eyes and smiled as if he had anticipated her arrival. She stopped inches from him. He was seated, which gave her a slight physical advantage, and she looked down at him, seething. She didn't let the scent of lavender wafting about the garden dispel her anger. "Who the hell are you? And what the hell were you doing in Bir Tawil? Why did you kill all those people? Are you some kind of terrorist?" She was shaking so violently she thought she would fall down. She was irritated by the tears flowing down her cheeks. Some part of her wondered if it was wise to charge up to a suspected terrorist and confront him, but she didn't care.

"I am not a terrorist, Elena. I'm not a murderer either, though I can understand why you might think so. I was there to ..." He seemed to search for the words, "... to protect you."

"Protect shit! I saw you. I saw all of them. You had a gun slung over your shoulder, too. They were following you!" As she spoke, something occurred to her. She hadn't seen him lead the group to the site. She'd only seen him lead them away. What's more, she'd never seen him fire the gun. It had just been slung over his shoulder.

Anurak remained calm, but he didn't smile. He just looked at her with those clear blue eyes. It was hard to look into those eyes and remain angry, but she held tight to her rage and indignation, pushing away the peaceful calm that emitted from him. She wanted answers, and she wanted them now.

"Perhaps we should go inside and have a cup of tea where we can have a little more privacy," Anurak suggested.

Elena glanced around. A few monks had stopped their gardening to stare in their direction. She didn't care, but maybe he was right. She was in no position to tell the world how she knew that Anurak had been in Bir Tawil. The discovery of the Ark was still a secret, and there was no proof they'd actually seen it. People would think she was insane and she wasn't entirely sure they would be wrong.

"Fine. Lead the way Anurak, or Aidan, or whatever the hell your name is."

Anurak led her inside the monastery to a small sitting room and then left to get a pot of tea for them. The temple was cool despite the lack of air conditioning and the rising temperatures outside. It was a peaceful place, but Elena was still angry. She had no intention of letting this peaceful place quiet her emotions, at least not until she got answers. She was here for a purpose, and until she understood what this man was doing in the desert, and now hiding in this New York temple, she was going to remain focused on that goal.

Elena sat on a low wooden stool with a firm, velvety seat. The pillows on the floor were too soft, and she didn't feel soft right now. On the small round table in front of her there sat an ivory, laughing

Buddha. She wondered what he was laughing at. Nothing seemed particularly funny to her at the moment, and a bitter, cynical side of her began to erupt.

Anurak returned with a glass teapot on a silver tray. If she weren't so upset, Elena would have been impressed by the delicate Jasmine flower unfolding itself in the hot water. He poured each of them a cup and set the pot down on the tray.

"I know you have lots of questions Elena. I can sense a whole jumble of them whirling about in your mind. I'll try to answer them one at a time. First, as I said, I did not try to kill you. The monks you encountered in the desert are an ancient order, bound to protect the Ark. I was there to protect you. I know that sounds crazy, but let me start at the beginning, of how I came to know about the Ark and the monks who protect it."

Elena nodded for him to continue. The tea and the calmness of the temple were settling her nerves a bit even if she did mistrust him.

"In my travels to different spiritual centers around the world," he began, "I learned about a church in Ethiopia that claims to be the home of the Ark of the Covenant. Actually, I had heard about it in seminary, but that had been so long ago and had seemed so far-fetched that I'd forgotten about it. I thought it was an unlikely place for me to visit because no one is allowed into the chamber where the Ark is alleged to be, except one monk, The Guardian who must vow never to leave." He took a sip of tea and went on.

"Anyway, in the back of my mind, I kept hearing my mother saying, 'it never hurts to ask.' She always assumed everyone would do exactly what she wanted them to do if she just continued to ask. In fact, I remember her saying once, 'If you don't get what you want, just nag, nag, nag until you get what you want.' Every time I hear those words in my mind, I chuckle to myself."

A soft harrumph escaped Elena's lips. She didn't feel much like chuckling. Anurak held the pot of tea in front of her, offering a refill, but she shook her head. The tea was not settling well.

Anurak nodded with a look that suggested he understood. "So, with my mother haunting me, I wrote to that church. It was months before I received a response, partially because I tend to move around a lot. But also, because it is just their way to allow things to occur in their own time. To my surprise, they invited me to visit. I had no idea how long I would be there, so I bought a one-way ticket and left the ashram where I'd been staying to fly to Ethiopia.

"When I arrived, they treated me like some kind of royal dignitary. They assigned me to a lovely, private room and saw to my every need. One of the monks was assigned to assist me with my research and shared the whole history of the monastery, the legend of the Ark – though he did not refer to it as a legend – and anything else I wanted to know.

"It was still not possible to actually see the Ark. It was hidden in an inner chamber guarded by the one monk who would never leave until his death. No one else was allowed in. But the young monk assigned to me did take me to visit an island on Lake Tana where the Ark is believed to have been hidden for an extended period before arriving in Aksum.

"About six months after my arrival, I received a rather startling invitation. I was invited to meet The Guardian of the Ark and visit the inner chamber of the monastery. I was dumbfounded, as was the monk who delivered the message. Never in all the centuries since the Ark had arrived in Ethiopia had an outsider been invited into the inner chamber to meet with The Guardian.

"I was very honored, and of course I accepted. The monk that led me there opened the door and gestured for me to go in. He closed the door behind me as I entered a vestibule; a sort of receiving area where the Guardian's daily meals were delivered. It was also the place he received supplies, messages, and on extremely rare occasions, a guest. The Guardian greeted me and said, 'Welcome. I've been expecting you.'

"He then led me to his sitting area and beyond that, the dining area with a small kitchenette. That room led to a library and finally a bedroom. The rooms all had one curved wall, encircling an inner chamber and each room had access to it. From the bedroom, the Guardian opened the access door, entered the chamber, and invited me to join him.

"The room had a brightness to it, not in terms of light fixtures, but in energy. It felt ..." Anurak's eyes seemed to search for the next words. "It felt sacred and peaceful. It felt more than that, but I can't find the words to describe it. In the center stood a curtained area, a sort of ceiling-to-floor tabernacle. The burgundy drapes were heavy velvet, gilded with golden fringe and trim. A delicate floral pattern was subtly embedded in the plush fabric. These were tied back at several intervals with golden ropes and in the empty spaces were another series of curtains; a layer of wispy white sheers, followed by a layer of black netting and finally an amber cloth with flecks of sparkling threads woven in an irregular pattern. It looked quite regal and was clearly the sacred space in which the famed Ark must reside."

Elena was impressed, but she was not entirely sure she believed him. How does an American ex-priest get invited into the inner sanctuary of a highly secretive monastery to view what no other human being has seen save a single, devout monk committed to never leaving again? Besides, she knew the Ark wasn't there. She had seen it in the Bir Tawil cave. Not only had she seen it, but she had been inside of it. And now, she had discovered she had access to it wherever... *Oh ... It can be accessed from anywhere.* A piece of Anurak's story began to click. Now she wondered which Ark was the real one, the one in the cave, or the one Anurak alluded to. She was thoroughly confused, but her anger was subsiding – just a bit.

"Go on," she said. "Did you get to go behind the curtains?" If he told her he had seen the Ark she wasn't sure if he would be lying, or if she had been delusional. All her senses told her the Ark was not there. If it was safely enshrined in that Ethiopian sanctuary, why the hell did Anurak lead a bunch of radical monks on a violent raid on their camp? It just didn't make sense.

"Well, that's the thing, Elena. I was invited in, in spite of being an American, ex-priest, which was a total surprise to me."

What was surprising to Elena was Anurak answering the question she hadn't asked aloud. When she had meditated with him and felt at one with him, his knowing her thoughts had seemed natural. Now, it was just ... creepy.

Anurak was still talking. "I couldn't imagine why I was being given this supreme honor. He kept referring to *me* as the Guardian, but that didn't make sense, either. Until we went inside the tabernacle."

Anurak took a long sip of his tea. "He pulled the curtain back, entered, and then held it open for me. Inside it was surprisingly bright given the weight of the curtains that ensconced it. In the center was an ornately carved marble pedestal, and on it…" He paused and looked intently at Elena. "…There was nothing."

Well, at least he isn't lying, Elena thought. "Nothing? Seriously? All the secrecy and the commitment to never leave the inner chamber… and there was nothing?" She wasn't really surprised. She knew it wasn't there. But she wondered why this fact was being exposed to Anurak, who clearly hadn't made any vow to remain there. He was sitting right in front of her.

"Why would he show this to you?" she asked. "Did they want their secret revealed? Or, had the Ark been moved?" She hadn't thought of that. Maybe it wasn't there because it had been stolen and the monks were hoping Anurak would help them retrieve it.

"I wondered that myself, but then the Guardian pointed to some small steps carved at regular intervals around the base of the pedestal. I looked at him with what must have been the face of total confusion because that's what I felt. I didn't know if he wanted me to stand on the pedestal or what. Being a monk, he was a man of few words, so he climbed the steps, sat on the pedestal, then motioned for me to join him. I thought this was kind of nuts, but I did as he requested. And then, everything changed."

Anurak placed his two index fingers over his mouth. He wasn't signaling silence or secrecy; it was just a gesture of deep thought. Then he spoke, "I suddenly found myself in another dimension. I was weightless. In fact, I felt bodyless, but I could see my body and I could see the Guardian's. I could hear his thoughts, and I know he could hear mine by the answers he projected. This place that I was essentially floating about was *inside* the Ark. The pedestal provided an opening or some kind of portal to it. The Ark itself is an opening too, in a sense. Inside the Ark …" He gave a long, penetrating look into Elena's eyes now. "Inside the Ark is another opening, to something beyond words. Wouldn't you agree?"

Elena felt chills running up and down her arms. The tingling didn't stop there. It seeped into her neck and face and the top of her head. She felt the faintest trace of Ark vibrations now but purposefully quelled them. She didn't want to be in the Ark just now. She wanted to know how he knew, what he knew, and why he was apparently stalking her now in New York.

"I'm not stalking you, Elena. I'm here to help you sort it out. You were allowed into the Ark for a reason, and you have questions. I know how challenging it is to bring the knowledge received there into this more mundane world. It's as if the physical world vibrates at a lower frequency that doesn't combine well with the higher one. At first, there is a lot of interference or what we might call static. It takes some time to assimilate. I came to help you make sense of what you are experiencing."

Elena scrunched her face and squinted her eyes to match the quizzical thoughts running through her mind. She didn't know which was more outlandish, this peaceful, loving monk taking part in a mass shooting or the idea that he had also been in the Ark and was intentionally here to help her. But then, she had seen him in the Ark. Most of what she saw was a memory, a replay, but not that look from Anurak, not those eyes staring at her as if they were both right there inside the Ark.

"We were," Anurak said.

"Stop that," she said. He was reading her thoughts, and it was disconcerting. He could read hers, but she could no longer read his.

"Then why the hell did you try to kill me? I know you were there. I saw you! I mean, not at the time, but later... in the ..." She was frustrated and stumbling with her words, but she was certain he knew what she was trying to say.

"I didn't try to kill you, Elena. I was there to stop the carnage. I knew who you were. Well, I didn't know it was Elena Rowan from grade school just then, but I knew you and your friends were about to discover the Ark. You were meant to find it, as were the others. At least those who survived. I was there to stop the monks. The only way I could get close enough was to be there with them, as one of them. They wouldn't have believed me if I had just told them who I was and who you were. They believed with all their hearts that it was their job to protect the Ark at whatever cost. And they knew the consequences, too."

Elena's mind was spinning like a Kansas tornado. "What do you mean, consequences?"

"First, they knew they were not killing the individual souls, just destroying their physical vehicles. They also knew, and you saw this

Elena, that with every shot they essentially killed a little bit of themselves. With every shot, they buried a little more of their own essential being. Their own frequency, as it were, slowed down. It got denser and further obscured their connection with the Divine. It was as if every shot they took buried a piece of their own souls.

"It's what happens whenever someone takes a life. People kill each other for a multitude of reasons, but mostly because they fear some part of themselves cannot survive or succeed at some self-imposed goal unless they do so. But the ultimate surprise is that they actually kill some part of themselves. Jesus taught, 'The measure you give will be the measure you get back.' The law works irrefutably. Give love, receive love. Give hatred, receive hatred. Kill, and something in you is killed. It's like the apostle Paul said, '... you are the body of Christ and individually members of it.' If we are all members of the same spiritual body, then harming another, harms the self.

"The monks knew this – at least on some level. But they did it anyway because they mistakenly believed it was their duty to protect the Ark. Their order is ancient. They have surrounded the Ark for eons, for so long that none of them have ever actually seen the Ark, nor have they entered it and understood its message and its power. They were afraid that if they didn't stop you, they would have failed their god."

Elena sighed. She knew what he was saying was true. She had seen it in the Ark. She had watched the *knowingness* paint an image of pieces of the monk's souls being shrouded in dark energy – and fragments of them apparently evaporating.

Anurak went on. "In this world, killing one another is unacceptable. Laws have been written in both social and religious traditions to protect the physical vehicles of individual souls. Punishment occurs for those who break these laws and are caught. This is good for two reasons. First, the world would quickly become total anarchy, a dangerous place to live, without these agreements. Secondly, the agreements are a worldly expression of a greater law. Adhering to the lesser law keeps you from further separating yourself from your essence and your oneness with all things. It's like the kindergarten version of a greater truth. You never throw away what you learn in kindergarten, you just continue to build on it and expand as you grow."

"What is the greater law? I have been able to grasp each of the commandments as blessings but not this one," Elena asked.

"In the greater experience? Nothing *can* be killed," Anurak answered.

"But that's just ... that seems like a dangerous path to walk. What would happen if everyone believed no one can be killed but just ran around destroying the bodies of anyone who got in their way? What if they believed there was no punishment for such behavior?"

"Most of the world is not ready for the greater statement yet, Elena. The kindergarten rule will remain prevalent until a greater understanding is reached. With a greater understanding comes the realization that there is nothing to kill, no need to fight, no need to protect, no need to possess. There is an understanding of All-ness and Oneness and a great desire to honor ALL the expressions of the Essence of Life."

It was all still a little overwhelming, but it felt good to talk to Anurak. She was surprised at how comfortable she felt now considering how infuriated she had been when she arrived.

"But what happens now, Anurak? What happens to the monks? Are they to be forever separated from their wholeness? Damned? Are their souls lost forever?"

"Forever is relative, but no. Their journey to wholeness will be longer, but not forever. They haven't actually killed anything – not the essence of the victims, not their souls – because nothing of Spirit can ever be killed," Anurak explained.

"But still." Elena was lost again. "I mean, I get it. I saw the souls of the victims leave their bodies. I know their essence continues – but their bodies were destroyed, brutally. I guess this is the area where I don't know how to reconcile the commandments vs. the blessings. Thou shall not kill seems pretty clear-cut to me."

"Once again you have broached a question with many answers. Yes, the body can be destroyed. Yes, it is a wrongful act to take a life before its time. Yet, the true life lives on. So, let's look at the deeper meaning of the teachings, because there is a real shift when Jesus comes along and says to disregard the idea of an eye for an eye and instead turn the other cheek, forgive, and pray for those who hurt you. What he was acknowledging is the continuous growth of the spiritual being and the eternal life of the soul. This is impossible to kill. But attempting to do so not only harms the body of the victim, it harms the perpetrator who has become so ingrained in the physical world, he has shut himself off to his own essence, to God. In this way, he has actually served to kill himself."

"So," Elena said. "'Thou shall not kill' is both a command, a rule of religious and social governance. And, it is a blessing, meaning *you cannot kill, or nothing can be truly killed.*"

"True," Anurak said. "And, there's another more metaphysical concept that explores the meaning of the word *kill.* To kill is to end prematurely. For instance, you can kill an engine, or you can kill a project or an idea. Killing something prematurely binds you to the outer condition rather than your inner power. In a sense, it sentences you to an experience of separation. For instance, someone could theoretically *kill* a painting."

Elena was speechless. Her mouth fell open, and her heart jumped into her throat. He was talking about her! She had killed her paintings! And yes, that had definitely caused her to feel separate and alone – as if her prayers and efforts were all in vain. The Ark, however, had taught her otherwise. She knew Anurak was right – about the monks, about the victims, and about the multiple meanings behind the statement of Truth, 'Thou shall not kill.' She'd understood it all the first time she entered the Ark. But here, in the world, it was so different.

"So, you see Elena, I'm not here to hurt you or stalk you. I'm here to help you to digest what you've received and to help you express it to the world because the world needs it so desperately."

"I know. Somehow, I just know," she said. "I think I knew right away, but some part of me could not comprehend it all. When I'm in the Ark, everything makes sense – even the challenging memories that play out in front of me seem to be teaching me something and allowing me to rise above them. But this ... this was terrifying. The attack was horrible when it happened, and I was not ready to experience it again. Then, when I saw you there ..." *Just like Zak said,* she thought, "... I just froze. It felt like I was suffocating and I pushed my way back into my ..." She was going to say studio, but that wasn't quite right. "I pushed my way back into myself."

"That's an accurate observation, Elena. Your body does remain in this realm when you enter the Ark, but it is possible, with practice, for your body to enter the Ark with you." Anurak stopped as if waiting for her next question.

Elena had plenty of questions. They were spinning in her mind, and she couldn't seem to land on one. *Wait, Anurak is saying something.* She pressed the internal pause button to listen to him.

"I was asking you what it was that Zak had said to you?"

Elena ignored his question. It was unsettling that he kept reading her thoughts when she was not privy to his. In the Ark, the entire team had been able to read one another's thoughts. But now, the mind connection with Anurak was one-way. Everything he said made sense but something still seemed odd to her. And there were all those coincidences that Zak had shown her, like the King of Bir Tawil.

"You want to know about Oliver, don't you?" Anurak asked.

"Stop it! How do you keep doing that?" Elena asked. "It's really making me uncomfortable; why can you read my thoughts but I can't read yours?"

"I'm sorry. I can't turn it off. I can pretend it's not there if you like. But the only reason you can't read my thoughts is the energy you are sending out. You are blocking it, not me."

Elena scowled at him. He was making this *her* fault?

"The King of Bir Tawil, my brother Oliver," Anurak was saying. "He's an eccentric sort of person. He spent a lot of years struggling financially. Then, when he was totally desperate, and his wife was ready to leave him, he made a decision to turn everything over to – well, I'm not sure Oliver would say, God, as he considers himself an Omnist, believing there is truth in all spiritual paths – but he turned everything over to the power he believed was higher than himself. He listened to an inner stirring and created a video game for children that encourages peace. He called it PAXman, meaning Peace Man. It was a play on an earlier video game with a similar name. The idea took off. He landed contracts with schools and churches all over the world, and his business continues to flourish. He vowed to use his good fortune to help others. He's become a bit of a philanthropist. And, the King of Bir Tawil? It really was a gift for his wife to show his gratitude for her sticking with him."

Elena half-listened to the story about Oliver. She was still trying to understand how *she* was responsible for the one-way communication. She had to admit that she was emitting some pretty intense energy. The colors shooting out from her were red and orange and black. They looked a lot like the energy she had seen Zak projecting when he'd told her about Anurak being mysteriously in New York.

The King of Bir Tawil faded from her mind. The question looming in front of her now was, how the hell did Anurak get here. According to Josh's research, he hadn't left Aksum. And if he was this *Guardian*, shouldn't he have taken a vow to remain there? How was it that he was sitting in front of her?

"That's a conversation for another day," Anurak said and stood as if today's meeting had come to an end. She hadn't asked the question aloud. She was definitely feeling better than when she'd arrived, but something about Anurak still frightened her and at the same time intrigued her.

Anurak walked her to the front doors of the temple and mentioned something about coming by to see her, but her mind was in a fog. She didn't really hear him. With an unconscious nod toward him, she walked out into a humid, spring day and headed for home. Low-hanging storm clouds threatened rain, but Elena hardly noticed them. Her intense anger and fear had subsided. She was no longer certain that Anurak had tried to kill them. She wanted to believe that he had been there to help, but how he had gotten there? How had he gotten *here*? A part of her knew he told the truth, but another part of her would not shut up.

Raindrops, large ones, plopped down on her head and pulled Elena out of the endless cycle of conflicting thoughts. It was raining, and she was getting drenched. She ran toward home.

CHAPTER THIRTY-FIVE

Too Much Smoke

Elena was out of breath when she reached the eleventh floor. She had run the last few blocks to Westbeth and then taken the stairs in an effort to still her rambling thoughts. The closed space and sluggish movement of the elevator would have added to her sense of disconnection, and she needed to feel firmly grounded in her body. As she rounded the corner, her apartment door came into view, and so did the empty chair sitting next to it.

There's no such thing as empty – not that kind, anyway. It is impossible to be alone. Loss is an illusion. The chair is just a chair. I can see it as an empty hole, or I can see it as a possibility.

Choosing possibility, Elena opened the locked door, picked up the chair, and placed it by the kitchen table. She picked the scattered junk mail up off the floor and resisted the urge to put it back on the chair. Instead, she put every piece of it into the recycling bin. While she stooped down, stuffing the bin, Moses began a dance of figure eights around her, nearly knocking her off balance. "Looking for manna, Moses?"

"Meow" replied the cat.

"Of course," Elena said. "How about something special today. I'm thinking a tuna sandwich for me and tuna from the can for you."

Moses purred so loudly at that, Elena was convinced he knew what she was saying before she even pulled the can from the cupboard. She continued talking to him as she prepared lunch. Moses jumped into the empty chair as if this place were made just for him. "No. Get down," Elena said. Moses paid no attention to the command, but he leaped immediately to the floor when Elena dropped a large spoonful of tuna into his bowl.

Elena's phone chirped in her back pocket. It was Zak. "Final grants approved. Booking flights. Sure you won't come?"

Elena let out an exasperated puff of breath and rolled her eyes. She no longer believed Anurak was a threat, but she was still concerned. There were so many questions left about their safety – namely *where are those monks now and what if they decide to attack again?*

But even if all her questions could be answered and concerns addressed, she couldn't go now. She had a show to organize, and it was going to take more than the usual amount of preparation. Renee was coming by later today, and she was going to be skeptical about Elena's plan as it was. Leaving town for several weeks or months would not help her case.

"Sorry. Can't. Be careful," She texted back, then added, "When do u leave?"

"Jun 9."

Elena took a bite of her sandwich, set it down, and began typing again. "That's the day of my opening." Then a few minutes later she added, "Tenant Exhibit here Fri. U coming?"

The answer was almost immediate. "Wouldn't miss it."

The Annual Westbeth Community Exhibit featured the work of resident artists. In addition to visual arts, the show included poetry readings, music, and performance art. It was not just an art show; it was a cultural event. Zak usually attended the show with Elena, unless she was dating someone who appreciated art, which hadn't happened for a while.

"Great. CU then," She replied.

Good. She'd see him at the Westbeth opening. She wanted to warn him about the monks but wasn't sure how to do it without causing him more concern about Anurak. She wished now that she had told Zak about her additional trips to the Ark realm – but he already thought she might be delusional.

Elena finished her sandwich while musing over the events of the past twenty-four hours – particularly her conversation with Anurak. Moses had long since finished his portion and was bathing furiously in her papasan chair. The unfinished Ark painting still sat on the floor surrounded by jars of paint. Should she lay down more paint? Maybe. Or, maybe not.

Placing her plate in the sink, Elena washed her hands before moving closer to the painting. *No. It's not time to finish it yet. It should be last.* She propped the canvas against the south wall, under the windows. There, she would see it as she worked on the next set of paintings, *Life* and *Death.* Or maybe she would call them, *Life* and *Life.*

Intent on starting the new pair of paintings, Elena realized there was not a blank canvas left in the studio. No canvas, no painting. Time to get busy. She pulled a worktable into the center of the room and began pulling 1x2s from the storage area behind one of her Shoji screens. Materials and tools assembled, she grabbed her earbuds and opened a playlist on her phone. Elena liked building things, but she hated the sound of saws and hammers.

Elena sang along with the music flowing through her earbuds. When she painted, Elena liked silence or soft, quiet instrumentals if she listened to music at all. But when she was building frames and stretching canvas, well, that was another story. She had a special playlist just for the occasion. It was like a workout playlist, but better.

Now playing was Cindi Lauper's "True Colors." Elena loved that song and hoped her neighbors couldn't hear her belting out the lyrics along with Cindi at the top of her lungs, most likely in an unpleasant key.

Elena recalled her mother using the term *true colors* differently, to describe discovering someone's devious, hidden nature. But that was not what this song was about. It was about the true colors that existed beneath the skin, beneath the emotions and even beneath devious natures. *I wonder if someone can intentionally hide their true colors – even from someone like me? Is it possible to build a faux aura, something colorful that could disguise a dense, cloudy one?*

As the playlist came to an end, Elena put the last staple in the second canvas and laid it on the floor next to its mate. They would be the foundation for the *Life* and *Life* paintings. And both would begin with a base of *true* colors, the brilliant beams of light that formed the essence of each individual soul. Everything else would be layered upon this original core of light.

Using jars of thinned paint, Elena began pouring swirls of pigment, watching as they permeated the canvases. These colorful underpaintings would be nearly identical, but the final images would be vastly different. One would be covered with a brilliant array of lights aligned perpendicularly. From the beams of light, the soft glow of rainbow color would expand outward, creating something that resembled a human form, but without the skin and bones. It was the spiritual being. It lived on. In her mind, Elena saw the finished painting, hundreds, thousands, millions of similar forms all in the process of movement, in and out of a multitude of bodies, floating within them, above them, free of them, and gently descending into them again. She heard the voice within her speak. *Nothing real can be killed.*

That may be so, she thought, *but that does little to fill the hole created when someone leaves their physical body and visible presence behind.*

With that thought, Elena began to imagine the other painting, *Life,* the same essence at its core, but a limited experience of it. Beings of light would be floating over scenes of carnage, hollow bodies discarded as the beings rose from them and gathered together into one greater light. Other beings, perpetrators, their light obscured by a cloud of dust, would remain amid the carnage, unable to merge with the greater light.

As the image formed in her mind, Elena was immersed in a cloudy, heavy feeling. The violence of her desert memories and the mounting cruelty of the world around her came crashing in on her. She reached for an empty jar and began mixing a thin wash of gray. She left streaks of black in the paint, and poured the mixture onto the canvas, swirling it around and around. *It looks like smoke,* she thought. *Too much smoke.*

A faint feeling of nausea arose as Elena thought about smoke. It happened whenever she thought about cigarette smoke, which inevitably brought back the visceral memory of the day Elena's mother had found the pack of cigarettes in her dresser drawer. They were hidden under her stack of blue, knee-high socks and Catholic school beanies. "Dreadful, smelly things. Deadly too. They put holes in your lungs, stain your teeth, and make you look cheap," her mother had said.

They could also make someone quite ill if they smoked enough of them too quickly. Elena's mother had decided that an excellent way to convince her teenage daughter to give them up would be to force her to smoke an entire pack all at once.

Elena remembered that day. She felt queasy just thinking about it. Her mother had sent her to the bathroom with a full pack of cigarettes and instructed her to smoke the entire pack before leaving the bathroom. She didn't finish the pack, and she didn't leave the bathroom anytime soon either. The overdose of smoke and nicotine kept her glued to the toilet for hours and she never smoked another cigarette afterward.

Elena grabbed another empty jar and squeezed a bit of Brick Red paint into it. She added thinner and a bit of gray. With a brush, she applied the paint, forming semi-transparent bricks in a wall-like fashion around the earthbound beings. In her mind, Elena could see each violent, deceitful, or malicious act piling on additional blocks, increasing the separation between the individual beings. The entire canvas was eventually covered; filled with bricks of varying hues and opacity.

Elena placed the wet canvas on one of the easels and stood back to get a sense of the overall effect. Brick walls were a good metaphor, and she nodded her head at the image taking shape. Sometimes a brick wall was protective. Sometimes it was exclusive. And sometimes, it begged to be broken through. An idea for the upcoming installation popped into Elena's head. Bricks. She would need a lot of them.

Just then, there was a hefty nudge against the back of Elena's legs. Moses, trying to break through the brick wall that governed his food. He purred and bumped and wound about her legs. "Okay, buddy. I know. Time for a break," she said wiping the excess paint from her brush and placing it in the jar of solvent. She tightened the jar lids, fed Moses another small portion, and settled into the papasan to ponder the paintings, the one on the easel and the one still lying on the floor.

The one on the floor had only the first wash on it, but in her mind, she could see it taking shape in a way that communicated life, a life that persisted beyond the physical manifestation of it. Her focus shifted then to the painting on the easel. The same underpainting existed, the same images of persistent life were present, but futile attempts at stopping it were scattered about the canvas, each attempt creating smoky blocks of dense matter resembling bricks. It expressed, for Elena, a vision of a preponderance of violence that seemed endemic.

Maybe violence and the fear that causes it are like smoking too many cigarettes. Maybe the human race can't fully comprehend that killing is futile until they've exhausted themselves in the endeavor and it becomes too distasteful to continue. Maybe humans like hitting their heads against a brick wall.

Reaching for her notebook to record her thoughts, Elena caught sight of her e-reader sitting next to it. *Hmm. I wonder what Paul's book has to say about life and death and killing.* She had devoured the first few chapters of *The Tomb of God* but had gotten distracted by the paintings, and Anurak, and Zak, and well, life.

She opened the reader and skimmed the chapters, most of which were titled to match Paul's interpretation of one or more of the traditional commandments. She stopped at "Nothing Real Can Be Killed." Of course, he would use the same words that had wandered into her mind. *Minds once linked reflect like-thoughts.* Elena touched the chapter title and began reading:

> *It is impossible to kill the essence of life, but it is possible to destroy the body it inhabits. Destroying the body of another can never succeed in bringing the perpetrator closer to God. It can never succeed in fulfilling the killer's desire for safety, connection, or well-being. Only total surrender to a power higher than one's self and seeing beyond "otherness," to our oneness with all beings can do that. In an absolute awareness of being one with God and all of creation, the directive "Thou Shall Not Kill," becomes an acknowledgment that there is nothing to kill, no desire to engage with what is not real, and a realization that nothing real can be killed.*

Minds once linked equal linked thoughts. Setting the e-reader aside, Elena pulled her cell phone from her pocket and flipped through the contacts. She didn't know Paul very well. They'd only met on a couple of field studies, but his number was in her phone from the last dig. Every member of the team had exchanged numbers for ease of communication. It worked better than walkie-talkies at the base camp where cell signals were reasonably stable.

She pressed his number and waited. "Hey, Paul ... this is Elena, Elena Rowan from the dig... I'm reading your book... Yeah, it's really intriguing... You're welcome... No, I'm not finished yet, but there's an uncanny – well maybe not so uncanny – similarity between your book and what I'm doing with my paintings ... I know, right. I was just thinking about how our minds were linked when we first returned. Anyway, I'm wondering if you'd be interested in collaborating with me on my upcoming show ... It's in June ... no, I'm not going on the new dig either ... Great! Here's what I'm thinking...."

Elena proceeded to tell Paul about the contrast paintings, the installation, and her painting of the Ark that was still in progress. She suggested they incorporate a few corresponding sentences or paragraphs from his book, either embedded in the paintings or as statements hung next to them, and they could have his book available for sale at the show. Paul loved the idea and agreed to come by the studio the next week to work out the details.

As she ended the call, the pile of junk mail now neatly contained in a bin by the door caught her eye. She grabbed a weekly news magazine. It wasn't junk mail, but she discarded them as soon as she had read them. She limited her exposure to the news now, not because she wished to hide from it, but rather because she chose not to focus undue attention on it. If she had learned anything from her conversations with Anurak, it was that focusing your attention on something caused it to increase. Your attention could give power to a problem, or to a solution, and she was choosing solutions from a higher realm of thought.

Sitting on the floor, next to the smoky painting, she began clipping headlines to be embedded in the work. She placed each one carefully in its ultimate position; *WAR BETWEEN UKRAINE AND RUSSIA RAGES ON, U.S. CRIPPLED BY DIVISIVE AND CORRUPT POLITICS, STARVING CHILDREN IN GAZA, HATE CRIMES INCREASING, ACTIVE SHOOTER APPREHENDED.*

Elena opened the jar of quick glaze, added a bit of brick red and gray, then held the clippings to the canvas as she applied the adhesive finish over it. The brilliant streams of color in the background were all but obscured by the brick-like shapes and the devastating headlines. The overall effect was a feeling of despair; *Life - but not Life.*

The other painting, still on an easel, caught Elena's eye. Maybe she would include a layer of the bricks and newspaper clippings in various stages of disintegration at the bottom of that scene. She saw the images taking shape in her mind, looking a lot like the discarded chrysalis of an emerging butterfly. Her heart felt suddenly lighter at the thought, and the whole direction of the painting became perfectly clear. *Nothing is written in stone.* She smiled at the memory. *Unless we choose to make it so. The current state of human consciousness "can" be transformed.*

241

CHAPTER THIRTY-SIX

Westbeth Opening

"Something's bothering me," Elena said as she walked toward a bench in the middle of the seventh-floor garden.

"What's that?" Anurak asked, walking alongside her.

"How does it work? I mean, the Ark. I saw it open up and it drew the team into what appeared to be inside of it. I assumed that the only way into that realm was there, with the artifact itself. But now, I'm able to enter anytime I choose, right in my studio. And from what you've told me, it can also be entered from the inner chamber in Ethiopia. How does that work exactly?"

Anurak sat on the bench, adjusting his robes as he did. He took a deep breath and said, "Isn't it an amazing day? Can you smell the variety of floral scents? They're blooming everywhere, and it seems as though there will be no end to their beauty."

"Yes. I can smell them. I wish there weren't the scent of carnations, though. That always depresses me – reminds me of funerals. But what about the Ark?"

"It's like the flowers. They bloom. They drop their seeds. They seem to disappear or fade, but the seeds pop up and continue to spread the same beauty and the same scent. The bees, butterflies, and even the wind help to scatter the seeds spreading their beauty elsewhere."

Elena understood how flowers spread, but she was a little confused by the analogy. "I'm not sure I get your point," she said.

"Everything and everyone who comes in contact with the message of the Ark spreads it a little further. Once opened, it cannot be fully closed. The one who carries the message will spread it, consciously or unconsciously."

"So ..." Elena paused thoughtfully. "You are saying that I am a carrier?"

"Indeed."

"And, every place the Ark has been becomes a portal?"

"For those who are open and willing – and sometimes those close by, yes."

"What do you mean by *open?*

"Able to let go of preconceived ideas and attachments. This is more difficult than you might imagine. We have beliefs and expectations that have been ingrained since birth, perhaps, even many lifetimes. They are hard to let go of. *Open* means you are ready to release all of that and see things in a new way."

A mixture of feelings stirred in Elena's chest. She could feel her heart pumping a little more rapidly as a fluttering feeling welled in her chest. "I'm not sure how I feel about being a portal. What about people who are not ready and open?"

"Most will be unaware of the opening. Some will be oddly attracted to you – not in a romantic way, but they will feel something intriguing when they are near you. They will want more of that. But for those who are truly ready to evolve, they will hear something you say, or see something you've painted, and it will open something in them. They may not have the experiences you have had, but enlightened thoughts within them will be set free, and they will bloom in their own way and in their own time."

This felt a little better. She was glad it didn't mean people were going to enter *through* her in a way that invaded her space. But she still had dozens of questions about this strange idea. "And what about ..." She searched for the words. "What if someone is not ready, but noticed or knew about the portals, would they ...?"

Anurak finished the thought for her. "You are worried that they will find a way in and abuse the wisdom. And you wonder if they might cause you harm. The answer is no. The Ark cannot be harmed and neither can the Ark that has opened in you."

Elena's mind wandered. *The Ark "in me" cannot be harmed? Okay, so the essence of me cannot be harmed, but what about my body? I know that it can be damaged....*

Anurak was still explaining, "The energy of the Ark cannot be stolen, it can only be shared. And those who are closed, or those who would misuse it, prevent themselves from entering it. The energy they project is too dense – not unintelligent as the word is sometimes used – but dense as in matter vibrating at such a low frequency that it cannot penetrate the higher one. However, the higher frequency can begin to dismantle the denser energy – it can scratch the surface and create an opening in the person. It's why Jesus told us to pray for our enemies."

Elena's breath moved through her a little easier, and the beating of her heart returned to normal. She wondered how she had ever suspected anything dangerous about this peaceful man whose wisdom had such a calming effect on her.

"Thanks, Anurak," she said, preparing to leave. "I hope you'll come to the Westbeth Opening this evening. I'm displaying a set of the *Contrast Paintings,* and it's really a fantastic event. It's not just a show – it's an art-world happening."

Anurak nodded, then held his hands in a prayer position and said simply, "Namaste."

***

The downstairs gallery brimmed with activity. The preparations for the annual exhibit of resident artwork was finally complete, and guests were beginning to enter. Paintings and mixed media work hung from nearly every vertical surface, pedestals displaying sculptural works in a vast variety of materials dotted the gleaming wood floor. Stages had been installed in the adjacent galleries for ongoing performance art. Westbeth was a beautiful place to exhibit. The lighting, the atmosphere, everything about it looked as though it had been designed by artists *for* artists. Because it had.

Elena stood near the two paintings that Renee had insisted she exhibit. One set of contrast paintings, "Life," and "Life," hung side-by-side, much to Elena's chagrin. A small table next to the paintings held postcard-sized announcements of her upcoming installation. In her small cross-body shoulder bag, she carried invitations to the private preview. These had been mailed to her patrons as well as those of the gallery and some of Paul's readership.

Being tied to the paintings was a bit annoying. Elena wanted to enjoy the show herself. This was an event she looked forward to all year whether she had a piece in the show or not. It was a *happening* in the artist community, and she didn't feel like part of it, standing here hawking tickets to her next show. She hoped Renee would show up soon before she gave in to the urge to abandon her post.

"Oh, Elena! These are wonderful!"

It was Mrs. Randolph; the woman Elena had walked away from at her opening right after the dig. Mrs. Randolph tended to love anything Elena painted, but it was really reassuring to hear her complimenting the new series.

"Mrs. Randolph, how good to see you again. I'm so glad you like them. Did you get your preview tickets to the installation?" Elena hoped that her previous rudeness had been forgotten.

"Oh yes, dear. I wouldn't miss it. But what's this about nothing is for sale at the opening – we have to come back on the final day of the show? That's quite interesting – I've returned to pick up my purchases, but I've never heard of that before."

"There are several reasons. First, sold-stickers would detract from the overall experience, but there's more. The "before and after" theme will be enhanced by a final addition to the exhibit on the last day. Patron tickets will get you into both The Opening and The Closing. Everyone else will need to purchase the limited tickets available for The Closing."

"Very interesting," mused Mrs. Randolph. "You know I'll be there. Can't wait to see what you have planned for us, dear."

"Thank you. I'm so grateful for your support. I'm really excited about this show."

Elena felt a tap on her shoulder. It was Renee. *Finally!*

"Go take in the show, Elena. I'll cover for you. There's so much happening, I know you want to take it all in. And there are people to meet, too." Renee said this last part as an instruction – '*get out there, and schmooze,*' was what she meant.

Renee continued the conversation with Mrs. Randolph, freeing Elena to enjoy the show and partake of the refreshments. The hors d'oeuvre table was near the front, and she saw Zak arrive just as she was filling a small plate with some gouda and a few crackers.

"Hi! Grab some cheese and let's take a look around while Renee fills in for me," she said.

"Sounds great," said Zak, grabbing a plate. He selected a few snacks and joined Elena on a walkthrough of the show. Their first stop was a poetry reading by Elena's neighbor, Margot. She sat on a wooden stool in the center of the stage. Eerie blue lights lit only her face. She gazed at her audience, then toward some distant place as she read:

I sit in the darkness,
Ensconced by thick walls.
Is this a cave, I ask?

Where is the light?
I search for a switch but find none.
I crawl about, jagged rock scratching my knees.

A ray of Light penetrates my darkened cask.
I reach for the beam,
But it slips from my grasp.

The stream of light cannot be won.
I close my eyes and there I see,
Another world inside of me.

Here there is Light, abundant and free.
It shines through the peepholes,
Of my long-worn mask.

"Zak," Elena began as they approached a small sitting area near the main gallery, "Have you read Paul's book? Or seen it?" she asked.

"*The Tomb of God*? Yes, I've seen it. Haven't read it, though. There's a lot of umm ... criticism about it in the field," he answered.

"You should take a look, Zak. I know it's not what the archaeology world was expecting, but he's really put into words some of what we experienced in the Ark."

Zak stared at her, his eyebrows arched. "He talks about the Ark?"

"Oh no. Not specifically. He doesn't give anything away, but he's put into words the same ideas I've been trying to capture with my paintings. I've asked him to collaborate with me on the installation."

"You. And Paul? That's an interesting combination," Zak said, his eyebrows now furrowed as if he were trying to imagine the two of them together.

"Oh, *c'mon* Zak! Not like that. We're working on an artistic statement together. Besides? What's so strange about me being friends with an archaeologist?" she said with a laugh.

"Touché," Zak said, swirling the last bit of wine in his glass. "Want some more wine?" he asked.

"Yes, but I want to tell you something first." She didn't even know how to begin. Taking the last swig of wine from her own cup, Elena set it down and said, "It's about Bir Tawil."

"It's a little late, Elena. We're leaving soon."

"No, I'm not trying to stop you, though I wish I could. It's just that ... well, Anurak suggested something I think you should be aware of."

Zak stiffened, his lips stretching flat across his face as he let a long breath seep out through his nose. "Not my favorite person, Elena. I suppose he has some explanation for why he's here in New York? And that he and his brother don't have anything to do with what happened in Bir Tawil?"

"No. Not exactly." She should have told him about entering the Ark again. She could leave Anurak out of it if she had. She could just tell him she'd had a vision. Instead, she said, "He just mentioned a group of monks that live in Bir Tawil. He thought you might want to be aware of them. They're an ancient order with ties to the priestly tribes of Israel. He thought you should know. It's *possible* they had something to do with the shootings."

Zak looked skeptical. He rubbed his open fist over his mouth, apparently thinking. Elena could almost see the internal calculator behind Zak's eyes, adding a ticker tape of facts and hunches.

"It's plausible," he said at last. "Though how or why Anurak would know about them without being part of them, I can't imagine. There are some Bedouin tribes in the area. It's what the Egyptian police first mentioned. But besides that, our contacts in Egypt detected an area on LiDAR that looks like it might be a dwelling or temple built into the side of a mountain near the cave. There's no indication that it's being used, but Josh did mention it to the Egyptian military. They're keeping some satellite eyes on the area while we travel through."

"Great," said Elena. "I don't know if it will help me sleep, but at least I've told you. Let's get that wine. Or, better yet – can you get some for me? I better get back to my post before Renee sends out a search party."

"Sure," he said, grabbing her cup and heading toward the hors d'oeuvre table.

Rounding the corner near her own display, Elena saw Renee speaking with a potential buyer. She was explaining that these paintings were not currently for sale but would be a part of the upcoming installation. The man was well-dressed, with expensive shoes, well-pressed pants, and a Brooks Brothers shirt and tie. It was a little over the top for a Westbeth opening, but then some wealthy patrons frequented the show – not just artists admiring their peers. She'd never seen this man before, but there was something vaguely familiar about him.

"Oh! Here she is now!" Renee exclaimed. "Elena, come tell us about your paintings and what they represent."

Elena explained to the guest that her paintings were a contrast between what she saw occurring in the world, and what the ideal expression of life might be. The paintings and their contrasting images represented a before-and-after consciousness, suggesting the implications of the spiritual evolution of humankind. She avoided mentioning commandments or arks. It wasn't really necessary and might be off-putting to some people. She wanted people to experience the paintings and the message, not form a new religion around them.

The man nodded and smiled. "Your theme reminds me of something I read recently. Are you familiar with *The Tomb of God,* by Paul Silva?" he asked.

"Yes. Absolutely!" Elena said. She was delighted that he had noticed the connection. "Paul is actually working with me on the exhibit. I hope you'll come."

"I wouldn't miss it. I imagine that's quite a financial undertaking. I represent a foundation that promotes the arts. We might be able to help if you need us." He handed Elena a purple and black card. Glancing at the card as she slid it into her small shoulder bag, she noticed there was no name on it, only a company and phone number.

"Thank you so much. Did Renee give you a preview ticket Mr...?" She waited for him to fill in his name.

"Indeed, she did," he answered. "Please excuse me. I see someone I've been waiting for. Do you mind?"

"Oh. Of course not. I'll see you at the show then," Elena answered, confident that Renee had gotten his name.

Elena greeted the next guest, allowing the mysterious patron to slip from her mind, but not without glancing at the man's energy as he departed. Overall his colors seemed bright, turquoise being the most dominant hue. There were, however, unusual rays of orange and green radiating outward. Just as the man rounded the corner of a display wall, Elena noticed a small cloud of dark energy following him near his feet. A slight chill ran up her arms leaving a trail of little bumps.

"Who was that?" Zak asked, handing Elena a glass filled with Sauvignon Blanc.

"No idea," Elena said taking the glass. "Thanks for this. I needed something to warm me up a bit." Taking a sip, Elena peered through the gallery windows, catching one last glimpse of the mysterious man before he disappeared into the night.

***

The tarp covering Elena's studio floor crunched as Paul walked back and forth, viewing the paintings on one side of the room, then the other. He paused at each one, glanced at Elena with a knowing smile and continued to the next. Watching him, Elena felt a bit of the former sense of connection. She could almost hear his thoughts and acknowledgments. No words seemed necessary. Their understanding of the message of the Ark was ultimately the same.

"Elena, I'm *so* delighted to be a part of your exhibit. My mind is racing with snippets from the book that work with these – especially the, what did you call them? *The Light Paintings?"*

"Yes. *The Light Paintings.* I was thinking the same thing. The quotes would work best with those. The installation design calls for the darker paintings to be hung first, then the light-filled ones will be hung in the same order, but after an experiential chamber between the two," Elena answered.

"What kind of experiential chamber?"

"Let me show you," Elena said, gesturing toward the empty chair at her kitchen table. Paul sat, and she opened her folder of drawings and engineering plans and turned them around to face him.

Paul scanned the drawings then homed in on the engineering plans. "Whew. Lasers? Holograms? Video Cubes? It sounds like a huge investment. Who's funding it?"

Elena arched her eyebrows and let out a sigh. "Well, the gallery is fronting some of the funds and banking on ticket sales – especially for the closing event. I'm also fronting some of the expense myself and calling in student volunteers from the Schools of Engineering and Computer Sciences. But the budget is getting a little tight. I'm not worried, though. I know this is going to be a huge success. The Closing will reveal an unexpected piece, and the gallery will be grateful they said yes. I have this feeling that funding will show up and I'm focusing my attention there rather than on a fear of lack."

"Of course. I totally get that. That's just how I felt about the book. I came back from the dig with plans of completing the book I started before the trip. It was almost done. The publisher was lined up, and the editor was just waiting for my final insertions. But when I started writing something entirely different came out of me. The publisher was expecting an educational work, and of course, that's not what came out at all. They dumped me like a hot potato. But I didn't give up. I knew it was meant to be published – and fast, before the Christmas rush. Then, just as I was about to indie publish and foot the bill myself, an unexpected resource just showed up.

"A guy from this place called the Seventh Light Foundation contacted me – said he had heard about the manuscript from my other publisher's editor and he wanted to back the book. I was like ... okay, cool. Let's go. They published it and set up a bunch of book signings and other marketing opportunities. In fact, he's arranged for me to do a TED Talk the day after your opening! Never in my wildest dreams did I think I would be doing that."

"Amazing!" Elena said. An invitation to a TED Talk was an amazing accomplishment. The TED Conference posted dynamic, twenty-minute presentations from innovative leaders around the world under the maxim of *Ideas Worth Spreading*.

"Yes, like that," Elena added. "I think the funds to complete the installation will show up like that, too. I can just feel it, and I know that's where I have to focus my attention – as the saying goes, 'Where attention goes, energy flows,' right?"

"Yes!" Paul said. "I hear people say that a lot, and it's true. I think I first heard it from an author named James Redfield. I try to remember it and avoid putting too much attention on what I don't want. It seems to work if I can stick to it. Another way of saying it is, 'believe it until you achieve it.' No idea where I first heard that, but the man from the Seventh Light Foundation said it when he handed me this card." He pulled the card from his pocket and handed it to Elena.

"Here," he said. "I don't know if this is the resource for you or not, but try calling them."

Elena took the card. It looked familiar for some reason. It read, "Seventh Light Foundation, Supporting the Arts" and listed an 800 number, but no name.

"Thanks! I'll give them a try."

CHAPTER THIRTY-SEVEN

Preparations

Zak glanced away from his computer screen, eyeing the series of satellite photos spread across his desk confirming the vast potential of the dig site. The images had been pivotal in obtaining the necessary grants and university permission to further explore Bir Tawil. The LiDAR shots Mason had been able to procure through his contacts in Egypt provided further evidence of a lost civilization; traces of underground mounds that indicated ruins of buildings, better views of the winding, indented pattern suggesting a possible dried riverbed, and wide-spread scatterings of shapes with distinctly human markers.

Permission from Egypt and Sudan had been tenuous. Neither country, even with the potential of archaeological discovery, was willing to assume jurisdiction for the disputed borderland. To grant permission would be to claim the area – and that would bequeath ownership of the much more valuable Hala'ib Triangle to the other. In the end, it had been determined that the American group could move forward with excavation plans provided they adhered to the conservation guidelines from both countries and included them in all relevant information.

The Egyptian military had agreed to monitor satellite imagery and warn the group of impending danger, but they would only enter the area for "search and rescue." The Sudanese military agreed to ignore their presence provided they stayed clear of Sudan's border. The Egyptian police had worked with Josh on gathering a reputable group of guides who would offer the only onsite protection politically feasible. Not the greatest situation, but far better than what they had for their previous venture.

The glass door wall behind Zak revealed a flurry of activity in the lab. Gina was overseeing the packing of various artifacts from the Qasr Ibrim dig to be returned to Egypt, and Dr. Mason was directing a flock of grad students as they gathered and packed items for the two field labs, one at base camp in Abu Simbel, and one onsite in Bir Tawil. Zak was grateful for the buffer the glass doors provided from the boisterous activity – but it was not enough. Rubbing his ears as if he could blot out the sound, he rotated his neck and stretched his back, then turned his attention to the survey plans. The six areas targeted for the survey were selected by their likelihood of success, based on the photos Zak was reviewing. The teams would begin with metal detectors and ground-penetrating radar, then stake the parameters for suggested pit squares based on their findings. Each group would be accompanied by a security detail and a photographer.

A seventh site was known only to Zak and Josh, and it would remain that way until the two of them had adequately secured the artifact. They'd gone back and forth on the importance of including a photographer for this initial inspection, but without Elena there, they had finally decided against it.

A rap on his office door drew Zak's attention away from the photos. The door opened without his verbalizing an invitation and Josh appeared. "I've got the final paperwork for all the team members," he said. "No issues were found with any of them. I thought we could review my suggested assignments before I head out for the day? I think the teams are pretty well-rounded, but I thought you'd want to take a look."

"Sure. Absolutely. Come on in. Your timing is great, actually. I'm making some final notes for each site, and it would be helpful to add the names of team members assigned to each site before we go. We still need credentials printed, and they should have the team numbers on them."

"Okay, so I've reviewed all the data available on each person and tried to include at least two experienced members on each team, plus the security team, which we'll assign when we get there."

"Where have you placed Dr. Mason and Gina?" Zak asked.

"Like you said, I put them together, setting up the field lab at the Bir Tawil camp so they'd be close by when you're ready to open the seventh site."

"And photographers? Who will be close by?" Zak asked.

Josh twisted his mouth and sighed. "Well, since you haven't been able to talk Elena into coming, I've got Barrette remaining in camp as coordinator for his team. His assignment is to be ready and available when the first survey-team reports findings."

"Perfect," Zak said. "Thanks for working on the team rosters. It's a bit above and beyond security but we needed the help and it seemed like your background information on people might prove helpful in creating balanced teams. Lots of time together in close quarters is a recipe for personality-trait issues and ego clashes."

"Yeah," Josh said as he handed the lists to Zak. "I considered their psych evaluations as well as their strengths when I assigned them. The groups should be pretty well balanced."

Zak scanned the lists, made a couple of modifications and handed it back to Josh. "Can you make those changes and then email the list to me? I want to enter the teams into the individual site plans and distribute to the team leaders before we leave."

Josh nodded, made a note of his own and said, "I'm on it."

A buzzing sound came from Josh's hip as he walked toward the door. He checked his cell phone and stopped abruptly.

"What is it?" Zak asked.

"It's about Oliver Quinn," Josh replied. "He's in New York."

A crash from the lab interrupted their conversation. Zak gritted his teeth and wiped his mouth with his hand. With trepidation, he turned in his chair to assess the damage. "Oh, Christ. It's just a monitor, but for God's sake, you'd think we were going to the moon."

The sound of Zak sliding the door along its track stopped the commotion as everyone looked up, sheepish. "Settle down, people. It's not a sprint – it's a marathon. Please take your time with the packing. We need everything packed carefully because replacing equipment in the middle of the desert will be next to impossible." He slid the door shut and watched them return quietly to their tasks, shaking his head.

Grabbing his jacket and scooping up his laptop, the photos, and various folders, Zak said, "Let me know if you get any more information on Oliver – or if he moves again. And send that email to my home address, will you? I've gotta get out of here before I strangle someone. I need some peace and quiet before we leave tomorrow. I can't think straight here."

"Sure thing, Zak. See you in the morning," said Josh as he left the office.

Before Zak could reach the door, there was a knock on the glass behind him. He took a deep breath, controlling the desire to roll his eyes. He loved the glass doors and being able to monitor the activity in the lab, but he was not so much in love with the lack of privacy. He wished he'd pulled the blinds shut. Mason was at the glass with folders in his hands. *Crap!* Zak had forgotten they were supposed to go over the basecamp plans.

Setting his laptop and files back on the desk, Zak nodded at Mason and opened the glass door. Mason closed it behind him, aware that the activity in the lab was distracting. "One last look at the base and site camp plans?" he asked.

"Of course. Sorry, I almost forgot. Thanks for catching me before I left. I just need to finish a few things without all the umm ... activity," he said.

"No problem. I know it's crazy in there. The students are so excited they can barely contain themselves. No amount of chiding seems to settle them down – I'm thinking we should remove the coffee machine," he said with a smirk.

Zak had to laugh at that. His own addiction to coffee would never allow the coffee machine to be removed, but he appreciated the sentiment. Caffeine was definitely not needed in the lab today.

"So, what've you got, Mason? Are we all set to go?"

"Yes. I've finished the layouts for both sites." He pulled two diagrams from his folder and turned them to face Zak. "We won't spend a lot of time at base camp, but it will be where we stage the trips to and from Bir Tawil. There is a field lab in each – though the one at base camp is more thorough. I worked with Josh on staffing it with volunteers willing to stay behind and do only research. The grad students working on research theses were reluctant to miss the action but grateful for the lab opportunity."

Zak placed the layouts side-by-side and examined them. Assured that each had the basic team necessities; sleeping quarters, dining, cooking, and most importantly, water; he flipped the page to review details of the field lab setups. Base camp had more sophisticated equipment, but the site camp had the proper cleaning, washing, and storage setups. It would be equipped with computers for logging items found. Both sites would have internet capabilities, the Bir Tawil camp using a satellite connection.

"Looks great, Mason. How much of this will be set up when we arrive?" Zak asked.

"Not everything. A local contractor will start things up, but we'll need to spend a couple of days setting up the base camp and prepping for Bir Tawil. Nothing will be set up in Bir Tawil when we arrive. It will take at least a day to set up enough equipment for the site teams to start exploring and we can set up the lab while they begin the surveys. I'm sure you know this, but Josh has arranged local guides to join us at the base camp when we arrive so we can coordinate with them before we head out."

"Yes, Josh mentioned all of that in his last report. Seems like we're pretty well set to go." Zak shot a doubtful glance toward the lab, "that is, if this team survives the anticipation." He and Mason both chuckled at that. They'd each been that excited on their own first digs – and this one was already expected to be extraordinary.

"All right then," Zak said standing and gathering his things. "I'll see you in the morning."

"Can't wait," Mason replied as he gathered his notes. He smiled with a look of pride at his former student, then another, more puzzling look crossed his face as he returned to the lab and shut the glass door behind him.

Zak pulled the blinds, shutting out the lab scene, turned off the lights, and left for home. In the hall, he remembered that Oliver Quinn was in town. He sent a text to Elena "Oliver Quinn in NY." He had no idea what Quinn being in New York meant but wanted her to know.

***

Gina double-checked the packages against her log records as an irritated delivery man loaded them onto his cart. The process was tedious, but each artifact had to be accounted for, and the delivery guy was going to have to sign for each of them before they left the lab. Only one student remained behind, helping her with the task. Mason and the others had departed as soon as the last shipping crate had been labeled and had been handed over to the airport delivery service.

Finally, the last package accounted for, Gina closed the book and dismissed the student and the delivery guy. She was alone in the lab, a rare occurrence lately. The quiet was lovely. She felt a sense of release as she placed the log book on its shelf and began gathering her files and belongings. Turning the computer off seemed so final that she hesitated before clicking the mouse to close it down. She wanted to explore more, but it was getting late, and there was packing to do – and then there was Mason. She licked her lips at the thought.

If it had been quiet before, the silence only increased as the computer fan stilled. Gina took one last wistful glance at the vault in the corner fingering the key in her pocket. She wanted desperately to touch it one more time ....

"Gina!"

Her desire was abruptly interrupted by another, more urgent desire. Mason. He was standing at the lab door, waiting.

"It's time to go. Nothing left to do tonight. Let's get dinner and ... *drinks* at my place after?" he said, winking at her.

Gina smiled. Her silky red locks waved rhythmically over her shoulders as she shook her head giving him an *oh, you naughty boy* look. She took her time removing the lab coat, making sure the plump mounds underneath would be revealed with enticing slowness. She hung the coat on a hook near the table and joined Mason for what would be a decidedly relaxing evening.

CHAPTER THIRTY-EIGHT

The Installation

The gallery had undergone a complete transformation in preparation for the evening's preview. A floor-to-ceiling brick façade now covered the stark white gallery walls. Nine *Dark Paintings,* as Renee called them, were hung on this brick backdrop. A half-wall, also made of bricks, formed a spiral path leading from one painting to the next in the intended order. The half-wall sloped upward along the curved path until it met the ceiling, obscuring the opening of the experiential chamber of the exhibit to those who had not yet entered the pathway.

A deep swelling sensation radiated from Elena's heart, and tears brimmed her eyes as her feet touched the entrance of the brick-lined pathway. The installation was complete, and months of painting, self-exploration, and working with engineering and computer-science students, and then collaborating with Paul had given birth to this grand culmination of her work. Heart palpitations wormed their way up into her throat as she viewed the first painting, the crocodile, now titled *Fear: The Greatest of False Gods.* The distance created by the pathway brought the viewer intentionally close to the painting to increase the feeling of being swallowed by its image. The tremors in her throat subsided, and a breath of deep satisfaction emerged.

Elena followed the brick-lined path, stopping at each of the dark paintings. The final piece in the dark series, *The Grass Is Greener,* was followed by an opening in the brick wall. An assortment of broken bricks and mortar dust lay scattered about the entrance, giving the appearance that the wall had been smashed open. Stepping onto the exposed walkway, Elena entered the experiential chamber.

She stood in the middle of the installation, surrounded by undulating, colorful waves of light. Harmonic sounds filled her ears and pulsed through her body. There was a sweetness to the sounds that both relaxed and excited her. Here, there were no brick walls. Lasers, hanging strips of projectable scrims, 3D projection cubes, and holographic images gave the impression that there were no walls at all. Under-floor projection created the illusion of walking on clouds.

It was thrilling. It was peaceful. It was unearthly. Subtle imagery floated into the scenes that surrounded her and then disappeared into the light. Multiple variations of the *Power of a Comma*, painting floated by on giant 3D video cubes. Towering images of commas hovered before her, then glided away, replaced by the letters I, A and M. *I am, that I am ... I am, that I am ... I am, the Lord your God ... I am ... I am ...* The combination of projected and holographic images, the sounds, the cloudlike images stirring beneath her feet, all created an experience that resembled being inside the Ark. It wasn't perfect. It didn't whisper words of Truth into her mind, but it did evoke feelings of joy and utter serenity. *So close,* she thought.

The spiral-like pathway led to the next chamber of the exhibit where the "Light" paintings were hung in an order matching those at the beginning of the tour. The first image was the goddess steering the crocodile, reins held deftly in her hands. The mirror-like substance embedded in the paint created the subtle effect that she might be the one riding the beast. Gentle wavelike movements of the floor enhanced the effect. It was just as powerful as she had hoped it would be. A plaque next to the painting displayed a quote from Paul's book:

> *When the power within you is recognized as greater than what threatens you, you will have eliminated a false god. It is in the taming of this false god called fear that the true salvation of humankind is attained.*
> *– Paul Emerson Silva.*

When the motion of the flooring subsided, the lighting on the goddess painting dimmed, and the next set of lights came to life encouraging the viewer to move forward toward the next painting, *Nothing In Vain,* then *Nothing Engraved.* Then the lighting shifted to a warm bluish glow highlighting the next work of art titled, *Mother-Father.* Elena stood before it now, the lump in her throat growing larger. The colorful wash saturating the canvas was visible through the semi-transparent images of a man and woman holding a child. At first glance, it was a simple, loving family portrait. But within each of the figures were infinite repetitions of two more ethereal figures, entwined together, in an energetic braid of light and energy. A perfect yin and yang, the male and female energies, joining as one light within each figure, expanded beyond them into one harmonious blend of light merging into the colorful wash of the background. The inscription below the painting was from Paul's book:

> *In the purest state, each of us is an expression of the One, the Divine that is neither male nor female, yet gives birth to both; a mother, father, everything God. When we honor the mother and father in ourselves and in others, we honor the Essence of Life which gives birth to all. – Paul Emerson Silva.*

Elena continued through the winding pathway, stopping at each of the light paintings. Each presented a contrasting view of the first set of paintings, depicting a higher, light-filled perspective. They were brilliant, colorful, and inviting. The message was clear in Elena's mind. The experience of Light and harmony in the space between what appeared as *darkness* and *light* changed everything.

At the last of the light paintings, another pathway opened to the final chamber of the exhibit where the eight-foot by four-foot painting of the Ark was hung. The resemblance to an actual Ark was only subtly implied, a translucent image floating above a ground of color and light. From its subtle top, streams of sparkling color emerged upward toward projectable strips of fabric and holographs, giving the appearance that light was flowing right out of the canvas into the space above it.

In front of the Ark painting, stood a pedestal, six-feet wide by four-feet deep. On its front, a brass plate was attached with nothing inscribed except the closing date for the exhibit. The pedestal was lit, spotlights shining down on its center. A thick acrylic cube was secured to its top with locking bolts. Inside, there was nothing.

As Elena walked toward the showcase, a tunnel to her right lit up, inviting her toward the lobby. It was lined with soft, padded fabric and lit with rippling purples and blues. Even the floor was covered in a soft, spongy material that gave the impression that one was walking on clouds. At the exit, strips of silk-like material caressed and brushed over her as she arrived at the lobby where the patron's reception would be held in less than an hour.

A mixture of feelings arose in Elena. She was beyond pleased with the installation. She knew she could not control what others gained or understood as they experienced the work. That was art. She knew that now. But what was this other feeling welling up in her? It wasn't anger. It wasn't frustration. It was something else. It was a deep knowing. It didn't matter what she painted before or after the experience in the Ark. It didn't matter how well she depicted the experience. She could paint for the rest of her life and not convey the experience or the knowing that accompanied it. The only way to do that was to live it. By living in this world of clay and limitation with eyes that had seen it all as Light, and bringing that understanding to every experience, she would be different. She would express Truth. She would be the portal of Light awakening it in some small way in others. Replicating the Light was impossible. Living *as* the Light was the only way to reveal the mystery of what had never been lost, only hidden.

***

In the lobby, Renee was waiting for Elena, a huge smile on her face and arms open for a congratulatory hug. "You've done it, Elena! You told me I would want to be a part of this and ... well, it's amazing. Blake and Judith couldn't be more pleased. This is going to be huge."

Elena returned the hug and smiles. Tears were brimming in her eyes, but they were tears of joy and accomplishment.

Renee was still talking. "And just when I thought we were doomed, that grant money showed up too."

Elena had been dialing the number for the Seventh Light Foundation on the card Paul had given her when Renee had called with the news. The foundation had already heard about the show and had awarded a grant before they could even apply for it.

"How did they know about the show in the first place?" Elena asked.

"The mystery man from the Westbeth show, darling. Remember? He mentioned he might be able to help and gave us his cards. I guess he just went ahead and started the ball rolling from the information on the flyers. It's crazy, but hey – who's complaining?"

The Mystery Man? Something clicked in Elena's mind. She remembered thinking there was something familiar about the card when Paul had given it to her saying the foundation had just shown up and helped him publish. She reached into her small shoulder bag. The card was still there. She pulled it out and stared at it. *Seventh Light Foundation.* Then below it, in small print, she read, "Subsidiary of PAXman International." *PAXman? PAXman ... Oh!* She remembered the report from Josh now. *Oliver?*

Elena's cell phone buzzed inside the bag. A text from Zak. *Maybe he's saying he's sorry he can't be here,* she thought.

Swiping the screen, she discovered an unexpected message. "Oliver Quinn in NY."

Elena didn't know if the chills running up her arms were fear or joy. Oliver Quinn was in New York, and he had just financed the greatest-ever display of her work. Anurak did say Oliver was a bit of a philanthropist. She chose joy. She was damned if she was going to let Zak's paranoia about Anurak and his brother spoil this incredible evening. She shut the phone off.

***

That damn empty chair! It was the morning after. Elena sat at her kitchen table drinking a cup of green tea in an attempt to revive her tired body. The opening last night had been incredibly successful. They'd sold nearly every ticket to the finale, and Judith and Blake had beamed at the thought of printing more tickets. They'd even discussed adding a second day to the finale.

But now, sitting across from the empty chair, the post-show blues began creeping their way into her consciousness. It was a common response. Weeks, months, sometimes even years would go into the preparation of a major show. And then it was over. The human mind did not switch on and off that easily. The brain would try to continue what it had been absorbed in and would cry out, *What now?*

Now, the empty chair across from her seemed to cry out as well. Zak was gone – back to the desert, and she was intensely worried about him. Paul was off to his TED Talk and a book tour. Anurak no longer came to the studio. It was as if he got the message from Zak that they should only meet at the temple without Elena ever mentioning it. Even Moses was too busy for her as he chomped away at the kibble in his bowl.

The overflowing bin of junk mail by the door caught Elena's eye. She resisted the urge to bury the other kitchen chair with a pile of papers. Like the chair, something in her had opened up, and she no longer wished to close it, but she did wonder what might begin to fill that space.

The studio was nearly empty now, the contrast paintings all serving their role in the installation. What remained were two empty easels, one blank canvas, and an unopened box of clay. There was one more piece of the installation to be added on the last day, and she was not yet sure what it would be, though she doubted it would be a painting. She eyed the box of clay, but it wasn't speaking to her just yet. She sat in her papasan chair waiting for inspiration, but nothing occurred.

Anurak. She hadn't realized it until now, but she was a little disappointed he hadn't attended the opening. She had given him a patron's ticket, but he hadn't shown. Of course, he had seen all the paintings and reviewed all the sketches and plans for the installation, but she had hoped he would join her in the celebration of its completion. He had, after all, influenced some of the work. He had been her sounding board for all the ideas that had filled her mind following the Ark experience and helped her make sense of it all. And, as it turned out, his brother had helped to fund the show. Oliver hadn't shown either, which seemed a bit odd. She needed to see Anurak.

Grabbing her keys from the bowl, she laughed as Moses stopped eating mid-bite and bounded across the room to the window. *Crazy cat. I guess he loves tiny me more than food.*

***

At the temple, Elena was surprised to find Anurak was not in the garden. He was nearly always there when she arrived unless he was right at the door waiting for her. He had an uncanny ability to anticipate her arrival without any communication on Elena's part. But today, he was not there. He wasn't in the lobby. He wasn't in the open receiving room. He wasn't in the cafeteria, either.

"Excuse me," Elena said to a monk walking through the lobby. "Have you seen Anurak today?"

The young monk looked quizzically at her. "Anurak?" He paused, then smiled as he recognized the name. Elena's pronunciation was not quite correct.

"Anurak. No. I have not seen him today. He is no longer here. He left yesterday."

"He left?" Elena was surprised, maybe even hurt. *Why would he leave without even telling me?*

"Do you know where he went?" she asked.

"No. I'm sorry. He did not say, just that he must leave immediately, something about catching up with a group traveling yesterday," the monk replied.

"Okay, thanks," she mumbled as she walked toward the front doors, the feeling of emptiness growing exponentially in her heart.

The day outside was warm and bright, but Elena did not notice. She felt cold inside as if the heat had been turned off on a frigid winter's day. She took no notice of the birds singing in the trees or the flowers blooming in planters along the sidewalks. The park, which usually brightened her day, passed by without notice.

Anurak was gone. Just like that. Zak was away. The installation was complete. What now? Where the hell was Anurak, anyway? And what group was he *catching up* with? Was he catching up with Zak? Had he completely pulled the wool over her eyes? Was he on his way to ambush them? Her mind would not stop, and she felt a black cloud rising up around her.

She stopped and sent a text to Zak, hoping he would get it before losing WiFi in the desert. "Anurak and Oliver both gone."

Elena made polite pleasantries as she passed a few tenants on her way to the elevators but had no recollection of what she said. The elevator ride seemed excruciatingly slow and endlessly long.

The apartment looked and felt empty as she entered and fastened the locks behind her. The only warmth seemed to be a single ray of sunlight pouring through the window, landing on her papasan chair. She took the hint and sat there. Moses appeared out of nowhere and climbed into her lap. The warmth of his furry body and the vibrations of his purring had a calming effect. She stroked his ears and hugged him. "Thanks, buddy. I needed that," she said as she settled into the chair hoping for a little insight and some relief from the emptiness of the room.

CHAPTER THIRTY-NINE

Bir Tawil

The trip to Abu Simbel had been an arduous one, an eleven-hour flight from New York to Cairo, two hours on a smaller plane to Aswan, and another two hours by bus. Zak would have been exhausted if he were not so fired up to finally be here. It had been almost a year since he had set foot on Egyptian soil and made that ill-fated journey into Bir Tawil. Finally, he would be able to justify his actions and validate the discovery. But not as quickly as he had hoped.

The base camp was to be partially set up by the time they arrived. They were expecting the local team to have erected the temporary buildings and connected the generators, but they were drastically behind schedule.

"You Americans need to slow down," said Lateef. "Life is not a short race. It is ... how do you say it? A marathon? Work will be done when it is done."

Irritated by the cliché almost as much as the delays, Zak gathered his team and devised a plan to get them back on schedule – or at least close to it. They would pitch the site tents for now and everyone on the team would help with the construction. Signing on for a dig was not always about the glamour of finding artifacts or doing field research. It was hard labor, digging, schlepping, and in this case, building.

The advantage of the delay was additional time for Josh and Zak to meet with the local guides who would be leading them through the desolate landscape of Bir Tawil and providing security for the team. They met with Jabare Fakhoury, who had been recommended as co-ordinator of the local guides and security personnel by Major Karim Al Hadad of the Egyptian National Police. Jabare was a retired police officer with extensive military experience.

Josh and Zak shared topographical and satellite photos and discussed watch schedules with Jabare. Together they paired guides with the site teams. Meals taken as teams during the construction allowed the groups and their guides to bond, which would be a useful asset in the field.

Three days in, they were getting closer to the original schedule, and the delay was looking more like a gift than a setback. Zak watched the activity with a growing sense of assurance. The work was preparing them for the field in a way he could not have planned. *Always a silver lining if you look for it.*

"Water trucks and buses will be here tomorrow," Josh was saying. "And the Jeeps are all set to go."

"That's great. Has the lab equipment arrived yet?" Zak asked. The shipment had been delayed at customs in Cairo.

"It's on a truck and due here late this afternoon," Josh replied.

"What about WiFi? Are we up and running yet?"

"Should be ready this afternoon. A couple of students have IT experience, and they're pitching in to help the local techs."

That was good news. Even if construction were complete, they wouldn't be able to leave until the internet connection was up and running.

"Oh. There's one more thing I think should make you happy," Josh said.

Zak raised a tired eyebrow. "Oh? What's that?" Lack of sleep was apparent on his face; the crevices under his eyes were returning and his "field beard" as he liked to call it, was filling in.

"Lateef has arranged delivery of something special for breakfast," Josh smiled. He knew this would be a treat for everyone, but especially Zak. "It's Starbucks."

"Yes!" Zak exclaimed, then "Wait. There's a Starbucks in Abu Simbel?"

"No. Closest one is ten hours away, but Lateef knows the owner and says he owes it to your team to have a special *American* treat before we head out into no-man's-land. They're bringing in a temporary kiosk."

Zak nodded with a smile. Coffee in Bir Tawil would not be Starbucks. Not even close. "Have you seen Mason?" Zak asked. "I need to go over some plans with him and see how the lab set-up is coming."

"Last I saw he was on his way into Gina's tent."

Zak rolled his eyes. The two were inseparable. They were like teenagers on a field trip without chaperones. Even in field clothes, Gina had an enticing air about her that Mason could not seem to resist. Field clothes was a bit of a stretch, but at least she'd left the stilettoes at home. Watching her move around camp and fuss over Mason, Zak wondered how she had gotten through her undergrad work. Didn't they require fieldwork at the University of Chicago?

Zak grabbed his mug, filled with what was decidedly *not* Starbucks, and headed toward Gina's tent. He hoped the two would be able to focus more on their work than each other when they got to the site.

***

In the distance, Zak saw the familiar formation of rocks and sand. His entire body began to vibrate as he glimpsed the unforgettable terrain coming into view. Fear, grief, excitement, and an indescribable elation caused every part of his body to tingle, and a small lump began to form in his throat. He wasn't sure he could speak. Looking down at his boots, he loosened and refastened the shemagh about his head, adjusted his sunglasses and unclipped the water bottle from the carabiner on his belt. He popped the lid and took a long, slow swallow, trying to steady himself.

Gina sat next to him in the back of the Jeep, Mason was in the front passenger seat scouring maps and directing the driver. Gina, noticing Zak adjusting his glasses, asked "What? Something familiar?"

"Yes. Vaguely. I think we are close to the spot where the shootings happened." Zak motioned to the caravan behind them to get ready to take a turn. "Over there," he said to their driver, pointing to the left of a rock formation at the edge of a vast open area. Nearby, a long, shallow depression in the earth hinted at the long-dried riverbed spotted in the satellite photos.

"Follow that dead river and come up behind the foothill of the rocky cliffs over there." He pointed toward the base of the rocky terrain they had climbed in the dark after the shootings, but he directed them around it to an area sheltered by rock formations and the base of the mountain. It would be safer there. He had no desire, even with the extra security, to be in the same open space they'd been in before. The thought sent a shudder up his spine, and he took another long, slow drink from his water bottle.

The Jeeps, buses, equipment trucks, and water trucks circled up, forming a perimeter for their site camp. Zak couldn't help thinking they looked like a circle of covered wagons from an old western movie. There were definitely some similarities. Red and beige cliffs towered over them, blocking the falling sun and giving the illusion of protection. But glancing up into the backlit rocks, Zak feared that at any moment some silhouetted figure could appear at the top of the ledge ready to raid their camp and crush their pioneering spirits – if not their lives.

Darkness had no effect on the tiny camp as the sun slipped behind the rocky cliffs and then below the distant horizon. A combination of solar and battery-operated halogens fastened to telescoping tripods lit the area as if it were still daylight. Zak thought they looked like something out of *The War of the Worlds*, pointing their watchful eyes at the occupants of the camp. Sleep would be difficult for everyone. Even veiled by canvas tents, the lights were very bright. And, the nervous, watchful eyes of the security team did as much to frighten everyone as it did to comfort them. Zak laid awake on his cot, his stomach clenched and eyes unable to close. He wondered how much of the twitching in his abdomen was anxiety and how much was excitement. Either way, sleep was not coming anytime soon.

The night was long but uneventful. No robbers. No vigilante groups bent on quelling their expedition. Only a hot, yellow disk rising over the barren eastern horizon announced a new day. Zak watched with weary eyes as the camp slowly came to life with the appearance of the sun. The halogens were extinguished and lowered for the day. A camp kitchen was being erected near the cover of the rocks in the hopes that the afternoon shade provided would keep the cooking area from becoming a virtual furnace. Raised boxes held sealed food containers out of the reach of wandering wildlife.

On the other side of the camp, a field lab was being assembled. Generator trucks were positioned beside it to power the equipment, yet remain visible to security. Another truck lowered its tailgate to aid in the unloading of high-tech equipment and supplies. Zak breathed a sigh of relief. The official site survey could finally begin, and the lost artifact would finally be uncovered and documented. A profound, historic moment was being carefully orchestrated, and his name, his reputation, and his potential for tenure at the university would soon be restored. "Wait. Bring that over here toward the rocks," Zak said as he saw his plane table coming off the truck. "We'll need the afternoon shade for that. We'll be spreading maps and hovering over it through-out the day."

The table in place, he pulled a box of papers and books from his tent and spread out the maps he and Mason had charted. They would need the survey teams deployed to the six sites chosen from the re-search photos. There was more than enough GPR equipment to supply all six teams. The sites each promised to reveal significant remnants of a lost civilization and what had happened to them. But the seventh site, the one up the rugged mountainous path right next to him, that one would be his. He already knew what was hidden there and needed desperately to rediscover it.

CHAPTER FORTY

The Seventh Site

It had been three days, not two, since they had arrived in Bir Tawil. It had been grueling work in the desert sun, but it looked like a camp now. Platform tents, a functioning field lab with satellite WiFi, and a bustling mess hall. Breakfast was being served, and the coffee was not Starbucks, but it would definitely wake you up.

Zak watched over the top of his laptop screen as the survey teams took their packs, equipment, and satellite images in preparation for the day. They wouldn't need shovels or trowels yet, just GPR, metal detectors, stakes, and plenty of water.

Zak continued working at his laptop until all six teams were on their way, then began gathering his own equipment. He didn't really need the GPR. He knew where he was going and what he was about to find, but he took it anyway. He wanted it to look as if he were discovering it for the first time. No one would understand that he had found it and left it behind. The world believed he and the other survivors had simply hidden up the mountain behind rocks until help had arrived. Zak had no intention of changing that story. He simply wanted to rediscover the Ark, be sure it could be touched, and then give it to the world.

He gathered maps, printouts, and a full water bottle, then pressed the button on the radio attached to his shoulder. "I'm headin' up the hill by the camp to get a better overhead view," he spoke into the microphone.

The radio on Josh's shoulder squawked Zak's message. Surprised, Josh glanced up from his security detail lists in time to see Zak heading toward the hill. He knew where he was going. It wasn't a good idea to go alone. *What the hell is he thinking?* It was going to be a good hour before Josh could follow him up there and he couldn't send anyone else. He knew Zak would not want just anyone showing up. "Copy that. I'll join you as soon as I can," he said. He assigned a security team to monitor the far side of the hill. At least he could make sure no terrorists approached Zak from that direction. The next survey team stepped up, and he went over their assignment and security protocol, gave them their equipment list and pointed them toward the storage shed and water truck.

***

Across camp, Gina peered out from behind the flap of her tent to see Zak climbing up the hill. She scurried undetected toward Mason, who was reviewing photos of the Karta. "He's on his way up that hill. Alone. Let's go," she said. Mason moved quickly, shoveling the photos into a metal briefcase and snapping it shut. They gathered scouting equipment and water, then followed the path Zak had taken.

The cave was so obscure that Gina and Mason never would have found it if they hadn't been following Zak. They rounded a curve just in time to see his pack disappear into a crevice between some tall, flat rocks. "Give him some time," Gina said. "Let him find the spot and start digging. No need for us to do the hard labor."

Mason nodded. The sun was beginning to peek over the horizon, and he was already hot. They found a small area behind a group of boulders shaded from the rising sun and sat.

As the already minuscule piece of shade dwindled with the sun's westward movement, Gina's leg began to jiggle. She shifted her position, groaned, and took a long swig of water. Her patience was giving out from heat and the growing anticipation of attaining her goal. She held her knee with one hand to stop the jiggling and used the other to lift her water bottle to her drying lips when they heard something from inside the cave. Was it laughter? Or was it screaming? They weren't sure which. Maybe it was both. They stared at one another, wondering. "This is good," said Gina. "It gives us a reason to show up."

They squeezed through the hidden crevice leading into the cave and found Zak sitting next to a pile of rock and dust. There was a small tripod light standing over an opening in the cave wall, an entrance to a hidden chamber. Zak was covered in dust, and he was laughing. And he was screaming, carrying on about someone stealing *it*. He was babbling now. "It should've … we should've … I knew … delusions ... ha, hah … it's over. It's all over."

"What's all over?" Gina asked. "Dr. Erdmann. Are you okay? Why were you digging all by yourself? We could have come and helped you. We just heard you from outside and wandered in. What's over? What should we have done?" Gina feigned her best look of sympathy. Kindness tended to get more information from people than aggression, especially when they were freaking out like this. He was so incoherent now she half expected foam to come out of his mouth. "Dr. Erdmann?"

Zak looked up at her, his eyes red from lack of sleep. "It should have been here. Right here in this spot. I was certain of it."

"How could you possibly know that?" she asked. "The tablet is not specific. We've got dozens of satellite shots, and not even LiDAR could have penetrated this cave. They are all potential sites but not confirmed. Why here? Is this location even in the plans? I don't recall seeing it before." She was baiting him. She knew there was more. She wanted that fragment. "Are you sure you dug in the right place? What kind of readouts did you get? Should we have a team come up here and dig some more?"

Zak shook his head. "It's no use." This is the only spot in the cave that had any readings," he lied. The equipment hadn't shown any readings at all. He'd only opened the hole in the wall because he knew where they'd left it, but he wasn't going to tell Gina that. He wouldn't tell anyone now.

"Where's the fragment?" Gina said abruptly. Her face and demeanor had changed.

Zak's eyes widened, surprised. "What fragment?"

"Don't pretend you don't know Zak. I've scoured the logs. You disguised it pretty well, but I finally found it. Why hide it anyway? Looking for the highest bidder?"

"Ha!" He let out a half laugh. "Here." He pulled a small packet from his pocket and tossed it to her. "It really doesn't matter now. "It won't help. It leads right here to this spot, and there's nothing here."

Gina pulled a glove from her pocket and opened the small package. "How could it possibly lead to this *exact* spot? You know that's impossible. A general area sure, but an exact location?" She looked baffled at the idea, but also intrigued. Her hands were almost trembling now as she carefully lifted the small chunk of stone from the packet.

There it was, a small beige-colored piece of stone, broken from the larger tablet. There were familiar glyphs and something else.

Ge'ez? Numbers? She wondered as she moved closer to the portable lights. She knew these symbols. It *did* give a very precise location. She calculated it in her mind. The place was precisely defined using Mt. Elba, Lake Tana, and the temple at Abu Simbel as three-point coordinates along with precise degrees measured by the constellation markings on the Karta that Mason had finally shared with her.

Gina's eidetic memory recalled the exact distance they had driven from Abu Simbel to the campsite, then adjusted to the temple's original location. This was gold. She would be rich. Millions, maybe even billions would be offered for the Ark on the black market. She had buyers standing by, waiting for her instructions.

She looked at Zak with disdain. "You're wrong, you fool! You read it wrong. You measured from the center of Abu Simbel. That's not what it says. You missed the reference to the temple, and you read the numbers in reverse. Reversing glyphs is pretty common. Only an expert would notice that. But really Zak, you should have known to measure from the temple and its original location, not the center of Abu Simbel. Doctorate in archaeology and all."

Zak? Gina had never called him Zak before. Always Dr. Erdmann. There was not only a lack of respect in her tone, there was also taunting and blatant contempt. Zak wasn't offended, just surprised. She was like a different person wrapped up in Gina's skin. He was about to tell her they'd already searched the other location but thought better of it.

"Go for it then," he said. "I'm going back to camp." He was devastated. All the months of planning, gathering data, manipulating the system, and preparing grant proposals were all a waste to him now. It was gone. There would be other discoveries in the area. The satellite photos promised that, but there was no Ark. His plan to reveal the Ark to a world that needed its wisdom had failed. Once again, the Ark was lost.

"Not so fast, Doctor." She spit the words out with that same ridiculing tone in her voice, but it sounded almost threatening now. She nodded at Mason who pulled a roll of black duct tape from his pack.

What's that for? Zak wondered and then noticed something red flash across his chest. He looked down and saw a small red dot on his shirt. It was bobbing about near his left pocket. Then he saw it. The line of light leading from his breast pocket to a gun in Gina's hand. *Is she going to shoot me?* Zak instinctively froze.

Dr. Mason covered Zak's mouth with tape first, then proceeded to bind his feet. Zak glanced at the radio button on his shoulder, but Mason saw him and ripped it from his shirt. He pulled his arms behind his back with a roughness that seemed out of character for the mild-mannered archaeologist. When Zak was sufficiently bound, tape running up from his wrists and around his throat preventing any movement at all, Gina and Mason took the fragment, the lights, and Zak's water, and left. There was some satisfaction in knowing they were embarking on a wild goose chase but not much. How long would it be before someone noticed he was missing? Josh was the only one who knew where the cave was. No one else from the previous team had come with them, and the cave wasn't listed on the scouting register. It was dark inside without his portable lights, totally obscuring it to anyone not knowing its location. It probably wouldn't be days, but it could be hours before Josh would look for him. That's a long time to be helplessly bound in a desert cave. The heat alone, with no water, could put him in a coma by then, or maybe worse. Then there were the snakes, enormous spiders, and mountain lions.

***

"Why didn't you shoot him?" Mason asked. "Someone might find him, and he'll tell." Mason was breathing hard. He was scared.

"Relax. No one's going to find that putz. Zak didn't bother to chart that cave. He was sure he knew where the Ark was and wanted to find it for himself. He wanted glory and prestige. He's too prim and proper to want the money. He's all about the recognition. Anyway, that cave is so obscure no one could find it even if they were looking for it. We wouldn't have known it was there either, if we hadn't seen him go in. Besides, I'm not done with him yet. We might need him if we don't find it right away."

"Relax!" Gina said again, looking at Mason. He was shaking now. He was clearly not cut out for this. Alone with his books and maps was his comfort zone, not this. Lucky for him she didn't plan on him being around much longer. "Why don't you go down to the camp. Let them know we're headed east, but show them this location." She pointed to the small satellite map she'd pulled from her pocket. Tell them Zak found something that led him to believe there's something there and he and I are already on our way there. Say you are gathering some extra supplies and arranging for security backup, but you are in a hurry to rejoin us." She pointed to another area and circled it for him. This is where we'll really be going, but we don't want them showing up there. I'll move ahead and meet you here." She circled another area. "This will keep anyone from looking for Zak for a while and keep them away from us."

Mason took the map with trembling fingers. His pale skin looked even whiter than usual. "Go on now. Be a good boy and momma will have a surprise for you when you get back." She kissed him gently then gave him a provocative smile, winking one gray-blue eye at him.

Mason smiled at her wink and stood a little taller. God, how she turned him on. Mason had never met anyone like Gina before. She was beautiful, kind, a fantastic lover, and as it turns out, pretty cunning. His desire for her was overwhelming, and she seemed pretty insatiable in that department too. Gina awakened things in him that he hadn't felt in years, some never. He'd never been a driven man. He'd been too wrapped up in his books and maps to even consider his status in the world. But Gina changed all that. She encouraged him. She recognized his talents. She dared him. And, he was pretty sure she loved him. He was certain he loved her and he would do anything to please her. Losing her would be like losing his life, his new-found life anyway. He took the map, grinned at her, and headed down the hill toward camp.

Gina watched as Mason's image receded into the distance and disappeared. She slung her pack over her shoulder, attached Zak's water bottle to her belt next to her own, and grabbed the lighting pack. She scanned the horizon. There was nothing but sand and rock ahead of her. Some might think the scene was beautiful, the light beige rocks set against a bright blue, cloudless sky. But Gina only frowned. It was too bad the terrain was so mountainous and strewn with rock. There was no way to get where she was going except on foot. Not even the sturdiest Jeep could make it up here. She headed east searching for a good place to ambush Mason when he returned. This prize was hers, and no one was going to take it from her or even share it, for that matter. He was such a fool, so easy to manipulate. Weak, quiet men were always the easiest marks. They needed recognition so badly they would do just about anything for it. Then there was the sex. What a gift that was! What a delicious way of getting what she wanted. She could have her fun and increase her fortune all at once.

CHAPTER FORTY-ONE

Revelations

Elena cuddled with Moses. Stroking his soft fur and being caressed by her papasan chair gave her a slight feeling of comfort as she contemplated the emptiness of the room. Zak was gone, at least for now. He may be in danger, but she didn't know for sure. Anurak was gone, maybe following Zak, but she didn't think so. The opening was over, and she had no idea what to do with the profound sense of emptiness threatening to engulf her.

Empty. Empty is not a bad thing. Empty is the ability to be open. I am open. She repeated the words, intent on remaining centered and not allowing fear to overcome her. She would keep her mind focused on what did not change. She would ride this fear and empty feeling like Akhilanda rode the crocodile, knowing she was one with the Essence of Life that did not change.

I am open. I am ready to receive. Elena repeated the words over and over, allowing the words to be a mantra drawing her into the quiet place within. The words, coupled with focusing on her breath, began to sooth and loosen her tightened muscles. She was not alone. She was one with all. *I am one with the One. I am one with All.*

Soon, Elena felt the comfort of the silence, the quiet place where she felt oneness and no longer felt alone. She felt love, harmony, and then, a faint vibration moving through her from the top of her head to the tips of her toes. She surrendered to it and allowed the waves of energy to draw her into the realm of the Ark.

There, in the Ark, the canvas that had presented so many images explaining the message of the Ark was blank. There was nothing on it at all. The brush that had rendered the magical visions was completely still now, unmoving.

Then something began to take shape on the canvas. No. Not on the canvas, but behind it. The canvas itself was disintegrating and a form, a human form, was moving toward her. The shape was draped in white and as it approached two blue eyes appeared. *Anurak!*

Elena felt chills along her arms and spine. She wasn't sure if she was excited to see Anurak or terrified. Why was he here? How was he here? He wasn't just an image appearing on the canvas. He looked different than he had in the replay of the desert scene. He was here, right here next to her, just as the team had been in the Ark with her when they had discovered it in the desert cave.

"How are you here?" she asked.

"The same as you, Elena. I've been in the Ark before as I told you, at the chapel in Aksum. I too can enter and exit at will."

"But," Elena was confused. "Are you back in Aksum then? I just went to the temple, and you are not there."

"I am not back in Aksum – not yet. But you are correct. I am not at the temple, either. I am here."

Elena's mind was spinning. She didn't even know what to ask, but knew she needed more information.

"It's not really that confusing, Elena. I'm here, mind, soul, and ..." he paused. "And body," he continued. "It is possible, with practice to enter the Ark with your whole being. You wondered how I got to New York without a trace of travel. This is how. I can enter the Ark, and I can *steer* it, for lack of a better word, and I can exit at will. You can do this, too. You simply have to believe it."

Elena let this sink in. She was hardly in a position to not believe it. The past year had been filled with things she would never have believed before – but here she was, talking to someone who was not really here, but somehow was.

"Why didn't you come to the opening last night? You have been an inspiration for so much of the show and I really missed you there."

"I was there. I saw. I just wasn't visible to others. It would have been a distraction for me to show up physically."

"Why are you here?" Elena asked. "I get *how* you are here, but why? Why show up this way now. The monk at the temple said you left, so I'm assuming you are going back to Aksum now – that is, unless you are following Zak and his team to their dig." She finished with a bit of sarcasm in her voice bordering on an accusation.

"I am headed to Aksum soon, but I'm here for more than just good-byes. You have questions that need to be answered, and you will need to expand your ability to access the Ark in the future. I've come to help you with that. This seemed to be the best way to demonstrate what you will soon need to do."

Questions. That's for sure. Elena still had lots of them.

"Go ahead. I'm here to answer," Anurak said with that uncanny ability to read her thoughts.

"Okay, so I've seen images of my own past in the Ark, but from a different perspective. The events that occurred didn't change, but the way I saw them did – and that has changed me," Elena started. "And that's good. I feel much freer without all the baggage I had attached to some of the events in my life."

"Yes. Seeing things from a higher view often changes us – though not always permanently at first," Anurak confirmed.

"Is it possible to see the future in the same way?" Elena asked.

Anurak raised his eyebrows and took a breath. "In the greater reality there is no future, there is only now," he said. "But I know that's not what you mean. From the human perspective, it is conceivable to see a *possible* future, but the future is always dependent upon the choices and actions of the people involved. What future are you interested in seeing?"

"Zak's future," Elena responded. "I want to know if he's safe. If he'll be attacked again, if he'll find what he's looking for, and what he'll do if he doesn't."

"Ahh," Anurak said. "Precisely why I am here. Sit," he said as he folded his legs under him and sat on the invisible nothingness that held them there. As Elena followed suit, he continued.

"Let's start with what Zak will find in the desert. He may not find what he thinks he is looking for, but he will find much more."

A riddle? That's helpful, Elena mused sarcastically.

"Not really a riddle. He looks for an object that will satisfy his logical mind and answer all his questions. He has already found that but doesn't realize it. His logical mind won't let him. The actual object he may find now is undetermined – but the result is not. He will find much more than he *thinks* he is looking for."

That wasn't the complete answer Elena was looking for, but it helped. "But is he safe? Is he in danger? Will those monks return and...." She didn't need to say more. She could feel Anurak's understanding. Finally, the link between their minds was reciprocal.

"He may be in danger. It is difficult to tell. The actions of others cannot be determined beforehand. But we can help him."

"How?" Elena asked. "I have no intention of joining them in the desert. I've made that pretty clear. I can't see how ... oh. You mean from here? From the Ark?"

"Yes. It's why I've come. To help you learn to enter more fully into the realm of the Ark and navigate to where you want to be."

"If he brings the Ark back with him, what then?"

Anurak smiled. "Too soon to tell, but the Ark can only be helpful to humanity. It is, after all, the portal to what gives birth to humankind. Like a parent, it delivers information a little at a time, taking care to not overwhelm its child or to give it more than it is capable of understanding. Time will tell whether the world is ready for the fullness of its message. But that should not stop you and the others who have experienced it from sharing what you've learned. People learn best from experience. Living what you've learned will have a positive effect on others – just like the paintings, your actions will speak to what is higher in others."

"I get that, Anurak. At least I think I do. But I still don't understand how we can help Zak. If someone's trying to hurt him how will our being there make a difference? How do you speak to what is higher in someone who is trying to hurt you?"

"It's what is higher in Zak that will make the difference. Whatever he finds in the cave, whatever is uncovered in the dig, none of it will compare with what he will find in himself. And that is what *we* will be speaking to, Elena.

"*We?* What do you mean? Zak is there, we are ... oh, we're going *there? Now?*

"Yes, Elena. There and now. So, if you're ready, go back and feed your cat and make arrangements for your neighbor to look in on him. We might be gone for a while. Oh, and you might want to change into field clothes and grab last year's credentials while you're at it."

CHAPTER FORTY-TWO

An Imposter

Tom Majors looked annoyed as the junior analyst broke his concentration, bursting into his NSA office without knocking. "What is it? Has the world ended?" He asked.

"No." said a breathless Marc Matthews. "But someone's world might be in grave danger." He held the printout in front of Tom, his breath and heartbeat slowing just a bit. He had run across the entire building and up three flights of stairs to deliver this information.

Tom frowned, pursed his lips and snatched the report. He did not appreciate being interrupted with no regard for protocol. Was the kid born in a barn? Did he not have hands to knock with?

Shaking his head, Tom glanced down at the page. His eyes widened. His heartbeat increased, and he felt clammy. He looked up at Marc. "Are you sure?"

"I've run it several times sir. There's no mistake. I've run face recognition algorithms, and this is what comes up. Here's the facial images and reports." He handed Tom the rest of the papers with shaking hands.

"Thank you, Marc. That'll be all," he said, dismissing the young but very adept analyst. He scanned the images, flipped through some files on his computer and brought up the photos from the university website. There was no mistake.

He grabbed his cell phone, his thumbs rapidly seeking the correct field number for Josh and typing out an urgent message. He clicked send, heard the whoosh confirming its send status, then began composing a short email summarizing the reports to Josh's encrypted NSA email. It would take some time for Josh to get the text let alone the email. But the text was enough to warn him of the danger of an imposter in their midst.

***

Josh was standing at the plane table gathering maps and gear. His security teams had all been deployed, and he was getting ready now to join Zak. They should have reached the cave by now, and probably even started to dig. He was grabbing a folding shovel and an extra lighting pack when he saw, or rather heard, Dr. Mason, trudging down the hill at a clipped pace. *What's he doing? Is he coming down for more help? Or to announce the find?"* Josh set his packs down. "What's up, Mason?" he called out.

"Are you okay, man? You seem out of breath. Should I call the medic? What's going on anyway? Is everything okay up there?" Josh was more concerned about the worried look on Mason's face than he was about the shortness of breath. He'd heard that sound from Mason before. Sometimes he panted so loudly you could hear him coming around the corner before he got there.

"No. No." He stopped to catch his breath. "Everything's fine. Zak just found an artifact that he thinks leads to something unprecedented. He and Gina are on their way there now. He wanted me to get some more gear and a security team."

Josh noticed Mason's hands were trembling as he pulled a map from his pocket. "Here's where they're headed now," he said pointing to the map.

Josh studied Mason as he took the map. He glanced at the printout and saw a circled area. It was several miles northeast of the camp, unnavigable by Jeep. His team would have to walk there. They would need more gear; food, extra water, maybe even overnight supplies. It all seemed a bit fishy to Josh. Why would Zak go off on another search? He already knew where the Ark was. They should be uncovering it by now. And why the hell would they send Dr. Mason down for the gear? Gina was the assistant. It would be her job to gather equipment, not the Associate Director of Egyptology. He sized Mason up some more. He was a bit of a pushover for Gina. She seemed to have him pretty well wrapped, just the way she wanted him. Poor guy. But there was still something wrong with this picture. Zak had no need of scouting yet another site, and he sure wouldn't run off that far without a plan and a security team after what happened last summer.

Mason was sweating, but it wasn't from the heat. He was lying. Josh could see it written all over him. "Okay," he finally replied. "I'll call for a team to join us."

"Oh no. I can't wait," Mason said. His eyes blinked a few too many times as he said it. "I need to get water to them right away. You … You've got the map. You can catch up with us once you have a team together."

Josh sighed. "Okay, fine. Go ahead. Grab what you need. We'll catch up." He waved him off and began speaking into his shoulder mic. "I need a team over by the plotting table fast," he said. Josh observed Mason as he headed back up the mountain. He let Mason get just far enough ahead that he wouldn't be able to detect Josh following him. The map was going to be useless. He was sure there was something suspicious about this, and if he was right, the map was going to lead him nowhere. He couldn't wait for the team, either. They were all out on assignments. It would take a while to call one in. He would have to explain by radio and update them with his position.

There was an insistent beep from the satellite phone on Josh's hip. Grateful for the audible beep rather than a silent buzz, he pulled the phone from its holster intending to silence it before following Mason. But instead, he set down the map and tapped the screen to open the message. It was from Tom Majors and the firsts few words were "Urgent. Impos ...."

Two rapid swipes of Josh's thumb brought up the full text. "Urgent. Imposter with you. Gina Edwards is Jordan Phillips. Criminal history. Check NSA email!"

A chill ran down Josh's arms and legs. In spite of the hundred-degree temperature and the already blazing sun, he felt ice cold. He didn't need to check his email. Not now anyway. This confirmed his suspicions about Mason's behavior. Something was up, and it wasn't good. He grabbed what he needed from the supply bin, reattached the phone to his belt clip, patted the firearm on his other hip and followed Mason.

Josh kept a short distance away, laying low to stay out of sight. Mason walked right past the cave, but glanced nervously at it as he walked by. *He knew it was there! They must have been in there at least,* Josh thought. And there was something strange about that sideways glance at the cave. Mason seemed to pause, as if he wanted to go in, then hurried forward again. Josh was torn. Should he check the cave? There was no light coming from it. They must have left it. He continued to follow Mason who, as expected, quickly veered from the charted path.

What Josh hadn't expected was Mason dropping to the ground. He heard a muffled shot and watched him crumple and fall. Josh started to run to him, but instinct told him otherwise. He hid behind a rock and watched as someone pulled Mason's motionless body behind a large boulder. His view was obstructed, but there was just enough space between the boulder and the cliff to see Mason's body pushed over the edge. Then a figure emerged, with bright orangish-red hair poking out beneath a beige safari hat. Three water bottles. Two backpacks. Two lighting packs. And a gun. It was Gina, and she had Zak's gear – and now Mason's. She was heading southeast, and at a quick pace considering the extra equipment she was carrying.

Josh's heart was beating so fast he thought it would jump out of his chest. She'd killed Mason, for Christ's sake! Had she murdered Zak too? Where the hell was he? *Oh my God,* he thought. *Is he in the cave? Is he alive? Should I save Zak or follow the murderer?*

Tactical training said to follow the murderer. Prevent more damage. Josh gave her just enough lead to not be heard as he informed his team by radio. He briefed Jabare on the murder. "Split up," he said. "Zak is missing, but I've got to stop Gina. Zak may be in a cave. There's a map in a file on the plane table marked Site Seven."

Jabare's voice squawked back through the shoulder radio. "Site Seven?"

"Yes," said Josh. "No time to explain now. Call the survey team from Site One and their security detail and have them meet you at the cave." Josh had no idea what the team would find at the cave, but if the Ark were there, it would be safer to have a trained team present to handle it.

"And Jabare, the cave is hard to find. Look for a photo in the file of a small piece of rock. It has a drawing chiseled into it that resembles the rock formation hiding the entrance. And hurry!"

"Copy that."

CHAPTER FORTY-THREE

A Light in the Darkness

Damn, it's dark in here without the lights, thought Zak. He was squint-ing, trying to adjust his eyes to the darkness. It was unsettling not knowing what might be creeping around him. His initial terror was subsiding a bit though the blood still felt cold in his veins. He was shivering even though the temperature was climbing, even inside the darkened cave. It was hard to tell the difference between the adrenalin rushing through him and the subtle vibrations that had begun pulsing up and down his arms and legs. He wasn't sure, but he thought it felt like the vibrations from the Ark. But the Ark was gone. It must be just the fear that was causing the feeling. After all, he'd never been tied up and left for dead in a cave before. If there was something that could cause someone to feel fear rushing through his body, he was pretty sure this was it.

I sit in the darkness, ensconced by thick walls.... Margot's poem from the Westbeth Exhibition meandered through Zak's mind ... *I close my eyes and there I see, Another world inside of me.* He closed his eyes for a minute. The cave was so dark he could see more light with them closed.

Zak opened his eyes and was surprised that they had adjusted enough that he could make out a pile of rocks across from him and even some of the shapes on the wall ahead of him. He blinked, then blinked again. There was something there, something shiny. About four feet from his tightly bound feet there was a tiny glint of something that looked like gold protruding through the dusty cave floor. The sun outside was moving westward in the sky, and its rays now ricocheted off the oblong rock that obscured the cave opening. A narrow beam of light landed precisely where the gilded object poked through the ground. Light was peeking in now from an open space just above the entrance to the cave. *My God, it's a roof box!*

A roof box was an opening built into ancient tombs that allowed the sun to shine in on the remains. Most were designed so that the sun's rays came in at dawn on either the Winter or Summer Solstice. The formation disguising the opening to the cave had appeared to be a natural formation, but Zak knew better now. This place had been constructed purposely to shroud its sacred contents. They'd been here in July last year, too late for the sun to shine through. Today was June twenty-first, the Summer Solstice.

But it's past dawn, Zak thought. He turned his head as much as possible toward the opening. It's facing south, not east. *It must be aligned for noon.*

The light was pouring in now, and the sight of the rays hitting the shiny object across from him was almost surreal. He could practically hear Margot's voice reciting her poem. *Here there is Light, abundant and free. It shines through the peepholes ....*

Zak felt the familiar phantom vibrations moving through him more strongly at the sight of the glittering object. There was no mistaking the feeling now. He felt as if his cells were splitting apart, as if every particle that formed his physical presence was involved in some whirling dervish of activity. It wasn't painful. But it was disconcerting, yet familiar.

The golden sherd could not be the Ark. That was gone, and this thing was too small, too shiny. *What the hell is it? If there's a sharp edge on it somewhere, maybe I can free my hands.* He had to get a better look at it, but how? He tried to inch his way toward it, but every movement was excruciating. If he moved his feet, it pulled on his arms, which pulled on the tape wrapped about his throat. It made it hard to breathe or swallow. He took as deep a breath as he could, held it and moved his butt just a bit to the left, then forward. Another breath. Another small skootch. It was possible. If he took his time, and apparently, he had plenty of that, he could slowly inch his way toward the object.

Breathe. Inch. Breathe. He repeated the moves over and over. He got closer. It was definitely gold or some gold-colored metal. More light was hitting it now, and the air was beginning to feel warmer. The vibrations were getting stronger, too. He was closer now but still was not able to touch it. He would have to turn himself around so his hands could reach it. Breathe. Inch. Turn. Breathe. Little by little, Zak inched himself in a semi-circle until his fingers were just an inch from the object. The tingling in his fingertips was incredible now. Breathe. Inch. Touch! He made contact. He could feel the cool, smooth surface of the object. Breathe. Inch. Pull. It was buried deeply. Breathe. Pull. It moved. Slowly he pulled the object from its earthen crypt. It was in his hands, but he couldn't see it. He twisted his head as much as he could without suffocating and looked down while he moved his hands just a little more in line with his sight. It was long and slender with elongated ripples that ended in graduating lengths. It was caked with dirt, but it looked like there was a pattern engraved on it. *Where is Elena and her brush when I need her?* Zak thought. *Damn her for not coming back with me! It would have been great to have her here, and not just for brushing away the dust.*

Zak rubbed the golden object with his thumbs, wiping away as much dirt as he could. It wouldn't hurt the artifact. It was gold, soft but not brittle. He twisted himself again to get another look. *It's a wing!*

Zak's fingers began to vibrate so violently he could hardly grasp the golden wing. It was a broken piece from the Ark. He was sure of it. And the edges felt sharp enough to free his hands if he could maneuver it just right. But the vibrations in his fingers were overwhelming. He couldn't turn it. He couldn't let it go. The sensation was moving up his arms and through his entire body. He tried to resist it. He'd felt this before. It was the same feeling he had when he had been pulled inside the Ark. *No, I have to stay....*

Zak's words were cut off in mid-thought. The feeling of being torn apart, then drawn into another realm overcame him. He was back. He was in that mystical place again, inside the Ark. But how? He was nowhere near the Ark. It was gone. Somehow, the small golden sherd of the wing had pulled him into this strange place once again. He was amazed at how instantly relaxed and safe he felt, considering he had been tied up and left for dead, but this was not nearly as traumatizing as the night before they had discovered the Ark. Perhaps it hadn't been a mass psychosis after all. Elena wasn't even here. He had experienced the same mystical feeling as the others when they encountered the Ark, but he had begun questioning its reality almost immediately afterward. Zak was a man of facts and science. His view of life did not allow for such fantasy worlds, yet here he was, in a realm unlike anything remotely earthly. Again.

He felt the tension in his shoulders loosen. His face muscles relaxed from the tight grimace they had held for months. He took a breath, and it felt as if it were the first he had taken since the ill-fated expedition. All the worries and concerns that had beleaguered him dissipated, and the sense of knowing he'd experienced the first time in the Ark gently caressed his entire being.

Swirls of light surrounded him and began to shift and take shape. Zak found himself viewing the previous expedition as if he were atop a mountain. He could see himself and the others as they discovered the stone map and its broken fragment. He watched as the survey team gathered equipment; ground-penetrating radar, simple metal detectors, several days' supplies, and water for the exploration. The team was excited about the map and its possibilities. If they gathered enough conclusive information, they would be the first explorers of a new site. Grants would be plentiful if the site proved valuable enough. The entire team was energized by the exciting possibilities suggested by the map, but only a handful of them had been aware of the broken fragment and its incredibly accurate content.

Zak watched the entire expedition; its hazards, the tragic accidents, the shootings, and the eventual discovery, with a calm he had not experienced in months. From this mystical realm, everything seemed to unfold in a natural, anticipated order, even the events the night before the discovery. He could see what appeared to be the spirit or life force of each of the victims hovering over their own lifeless bodies, unharmed. They were not dead at all. In fact, they seemed to be peering at him now with a serenity that quelled any inkling of fear or dread. The scene continued as the small team of survivors escaped into the final peaks toward the hidden treasure. Zak watched as they uncovered the hidden chamber and stared at its secret contents in disbelief; one-by-one they attempted to touch its unearthly surface. Then, Elena touched it, and it opened. Their bodies seemed to glow as if they were experiencing something mystical and the energy of the box had completely enveloped them. An instant later, they worked in unison to restore the box to its secret place, hiding all signs of the ground ever having been disturbed. Zak recalled now the serenity he had felt at the time. He remembered how their thoughts were all intertwined and the deep knowing that caused them to conceal the treasured relic without speaking a word.

Why, Zak thought, *is it necessary to conceal what might finally make a difference in this war-torn, beleaguered state of humanity? If everyone had the opportunity to experience this realm of being wouldn't the greed and hatred of the world finally subside? If one knew without a doubt that there was nothing to fear, nothing to steal, nothing to be taken away, wouldn't that change everything?*

Zak had spent his entire life digging through ruins trying to answer the fundamental questions of life, "Who are we? Where did we come from? Where are we going?" The objects he found buried in the earth gave clues to what ailed our human ancestors and what inspired them. Each artifact was another piece of the puzzle of human life and a possible clue to its preservation. This find was beyond anything discovered before. It answered all the questions ever uttered by humankind. It quelled every fear. Yet it was hidden and apparently destined to remain that way. He doubted that Gina's plans included revealing the sacred treasure to the world.

Zak's thoughts were interrupted by a shift in the scene laid out before him. Although time was irrelevant in this realm, Zak could see both the future and the past playing out on a virtual screen before him. He saw the events of the excursion in detail. He even saw the shrouded figures of the shooters that had wreaked the disturbing, violent scene on his team. He saw them lower their weapons and follow someone away from the scene, a figure with brilliant blue eyes that glowed like the topaz stones in an ancient Egyptian queen's earrings. They were clear, and blue, and penetrating, but they were chilling. They were out of place. They seemed to be looking right at him. Zak felt no fear because he was enveloped in the energy of the Ark, but his questioning mind could not let go of those eyes.

Zak blinked, and the scene changed. He could see the stars and planets in motion, creating the illusion of time and space. It was a fascinating activity that somehow resonated with his breath, his heartbeat, with every cell of his being. He watched the sun as it glowed and saw its energy radiating out toward the planets that encircled it, Mercury, Venus, and ... an ashen white planet resembling earth's moon. His attention was captured by this cold, white orb and its path. As he watched, the planet grew closer – or he was growing closer to it. He was directly over it. He was floating just above its surface observing some silent activity.

It was a dig site. The equipment was strange, nothing Zak had ever seen before. New tools for discovery were always being invented and adapted for archaeological purposes, but these did not appear even a little familiar. The site was surrounded by a wall made of some strange material, translucent yet strong and impenetrable. The researchers looked vaguely human yet vastly different. They were small, thin, with appendages that seemed too delicate to support them. The diminutive beings rode instead on some type of air-powered apparatuses. Tiny bots held fine brushes, delicately whisking away layers of unfamiliar dust-like silt. *What were they finding? Where were they digging?"* It was not a desert dig. That much Zak could discern from the landscape surrounding the site. The gaping crater revealed rock layers that were foreign to Zak. One, two, at least three layers of strata he had never seen before. The first resembled some kind of ash.

Several of the researchers gathered around one archaeological square. There seemed to be much excitement as small objects were hauled to the surface. One by one, small rectangular objects were dusted and set on a large white slab. Zak squinted his eyes, and the scene enlarged itself. He realized he could zoom in with a squint of his eyes or by swiping his thumb and forefinger as he would on his cell phone. And that's what they were! Hundreds of small rectangular objects set aside for archeological research. They were cell phones, long silenced in what appeared to be a single devastating event. *We finally did it*, Zak thought. *We blew ourselves up!*

The scene shifted to another area of the futuristic dig. Here there were other artifacts from Zak's time; beer cans, rifles, plastic bottles, circuit boards, Styrofoam boxes that hadn't changed much at all, and something else. At the bottom of the pile, a small brigade of sweeping bots cleared the dust from what appeared to be a wooden sign. It had an irregular shape, like a rectangle with two humps. It had been painted at one time, but most of the pigment had worn away. Remnants of characters or letters showed faintly on the weathered surface. They were not hieroglyphs; they were English letters. The object was a replica of the tablets. The ones that didn't exist in the Ark, the ones that had been misinterpreted for eons as rules rather than the blessings revealed to Zak and his team in the Ark. The artifact was riddled with holes. Had it been ravaged by insects? Zak swiped his finger and thumb for a closer look. No. Those were not the holes of an insect or organism of any kind. They were bullet holes! The tablets had been shot at. Repeatedly. Zak's mind whirled in a flurry of theoretical deductions. The end of times had occurred and the tablets revered for centuries as the code of a very human god had been desecrated in the midst of it. What did it all mean?

Brilliant blue orbs emanated from two of the bullet holes, and the tablets faded away, revealing a blue-eyed monk garbed in white linen standing silently in front of him. This was not a future vision. It was not an image on the virtual screen at all. A man, dressed as a monk with brilliant blue eyes, was standing right here with him, and next to this seeming holy man, stood Elena.

Zak squinted, swiped his thumb and forefinger, and blinked. Nothing changed. He felt the merging of minds, but he resisted. He wanted to talk.

"How on earth did you get here Elena? I begged you to come on this expedition, and you wouldn't. And now you're here? Inside the Ark again? How... and you're with him! What the hell is he doing here? You know what he did!" Zak was confused beyond belief. His logical mind fought with the evidence in front of him. But something about the surrounding energy calmed his nerves, and he sat down on the invisible ground and waited patiently for a reply.

Elena smiled. God, she was beautiful when she smiled. It didn't seem to matter how many women Zak met or dated, none of them compared with the feeling he got when Elena gave him that look. It was as if he were engulfed in a stream of perfect peace and joy. He wondered why they had never dated or become a couple. His suspicions about her causing mass hypnosis or delusion melted away.

"I'm here, Zak, because it is not necessary to enter this realm through the Ark." Elena hesitated, then went on. "I've found that I can enter and exit at will wherever I am. You can do this too, as you discovered when you touched the wing. The wing did not bring you here, it just reminded you of the way in."

"But what about him?" Zak asked pointing to the blue-eyed silent figure. "Why the hell is he here? Do you know who he is?" The monk remained mute, but his eyes softened as he gazed at Zak. Something peaceful and calming flowed from him. Zak could almost see the stream of quiet energy flowing toward him. He didn't fight it. He knew somehow it was not intended to harm him.

"Anurak is here because he is the Guardian of the Ark," Elena said. "He has been with us all through this journey. He didn't orchestrate the shootings, he stopped them. He's here because it is time for the message of the Ark to be revealed, but not the Ark itself. He's here to help us give the hope it contains to all of humanity."

"Moses – not my cat – but the stone-tablets one, was a lot like us," Elena said. "He had a mystical experience that exceeded human words. He understood the blessings just as you and I do, as everyone who entered the Ark does. But he was unable to express the enormity of the blessings to his people. There just were not words that could describe his adventure. His new-found wisdom and knowledge seemed to shatter when he tried to apply it to the everyday lives of his people. He did the best he could to record it in a way that would help people understand, and guide them on a path to learning what he knew. What he wrote kept people on track for millennia.

"As humankind evolved, and people began to realize that God was more than a superhuman being judging their every action, the texts of ancient religious movements began to wane in their power to govern. People's enchantment with the mystical began to fade. Unfortunately, a belief in a bigger God led many to believe there was none. And if there was none, of what importance could these rules for living possibly have. To show the human race an empty Ark now would exacerbate this sentiment. Many would say there was no God and this was proof of it. They would not be able to assimilate the true message of the Ark. They wouldn't be able to grasp the enormity of the hidden meaning of the words Moses transcribed. Their anger and sense of futility would be their end. That was what you viewed in the future dig. But that was only a possible future, the future of a world asleep to its true nature given an empty container with no understanding of its actual contents.

"Many people are beginning to understand God in a greater light. Many are ready to experience the realm of the Ark, but many are not. To enter this realm where thought can instantly be made manifest would be dangerous to a person engulfed in anger, hatred, or fear. It would be like giving a child the keys to a Cadillac and expecting him to drive. For now, it is enough that people know the Ark existed. The wing will do that. For many, it will give hope and meaning. For some, it will trigger a greater thought and perhaps even a mystical experience such as we have had. As more and more people tune in to this greater understanding, their actions will have a slow but steady impact on those around them. It is slow, of course, only in the earthly realm where the illusion of time exists. In this place of wholeness, though, it is already done."

Zak considered Elena's words. He knew what she said was true. It was what he knew beyond a shadow of a doubt when they returned the Ark to its hiding place in the first place. But this knowledge had seemed to fade when he had returned to the world of reports and scientific analysis. Maybe he was still a little bit asleep himself. Or maybe it was just easy to fall back to sleep in a world that didn't understand there was so much more to life than met the eye.

Anurak took over now. "It's only a possible future, Zak. The world at large is not ready for the full message of the Ark. The logical mind will fight it, grasping for something concrete. When a child is young, we teach them about God with a humanlike image because their ability to understand the abstract has not yet developed. So it is with much of the world.

"If the contents of the Ark were to be revealed to everyone right now, its apparent lack of content would cause greater doubt and chaos. People need something solid to grab hold of while their spiritual mind is growing and expanding.

"As a scientist, you know that nothing is really solid, it only appears that way. Most people believe that the world, which appears to be solid, shapes their lives. They are not aware yet that it is their thoughts and actions that shape the world. You have experienced this in the Ark. You saw your thoughts taking shape before you.

"The world is on the cusp of a greater awareness, and a greater ability to grasp the abstract. Until now, most of the evolution of life on earth has been physical, things that can be seen and touched. Now, humanity is reaching a new level of development – a spiritual evolution, or the evolution of the mind.

"The wing will give hope to those who need something concrete. Paul's writings will speak to those whose minds are opening to a greater reality. They will open ears. Elena's paintings will open hearts, as well as eyes. Josh will take his experience with him into the world of politics and international relationships. He will begin to penetrate the logical minds of those who govern and protect. He will demonstrate that all needs can be met and that giving and compassion are the tools that create harmony."

"What now?" Zak asked, looking at Elena and Anurak. "What should we do with the wing? With the site? With all of this?"

Elena and Anurak laid out the plan. First, Zak would need to learn how to steer when inside the Ark's energy. The discovery of the wing would be made public. The site would be approved for further excavation. More evidence of the Ark's existence would be uncovered, but the Ark itself would remain hidden. The wing would simply be proof to some, but it would provide a portal for those ready to awaken to a greater experience.

"But," Anurak said, "there's work to do at the cave before returning with the wing. Your friend Joshua is in trouble, and you will need to help him. Here, you are no longer bound, but your body remains bound in the cave. Elena will go with you and help to loosen the bindings before you go to assist Joshua."

Zak looked down at his hands and feet. He hadn't realized there was no duct tape on his body while in the Ark. He understood now that the tape was only an obstacle in the material world. In this higher awareness, nothing could bind him, and nothing could harm him.

He closed his eyes and imagined himself back in the cave, bound but not imprisoned by the tape. He felt his body shuddering and stretching as his entire being was pulled back into the cave. His feet were bound. His mouth was covered, his ankles and wrists were still dangerously bound to lengths of tape that circled his throat and neck. His hands were bound, but the wing sherd was in them, and he maneuvered its sharp edge to snag the tape. It was an agonizingly slow process, but then ... he felt small, cool hands working the wing with him. He turned slightly and saw Elena. She was here, wearing one of her tie-dyed field shirts. He was glad she was here, and that they could hear one another's thoughts again. She was glad, too. And, his hands were free! They worked together to remove the rest of the tape. They could hear Josh's thoughts now as well.

Zak knew where Josh was. He could sense it as if he were right there with him. He was about to encounter Gina, and he was alone. Zak tried to merge with Josh's thoughts, but they were chaotic, emitting an impenetrable energy. He tried again. "I'm coming, Josh," he said and hoped that Josh could hear him. He started toward the door, but Elena stopped him.

"There's no time, Zak. Use the Ark. Anurak will show you how to get there," she said

"You're not coming?" Zak asked.

"No. I'll need to stay here and secure the wing. There's a survey team and security coming. They'll never find this place without my help."

Zak nodded in agreement and closed his eyes. He concentrated on the wing-sherd still in his hands. He coaxed rather than resisted the vibrations it sent through his fingers and arms. He swiped his hand across the swirls of light engulfing him, and a mountainous desert scene emerged. Anurak was waiting for him, already navigating toward the abandoned excavation site.

CHAPTER FORTY-FOUR

The Abandoned Site

It wasn't hard to find her. Josh knew she was headed to the first place they had dug for the Ark, though he could not imagine why. The author of the Karta had been unfamiliar with Egyptian hieroglyphs and had done his best to divulge the information, falling back on Ge'ez at times. He had transposed the glyphs measuring the distance to the cave, which had led them to this small clearing nestled in a desolate, rocky terrain, miles from the actual site.

The whole team had still been together then. Digging hadn't taken very long with so many hands doing the work. A faint reading on the equipment had seemed to confirm the spot. The signal was so weak they probably wouldn't have bothered to dig if they hadn't been convinced that it was the precise location. But they had found nothing there, except for the scattered remains of a small fox and a heavy concentration of ore that had caused the false reading on their GPR.

Josh deftly scaled the last remaining ridge concealing the abandoned site. Silently leaning around the edge of his hidden alcove, he saw Gina, hat discarded, red hair dampened by the heat. She had reached the useless and abandoned site where the carefully dug square remained open. She stood in the pit, mouth open, a multitude of obscenities flowing from it. Her face was nearly as red as her hair, and her verbal anger gave rise to a full-fledged tantrum. She threw the equipment she had lugged for miles on the ground. She kicked at it and screamed. She cried. She fell to the ground and sat there, whimpering like a child.

"All that work for nothing!" Gina sobbed. "Months of research and grooming Mason, all in vain. Someone's been here, and it's theirs now." She kicked at the sand, then stopped. She stood, looking around the landscape.

Josh had been soundless in his maneuvers. It was part of his training. She couldn't be looking for him – at least he didn't think so. He held his breath and waited.

"Zak!" she screamed. "Damn him. He knows who has it! He doesn't have it, but he knows who does and how to find them!" Gina dried her wet, gray-blue eyes with the back of her hand, swallowed some water, and drizzled the last few drops of her near-empty bottle over her head. She reached for one of the two remaining bottles and started to pour it too, but stopped, apparently realizing she would need every drop of for the return trek. She stuffed her sodden red hair into her hat and began collecting gear. She tossed the lights, the empty bottle, and several small pieces of equipment over the cliff into the no-man's-land below then slid her arms into the straps of her lightened pack and turned to head back to camp, two water bottles clanging against her hips.

A distorted voice came through the radio on Josh's shoulder. "Josh … Josh … We're at the cave. No sign of …." Josh turned the radio off, but it was too late. Gina stopped in her tracks, remaining motionless for a moment, then slowly stepped back into the pit.

Damn. She heard it. She was looking for him now, scanning the jagged rocks that hid him. Waiting. This complicated matters. He'd planned to take her by surprise. Now she was armed and ready, the red laser sight searching the rocks in front of him.

He needed backup, and there wasn't any. It would be hours before the team caught up with him. And where was Zak? No sign of him at the cave? Images of him lying lifeless behind some rock, or worse, at the bottom of the mountainside with Mason, haunted him.

He drew his sidearm and carefully aligned the sight on Gina, his finger not yet on the trigger. His position was just enough higher than hers to thwart any protection the pit might have provided. Squinting his right eye to sharpen his view, Josh was startled by what he saw. He opened his eye and moved his head back. Same image. A dense and heavy cloud surrounded Gina, nearly obscuring her. He blinked. He squinted again. No. He wasn't imaging it. She was enveloped in a heavy, dark cloud that moved like something familiar. It moved like the lights and energy he'd seen in the Ark! But it was different. It was dark. It moved slowly, almost indiscernible, and it appeared nearly solid. He squinted again and saw through the darkness, through Gina's physical presence, to a tiny, almost imperceptible light. It sparkled and stretched upward as if trying in vain to penetrate the heavy cloud. Images of Gina's past appeared before him; trauma, isolation, humiliation, anger, retaliation. The shadow grew darker and heavier with each image.

Josh felt his heart swell within his chest, and a warm, tranquil feeling spread over his body. Gentle vibrations traveled from his chest to his arms and legs and head. *To kill another is to kill the self. The Essence of Life cannot be killed. Reverence for Life in all its forms is the only way.* Josh recalled the revelations of the deepest mysteries of life that had been made known to him in the Ark. *The voice that is not a voice,* he mused. He could hear it now, loud and clear. He lowered the weapon and returned it to its holster. He would not use it.

Josh took a breath, quieting his busy mind. He had to remain focused, frosty, and calm. It was only a matter of time before she gathered the courage to come looking for him. He'd have to climb farther above her or somehow maneuver behind her. He couldn't harm her. He had to outmaneuver her, outthink her, outwait her.

I'm coming, Josh.

Josh heard the words but shook his head. Gina hadn't moved her mouth. He looked around and behind him. There was no one else there. *Too much sun and not enough water,* he thought.

I'm coming.

He heard it again. It sounded like Zak. He kept his eyes on Gina, but he listened intently now. The voice was Zak's, and it was coming from … from within his head! He remembered the intertwining of their thoughts when they had been in the Ark and on the way down the mountain. *Be still* he thought. *Be still. I hear you, Zak. I'm here. Right here.*

Suddenly, Josh felt his skin begin to prickle. He looked down to see the hairs on his arms standing at attention and then wave in unison with a vibration that originated in his toes and traveled rhythmically through his entire body. The vibrations. They were back. The feeling of cells separating and being pulled into some other shape or form was overwhelming and quite disconcerting. Was he being pulled into the Ark again? But, it wasn't here. No. This was different. *I'm coming.* He heard it again. Then, with a strange whooshing sound, the particles of light that made up the air and the space around him became visible, parted, and through them appeared Zak.

Am I in the Ark again? Is this a vision, or what? No. It was not a vision. It was not a hallucination. Zak was standing right in front of him, index finger across his lips, signaling Josh to remain silent.

Their minds were linked again. Josh knew Zak's thoughts. He understood everything that had happened and why Gina had ended up here at the barren site. Josh heard Zak's thoughts now. *She won't shoot me. At least not right away. She thinks I know something that will lead her to the Ark. You can maneuver up and behind her while I distract her. Wait. Give me your radio first.*

Zak clipped the radio to his shoulder and carefully, soundlessly, climbed just a bit higher, circling to Gina's right. Her eyes were fixed on the spot where she had heard Josh's radio. Zak moved like a cat, stealthily picking his way down the jagged rocks toward the clearing until he was just a few feet from the square crater where Gina hid.

A pebble skittered down the rocks near where Josh had been, and Gina fired at the rocks, causing them to splinter, raining pebbles, and dirt. She pursed her lips in irritation and aimed the gun again.

"Come out, come out wherever you are," Gina taunted as she moved closer to the edge of the makeshift bunker.

Zak was in the hollowed space now almost next to her and slightly behind her. "It won't do any good, Gina. He's not there."

Startled, Gina swung around and pointed the laser at her new target. "Zak. How good to see you," she sneered. "You're looking … well. How did you manage to get yourself free? And where is Josh?" She glanced again at the splintered pile of rock and moved back a bit trying to keep her eye simultaneously on both Zak and Josh's hiding place.

"Josh is gone. He found me. Got me out of the sticky mess someone left me in," Zak said with exaggerated sarcasm. "But I took care of him. It's just the three of us now. Or is it just two? Where is Mason?"

Gina eyed Zak, suspicion etched in her eyes. Her eyes fell on the radio attached to his shoulder. "He's gone off the deep end, you might say." She turned and pointed the laser at Zak now. "So where is it?" She paused. "Umm … *Partner*."

Zak looked down at the red dot on his chest. Funny, he didn't feel as frightened by it now as he had earlier. Instead, he felt a deep calm and a peaceful harmonic vibration continuously flowing through him.

"It's been stolen," He said.

"Well, no shit Sherlock. By who?"

"I didn't know they had stolen it until just before you found me this morning." He was buying a little time now.

"And who do you think *they* are? Who got to it first Zak? I thought you had tightened security for this dig after your … *mishaps?* Last summer," Gina mocked.

"They didn't have to get here. They live here. There's a Bedouin tribe nearby. That's who attacked the first team. They took it as soon as we left."

"Nomads? Really?" She seemed skeptical.

"They're the only people who knew where it was other than the first team, and none of that team are here, except for Josh and, well … just me, now. We researched this group in depth back in the states. I know where they are."

"You have a map? Coordinates? Where are they?" Gina pointed the laser more precisely over Zak's heart now.

Zak felt the subtle vibrations flowing through him increase in intensity. As he breathed into them, he felt the tingling energy around him expand. He could see subtle streaks of light emanating from his whole body, forming a virtual shield. A darker, nearly motionless energy clung to Gina. He saw the same traumatic images Josh had seen buried within Gina's mind. Beneath the darkening cloud, a tiny spark of light flickered. Using the rhythm of his breath, Zak projected streams of light toward Gina.

A slight, very slight increase in a tiny wavering light gleamed within her. It might be a long time before the darkness left her, but enough of a crack had been made … enough that she wouldn't likely pull the trigger … at least not yet. He saw her finger slide off the trigger and subtly grasp the outer guard instead.

"No maps, just inside information. Right here." Zak pointed to his head. He gave a sly grin and watched Gina's face as she calculated her next move. He didn't have to glance up to know that Josh was skulking down behind her. He knew every move Josh was making as if he were doing it himself. He continued to surround himself and the entire scene in the light emanating from his heart.

"How far? How long?" Gina said squinting at him, the redness creeping back into her face. Her finger slid back and forth from the trigger to the guard as if she couldn't decide whether to pull or not.

With every touch of the trigger, the murky cloud around her grew thicker. With every pause, the tiny flicker grew slightly brighter.

"Not far. We can get there in a couple of hours." He tossed his head a bit to the right and over his shoulder indicating the direction was behind him. Gina would have to join him or follow him to get there.

"How do we know it's there? How do we know anyone is there? They've probably sold it by now," Gina said.

"They're there, all right. I've got a surveillance team watching them. I've been spying on them since before we arrived. No change since we got here. Lots of activity within the dwelling, but no one coming or going. It's there, all right," Zak lied. He hadn't lied about the team watching. The military was monitoring satellite images. But he also knew it was unlikely the treasure was there. He watched as Gina fumed and finally spoke.

"Here," she said, sliding the pack off her back. "If we're walking, you can carry this crap and I'll ...."

Josh had her arms locked behind her now. He had sprung into the pit so swiftly and silently that she hadn't had time to react. The gun lay out of reach on the ground beside her, useless. Gina struggled and cursed, but Josh wrapped his huge body around her, completely immobilizing her.

Zak pulled what was left of the duct tape from the side pocket of his pants. Kicking the firearm further away, he began wrapping the tape around Gina's wrists. "Should've taken the rest of the roll of tape with you," he said.

CHAPTER FORTY-FIVE

Bir Tawil Summit

The Bir Tawil field lab was brimming with activity. Grad students who had assumed charge of the lab after Dr. Mason's demise and Gina's arrest were thoroughly enthralled with the abundance of artifacts found at Site Seven. In addition to a golden wing sherd that appeared to be an authentic ornament of the Ark of the Covenant, they had discovered other items in the cave that suggested the Ark had once been housed there. A ceremonial breastplate forged of copper and in-laid with seven colorful stones was the finest of the additional artifacts. It was surmised to be a vestment worn during sacrificial ceremonies by the descendants of the priestly tribes of Israel. A large, shallow bowl was also uncovered, and early testing indicated particles of goat and sheep blood residues. The more surprising find, though, was the assortment of Ethiopian coins and pottery connecting the Ark to the Ethiopian claim that Menelik had carried it through Egypt and then to Ethiopia. The objects would provide many years' worth of research material for the university and various antiquities museums. The Site One team had still not determined the identity of the mysterious woman in the tie-dyed shirt who had directed them to the cave – but they were grateful for the find.

Zak was working closely with the students, overseeing the testing and making arrangements for additional research back in the states. Permission to remove the items was still causing a political nightmare for Egypt and Sudan. Both wanted possession of the objects, but neither wanted to claim jurisdiction in Bir Tawil. His satellite phone had been in almost constant use since he and Josh had returned to the lab with Gina, or as it turns out, Jordan, in tow.

Gina was currently being held by the Egyptian National Police, but they were in a quandary as to what to do with her. The crime had occurred in Bir Tawil, and they had no jurisdiction. Extradition to the states was the preferred course, but who would sign the extradition papers was the subject of Josh's current phone conversation with Major Karim Al Hadad. "Can Dr. Erdmann sign the papers? ... Would his role as Field Director of the expedition qualify? ... Wait... Sorry, I have another call coming in. Can I call you back?"

The call was from Tom Majors. Josh had opened his email as soon as he had returned to the field lab. Gina was an imposter. Her real name was Jordan Phillips. Gina Edwards, the graduate student with a degree in Near Eastern Languages and interest in cartography, had died in a car accident a year and a half ago. Jordan had stolen her identity, crammed on ancient languages and maps, and taken over Gina's hard-earned Research Assistant position. No one at the university had ever met Gina. They'd only seen her application and records, so no one noticed the imposter – except for Tom Majors. Tom had become suspicious when his staff intercepted an email to PAXman International that appeared to come from someone on campus. Innocuous other than where the email originated, it was a flag that led Tom to scrutinize the team members a little more closely. And something about Gina's history had looked a bit too clean to him, so he had run facial recognition algorithms to investigate further, leading him to Jordan Phillips. Jordan's criminal history was quite extensive and included several assault charges and numerous fraud cases. An archaeologist was not the first role she had impersonated.

"Hello?" Josh said, taking Tom's call. "Anything new?" He put the phone on speaker so he could take notes if needed.

"Hey, Josh. Just wanted to let you know that Oliver Quinn just landed in Aswan. He appears to be headed to Abu Simbel."

"Interesting," Josh replied, no longer worried about Oliver's intentions. "Thanks for the update, Tom. We'll keep an eye out and let the Egyptian military know he's here."

"Okay, take care. I'll let you know if we discover anything else."

Josh ended the call and circled Oliver's name on his pad. What was Oliver doing here? He didn't seem to be a threat anymore, now that Josh understood what had occurred in the Ark with Anurak. But why was Oliver *here*?

His musings were cut short by his ringing phone. It was Moshir Nkosi Nazari, the Field Marshal, or Commander-in-Chief of the Egyptian Armed Forces. This call, he did not put on speakerphone.

"Hello, Moshir ... yes, I know who he is ... Really? Hmm, interesting idea ... Yes, I'm sure we can arrange that ... No problem, just let us know when ... Okay. Thank you, sir." Josh ended the call.

"Hey Zak, you're not gonna believe this!" Josh said.

"What," said Zak, not lifting his eyes from the test data he was reviewing.

"That was Moshir Nazari. The King of Bir Tawil just arrived in Abu Simbel. He's suggesting a summit with Egypt and Sudan – here at the field lab. He wants to present a diplomatic solution that will allow both countries to maintain their positions on Bir Tawil. He will assume temporary control of the territory, maintaining jurisdiction but allowing both countries' input on his actions and giving them both access to the archaeological finds. If and when they work out their political differences, he will defer to their decisions."

Zak was staring at Josh now, his mouth open and the test results nearly forgotten. "That's ... incredible! There seems to be no end to the surprises from the brothers Quinn!" Then to his team, Zak said, "What are we waiting for? Let's get this place fit for a king! And a couple of prime ministers too, while we're at it."

CHAPTER FORTY-SIX

Closing Day

Elena struggled with the bulk of the oversized open purse borrowed from Renee as she passed through the lasers and holographic displays of her exhibit. It was the last day of the show, and she carried the final pieces of the installment – well, parts of it anyway. She smiled as she passed through the last of the holograms and the light-filled paintings came into view. For her, they had a life all their own. They were not flat engraved images but multi-dimensional windows into ever-evolving conceptualizations. The images moved as she looked at them. She wondered if the viewers experienced this sensation. Did they see them as two-dimensional pictures? Or did they see the continuous movement Elena saw?

In the center of the final chamber stood the empty pedestal, its brass plate fastened with four small brass screws bearing only today's date. Reaching into the unwieldy bag, Elena pulled out a screwdriver and set about removing the brass plate. As the last screw fell neatly into her hand, she felt the familiar vibration, a tingling that started at her fingertips and rippled through her entire body. An unruly strand of hair fell from tightly wound combs as she turned to see the laser display rippling in unison with the sensations. The visual effect of someone traveling through the laser tunnel was exquisite. The lights danced in harmony as they virtually birthed the person traveling through them. She felt herself falling into harmony with the movement, rising up as though she was no longer anchored to the floor. It was not a frightening feeling. It was comfortable and familiar now. She was in the room but not entirely. Her body was still planted on the floor, but her essence floated above, enveloped in the harmonious realm of the Ark. She was standing between two worlds. She focused some of her attention on her feet, willing them to remain in the room.

The rippling of the lasers grew more intense as the figure neared the opening. She could already see the outline of his frame, tall and lean. His silhouette was lit from behind, reflecting a rainbow of color glinting off the shadows of wavy hair, gently moving with the pace of his gait. A foot appeared, wrapped in a worn hiking boot. Legs, clothed in field khaki's, emerged, and then his beaming face. It was Zak, a little scruffy from the field, but glowing. To Elena, he had never looked so wonderful.

From his backpack, Zak lifted the golden sherd. The lights of the lasers glinted off its shiny surface in a cascade of color and light. Elena used a remote to turn off the alarm system embedded in the pedestal, then pulled a specially keyed wrench from the bag and began removing the bolts. Together, they lifted the plastic cover, set it on the floor and placed the ancient artifact carefully on the pedestal. Next to it, they arranged the copper chest-plate and other artifacts Elena had carefully packed in the oversized shoulder bag. They replaced the cover and secured the locking bolts.

The pedestal was equipped with the most up-to-date security measures. Nothing could penetrate the clear acrylic cover and once fastened, it could not be removed without the digital combination – something that was secured in a safe deposit box – one key to the box remained safely with Zak, the other had been given to Oliver Quinn, the King of Bir Tawil.

The cover protected more than just the artifacts; it protected the viewer as well. Those who were not open would be protected from the intense energies projected by it. Those who were ready to awaken to a higher spiritual understanding would feel its magnetic energy through the cover. They may even be drawn into its portal and understand that all the rules for living, all the sacred keys taught by the prophets and saints, the teachings of Buddha, Jesus, and Mohammed, the golden rule of all the world religions, the commandments of Moses, were all hints, precursors to an awareness that there was always only one law – a law that was a perfect principle of perfect balance – a law that preceded all things, permeated all things. This was the principle upon which all things were made manifest, and it was this: There is only one power, one presence, one activity in all the perceived universes and the power is called "I am that I am."

Elena drew a new brass plate from the purse and fastened it to the pedestal. With the remote, she set the electronic alarm, placed it back in the borrowed bag and reached for Zak's hand. They stood for a moment admiring the artifacts and all that they represented. Light began to pour out of them as if each cell of their bodies were somehow separate, revealing an inner source of light. It beamed in all directions and the light that began as two melded into one vibrant ray that reached through the ceiling and below the floor. It shot out in multiple directions and became so bright that the forms of Zak and Elena were obscured by the intense glow. And then it began to recede, slowly at first; then with a quick snap it was gone. And so were they. There was no trace of them.

***

Renee arrived at the prescribed time. It was the last day of Elena's show. She still wondered how they were going to sell these paintings. The reviews had been good, but nothing that would indicate people would be putting this date on their calendars to come and purchase artwork. Judith and Blake were still drinking their morning coffee and appeared to be reviewing spreadsheets at the small conference table near the front of the gallery.

"Elena arrived a little while ago while we were still brewing coffee in the kitchen," Blake said. "I think she went into the laser chamber to place the mysterious final piece. She had a heavy bag with her but said she didn't need any help. I guess she wants to get it set up before she invites us in to see it."

The three of them sipped coffee and nibbled on anisette toasts as they discussed the possibilities for this evening's Closing. Openings were a predictable staple for galleries. But a closing? This was a first as far as they knew. Who celebrated closings? Judith and Blake had agreed to try this new idea partly because they both felt there was something special about this event. They didn't know what it was yet. They knew they had gone out on the proverbial limb, but what did they have to lose really? If they hadn't done something to revive the gallery, they would've lost it anyway. Now, reviewing their books they were a bit more pensive, but the grant money from the Seventh Light Foundation had provided them a cushion. They went over the plans for the evening, checked with the caterers and then began setting up the food and wine tables in the outer lobby.

"I've got to go in there," Renee said. "How long can it take to set up one small piece of art on a pedestal anyway?" Recalling the breakdown that Elena had after the last show, Renee's concern was more than curiosity about the final piece. She was just plain worried. What if Elena was as worried as the rest of them about this final day of the show? *Dear God, I hope she's not back there destroying the artwork we plan to sell tonight!* Renee thought, remembering the scene that had followed Elena's last show.

She slowly made her way through the laser tunnel. The effect of the lighting was definitely amazing, a little disorienting, yet fascinating. The soft billows of air that came through the floor and from the sides added to the effect of walking through a cloud. Halfway through, there was a subtle vibration built into the flooring that started in your feet but traveled upward through your whole body. Losing all sense of direction, the viewer was guided by the movement of the lights that not only glowed but seemed to penetrate the body right along with the floor vibrations. Soft, ethereal music began to play somewhere past the midpoint. It grew more intense as you moved toward the chamber where the light-filled paintings were hung. Renee still wondered how Elena had gotten the paintings to have such a glittery effect and how they seemed to move, even though she knew they were two-dimensional, flat pieces of artwork. They seemed more like windows to some fantasy world where everything sparkled with colorful light. They hadn't looked that way in her studio. They were good. They were fantastic, in fact. But they hadn't moved and sparkled.

Renee caught the first glimpse of the Ark painting as she neared the entrance to the final chamber. There was a new lighting effect in the center of the room. It hadn't been there before. It beamed down from the ceiling onto the infamous pedestal. There was a soft, glowing light coming from within the cubicle where several objects had been placed. They appeared to be made of tarnished copper. A small, golden object in the middle seemed to be the centerpiece, emphasized by the additional lighting. What could possibly be so spectacular about something that small? She sincerely hoped that Elena had not lost her mind. Where was she, anyway? The chamber seemed deserted. Had she just dropped the piece off and left?

Renee peered into the cube as she drew closer. It was a small piece of gold, about the size of a woman's hand. Long, slender semi-cylindrical shapes had been carved or cast into it, so it almost looked like elongated fingers. But there were markings, lots of them, along the fingerlike shapes. Crosshairs of some kind and it appeared to be broken on one end. Was it only a piece of something larger? Was this another artistic puzzle? Would there be a reveal of a larger piece during the Closing? What were those markings? Renee leaned over the cabinet for a closer look. She pulled the dreaded reading glasses from her purse and donned them. Were they scales? Wrinkles? No. They looked like feathers! It was a wing. But a wing from what?

Renee stepped back and saw that the brass plate had been replaced. The new one had an inscription. It read:

> *Wing Sherd. Gold. Circa 1400 BCE. Believed to be an ornament of the Ark of the Covenant. Additional artifacts dated Circa 950 BCE discovered nearby. Property of the Kingdom of Bir Tawil. Displayed courtesy of the Seventh Light Foundation.*

***

The camera crews arrived several hours before the Closing. A barrage of vans with portable broadcasting equipment littered the street. Orange barricades blocked the passage of thousands of onlookers. People with advance tickets to the Closing were beginning to form long lines as they were carefully screened before being allowed to pass through. Judith, Blake, and Renee were all busy talking on cell phones to various museum curators, antiquities experts, and heads of a variety of archeological programs seeking special admittance. Judith and Blake no longer spoke about adding days to the exhibit, they spoke of months.

After determining that Elena and Zak had indeed vanished, Renee opened the sealed envelope Elena had handed her yesterday morning with instructions to open it at precisely 2:00 p.m. on the day of the Closing. *More mystery,* Renee had thought sarcastically. The letter conveyed the entire story of the original discovery, including the mystical experience of the team. It concluded with details about the wing sherd, where it was found, and photographs of Zak and his team uncovering it along with other ancient artifacts. They had gone to great lengths to have the objects carefully placed within the exhibit to ensure they would be seen by the public before being subjected to the inevitable scientific testing that would ensue. Given the location of its discovery, no country had a legitimate claim to the artifact. Oliver

Quinn, the self-proclaimed King of Bir Tawil, had diplomatically diffused the controversy by holding temporary ownership as the ruler of record, arranging a worldwide reveal, and granting research to the Smithsonian Institute and the Ministries of Antiquities in both of the bordering countries.

The disappearance of the actual Ark was a mystery that would likely be a significant focus of continued excavation of the area for years to come. Remaining members of the original team knew, however, that the Ark was not lost. In fact, it had never been lost. It was only hidden and would be rediscovered in its own time.

***

A soft glow appeared in the middle of Elena's apartment. Moses, poised at the window awaiting Elena's return, let out a timid meow and ran to the loft for cover. The golden glow expanded, becoming more brilliant and at the same time diffused. Particles of light sparkled, then gathered into form, two forms. Zak and Elena stood facing each other, hands clasped as they had been in the gallery. What moved and vibrated between them was fascinating. The light of their energetic bodies emitted a vibrant gold, red, and orange glow. The colors swirled between them, the light of one joining the other. They were irresistibly drawn together. A soft meowing sound surrounded them as Moses, who had slithered cautiously back down from the loft, wound himself in figure eights around their feet. Their hands unclasped and reached for one another in a gentle but longing embrace, and for the first time ever, their lips sought each other. They kissed. Their energy became one brilliant glow of light. The earth had finally met the sky, and it was delicious.

CHAPTER FORTY-SEVEN

The Guardian

Anurak washed his face and brushed his teeth. He walked from room to room of the circular apartment, making sure everything was in its place. The bed was already made. He hadn't slept in it for nearly a year. There was little out of place. He'd only been there long enough each day to be sure the trays of food left for him were emptied and returned.

Satisfied that all was in order, Anurak pulled the golden cord hanging next to the heavy mahogany door. He heard the muffled sound of a bell ringing on the other side and the soft padding of feet. Then there was a quiet knock, to which Anurak replied: "Come in."

The door opened, revealing a young Ethiopian monk who silently offered his assistance.

"Please bring the priest, Abba Biruk, to me."

A subtle look of surprise flashed behind the dark brown eyes, then disappeared. The monk bowed slightly and closed the door. There was little to do now but wait. Abba Biruk would be nervous and surprised, but Anurak would put him at ease.

A few moments passed before a second, timid knock on the door. Anurak opened it to see a slightly nervous older man dressed in yellow robes and a pillbox hat.

"Come in," Anurak said, gesturing for the priest to follow him. "I'd like to show you around."

Biruk took a noticeable breath and timorously followed him. Anurak started with the room they were in. He explained how meals and other necessities were delivered. He then led him through the sitting room, the small, efficient kitchen, the library, bathroom, and finally the bedroom with its curved wall and access door to the inner chamber of the apartment. All the rooms had access, but this is where Anurak had first entered the sacred realm of the Ark.

Anurak looked into the deep brown eyes of his successor; he saw recognition as well as a little apprehension. The priest's yellow sleeves nearly vibrated with the trembling of his hands. Anurak smiled his most loving and reassuring smile, sending calming energy toward the nervous priest. In moments, the priest's energy softened and expanded. Anticipation, excitement, and acceptance were replacing the hint of fear in Biruk's eyes.

Nodding, Anurak opened the door, revealing heavy velvet drapes and sheer, wispy curtains. He stepped inside, gesturing Biruk to follow and pulled the curtains back to reveal the ornate, empty pedestal. It had two cushions on it; Anurak took his seat, then gestured for the priest to join him. Still calm, but clearly confused and perhaps a little disappointed, Biruk took his place on the cushion next to Anurak.

Anurak smiled. He knew that feeling of confusion and disappointment well. He had felt the same when he had been invited into this sacred space and found there was no physical ark. He also knew the confusion and disappointment would soon disappear. He folded his legs into a lotus position and watched as Biruk did the same. Without a word, Anurak began a guided meditation, and Biruk closed his eyes to listen. After a few moments of breathing into the experience, both men's bodies began to glow.

Inside the realm of the Ark, Anurak spoke to Abba Biruk. "This is where you will spend most of your time. The Ark itself is not in the sanctuary, only the portal to it lies behind the curtains. The Ark remains hidden, and yet its essence is everywhere. It does not need protecting but those who find it will often need your assistance. Much of the world still needs guidance, but little by little, they begin to understand the true message of the Ark, the absolute blessings of oneness with God. Many more will discover where the Ark actually lies, for it is not truly lost. It is not hidden in the ground, a cave, or even this sanctuary. The physical Ark is but a manifestation, a portal of sorts to the true Ark, the one hidden in the hearts of humankind.

"As the new Guardian, you will know where the physical Ark is at all times, but more importantly you will witness the true Ark as it is rediscovered in human consciousness. It is opening now within the hearts of many, and you may be called to assist in their transformation. I was called for only a short time because of my connection with Elena who has made a fissure in the division between worlds – and she and her friends needed assistance.

"Understanding the Absolute requires an enormous shift in consciousness and can only be assimilated into the human experience one small piece at a time. This is the meaning of the shattering of the first set of tablets Moses brought down from the mountaintop. He was frustrated and needed to return to a higher place once again in order to bring his newfound spiritual understanding to the earthly experience, bit by bit.

"Like Moses, Elena shattered her first attempt at sharing the message of the Ark, but little by little she found her way back into the realm of higher knowing and began to incorporate her understanding into her life on a more conscious level. Those who traveled with her into the Ark did so primarily by being in close proximity to her. They had varying degrees of resistance to the experience but over time reconnected with their increased understanding. The four are now living a more authentic demonstration of a higher law, expressing it through their varied paths and callings. As they live this greater Truth, they will have a beneficial effect on those with whom they come in contact.

"A great unfolding is occurring in human consciousness, and as the new Guardian of the Ark, you will be the master teacher appearing whenever a student is truly ready to evolve. You will remain the Guardian until the time comes for you to transcend higher and your successor to be inducted. You will know the time, and you will know the successor – there will be no doubt."

With that, Anurak closed his eyes, and his face became incredibly serene, almost translucent. His body became more brilliant still, and then it began to pulsate. Each cell, each particle of light that formed Anurak's body began to separate. They twinkled and sparkled and then vanished altogether.

Abba Biruk watched in fascination as the young American disappeared into a realm that must be higher still. He had questions. Lots of them. But as he thought a question, the answer appeared. He remained in the portal for some time, surprised, still a bit nervous, and decidedly elated.

About the Author

Eileen Patra, is an ordained Unity Minister, Licensed Unity Teacher, Certified Spiritual Educator, and life-long student of spiritual studies. She resides in Michigan with her husband Steve and their two pets, Jessie & Shadow. She considers herself extremely fortunate to have both her grown children and their families living nearby.

In 2014 Eileen received the Ruth M. Mosley Award for Outstanding Achievement in Ministry while serving as the Senior Minister at Unity of Livonia, Michigan. Eileen has also served as the Teen Ministry Consultant, for the Great Lakes Region of Unity and as the founding minister of Unity of the Lakes in West Branch, Michigan.

Prior to her call to ministry, Eileen earned a Bachelor of Fine Arts Degree from the College for Creative Studies in Detroit, Michigan. As an author, she strives to paint an image of innate wholeness and un-limited potential in her reader's mind.

Eileen Patra is an inspiring and passionate speaker and writer who brings her love for spiritual principles and their power to transform lives to people of all walks of life. She has published dozens of spirit-ually themed articles in local periodicals and online journals as well as her own blog, eileenpatra.com. The Mystical Ark is her first novel.

www.eileenpatra.com